Praise for *Quill of the Dove*

Most authors try to keep their plot lines as simple as possible to avoid getting inextricably bogged down in the convoluted details of local reality. But by doing so, they tend to oversimplify, even ignore, the overwhelming complexity that burdens the daily lives of those who live there. So it is very uncommon to find an author who not only sets his story in the Middle East, but who can both keep the facts straight and also avoid turning individuals and regional populations into two-dimensional caricatures. Ian Thomas Shaw is one of those rare authors. Having served as a Canadian diplomat and aid worker in the Middle East for several years, he knows the land and people well, and has a firm grip on hills and valleys, swamps and jungles of the political topography as well.

—**Timothy Niedermann**, *The Ottawa Review of Books*

Quill of the Dove is an impressive debut, and Ian Thomas Shaw brings a new voice that's strong and confident, weaving a tale with a knowledge of culture and history that draws and transports the reader right from the beginning.

—**Dietrich Kalteis**, *award-winning author of Ride the Lightning,
The Deadbeat Club, Triggerfish, House of Blazes and Zero Avenue.*

Quill of the Dove is a suspenseful, powerful and ambitious novel.

—**Sonia Saikaley**, *author of The Lebanese Dishwasher*

Quill of the Dove approaches the history of Lebanon through the eyes of international journalists called upon to take huge personal risk to report the complicated facts. This is a terrific way for Shaw to tell his tale. Richly drawn characters, enhanced by his profound knowledge of the Middle East, ensure that we are along for the whole ride with men and women trying to make a difference, while trying just to stay alive. With journalists dying in disturbing numbers across the world, this novel may be providing the timeliest perspective of any on the Middle East.

—**David Whellams**, *author of The Verdict on Each Man Dead*

Shaw's intimate knowledge of Israel and the Palestinian Territories grounds the drama in this heart-stopping political thriller.

—**Claire Holden Rothman**, *author of My October and The Heart Specialist*

Quill of the Dove brims with heartbreak and love for a troubled region. We so soon forget even recent history, and Shaw's inclusion of the Phalangist massacre in Beirut from the point of view of a French journalist offers insight into current Arab-Israeli conflicts; this novel is both timely and needed. Shaw's characters are memorable and his sense of place, steeped in personal experience, is powerful; the scent of orange and olive groves lingers long after the last page is turned.

 —**Ursula Pflug**, *author of Down From*

Quill of the Dove is a gripping political thriller driven by memorable characters, both noble and nefarious, whose destinies are inextricably determined by war zones and conflicts. Spanning the Middle East, Europe and Canada, the novel delivers a fascinating quest for truth and love that illuminates the legacies of violence in our complex world.

 —**Cora Siré**, *author of Behold Things Beautiful*

Ian Thomas Shaw writes with the intensity and the scorched vision of nation states in crisis evocative of the late style of John le Carré. *Quill of the Dove* is a searing portrait of lives caught in the imbalance of a fractured Middle East where no one, not even, say a "quiet Canadian" can remain untouched by the bitter legacies of the conflict for long.

 —**John Delacourt**, *author of Ocular Proof*

Quill of the Dove is brilliantly plotted, bursting with suspense, and populated with characters one cares about immensely. Shaw proves himself resoundingly as a master of the political thriller. Easily one of the best novels I've read in recent years.

 —**David Joiner**, *author of Lotusland*

Quill of the Dove by Ian Thomas Shaw is about identity—family, political, cultural, and religious. The novel is an expansive narrative with deft insights centred in the Middle East. Shaw's use of meticulous and extraordinary research moves us backward and forward in time, shedding light on the complex motivations of a region rife with conflict. In the telling, we are reminded that the multi-faith Lebanese, Syrian, Israeli and Palestinian nations have endured a long, tortured history. But at the core of this unputdownable novel are ordinary human beings searching for meaning, love, and mastery of their rightful heritage. A finely told history lesson about sectarian violence, mutilation and territory, and yet Shaw writes: "Despite the war, the hearts of the villagers have not hardened." *Quill of the Dove* is a love story, a political manifesto and a voyage into the depths of war where life and death lie down together.

—**Susan Doherty Hannaford**, *author of A Secret Music.*

A young Canadian woman's search for her origins. A maverick French journalist on a quest for peace in the Middle East. These two intriguing stories mesh seamlessly in Ian Thomas Shaw's riveting novel *Quill of the Dove*. The final vision of a Middle East that could have been left me longing for more.

—**Caroline Vu**, *author of That Summer in Provincetown and Palawan Story*

Ian Thomas Shaw spins a memorable tale that intertwines the personal with the political. A fast-paced thriller, lyrically told, that moves seamlessly between Europe in 2007 and the Middle East in the mid-late 1970's, *Quill of the Dove* is a riveting novel that tells the story of a Canadian woman's quest for identity amidst the turmoil of the Middle East. It's not possible to do justice in a few sentences to the wisdom and intricacies of this very interesting and powerful novel. This page-turner will keep you engrossed throughout, providing not only insights into the very complex and layered political history that is the Middle East, but also into the deepest longings of the human heart.

—**Jerry Levy**, *author of Urban Legend and The Philosopher and the Golem*

Quill of the Dove is a novel that both delights and instructs. With its intriguing, fast-paced and riveting plot it takes the reader on an adventure into the world of entangled Middle East politics, a tapestry interwoven of intricate and insidious political games, and tragic stories of ordinary people showing extraordinary valour and endurance. The literary technique of shifting timeframes, as well as a multi-layered plot keep the reader in a delicious state of suspense. Definitively, a book of notable literary merit that satisfies a craving for an interesting read, and the desire to understand better a part of the world embroiled in turmoil.

—**Jana Begovic**, *author of Poisonous Whispers*

Quill of the Dove compels you to believe that the power of love and a determination for peace will triumph against hatred, betrayal, and brutality. While vividly painting the horrors of war, the novel also places on its canvas the power of human goodness, yet keeps the reader uncertain to the end as it slowly reveals the hidden truths between the characters and realpolitik.

—**Norman Hall**, *author of Four Stones*

Quill of the Dove is an intense political thriller written with an insight that can only come from a deep understanding of international intrigue. Spy novel lovers will find everything they want and more.

  —**Benoit Chartier**, *author of Red Nexus*

Quill of the Dove is a compelling novel that quickly plunges the reader into the depths of conflict rooted in the Middle East. The author's vivid characters and keen sense of history reveal the intricate layers of political nuance and fanatical allegiance that lead to entrenched positions and hostile environments. *Quill of the Dove* is a noteworthy addition to fans of international intrigue and political thrillers. This passionate tale of lives shattered by conflict will keep you turning pages long into the night.

  —**Sean McGinnis**, *author of Stark Nakid.*

The reader is immediately drawn into this tale of intrigue. The characters are complex and engaging, guiding the reader through Shaw's scholarly account of a dark history in the Middle East.

  —**Geri Newell**, *author of Quite Perfectly Dead*

This is a fast-paced story told in generation-crossing firsthand, casting love and hatred, good and evil, against the backdrop of a turbulent Middle East, with all its complexity and intricacy of religious and political allegiances. Shaw holds back no punches in his vivid and disturbing description of horrors, while simultaneously word-painting acts of breathtaking kindness and sacrifice. His deep knowledge of the political and religious landscape of his story lends an astonishing credibility to the narrative.

  —**Robert Barclay**, *author of Death at the Podium*

Drawing on his extensive experience and knowledge of the Middle East, Ian Thomas Shaw has crafted an exciting political thriller of intrigue and romance. As his protagonists reach toward a peace that might have been, they battle the in-grown political, religious and tribal forces that are the root cause of this instability. In the process, Shaw succeeds in bringing to life the horrors the inhabitants of this war-torn region have been living through over numerous generations. This is definitely a page-turner that will keep you reading well into the night. Enjoy!

  —**Geza Tatrallyay**, *author of the Twisted trilogy of international crime thrillers and the Cold War Escape trilogy of memoirs*

Ian Thomas Shaw's new thriller, *Quill of the Dove*, is a compelling story of the struggle between identity and destiny set against the turbulent backdrop of Middle East politics. It focuses on a woman's search for her own identity as she tries to find her birth parents, and a man's personal mission to overcome generations of communal conflict with a multi-stakeholder peace plan. Both characters encounter danger, sudden and brutal violence, hope, despair, betrayal and ultimate resolution as they follow their intersecting destinies. Shaw's ability to depict all sides of the conflict humanely are a testament to his time in the Middle East and his skill as a writer and story-teller.

   —**Susan Taylor Meehan**, *author of Maggie's Choice*

Quill of the Dove is a fine account of the impact of bigotry, the dehumanizing effect of violence, and a chronicle of the tensions within families and of the challenges of trying to broker a peace among polarized groups whose turbulent histories reach back generations. It is a first-rate effort, and it has paid off handsomely in a richly-told and layered tale that succeeds on many levels: thoughtful readers whose goal is to gain a better understanding of one of the most troubled regions of the world will be rewarded, but so too will the casual reader simply in search of a gripping and well-told tale. *Quill of the Dove* is one of the most rewarding novels I've read in a very long time.

   —**Jim Napier**, *author of Legacy*

Quill of the Dove is both a fast-moving historical novel and a fascinating and compelling view into the shadow world of middle east politics and violence in one of the most fragile of democracies—Lebanon in the 1970s. Well researched, intense, and believable, Shaw's novel does not shy away from exposing the shifting alliances, tribal jealousies, and foreign meddling that created this tragedy. Nor does it provide cover for the continuing aggression of State players who are still heavily invested in continuing conflict in the region well into the new millennium, and for whom the cost in human lives and human misery seems of little or no concern.

   —**Dr. Bob Abell**, *author and filmmaker (Corporate Prey)*

Ian Thomas Shaw has drawn on his long experience as a Canadian diplomat to produce a gripping novel that enriches and enhances the reader's knowledge of ethnic cultures and conflicts of the times. While multi-faceted, the time transitions are easy to follow. Character descriptions and development are well examined and presented. A good read for virtually any audience.

   —**Bill Horne**, *past President of the Ottawa Independent Writers*

IAN THOMAS SHAW

Quill

of the

Dove

MiroLand
p u b l i s h e r s

MIROLAND (GUERNICA)
TORONTO · BUFFALO · LANCASTER (U.K.)
2019

Connie McParland, series editor
Michael Mirolla, editor
Cover and interior book design
Rafael Chimicatti
Guernica Editions Inc.
1569 Heritage Way, Oakville, ON L6M 2Z7
2250 Military Road, Tonawanda, N.Y. 14150-6000 U.S.A.
www.guernicaeditions.com

Distributors:
University of Toronto Press Distribution,
5201 Dufferin Street, Toronto (ON), Canada M3H 5T8
Gazelle Book Services, White Cross Mills
High Town, Lancaster LA1 4XS U.K.

First edition.
Printed in Canada.

Legal Deposit—First Quarter
Library of Congress Catalog Card Number: 2018954208
Library and Archives Canada Cataloguing in Publication
Shaw, Ian, 1955-, author
Quill of the dove / Ian Thomas Shaw. -- First edition.

(MiroLand imprint ; 21)
Issued in print and electronic formats.
ISBN 978-1-77183-378-3 (softcover).--ISBN 978-1-77183-379-0 (EPUB).--
ISBN 978-1-77183-380-6 (Kindle)

I. Title. II. Series: MiroLand imprint ; 21

PS8605.U22Q55 2019   C813'.6   C2018-904697-X
                                             C2018-904698-8

To my mother Marie and brother Mark,
travellers of the world

PROLOGUE

They race along the camp's perimeter. She trips and scrapes her knee. "Don't cry," her cousin whispers. "They will hear you." He picks her up. They must find a breach in the wall. Beyond it is her uncle and safety. Her mother's words to her cousin echo in her head: "Munir, bring Meryem to your father. Go quickly. Take this money. And these photos." They scramble along the wall but find no opening. Finally, they see a spot where the debris of a bombed-out house is piled against the wall. A bridge to safety. Munir is sure-footed. He confidently climbs onto the broken concrete and twisted iron rods, holding Meryem tightly in his arms. He lifts her to the top of the wall and then pulls himself up behind her. The drop to the other side is steep. She is afraid. He leaps to the ground, turns and raises his arms. "Jump! I'll catch you." She trusts him, closes her eyes, and pushes off the wall. In mid-air, his hands clutch her tiny waist. She looks down at him and smiles. The crack of a single rifle shot. He collapses under her. Her face is wet with his blood. Struggling to breathe, he presses one of the photos into her tiny hands then falls against her. Steps, heavy steps come toward her. And the nightmare rewinds.

Chapter

1

Nicosia, Cyprus – *January 2007*

THE FRAYED CURTAINS dance in the warm Mediterranean wind. The modest hotel has seen better days, but it is close to the crossing and within her budget. She shifts her body on the sheets drenched with sweat from another night of turmoil. Dreams half-started and memories resurfacing from the unexplainable. She opens one eye to greet the sunshine streaming into the room. *No, one more hour of sleep*, she pleads. But the wind has picked up and is causing a loose shutter to bang against the outer wall. Sound and light will not leave her be. She rolls out of bed and drowsily walks across the cold tiles to the windowsill. She reaches outside to secure the shutter's latch. On her second try to get the latch in place, she notices reflected light from across the courtyard. She pulls back to hide her nakedness. From the corner of the window, she glances out. On a balcony directly opposite stands a man, his dark glasses like mirrors in the sun. He is tall, athletic and blond. Marie Boivin shakes her head and draws shut the curtains. Today is not a day to worry about voyeurs.

In the darkness of the room, she slowly finds her way back to the bed. Exhausted, she falls on it, closes her eyes desperate to find some respite from the thoughts and doubts racing through her head. Eventually, a half-slumber takes hold, one that barely dulls her anxiety. The minutes turn into hours, and the temperature in the room rises. She stares at the peeling paint of the ceiling as the perspiration rolls off her forehead onto the cotton pillow. She knows that it's time to meet the day and all that it will entail, but her body resists. The sweet music of Scriabin's *Piano Étude* begins, first softly, then more intrusive. She reaches for the cell phone in her jacket and clicks on the speaker button.

"Hello!"

"Hi, it's Marc Taragon."

Her vocal cords instantly freeze at the sound of his voice. It is deep and orotund, gently laced with a southern French accent, and so different from how she had imagined it.

"Is everything okay?" he asks.

"Yes, yes, everything's fine."

"I'm wondering if we could delay the interview by an hour, and start at noon."

"Of course, Monsieur Taragon. Noon will be fine."

"Do you know the Black Sea Café? Two hundred metres from the Ledra Street crossing. They can show you the way at the checkpoint. Ask for Ibrahim. He's a friend who works there."

"Excellent. I'll be there at noon."

"Oh, how will I recognize you?"

Marie wants to say frazzled with dark circles for eyes, her hair tangled like a bird's nest, but then looks at her open suitcase, and says: "I'll wear a light lavender dress."

"Lavender. A pretty colour. *À bientôt.*" His words disconcert her. There's an uncomfortable familiarity. Could it be he already knows?

David Levi senses Ari Epstein's presence behind him. The old man has been trained to move silently like a ghost, but there is still an aura around him, a field of rage, that betrays him. David turns around.

"What?"

"David, you're going to screw up the mission if you continue to take chances like that."

David bites his tongue. He looks at Ari, squat and balding with a long lumpy Balkan nose. He wants to tell his superior what an old ugly prick he is. Instead, he mutters: "Did you see her? She's magnificent."

"You're not listening to me."

"But I think we should talk to her. She might know something."

"No! Keep your distance. My gut tells me that she isn't what she pretends to be. Besides, there's something in her file that bothers me."

"What?"

"It's above your pay grade."

David walks over to Ari. His six-foot-three muscular frame towers over the little man. He would like to press him for details but knows it will be of no use. When the old Mossad agent decides to clam up, nothing will pry anything from him. Anyway, David doesn't care what Ari thinks. The girl has a beautiful body—full breasts framed by wide shoulders and a narrow waist, hips that swivelled effortlessly as she walked toward the window. This assignment could be a lot of fun if only he can get the old bastard out of his way.

Marie rushes to the checkpoint. She's late. Why did she spend so long comparing the faded photo of the couple to the one on the flap of Taragon's book? She brings her breathing under control and steels her nerves, then again compares Taragon's face to the young man beside the beautiful woman in the old print. There's nothing certain about her theory. A resemblance between the two men, nothing more. Both share a sternness in their angular features, low hairlines and thick eyebrows, and in their eyes, a rare shade of turquoise glistens. She finds their faces mesmerizing and feels they beckon her to reveal her darkest secrets. But those secrets are locked even to her.

The checkpoint is newly renovated, meticulously painted white—a symbol of Greek order, a small monument of racial superiority. As she stands in front of the door, a gust of dry Mediterranean air lifts her lavender dress, much to the delight of the Greek-Cypriot guards. They flirt outrageously when she hands them her passport.

"Miss, we don't believe that this is you in the passport. We might have to keep you a bit longer to check things out," a young soldier says grinning, while his companions chuckle in chorus.

"What?"

"You're much prettier than in this photo. Do you have any other photos? Perhaps one I could keep?"

She levels a look to kill at the young man, who only smiles more lasciviously, his eyes washing over her body. When she opens her cell phone and begins to punch in a number, his grin vanishes, unsure of who she is and whom she knows.

"No problem, Miss. Here's your passport. Enjoy Nicosia! If you need someone to show you around, I would be delighted to. But watch out for those Turks. They don't respect women, especially beautiful women like you."

Marie grabs her passport and leaves without acknowledging the young soldier's last remarks. She walks quickly to the Turkish side, to the unwelcome accompaniment of low whistles from the Greek guards.

Her thoughts are spiralling in a swirl of apprehension and uncertainty. She stops and braces for what might be in store with the Turks. It's true that their reputation is worse than the Greeks'. It was a mistake to put on this flimsy dress, a replica of the one worn by the woman in the photo. It shows too much cleavage, and it's far too short. She had it made in Montreal just for this occasion. It was a foolish, childish thing to do. Ibrahim, that was the name Taragon had said. Repeating the name calms her—why, she doesn't know.

Marie steps inside the small hut on the Turkish-Cypriot side. The paint on the walls has yellowed and the glass is cracked in some of the windows. Still, there is a sense of order although different from that of the Greeks. The customs officials sit behind wooden tables, scratched from years of use but adorned with legs engraved with Ottoman calligraphy. They witness the longevity of the Turkish presence on the island and convey a note of defiance as if to say: *We are still standing—we are still here.*

A dark face looks up from the desk. It's a beautiful face, but so out of place. Yes, she's heard of black Cypriots, descendants of Ottoman slaves, but she's never seen one. And now here before her is the face of Othello, strong and muscular with such inviting eyes. She hands the young immigration official her Canadian passport. He smiles broadly and asks: "*Vous parlez français?*"

Marie takes a step back and answers: "*Oui. Êtes-vous Ibrahim?*"

"*Oui,*" the official says and quickly stamps her passport. She asks for directions to the Black Sea Café.

"To see Monsieur Taragon?"

"Yes."

"Go down this street and turn left at the second corner. You'll see the sign after one hundred metres."

"*Merci, Ibrahim.*"

"*Au revoir, Marie.* I hope to see you again."

Marie flashes a smile at the young man and starts down the road, thinking how she has forgotten to ask him where he learned such perfect French. She hopes that he'll be there when she returns. For a moment, she's no longer a woman on a mission, but a girl succumbing to her youthful desires. She glances back. Ibrahim is now processing two men. The younger one looks vaguely familiar. He is tall with blond hair. His shoulders are broad, like a swimmer's. His companion is short, bald, perhaps sixty. *Tourists*, she thinks. She turns and breaks into a run to make up for lost time.

The younger man watches her. He likes her athletic stride, the way the dress pulls tight to her in the wind. Ibrahim frowns and, with a particularly violent passport stamp, catches the men's attention. He sends them on their way with a sharp *Shalom* and reaches for the phone. The older man looks back, worried. Their Canadian passports are genuine, but the black Cypriot seems onto them. The young man ignores Ibrahim, puts on his dark glasses and saunters forward with the swagger of a movie star.

Chapter

2

Nicosia – January 2007

TARAGON WALKS TO THE EDGE of the rooftop terrace. The divided city pans out before him. On each side of the Green Line, Greek and Turkish Cypriots go industriously about their business. How similar they are. So different from their kinfolk on the mainland. And yet how viscerally they hate one another. Still, Cyprus is prospering, and the influx of euros and Russian gold have tempered the two sides' desire to re-ignite their centuries-old conflict. Occasionally, war is bad for business.

Taragon remembers the first time he was here. Then, no building was higher than six stories. The centre was a ghost town, scarred by barbed wire and Greek and Turkish watchtowers, and the Green Line manned by Canadian peacekeepers snaked its way through the city.

A hint of lavender catches his eye, the lavender of thirty years ago? He quickly brushes the thought aside. He shades his eyes from the glaring sun. The lavender takes form, and in it, a tall blond woman comes into view. She is running. Her stride is strong and determined like a marathoner. He wonders what can be so urgent. He watches the woman slow her pace until she's directly beneath him. He realizes that it must be the Canadian although she appears younger than Leyna had described her. He waves as the lavender disappears under the awning of the café's entrance.

Marie stands before the blue door. Sweat streams down her face. Her linen dress clinging to her body. She feels inhibited by her dishevelled appearance and self-conscious of the sensuality that it might exude.

For a moment, she ponders turning back, abandoning this quest for the truth to return to the comfort of her past existence. She regains her composure and turns the knob.

The café is dark and cool. A few old men in outmoded suits and wide ties sip Turkish coffee and play backgammon. One even sports a red *fez*. A young married couple feed their toddler bits of pita bread dipped in hummus. Over the bar is the obligatory portrait of Kemal Ataturk beside a framed business licence. But Taragon is nowhere to be seen. She is about to sit and wait when a barman, a black Cypriot like Ibrahim, emerges from the kitchen. He stares at her for a moment and then motions to the stairs leading to the rooftop terrace. She walks across the cracked marble tiles and looks up the winding staircase. One short breath before her long legs take the steps two at a time. As she reaches the top, the door opens before her. The intense sunlight is blinding. At first, all she can make out is the outline of a dark figure. When her eyes adjust to the light, there before her is the face that she has scrutinized for an eternity.

Taragon offers his hand to help her over the tall sill of the door. His face betrays little emotion, just a faint smile as he leads her to the table. Somehow, she already feels disappointed by his dispassion, but why should she? After all, she thinks, there is no reason for him to suspect she is anything more than a fellow journalist looking for a good story.

"Leyna has told me much about you," he says. "You know, I rarely give interviews, but she assured me that you are honest, and, more importantly, her friend. I trust Leyna's judgement. She's my oldest friend. I hope you understand there are some things that I need to say, things which may damage people's reputations or even put their lives at risk. So I'll ask you to be careful in how you write up the interviews."

Marie hesitates. She lowers her eyes.

"Yes, of course. I'm flattered Leyna said such kind words about me. I'll do my best."

Taragon smiles. This time an engaging smile. No sign of the arrogance her editor at *Le Devoir* had warned her about. She takes him in. His hair is grey, and his aquarelle eyes are framed in deep wrinkles, cutting into a very tanned face. Noticeable scars start beneath his right earlobe, disappearing into the collar of his blue cotton shirt. Leyna hadn't mentioned them. But then, Leyna would be the last person to speak of scars. Marie looks down at her own scar crossing the palm of her left hand and quietly clenches her fist to hide it. She looks up at Taragon. Did he see it? Suddenly, she realizes that Taragon is speaking to her.

"*Pardon, monsieur?*"

"I said, I hope you don't mind that I've ordered a *mezzeh*. It's an assortment of Turkish hors-d'oeuvres. Perhaps, you'd also like some *Buzbaj*? Red wine from Anatolia, and very good!"

"Yes, yes, that sounds wonderful."

The barman appears at the door with a large tray of assorted dishes and wine. He offers them a broad smile as he approaches the table. He pours the Buzbaj first into Taragon's glass. Taragon raises the glass to assess the wine's clarity. Marie seizes the opportunity to study his face further. It is different from both the photo on the book flap and the faded one from her childhood.

"Shall we begin?" he asks.

"Pardon?"

"The interview?"

"Yes, of course."

Marie straightens. Her distraction must seem odd to Taragon. She needs to stay focused. She can't let him guess why she's really here.

She brings out a small recorder from her purse and places it on the table. Every nerve in her body twitches. She suddenly feels her life will never be the same now she has met him.

She takes a sip of Buzbaj. The savoury liquid releases the muscles in her throat. She presses the ON button on the recorder and begins.

"This is Marie Boivin with the celebrated French journalist and Middle East expert Marc Taragon. Monsieur Taragon, can you tell us what brought you to Lebanon in 1975?".

He pauses, looks to the east and, with a mischievous glint in his eyes, replies: "The letter *'ayn*."

Chapter

3

Shemlan, Lebanon – April 1975

ABU WALID'S FRUSTRATION IS PALPABLE. For years, he has trained foreigners to master the intricacies of the Arabic language at the prestigious Middle East Centre for Arabic Studies, high up in the mountains above Beirut. But this class is the absolute worse. For the past two weeks, he has drilled them on the pronunciation of the Arabic alphabet. Only one, Marc Taragon, a young French journalism student, is making any progress. He has mastered all of the letters, except the elusive 'ayn. The others, aspiring British and Australian diplomats or perhaps spies, are dullards.

No matter—the school's director has already agreed to Abu Walid's request for a month's leave. He has packed his bags and will travel after lunch to visit his ageing mother in the Druze-Christian village of Maaser in the nearby Shouf Mountains. Unrest is stirring there, and he is worried. Militiamen from Beirut have been brainwashing the local Christian youth with stories of century-old massacres, and the Druze are preparing for confrontation. Beirut merchants, always keen to make a little money, have been visiting both sides with offers of arms shipments at rock-bottom prices. Druze with unfamiliar accents are passing through the area—Israeli or Syrian spies or simply visiting distant relatives from America? No one is sure. This morning, Abu Walid puts all that aside to teach at least one student how to pronounce 'ayn. He chooses his first target, Evan O'Shea, the class clown who occasionally surprises him with a close resemblance of a Damascene accent.

"'Arabi. Repeat 'Arabi!"

"R abee," the Australian replies, grinning.

God, how he hates that silly grin, more ridiculous than Arafat's. Abu Walid, a life-long Arab nationalist, has become increasingly intolerant of the Palestinian leader. Secretly, he wishes that Arafat and his men would reconcile with King Hussein and return to Jordan. Lebanon is fragile, too fragile to be in the crossfire of the Palestinian-Israeli conflict.

Abu Walid scans the class, desperately seeking just one student who can give him a decent *'ayn*. His eyes fall on the young Taragon.

"Marc, you say *'Arabi.*"

For a brief moment, Abu Walid holds out a faint hope that his favourite student will produce the elusive letter that distinguishes the Arabic language from all others. After all, Taragon is the anomaly in the class of pretentious neo-imperialists. The young man is focused, hard-working and genuinely interested in the Arab world. The rest are … Well, they are what they are.

"A rabee," Marc replies meekly.

Abu Walid sighs. "Class, I will be going on holidays to my village. You will have a new teacher after lunch. And may God help her!"

"*Aiwa*—yes!" Evan shouts. "Did I get the *'ayn* right?"

"No, Evan, there is no *'ayn* in *aiwa!*"

And with that, the old professor marches out of the classroom.

Evan turns to Marc. "A little melodramatic. It's only one fucking letter! Well, I can't wait to meet our next torturer."

"Hey, I like Abu Walid."

"Right. Let's get a shawarma in town. I'm famished."

Discussing who might win the rugby championship, Evan and Marc stroll down Chehab Street. As they approach the Al Sahra Restaurant, a girl steps out of a side street. A white hijab rests on her shoulders, framing long black hair. Her dark almond-shaped eyes have a slight feline slant to them, resting above high cheekbones. There's a bronze tinge to her skin, a gift from the Mediterranean sun. She blushes and lowers her head as the two young men stop in their tracks to stare. She gently raises her eyes to meet theirs. Blood rushes to Marc's head, forcing him to involuntarily look away.

Evan nudges Marc, and says: "Wow, isn't she a looker?"

The boisterous Australian's remark makes a number of villagers turn in their direction. The girl's face reddens and she quickly pulls her hijab over her hair. An old man sitting on a doorstep, mutters: "*Franji, haram*—foreigner, shame."

Evan is undeterred. He steps toward the girl, blocking her way. Then smiles expansively and offers his hand.

"Hullo. Do you speak English? I'm from Australia. You know Kangaroo Land! Ever been there? I can get you a visa."

The girl ignores his hand and looks straight past him.

"Evan, you're embarrassing her," Marc says.

"Thank you, but he is only embarrassing himself. And no, I don't want a visa!" the girl replies in flawless English before sidestepping Evan.

"Beautiful, fucking beautiful. Nothing like the rest of the local talent here."

"Don't be an asshole, Evan."

"Hey man, cool it. It's only a sheila."

Marc is tempted to cuff his arrogant friend, but a commotion at the restaurant distracts him.

A large crowd has formed in front of the restaurant's TV. Even with his limited Arabic, Marc can make out the key words—*harb* (war), *Filistini* (Palestinian) and *Falanj* (Phalangists). A Lebanese Broadcasting Corporation's correspondent is standing outside a Maronite Church. A photo of Pierre Gemayel, the leader of the Phalangist party, appears in the corner of the screen. The men in the restaurant look worried. Evan is no longer at his side.

A firm hand lands on his shoulder. He turns to see the grim face of the owner's son.

"*Fransawi*—Frenchman, it is very bad."

"What's bad?" Marc asks.

"There will be more bloodshed now. Some fools have killed four Phalangist militiamen in Beirut."

Marc looks past the worried faces of the men around him for some sign of Evan. Finally, he sees him badgering the young cook to hurry up with making two sandwiches while the other customers remain glued to the television.

Marc chooses an outside table near the stone wall separating the restaurant from the street. The grape arbour there provides at least some shade from the noon sun. The adjacent tables are littered with local newspapers. He picks up a few and tries to decipher the Arabic headlines.

Evan triumphantly returns with two shawarmas and cokes. "So what is the hoopla all about?"

Marc briefs him on the latest incident and tries to explain the broader political context. For the first time, his Australian friend actually shows a little interest in what he is saying.

Marc explains that the National Compact between the Lebanese Christians, Muslims and Druze is breaking down since the arrival of tens of thousands of Palestinian fighters from Jordan.

"So the Palestinians are to blame?" Evan asks.

"Yes, and no."

"Meaning?"

"The Palestinians didn't create the problem. Lebanon inherited an unsustainable political system from the French mandate, which gave most of the power to the Christians, particularly the Maronite Christians."

"The Christians are the majority, aren't they?"

"Maybe once they were, but their numbers are declining, and the Muslims have had a significantly higher birth rate for several decades. So they're lobbying for equal power."

"And where do the Palestinians fit in?"

"Arafat believes that the only way to force Israel to let Palestinian refugees return and to get it to agree to a two-state solution is to keep up military pressure. Since being booted out of Jordan and Syria, the only place he can do this from is Lebanon."

"Okay, so why is he meddling in the problems between the Christian and Muslim Lebanese?"

"Because he's a fool. Pierre Gemayel, the leader of the largest Christian party, the Phalangists, had originally supported the Palestinian cause, but now he is advocating that they should all leave Lebanon."

Evan polishes off his sandwich and sits back to sip his coke and crack a few lewd jokes. He has already mastered the first lesson of his new profession—dissimulate your own knowledge behind buffoonish behaviour and people will speak freely around you. He appears to be just a boorish foreigner to the restaurant's patrons who exchange views on what will happen next in Beirut. Their accent is rougher than the dialect that his Syrian grandmother had spoken when he was a child but still understandable. No one in Shemlan is onto his Arab origins, not even Marc. And he'll be sure to be the last to pronounce a decent ʿayn to keep it that way.

"Evan, shall we head back?"

"Lead the way. Maybe we'll cross paths with that young sheila again."

"Calm down! You have too many kangaroo hormones."

Hoda surveys the supplies in Abu Walid's desk—plenty of chalk, but a lot of the pieces are broken in two, some into even smaller bits. She's heard of Abu Walid's temper and wonders whether her class of *Franjis* could really be that bad. She takes out a piece of chalk and writes her name Hoda 'Akkawi in Arabic on the blackboard. She then adds: 'Akkawi is a person from 'Akka, Palestine—Acre in English. If she only teaches her students one thing in the four weeks she's replacing Abu Walid, it will be about 'Akka and why she's not able to return to Palestine, her country. Let the spies among them report back to their capitals that the Palestinians are steadfast.

"Hullo, are you lost?" comes a voice she's heard before.

Hoda turns, still holding the chalk. She looks confident but stern. Evan's face drops.

"You said you were from Australia, didn't you?" Hoda says.

"Yes."

"It is a country populated by criminals, isn't it? Well, there will be no criminal behaviour in my class. Keep your eyes and remarks to yourself, and you might just learn a little Arabic."

Great, a ball-breaker for a teacher, Evan thinks.

Marc stands at the door, not sure if he's also going to be blasted.

Hoda's stern look melts into a soft smile. "By your accent, you must be French. France is a civilized country. *Ahlan wa Sahlan*—Welcome! I am Hoda 'Akkawi."

And for the first time, Marc hears a distinctive *'ayn*.

"'Akkawi as in 'Akka?" he asks.

"Yes, that's right," Hoda says, smiling. "And your *'ayn* is perfect. Abu Walid has taught you well."

Trust the French to seduce the teacher, Evan thinks.

As if she could read his thoughts, Hoda casts a disapproving look at Evan. He sits down and begins to shrink in his chair.

Marc offers his hand. "That's right, I'm French. Marc Taragon. But my parents aren't French. They're refugees from Spain."

Hoda smiles again. *A refugee like me*, she thinks, as she places her palm in his.

The all-male class filters in, each noticing that Abu Walid's replacement is certainly a lot easier on the eyes than the old geezer. They soon also find her teaching a step-up. By the end of the class, most have mastered the pronunciation of 'ayn by reciting 'Akka medinah 'arabiyyah fi Filistin—Acre is an Arab city in Palestine.

At one point, one of the Brits in the class puts up his hand to ask: "Can you take a few minutes to explain who's who among all these religions in Lebanon. I find it quite confusing."

"Well, I'm not really paid to teach that," Hoda answers.

"Please, just the basics."

"All right. The population in Lebanon is divided into five groups."

"Five? I thought it was just Christians and Muslims," one of the students says.

"No, the population is divided among three groups who see themselves as indigenous Lebanese and two groups who came to Lebanon as refugees. The first refugees were the Armenians. They're Christian and have been in Lebanon since fleeing their homes in 1918 in what is now Turkey. The newer refugees are the Palestinians, who are mostly Muslim. I am Palestinian, and my family has been in Lebanon almost thirty years."

"And the indigenous Lebanese?"

"The population is roughly split between Christians and Muslims, with Muslims being a slight majority. There's an important minority, which is neither Christian nor Muslim. We call these people the Druze."

"Abu Walid is a Druze," one of the students says.

Hoda hesitates. It's not her place to comment on the religious affiliations of other teachers. "Did he tell you that?"

"Yes, he said he came from a mixed Druze-Christian village in the Shouf Mountains. He didn't tell us much about the Druze though."

"Well, the Druze are often reluctant to explain their religion to others," Hoda says. "I can tell you though they consider themselves to be an offshoot of Islam, although their beliefs are different from Muslims."

Just as Marc was about to ask Hoda for an explanation of the role of religion in Lebanon's power structure, the school's headmaster walks in.

"Thank you, Hoda. We are going to close the school a little early today. There have been some unfortunate events in Beirut."

Chapter

4

Beirut – April 1975

E VAN PULLS MARC ASIDE, as they exit the school. He grins and says:
"You didn't waste any time, did you?"
"What?"
"You know I have first dibs on her. I saw her first."
"What are you talking about!"
"The bird, man, the bird. She likes you and she could teach you a lot more than just Arabic, but let me have a go first."

Marc smiles at his incorrigible friend. Evan is the first Aussie he has ever met, and he wonders whether the whole island is like him.

Several classmates, all young British diplomats in training, file by them without a sign of acknowledgement.

Evan glares at them. "Those pommies—they're a stuck-up lot. Mostly poofs, you know. They come looking for a Lawrence-of-Arabia experience."

"What?"

"Yes, like in Lawrence's little encounter with the Turkish Pasha in Deraa and again with his Bedouin boy servants. You've seen the film, haven't you?"

Marc hadn't but he had read the *Seven Pillars of Wisdom*, and had an inkling of what Evan was alluding to and just maybe what "poof" means. He adds homophobia to the long list of his friend's shortcomings and is about to lecture Evan on the values of tolerance and sexual diversity when the headmaster turns the corner.

"Hello boys, we have a problem. Maybe you can help us?"

"Sure, what is it?" Evan asks.

"One of our teachers lives in West Beirut. Since noon all the local taxi drivers are refusing to enter the city because of the roadblocks."

"Roadblocks? Set up by whom?" Marc asks.

"By all sides, but there have been reports of kidnappings, maybe even killings at the Phalangist checkpoints. The Maronites are on the war-path to avenge the four dead militiamen found at the port this morning. Our teacher is a Palestinian and a Muslim. It would be much safer if she travelled with you. I know it's an imposition."

"Well, Evan, you're the one with the car," Marc says. "If you want to help out, I can come along."

"I don't know. It sounds a little iffy and ..." Evan stops in mid-sentence when Hoda steps from behind the headmaster.

"Is this the passenger?" Evan asks with a grin.

"Yes, Miss 'Akkawi lives in Sabra camp, but you can drop her in the Fakhani district. She can make it home from there. Do you know where that is?"

"We can find it," Marc says. "Mademoiselle 'Akkawi, it would be an honour to take you to Beirut."

A hard nudge from Evan's elbow inflicts a sharp pain in Marc's ribs. "Remember, it's my car." Evan then turns to Hoda. "As my young French friend has so gallantly offered, it will be an honour and a pleasure to see you home safely."

Hoda looks at the headmaster who nods. She turns to Marc, ignoring Evan and says: "I'd like to leave now before it gets dark."

"Of course," Marc replies, giving Evan a hard shove to the back. "It's this way."

When they reach Evan's car, Hoda sits in the back. Marc is about to sit in the front passenger seat when she says: "Could you sit with me. I'd feel safer that way." Evan winks at Marc.

The headmaster's wife rushes up from behind him. The plump, middle-aged woman presses something into Hoda's hand. She then bends over to whisper in the young woman's ear. Hoda nods obediently. Marc looks at her, but she avoids his glance. "Can we leave now?" she asks.

Evan is eager to test out his new Peugeot on the mountain road from Shemlan down to Aley. He's an excellent driver, but like most right-hand-drive car drivers, he occasionally looks the wrong way at intersections. Marc sits back and takes in the breathtaking mountain scenery. That is until Hoda removes her hijab, unbuttons the top two buttons of her blouse and takes off her long skirt to reveal a pair of tight-fitting jeans.

She leans toward him to whisper: "If the Phalangists stop the car, tell them I'm your wife. It'll be safer that way."

Before Marc can respond, she slips a gold ring on her wedding finger. Marc is impressed by Hoda's directness. He hasn't met many young Muslim women, but she is definitely different. He silently relishes his new *marital* status.

Evan eases on the brakes as they approach the sleepy Druze town of Aley. Straddling the Damascus to Beirut highway and perched at the top of the descent to Beirut, Aley is a stranglehold for getting in and out of the capital. Marc can feel Hoda tense up. But militiamen just wave them through. As Evan accelerates past the checkpoint, Marc breathes a sigh of relief and looks at Hoda. Her chest rises and falls as she struggles to regain her composure.

"Are you all right?" Marc asks.

"Yes, I'm fine. For a moment, I was worried the Druze might mistake me for a Maronite Christian. I changed my clothes too soon."

"The Druze have no quarrel with women."

"I wish it was like that. But when their leaders give an order, the Druze execute it without mercy. One day, they're the gentlest of people, the next day killing machines."

Evan smiles in the rear-view mirror. "Lovers' quarrel back there?"

Hoda struggles to hide her own smile. Marc feels both warm and embarrassed. An awkward moment passes before he borrows a textbook from Hoda and gives Evan a hard tap on the head. "Keep your eyes on the road!"

"Hey mate, that hurt!"

"Next time, it will hurt a lot more."

Hoda turns away to conceal her delight. There is now a pleasant complicity among the three of them. As the descent into Beirut begins in earnest, Evan negotiates the multiple bends with the skill of a race-car driver. When they reach a flat stretch again, Marc and Hoda begin to relax. He asks her how she learned French. From her Aunt Meryem, she replies and then begins to recount her Jewish aunt's tragic journey from Algeria to Palestine and then to Lebanon.

Chapter

———†———

5

Nicosia – January 2007

IN JUST THREE hours, Taragon covers the outbreak of the Lebanese civil war until the first Israeli invasion in 1978. Marie sits entranced as the veteran journalist speaks of his personal encounters, and often friendships, with most of the young Lebanese and Palestinian leaders of the day. What fascinates her even more is Taragon's cogent analysis of the behind-the-scenes manoeuvres that resulted in the full-scale confrontation of the PLO and its allies with the Christian militias.

Taragon explains how the Lebanese order, brokered by the country's notables, disintegrated, and younger tougher leaders emerged in all the communities. Syria and Israel enrolled these young cubs in a vicious proxy war. And ordinary Lebanese and Palestinians became mere pawns in a power struggle of the large egos of small men.

Taragon is unsparing in his criticism of Arafat, the most cunning of the new generation of leaders. Without regard to the welfare of the Lebanese, Arafat has made the PLO the master of all Lebanon south of Beirut. The devastation that the 1956, 1967 and 1973 wars inflicted on the Arab world had convinced their rulers to keep a tight leash on the Palestinian fighters in their countries. Lebanon was the exception. The political vacuum there unshackled the *fedayeen,* and the Israelis' worst nightmare of a truly independent Palestinian army on their borders became a reality.

Marie reaches over to turn off the recorder. It is time to ask him. She reaches into her handbag for the photo.

Taragon looks at his watch then abruptly stands up.

"I'm sorry. I lost track of time. I have to meet someone in Kyrenia.

Please forgive me. We'll meet next week in Istanbul."

"But …"

Taragon hands the barman a wad of Turkish lira, much more than just for the meal. The younger man leans forward to whisper in the journalist's ear. Taragon nods. Marie now has the photo in her hand. He touches her shoulder and looks directly into her eyes. He displays a seriousness that paralyzes her from saying what she has rehearsed so many times.

"Marie, it would be better if you stayed a little longer here. Ibrahim has finished his work. He'll be here in a minute and can accompany you back to the checkpoint."

"Why? It's only two hundred metres away?"

"I'd feel safer if you went with Ibrahim. On the other side of the checkpoint, we have a friend called Spiros. He'll take you back to your hotel in his taxi. Please don't take any taxi but his and don't try to walk back to your hotel. Nicosia is normally a safe city, but we have reasons to worry."

"I don't understand. What's going on?"

"Some people don't like what I'm doing."

Taragon vanishes down the staircase. The photo is now damp with the sweat of Marie's hand. She shakes her head a little, surprised by her inaction. She sought him out to show him the photo, to ask a simple question, but his mere presence has overwhelmed her. Now she must wait another week to uncover the truth.

Marie moves to the edge of the roof to catch a glimpse of Taragon as he exits the restaurant. Instinctively, she senses something is wrong. A man wearing sunglasses stands in a doorway on the opposite side of the street—the same man she saw at the checkpoint. And it dawns on her—the broad shoulders, the height and wavy blond hair, it's the voyeur from across the hotel's courtyard. Turning the corner, an older man joins the watcher, and both stare in Taragon's direction.

Marie starts to shout to warn Taragon, but her vocal cords freeze.

"Don't say anything," a voice whispers in her ear.

She turns. Ibrahim's beautiful smile greets her.

"Don't worry about Marc. Everything is fine."

"But look! Look at those men! They were at the checkpoint!"

"We know. But Marc knows what he's doing."

Marie cannot hold back. "What exactly is he doing?"

"He will tell you himself. But don't worry. Uncle Khalid has everything under control. Those men are Israeli spies. I ran a check on them. Uncle Khalid will detain them until the boat leaves."

"Uncle Khalid?"

"Yes, Khalid Murat, our uncle. He is the new chief of police," Ibrahim says with a proud smile.

There is a warmth, a connection, perhaps the making of a conspiracy between Marie and Ibrahim. More importantly—there's trust. She feels safe. She knows that Taragon will also be safe. Marie reaches out to take Ibrahim's hand. "*On y va?*"

Chapter

6

Nicosia – January 2007

TARAGON WALKS ALONG the seafront in Kyrenia. The war hasn't touched the beautiful port city. At the east end of the old harbour is the *Girne Kalesi,* a 16th-century castle built by the Venetians over a previous Crusader fortification. He notices a few boarded-up homes, abandoned by their Greek-Cypriot owners. Taragon reflects on the irony of meeting at a café called Chimera. For the Greek Cypriots, it denotes a mythological combination of a goat, lion and serpent; for the rest of the world, a fanciful illusion. Chimera—a fitful double entendre for their peace initiative. Indeed, it will take the stubbornness of the goat, the courage of the lion and the cunning of the serpent to convince the world they're not pursuing a pipe-dream.

Taragon arrives at the café and looks for Jonathan Bronstein, the man he is to meet. The café's employees busily prepare for the evening meal. Most of the tourists are Turkish Cypriots working in London. When they can save up enough to escape England's dreadful weather, they come back for a cheap holiday stay with their relatives. But the new government is determined to attract more European tourists to lessen its dependence on Ankara. Taragon wishes it luck. Turkish Cypriots certainly need to shake off the shackles of the Turkish military, but more importantly, they need to make peace with their Greek countrymen.

Taragon is about to leave when a beefy hand lands on his shoulder. He resists striking back with a defensive blow. Instead, he slowly turns. Bronstein's face has aged since they last met at the funeral of Israeli Prime Minister Yitzhak Rabin in 1995. Taragon had been sent to cover Rabin's assassination by a West Bank settler. Bronstein was then still in his prime, a stalwart of the left-wing Meretz Party, a man Rabin had

listened to. His once flaming red hair has disappeared, replaced by a
crown of thinning grey. His green eyes have lost their glint, and are now
surrounded by deep wrinkles. And his smile shows a few missing teeth,
thanks to a violent encounter with Israel's ultra-right.

Taragon embraces Bronstein, who grins.

"So are we going fishing?"

"Yes," Taragon replies. "Did you bring the boat?"

"It's over there." Bronstein motions to a small yacht docked in front
of the café.

"Where did you get it?"

"A wealthy friend in Meretz. So where are we headed?"

"Istanbul via Mersin. And just maybe we'll pass by Gordiyon."

"To cut a knot?"

"Yes, to cut a knot."

The boat leaves the dock, cutting through the aqua-blue of the eastern
Mediterranean. It is perfect for the short journey to the Turkish mainland where Taragon and his companion will land undetected. Khalid
Murat's agents are already circulating rumours that Taragon has returned to France, and Bronstein's gone to Moscow.

Night falls. Taragon watches the constellations form. No better place
in the world to see the stars dance in the theatre of the Gods. Cassiopeia
is brightly lit up, perhaps to attract her lover Perseus.

Taragon looks over to Bronstein.

"Are we safe?" Bronstein asks.

"Yes. Thanks to Khalid and your boat, we're now ghosts. Let's hope
that we can keep it that way."

"*Tov*—good."

The two men take stock of each other.

"It's been a long time," the Israeli remarks.

"Indeed. You know that the Mossad had me banned from entering
Israel. They even accused me of being an anti-Semite."

"I know. Some of my old friends in military intelligence are trying
to get the Mossad back under control, but they too are under pressure.
There's a witch hunt in the intelligence services for anyone who believes that peace is possible. And the American Congress is now in the
hard-liners' pockets. Marc, can we really make this happen?"

"I hope so. Time is running out."

Chapter

7

The Road to Beirut – April 1975

MARC LOOKS ACROSS AT HODA. *Perhaps, he has misheard her,* he thinks. Did this young Palestinian woman just say her aunt was Jewish?

Hoda reads Marc's mind and continues.

"My Aunt Meryem was Jewish from Algeria. You look surprised. You shouldn't be. There was a large Jewish community there, but the French Vichy officials sold them out during the war."

"How did she end up in Lebanon?"

"She went first to Istanbul, and toward the end of the war to Haifa where she met my uncle, Hisham. They were both Communists and worked on the party's newspaper."

"My parents were anarchists who fled Spain during the civil war."

"Oh. It sounds like we may have something in common."

"I'd like to think so. Tell me more about your aunt and uncle. Marriage between Muslims and Jews must have been rare back then."

"Not as uncommon as it is now. Like many party members, my aunt and uncle fell in love and married. The party and the British authorities protected them from extremists. When the British withdrew and the party splintered, that protection vanished. My uncle was killed in 1947, and my aunt and my cousin, Abdullah, fled Haifa to Lebanon."

"How did your uncle die?"

"It was in the middle of the night. He was working on an editorial for the party newspaper pleading for a bi-national state. No one was sure if the assailants were Jews or Arabs. My aunt Meryem found him perched over his desk with a makeshift garrotte around his neck."

Marc looks attentively at Hoda. He isn't sure how much more he should ask.

"Life wasn't easy in Beirut for refugees," Hoda says, "but Aunt Meryem found a job teaching art in a French convent school. The nuns, some pied-noirs from Algeria, knew she was a Jew but didn't care."

"Were you close to your aunt?"

"Very. My brother Nabil and I often spent our weekends with her and Abdullah. She taught us art. Nabil loved it. He's become a very good artist. You should see his street murals in Sabra. They're stunning."

"Was she a religious person?"

"Not at all, but she was pragmatic. She raised her son Abdullah as an atheist at home but conceded to her Muslim in-laws that he would attend the mosque with his cousins. When the rabbi of Beirut's small Jewish community asked that Abdullah also be taught basic Jewish beliefs and Hebrew, she reluctantly consented to that but insisted that it be kept secret. Meanwhile, Abdullah was educated by the nuns at Meryem's school. They taught him Christianity and to sing hymns."

"He sounds like an interesting person."

"He certainly is. He can cite the Quran, Torah and New Testament, but he doesn't believe in any of them. When foreigners ask him about his religion, he recites back to them the Declaration of the Rights of Man in Arabic, French and even Hebrew. You should see their faces!"

"You spoke of your aunt in the past tense."

"Yes, she died two years ago from tuberculosis. She contracted it when she walked to Lebanon in the winter of 1947."

"I'm sorry."

"Don't be. She lived a full life and taught me a lot."

Marc hadn't expected such an intricate story from his new Arabic teacher—neither did he anticipate the intensity of his attraction to her. He looks out the window. The outskirts of the Beirut suburb of Hazmiyeh are coming into view. Signs of recent fighting are everywhere. Walls marked by bullet holes. Overturned cars. Burning tires.

Evan slows the car when he sees militiamen at the Hazmiyeh junction. He can't make out the regalia on their makeshift uniforms, but Hazmiyeh is a Christian area so he assumes that they must be either Phalangists or their main rivals, the Tiger militia.

Elie Labaki begins to sweat when the officer says: "It's your turn." For the first time today, he must be the one to approach an oncoming car. It's the most dangerous job at a checkpoint. You never know if the car is full of fighters ready to gun through it. He fingers the stylized cedar insignia newly sewn onto his jacket and curses how easy it was for the Phalangist militiamen to knock on his door at nine that morning and hand the patch to his mother. Like the mothers of all his friends, she dutifully sewed it on. Refusal was not an option, not for him, not for her, not for anyone.

Elie steps forward, his hand in the air to wave the car to one side. He looks at the diplomatic plates and scrutinizes the faces of the driver and passengers. Clearly, foreigners—he relaxes. But the shuffling of feet and cocking of guns behind him remind him to hurry. He's already witnessed how trigger-happy his comrades can be. The sooner he can send these foreigners on their way, the better. He motions to the driver to roll down the window.

"*Passeports, s'il vous plaît,*" he politely asks.

"I'm sorry. What was that?" Evan asks.

In halting English, Elie asks again for the passports.

Evan digs out his diplomatic passport and Marc hands over his French one. Hoda sits rigidly.

"Diplomat, good! French also good. Who is she?"

"She's my wife. She's left her passport at home."

"Is she also French?"

"*Oui Monsieur, je suis française,*" Hoda says.

At first, Elie looks suspiciously at her. His own French is strong, and although he cannot detect a trace of an accent from the elegantly dressed young woman, her complexion is olive like the girls in the refugee camps. Then he notices her fingering something around her neck. The silver of a crucifix reflects in the late afternoon sun. Elie breathes a sigh of relief. Thank God, she's a Christian. French or Arab, it doesn't matter. His orders are clear—no Muslims are to pass through. He shudders at the butchery he witnessed that morning. Old men herded into open fields to be eliminated *à l'arme blanche*. This car will not be a problem. No need to add its occupants to the rising toll of the missing. He hates this war. He has no quarrel with Muslims, but he's a Maronite and he has his duty.

"Please continue. But be careful. The Palestinians and their communist allies are everywhere."

Evan nods deferentially. Marc gives Hoda a side glance. She's still fingering the crucifix. So that was what the headmaster's wife had pressed into her hand. As soon as the checkpoint disappears from view, Hoda removes it, buttons her blouse and puts on her hijab.

"The next checkpoint will be at the Museum crossing. There they'll be Muslims."

"Good, your people then?" Evan asks.

"Possibly. I'm not sure where the Palestinian lines are now. The checkpoint might be manned by Lebanese Muslims. Some of them are as extreme as those young Maronites."

Elie watches Evan's Peugeot disappear down the hill, and returns to his companions at the checkpoint.

"Who were they, Elie?"

"An Australian diplomat and a French couple." He keeps his suspicions about the woman to himself.

The sun is setting over the Mediterranean. It'll be a long cold night. Elie slumps into a chair, and worries about his fiancée. Palestinian and Druze forces surround the coastal town of Damour where her family lives, and she has left her studies in Beirut to stay with them. He knows that his fellow militiamen are no match for the enemy forces there. Already so much blood has been shed in so little time. He wants to finish his studies and start work at the Banco do Brazil, where his uncle is the Beirut branch manager. All he wants is a peaceful life, but here he is in Hazmiyeh, toting an HK sub-machine gun. Elie leans back to dream of his fiancée and their life together when the war ends.

Hoda is right about Muslims manning the Museum crossing checkpoint, and they are the worst type. She recognizes immediately the red-rimmed octagon shoulder patches of the Mourabitoun.

Three young militiamen point their guns directly at the car, march toward it, and without asking for identification, pull Evan, Marc and Hoda out of it. Evan reaches into his vest pocket to bring out his diplomatic passport but stops when the muzzle of a gun is pressed hard against his temple. Another grabs Hoda by the arm. She curses him in

Arabic. Just as the militiaman is about to strike her, Marc lunges at him, wrestling him to the ground.

"*Ibn sharmouta*—son of a bitch!" the militiaman screams as Marc pins him down. Marc looks behind. Ten more fighters are racing toward them. He releases the man and stands up, his hands in the air. The kicks and punches are swift and vicious. Half-conscious, Marc feels himself being hauled up against a cement wall. Evan is beside him, sweating profusely, the revolver now pressed hard against the back of his skull. Hoda screams and curses as two militiamen pin her against the car. As she protests, "I am a Muslim," the crucifix falls from her pocket. The leader, a small, balding man, picks it up and grunts: "You're a liar and they're spies."

The militiaman whom Marc had bested is now on his feet and leering at Hoda. "Captain Yassin, let's rape the bitch!"

Yassin glares at his brother-in-law and shoves him away from Hoda. There will be no rape on his watch.

With his palms pressed hard against the wall, Evan can feel the bullet-holes in the concrete. He looks beyond Marc to where the wall turns a corner. A shoe-less foot peeks out. He breathes for a moment and begins to smell the human flesh rotting in the sun. As the guns behind them are cocked, Evan knows what he must do. He summons the courage to utter in perfect Damascene Arabic that he is a Syrian intelligence officer—a lie, but perhaps one that can buy them time.

Abdullah 'Akkawi lowers his binoculars. He has seen enough. He curses Arafat for having made an alliance with these scum who have laid their hands on his cousin. "*Yallah, Shabab.*" He orders his men into the back of the beaten-up Mercedes truck and squeezes his gigantic frame into the passenger seat beside the driver.

"Go!"

Seconds later, the truck screeches to a halt in front of Yassin's men. Twenty Palestinian fighters jump out, and Abdullah climbs down from the cab and walks forward as if to shake Yassin's hand. Instead, he grabs the smaller man by the throat and lifts him off the ground.

"What are you doing to my cousin?" Abdullah screams at the man now going blue in the face. The other Palestinian fighters train their guns on the bewildered and outnumbered Mourabitoun.

Hoda breaks free of her captors, and races to Abdullah's side.

"Thank God, Abdullah, they were going to shoot my friends. And that one threatened to rape me!"

"Don't worry. You're safe now. Who are these foreigners?"

"My students. Marc, he is French and Evan's Australian."

Abdullah turns to Marc and in flawless French says: "Monsieur, can you quickly take my cousin home? There's a problem near the port. We must go there."

Abdullah assigns a young fighter to ride with them to Sabra and then escort Marc and Evan back to the highway to Aley.

As Evan's Peugeot rumbles along the almost deserted streets of West Beirut, Marc turns to Hoda. "He spoke French like you, even better than you."

"Yes, he's Meryem's son."

Evan watches Marc and Hoda and makes a mental note—Abdullah 'Akkawi, a half-Jewish commander in the Popular Front, Hoda's cousin. This connection could come in useful for his real assignment in Lebanon. He decides then and there that he'll begin to show Hoda a lot more respect and win her trust.

The Mourabitoun leader sits on the ground with his disarmed men. His throat still aches from Abdullah's strong grip. The gigantic Palestinian returns towards him.

"Your name?" Abdullah yells.

"Yassin Ayoub."

"What will I find behind that wall?"

"Three men. They tried to run our checkpoint this morning."

"Did you execute them?"

"No, two died when we shot at the car. The third died in the crash."

"Bring him!" Abdullah orders his men, who drag Yassin to his feet.

He walks past the wall. Yassin is telling the truth—only three men, no women or children. He stoops to examine the first body. The dead man is clearly older than his two companions. His forehead is blood-ied—small shards of glass in his scalp, but no sign of bullet wounds. The two others have been shot in the head and shoulders. He checks their identity cards. All are from Ain Ebel, a border village in the South. The young men were students, Maronites, the old man an Armenian Catholic, a taxi driver.

"Look at their forearms," Yassin says.

Abdullah rolls up the young men's sleeves. Tattooed on their arms is "*Lebeyki Lubnan*—At your service, Lebanon," the slogan of the Guardians of the Cedars. There's no doubt. These young men are followers of the fanatic Étienne Saqr, who preaches that the duty of every Lebanese is to kill a Palestinian. Abdullah looks at the young men's faces—schoolboys barely old enough to shave, and already recruited to be Saqr's henchmen. In the distance, he hears the mortar fire near the port. He makes up his mind.

"I should still kill you for dishonouring my cousin."

"*Effendi*, forgive me. We were only trying to frighten them into confessing. Beirut is full of spies, and she was wearing a cross but claimed to be a Muslim! What were we to think? Forgive me, *Effendi*, I did not mean to dishonour your family."

"Only God can forgive you. But today you'll defend our Kurd brothers in Karantina. Gather your men. We leave now!"

"May I be a martyr for Islam, *Effendi*. Men, gather. We fight in Karantina for Allah!"

Abdullah 'Akkawi looks at his new ally. There is a fanaticism he detests. He decides to test this man, to compromise him, to ensure that the man won't turn on him later.

"There is one last thing. Did that man really threaten to rape my cousin? Yes or no?"

"Yes, but I didn't let him."

"You know the penalty?"

"The man really didn't mean it."

"Are you calling my cousin a liar?"

Yassin can see that the giant Palestinian is implacable. He looks over his shoulder at his brother-in-law. The man's shaking. Urine pools on the ground between his legs. Yassin curses his wife for talking him into taking her brother on. Now he might get them all killed. He feels Abdullah's presence beside him, and his neck muscles begin to ache again from the bruising left by the giant's grip. Yassin knows what he has to do.

"Give me a pistol. I will personally carry out the punishment."

Abdullah studies the Mourabitoun leader. Can he really trust him with a gun? The man's eyes betray a mixture of sadness and resolution. Abdullah places the pistol in his hand.

The condemned man looks up as the Palestinian giant hands Yassin the gun. He turns in all directions, looking for an avenue of escape. There is none. He sinks to his feet and whimpers. "No, no. Please don't!"

Yassin takes aim. Can he really execute his wife's brother? His vision blurs. His hand shakes. Just as Yassin feels he is going to break down, his brother-in-law lunges toward him, desperately trying to grab the pistol from his hand. In a reptilian reflex, Yassin pulls the trigger.

Abdullah looks at executioner and executed. He feels disgust overcome him. How can he trust a man who would kill one of his own?

But there are men and women dying near the port. He needs these Mourabitoun fighters at least for a while longer.

Abdullah puts his hand on Yassin's shoulder.

"Get your men into the truck. Today we fight together."

Chapter

8

MARIE PACKS HER BAGS for the flight to Istanbul. She'll leave from the Turkish side—a chance to see Ibrahim again. She likes the thought of that. She'll come back to Cyprus soon enough, and then …? There's a knock on the door. Could it be Ibrahim passing by to say goodbye? The thought delights her. Marie walks quickly to the door, brushing her hair back. She opens it to the two men whom Uncle Khalid took away in the police car. She steps back defensively.

"Don't worry," David says. "We only want to talk to you, and to warn you about Taragon."

"Yes, you should know what you are getting into," Ari says.

Marie looks furtively for a weapon. There is none. She acquiesces. "Downstairs in the restaurant," she says.

To her surprise, both David and Ari turn and begin to walk toward the stairs. Marie grabs a pen and notepad and follows them.

They choose a corner table. David scans the room. Ari pulls out a thick envelope with photographs. One by one, he places them on the table. They are of two men. One is obviously an Arab. The other she's not sure.

"Have you ever seen these men before?" Ari asks.

"No, never."

He then pulls out two more pictures. They're blurred but she recognizes Taragon in both. Each with one of the two other men.

"This man is Abdullah 'Akkawi, a.k.a. Abu Munir. He's a Hamas terrorist. This one is a radical Israeli politician—a traitor."

"I told you that I don't know them!"

"But you know Taragon."

"Yes."

"We believe that Taragon is brokering the sale of Israeli military secrets to terrorists. That's why we're here."

"What do you want from me?"

"Do you know where Taragon is going next?"

"No."

"Well, where are you going now?"

"To Athens," she says, lying.

"With a ticket on Turkish Airlines?"

Marie's face reddens. Then she sees her taxi driver Spiros standing
by the bar watching them and speaking into a cell phone. She suddenly
feels safe and leans forward toward the older Israeli agent, presses her
pen to the notepad and says: "You seem to know a lot about me so you
must also know that I'm a journalist. And I know that you are Israeli
spies travelling on fake Canadian passports. That's a story I can file
within an hour. So don't try to push me around!"

David spots Spiros. He whispers in Ari's ear. The two men rise from
the table.

"Ms. Boivin, we'll meet again. Remember that a reputation for helping terrorists won't help your career."

Va te faire foutre, Marie thinks. She notices David's eyes are firmly
on her. They're not like Ari's eyes, which are cold and dispassionate.
David's project desire, a menacing desire. She stands up, determined
to show her resolve.

"No, we won't meet again!"

Ari watches her walking away. For a moment he admires her courage.

Chapter

9

Ramat HaSharon, Israel – February 2007

T HE OLD MOSSAD AGENT closes the door to the director's office and fumes at the berating, to which he's just been subjected. He is even angrier over his own mistakes. It was supposed to be a simple operation in Cyprus. Confront Taragon, tell him to back off on his plans to broker a peace deal—that was all there was to be to it. The Mossad already knows the basics of what Taragon is trying to do. They're fairly sure that Bronstein and Abdullah 'Akkawi are part of it. Bronstein, they can handle. All they need is to fabricate a scandal to discredit him. Perhaps, Photoshop him into a picture with an under-age prostitute. The ultra-nationalist press would love that. They hate his pro-peace views. Someone suggested putting in a boy instead of a girl, but the director, himself gay, cringed at the thought of stirring up the homophobic tendency of the religious right.

'Akkawi is another matter. No one in the service knows now what he looks like. The Iranian surgeons did a good job, and his inner circle has proven impenetrable. Even Ari's main informant in Gaza, Muhammad Shehadi, hasn't seen 'Akkawi since the surgery, or so Shehadi tells him. Ari doesn't trust the Fatah commander though. The man has played both sides for too long for anyone to really know where his loyalties lie. Ari had proposed to his superiors that they reach out to the Iranians to make a deal. One photo of 'Akkawi against information on several Iranian dissidents in the US. Their friends in the CIA would oblige them, and the Iranian Revolutionary Guards would welcome such a deal, he argued. 'Akkawi is close to Iranian moderates and has spoken out against the growing influence of the Guards in the Hamas movement.

It pisses Ari off that his superiors are no longer listening to him. It's in Israel's interest that the peace initiative fail. When peace comes, it must be on Israel's terms, and the sick notion that any Palestinian refugee would return to Israel could never be part of that deal. It turns his stomach that Bronstein, a man with whom he had once hunted Arabs, is now part of this *conspiracy.*

Ari rearranges his desk. He knows that he has to get the case back on track. He's getting old, and his bosses have hinted more than once about retirement. Retirement? What would he do in retirement? He has served the state all his life, seen two marriages disintegrate because of it, and is childless. No, he'll track down Taragon and put an end to it. His superiors are clear that they no longer want to hear how he does it as long as he gets the job done.

David enters his office and takes a chair. How Ari despises this young upstart. An idiot who thinks more with his cock than his brain. Had David stayed away from the balcony at the hotel, Marie Boivin would have been none the wiser.

It chafes him how quickly they were made in North Nicosia. The Canadian must have tipped off Taragon's friend, the *schvartze* police chief. It could have been worse though. By sheer luck, a Turkish intelligence official was visiting when they were detained. The Turk had long been on Mossad's payroll, and he was senior enough to speak directly to the interior minister. Within an hour, they were delivered to the Greek side.

Suddenly, he realizes that David has been speaking to him.

"What?"

"Ari, like I just said, the cyber folks are telling me that Taragon must be back in Nicosia. He's making calls from there to Beirut."

"It's a decoy, *Shmendrik.* There's no way that Taragon would have returned so quickly. Anyone can make a call from his phone."

David bites his tongue. He hates it when Ari uses Yiddish words that he doesn't understand. The man has been forty years in Israel, and he still speaks like he's just off the boat. Just a few more months and the old man will be out of here. If he plays his cards right, he could get his job. All he needs is one more screw-up from Ari, and he can throw the old man under the bus. Few in the service will shed a tear for him when he is gone. But Ari has a lot of authority while he keeps his job. He still instils fear in more than a few of his colleagues.

Ari picks up the phone. "Get me the consulate in Montreal." If they can't track Taragon and the other two, they can certainly find out where the girl might be headed next.

Ari dismisses David. "Take some holidays," he tells him.

David grins. Why not? There's that Swedish stewardess who is flying into Tel Aviv for a twenty-four-hour layover. He could use some recreation, although he's found it hard to get the Canadian girl off his mind.

As soon as David leaves, Ari pulls out his stash of passports. Rumanian, Hungarian, Brazilian and then the prize of them all, the E.U. He doesn't like to use it often, but it's the *passe-partout*. From his filing cabinet, he selects a Belgian driver's licence and identity card. Perfect. European security services may be on the look-out for Mossad agent Ari Epstein, but Belgian businessman Hendrik Achterberg is free to travel wherever and whenever he wants.

Twenty minutes later, the call comes in. "Istanbul. She has a flight there tonight."

Mr. Achterberg dons his fedora and overcoat and heads to Lod Airport.

Chapter

10

THEIR MERCEDES-BENZ BUS speeds along the highway from Gordiyon to Istanbul. The visit to the city of the "Knot" wasn't just for good luck but has allowed Taragon and Bronstein to blend into the regular movement of foreigners from the ancient capital of Phrygia to Turkey's burgeoning metropolis. For good measure, they've taken seats far from each other and now feel confident that they've covered their tracks.

Bronstein silently watches the Anatolian plains roll by. It will be the first time in almost twenty-five years that he'll see Abdullah 'Akkawi. He's heard that 'Akkawi had changed after Sabra and Shatila. According to his sources, the young Palestinian fighter, an atheist with socialist ideals and open to European culture, has become a hardened Islamist.

Taragon has assured him that 'Akkawi is sincere about starting second-track peace negotiations. Bronstein hopes his friend is right. There's a lot of Israeli blood on 'Akkawi's hands—true they were all combatants, and Bronstein too has taken lives in defence of Israel. Still, military intelligence wants 'Akkawi dead. But he needs him to succeed— peace is made with enemies, not friends. 'Akkawi is the only enemy he really trusts, the only one who once spared his life, even if he repaid that debt many years ago.

Bronstein watches the Turkish army trucks headed to the east. He's heard that the Turks might be launching a major offensive into northern Iraq to fight Kurdish guerrillas. Another war in the Middle East. Will it ever end? He sees his friend begin to take notes. Taragon always the diligent journalist, can he now succeed as a peace-maker?

Minaret after minaret zig-zags against the dying light of the Istanbul skyline. The encounter with the Israelis in Cyprus still haunts Marie, but she feels safer now. She's met up with her friend Minh Chau Nguyen who's in Istanbul to represent the Canadian government at a UN conference. Her interview with Taragon is the next day. Today, they'll spend the afternoon in the Grand Bazaar.

Marie sits back in her chair and lowers her sunglasses. Minh Chau, always a lively woman, is radiant today as she talks about her boyfriend.

"Marie, Mathieu is an incredible man."

"I'm so happy for you, Minh Chau."

"There's something else."

"I'm listening."

"Well, I think that I'm pregnant."

"That's fantastic news!" Marie gently caresses her friend's face with the palm of her hand and smiles. "You will have a beautiful baby!"

A small tear of happiness runs down Minh Chau's cheek.

The splendour of their silence is broken by the ringing of Marie's cell phone.

"Hello. Yes, it's Marie. Oh, Monsieur Taragon! A letter. Yes, I can pick it up. What is the address again? 27 Hoca Paşa Muhammad Street. Hotel Yildiz. Got it. *Pas de quoi.* I'll see you tomorrow."

"So that was him?" Minh Chau asks. "Taragon, I mean?"

"Yes. He's asked me to run an errand for him tonight. Can you come with me? It's not far."

"Of course!"

Abdullah 'Akkawi watches the two young women laughing and sipping Turkish coffee. The Vietnamese girl is stunning, but it is the blond Canadian who reminds him of someone from his past. Remarkably so. The years have never healed the loss of those closest to him. He moves to see the girls better. 'Akkawi's network is world-wide. It didn't take long to learn everything that he needed to know about Marie Boivin, including her father's peacekeeping service in Lebanon and before that, in Cyprus. He hasn't had time to check out the Vietnamese girl, but he will. 'Akkawi must know everything—to survive.

Marie and Minh Chau leave a generous tip for the waiter and head off to the Hotel Yildiz to pick up the letter. 'Akkawi follows at a safe distance. He slouches to conceal his height. A short, bald man steps out of a taxi twenty metres behind the women. There's something familiar about the man. 'Akkawi watches him closely. It is clear that he's following the women. But why?

Marie turns and also notices the man. It's the older Israeli from Nicosia. Their eyes meet for a second, and then he steps into a doorway to strike up a conversation with a prostitute. Marie whispers to Minh Chau that they're being followed. She quickly tells her of the confrontation in Cyprus.

"The man in the doorway?" Minh Chau asks. She is trembling with anger.

"Yes."

"Leave him to me. Go get the letter at the hotel. I'll see you later."

"Wait! Don't!"

Marie reaches out to pull her friend back, but she's already on her way to confront Ari.

'Akkawi is also closing in on the Israeli. He recognizes the cold look in the man's eyes. It takes him back to Beirut—to his son's bloodied body collapsed against the wall. The repressed anger of twenty-five years rises within him.

Minh Chau reaches Ari Epstein first. She slaps his face.

"You bastard! What are you doing cheating on me with this ugly whore?"

"What!?" Ari says.

"Don't call me ugly, you Asian bitch!" the prostitute lashes out.

"I'll call you anything I want. Leave my husband alone!"

A crowd gathers. The prostitute darts off. Ari too tries to extricate himself, but Minh Chau holds him back, screaming: "Police!"

'Akkawi has his knife out. He's two metres from his prey. He knows where he'll strike. He finds an opening and moves in. The screech of rubber against the curb stops him. From the corner of his eye, he sees two officers step out of a police cruiser.

"What's going on here?" a young officer demands.

Minh Chau begins to cry. "This man grabbed my breast!"

Ari is baffled. Who's this woman? Why is she doing this? Is she an agent?

"You, come with us!" The policeman orders. Ari protests and reaches for his passport, but is slammed against the hood of the car and then forced to the ground. Stunned he looks up at a massive blurred figure approaching from behind the policemen. He strains his neck to get a better look. He sees the knife in the hulk's hand. Suddenly, his mind flashes back to Lebanon—the giant he had once hunted? And now he is the prey? He tries to move, but both policemen pin him down. Ari waits for the blade to strike.

'Akkawi hesitates. He could kill the Israeli, but he would have to take out the two policemen as well. He easily has sixty pounds on each of them and has the element of surprise. As he calculates the risk, Minh Chau steps in front of him and strains her neck to look up directly into his eyes. She whispers: "And who are you?" It is just enough to distract Abdullah while the policemen pull Ari up and push him into the back of the car. 'Akkawi moves away. Marie's young friend has a lot of bravado he thinks but is short on common sense.

The young policeman gives Minh Chau a card. "Please come to the station to press charges. If you don't want to, don't worry. We will teach this man a lesson. We don't like his sort in Istanbul."

Minh Chau briefly holds the policeman's hand in both of hers to thank him, and then turns back to 'Akkawi. The giant with the hardened anger in his eyes has vanished. But she already has his face etched in her memory.

Marie pockets her cell phone as she approaches the hotel. The call from Minh Chau has calmed her down, at least a little. The Israeli has been arrested, but Marie is angry with herself that she let her friend take such a risk. What was she thinking? What were they thinking? She needs answers from Taragon.

Marie first walks right past Hotel Yildiz. It must be one of the most nondescript hotels in all of Istanbul. Only a small sign above the doorway distinguishes it from the offices and shops on a run-of-the-mill street. Marie wonders why Taragon has chosen it. She enters the small lobby where an older man in a fez sits behind a desk. The man looks up from his newspaper. It's in Arabic. His eyes are piercing, bluer than the Mediterranean—Circassian eyes.

"Yes," he says in English.

"I'm a friend of Mr. Taragon. I believe that he has left a letter for me."

"What's your name?"

"Marie Boivin."

"Who do you work for?"

"*Le Devoir*."

"Show me the palm of your left hand."

Marie complies. So Taragon had noticed after all.

The old Circassian examines the scar the width of her hand, a souvenir from her earliest childhood. How she got it, she doesn't remember. It runs from above her thumb to the base of her little finger. Its perfect straightness gives it an oddly aesthetic quality. The old man switches to French, "*Très bien*," and unlocks a drawer to hand Marie an unmarked envelope. "Café Esmir. Mr. Black will find you there. Order a glass of Buzbaj. Drink it halfway and then put the envelope under the glass and leave the café. Don't look back."

Marie stares at the man. She had not expected such elaborate precautions. He returns to his newspaper. On the front page, she notices a photo of tanks moving in convoy. With her very limited Arabic, she deciphers two words, *Gaza* and *Israel*.

In Café Esmir, 'Akkawi watches the girl from two tables away. It disturbs him—such a resemblance to his cousin. The coincidence tears at his heart. Old wounds, but ones that will never heal. He knows that Marie will look back after she leaves the café. She's a journalist; she can't help herself. He knows many journalists, but Taragon is the only one that he trusts. Most of the others are vampires, feeding off the blood of the dead, always wishing for more killing to report. Some seek only to ingratiate themselves with the brutal regimes that rule their countries and pay them handsome bribes. But the worst are the apologists—trained from an early age to convolute the facts to cover up crimes inspired by an ideal. Yes, he has known them all: Zionists, Communists, Baathists and *Phoenicians*. And now in his struggle—his *jihad*—he is fighting liars again, those who distort the truth in the name of God. With the help of Taragon and Bronstein, he will defeat these fanatics within his own movement.

'Akkawi has ensured that Marie will never see him. He knows that his enemies will relentlessly pursue her if they think that she can identify him. He must spare her that danger. How many of his friends have already died to keep his new appearance a secret? The surgery in Tehran has helped, but he can't hide his height. When Marie leaves the café and turns around twenty paces later, she'll only see the fourteen-year-old waiter clearing her table. The boy will later bring 'Akkawi his bill, and tell him what he needs to know.

Marie rises from the table. She places the envelope under the wine glass and walks casually down the street. 'Akkawi waits, but Marie doesn't turn. Her lithe figure eventually disappears from view. Discipline, loyalty perhaps. 'Akkawi doesn't know. He usually abhors being wrong, but this time he smiles.

Chapter

11

Lebanon – July 1975

H ODA DOESN'T RETURN TO SHEMLAN. The trip from Beirut is simply too dangerous. The school's diplomat students also begin to take precautions. An armoured car is dispatched to the village to pick up the British students whenever they need to go to the city. Abu Walid brings his ageing mother back from the Shouf. Some other teachers do the same. Shemlan with its international students becomes a haven from the increasing sectarian confrontations across Lebanon.

Marc applies himself to Arabic. He feels an intense need to distract himself from constantly thinking about Hoda. Surprisingly, Evan also takes learning Arabic seriously and makes tremendous progress. When he has built up a good vocabulary, he begins chatting up Raja, a local Christian girl from the neighbourhood grocery store. She occasionally teases him that he is picking up a Syrian accent, and asks him if he has a girlfriend in Damascus. This is enough for Evan to apply himself to learning the purest Shemlan accent. He knows that his life may depend on it one day.

Every Saturday, Evan drives into Beirut for lunch with the Australian embassy's political counsellor. Marc tags along to visit the city while his friend meets with his minder. He wants to see Hoda again, but to reach the Sabra camp, he would have to cross the Fakhani district, the stronghold of the PLO. The area is thick with checkpoints, and the Palestinians have developed serious suspicions about French nationals, and with good reason. Marc has heard through his own embassy contacts that his country's foreign intelligence service has doubled its presence in Lebanon. France is also rumoured to be in negotiations with the Syrians to send in troops in a joint effort to curb Palestinian power. Even if Marc could conceal his nationality, few taxi drivers are now willing to run the gauntlet of checkpoints where the Palestinians and their Lebanese leftist allies routinely extort money.

With Evan ensconced with his "mentor" at the poolside of the luxurious Saint George Hotel, Marc decides to head to Librairie Antoine, one of the best bookshops in Beirut. It's not a long walk. The city is still booming despite the war, or perhaps because of it. The usual back-packing tourists have been replaced by a small army of foreign journalists, all out to file exaggerated reports, sometimes turning small exchanges of gunfire into major battles.

"Marc! Over here!"

Marc turns at the sound of his name. At a table outside a small coffee shop, a grey-haired man is waving at him. It takes him a moment to recognize Martin Riley, a journalist for the *Irish Post* who recently visited the school in Shemlan. Beside him is a young blond man.

"Hi Martin."

"Marc, I would like to introduce you to Marwan Kanaan."

"Pleased to meet you, Marwan."

"The pleasure is mine."

"Marwan is an excellent interpreter."

"What are you doing in Lebanon, Mr. Taragon?"

"Please call me, Marc. I am studying Arabic."

"In Shemlan?"

"Yes."

"I have a friend who was teaching there."

"Really, who?"

"Hoda 'Akkawi."

Marc pauses to think what next to say.

"She's hoping to return to Shemlan when things are safer," Marwan says.

"Really? She was my teacher but only for one day. Do you see her often?"

"Yes, once a week. She can't come to classes anymore. The area around the university is too dangerous for Palestinian students, especially young women. So I bring her notes from her classmates."

"How do you get through the checkpoints in Fakhani? I mean, Kanaan's a Christian name, isn't it?"

"Usually, and yes, I'm a Maronite. I borrow a taxi from my uncle. His company serves all of West Beirut. He has good relations with everyone."

"Marc, will you join us?" Riley asks.

"Yes, please do," Marwan says.

Marc pulls up one of the old wicker chairs. Librairie Antoine can wait.

Evan leans forward to hear more of the political counsellor's take on the latest developments in the city.

"We are all getting frustrated with Arafat. He just doesn't know how to or perhaps doesn't want to rein in the extremists in the PLO."

"From what I hear, it's more of the latter," Evan says.

"In any event, the old poof is putting the Palestinians on a collision course with both the Israelis and the Maronites."

"Will the Americans intervene?"

"For the moment, the Americans want to play it cool. Kissinger is on his way out. Philip Habib is now running the State Department. Habib is an odd bird. His parents are Lebanese Maronites, but he grew up in a Jewish area of Brooklyn. He definitely knows the key actors in the Middle East and many of the movers and shakers in the American Jewish community. Perhaps, he can use his connections to get things back on track here."

Evan smiles at how naïve the older diplomat is to think that the Americans could ever pull off something in Lebanon. They may have the firepower, but everyone knows they're at the beck and call of the Israelis.

Riley rises to excuse himself. He has a story to file. He exchanges numbers with Marc and leaves the two young men.

After a moment, Marc breaks the silence.

"I'd like to send a message to Hoda. Can you do that for me?"

"Sure."

Marc takes out a slip of paper and starts to write. He plays it safe. Just a few pleasantries. News of the class in Shemlan. Things that will conceal the burning desire he has to see her. He folds the paper and passes it to Marwan.

Marwan looks at Marc. The young Frenchman is obviously interested in Hoda, and he doesn't like that. But he can't blame him. Who wouldn't be interested in her? Her long silky hair, high cheekbones and a hint of a Roman nose.

Marc is speaking again. Marwan breaks away from his own thoughts of Hoda.

"Marwan, let's stay in touch. Do you have a phone number that I can reach you at?"

"Sure, let me write it out for you. It is actually my neighbour's, but she'll pass on the message and I can ring you back."

Chapter

12

Beirut – October 1975

MARWAN KANAAN LOOKS OUT the car window at the garbage piled up against the mostly drab grey walls of the refugee camp. A few walls close to Hoda's house are adorned with the exquisite murals painted by her brother Nabil. On others are crude stencilled paintings of Palestinian heroes and maps of Palestine shaped like Kalashnikovs. He admires Nabil's portrayal of an old itinerant water seller and Bedouin women baking flatbread on upside-down cauldrons. They remind him of the Lebanon he loves best, the country that is fast disappearing.

Several young boys play soccer in the alleyway. A young fighter approaches them and nods toward Marwan. One of the young boys whispers in the fighter's ear, who pats the boy on the shoulder and walks away. Marwan relaxes. He's been numerous times to Hoda's to deliver notes from her classmates and knows that the neighbourhood children will vouch for him.

This may be the last time Marwan comes to the house in Sabra. The university semester is over, and Hoda has decided to return to teaching in Shemlan. This time she'll stay in the mountain town to avoid the daily dangers of the checkpoints. That's why he's there today—to take her to the mountains. He doesn't like the thought that he won't see her for a while. He likes it even less that the Frenchman is still in Shemlan.

"Hi Marwan. Can we go?"

Marwan looks up. Hoda is as pretty as ever, even with a white hijab covering up her beautiful hair. Nabil is carrying her suitcase. Marwan steps out, shakes Nabil's hand and opens the trunk for the suitcase and the passenger door for Hoda. He feels good that she asked him to take her to Shemlan. They'll have time to talk in the car.

A relative calm has returned to Beirut, not that anyone counts on it lasting. Still, it's a nice respite from the chaos of the first months of the war. The initial confrontations only proved that neither side can defeat the other, and no one is ready to risk annihilation. The old politicians resurface from their *diwans*—ageing men preaching moderation, pretending wisdom, but still flawed by their arrogant beliefs in the superiority of their own communities.

Although astute observers understand that this is at best a hiatus in a drawn-out conflict, it's enough to permit Hoda to return to Shemlan. And just in time. Since the fighting, her father has been unable to work in the clothing factory in East Beirut, and the prices of food have sky-rocketed as the militias on all sides impose taxes on trucking into and out of the city. Her family needs the money from her teaching more than ever, and she wants to see Marc again.

She feels a gentle pat on her hand. She hadn't even noticed that they had entered Shemlan. Marwan motions to a pretty whitewashed house covered with bougainvillea. Its doors and window frames are painted in blue. There is a serene quality to it.

"That's it. Five houses past the Al Sakhra Restaurant. That's what you said, wasn't it?"

"Yes. It's beautiful, isn't it?"

Marwan pulls up to the villa that Professor Jamal Seifeddine, known to everyone as Abu Walid, has rented for his mother and sister. Abu Walid has offered Hoda a room in the house for a nominal rent. It's a good arrangement for everyone, one that Hoda was able to convince even her parents to agree to.

Hoda knocks on the door. An older woman opens it.

"Yes?"

"I'm Hoda."

"Oh yes, my son Jamal said that you were coming."

"I'm honoured to meet you, Um Jamal."

"And is that your fiancé?"

"Oh no, that is my friend Marwan. He very kindly drove me here."

The old woman leans up to whisper in Hoda's ear. "Only a friend? That's a shame. He's such a handsome boy. Tell him to come in please."

Hoda smiles as she enters the house and waves to Marwan to follow.

Over tea, Um Jamal tells Hoda and Marwan why she and her daughter finally left their town in the Shouf to join her son in Shemlan. While Beirut may be experiencing a reprieve from confrontation, things are going the opposite way in the countryside. Druze are no longer safe in her hometown of Maaser. She trusts her older Maronite neighbours, but their children have fallen under the influence of militiamen from the city. Marwan listens intently to the conversation and then begins to ask a some questions. Does she know which militia the young Beirutis belonged to? What precautions were the Druze villagers taking? Had they asked Druze Leader Kemal Jumblatt for help?

"Marwan, please. You're tiring Um Jamal out with all these questions."

"No, it's all right, dear. Marwan, I'll tell you all about it when you come back to Shemlan. Now I should start preparing dinner."

"Of course, Um Jamal. Excuse me. I should be on my way anyway."

"Oh, wait. Here's my daughter Nadia."

Hoda and Marwan turn to see a middle-aged woman enter the living room with bags of groceries and fresh vegetables.

Hoda settles easily into life with Um Jamal and Nadia. Both women are well educated, like many Druze women. Nadia had worked in the fashion industry in New York for many years in America before returning to take care of her elderly mother. She shares with Hoda many insights into American policies on the Middle East. President Ford was a weak president with no real understanding of the region, Nadia explains. So US policy was left in the hands of Secretary of State Henry Kissinger who used his influence to strengthen US support for Israel. There is a glimmer of hope that Kissinger's successor Philip Habib would change that, but Nadia is sceptical.

Hoda is assigned the advanced beginners' class, and she's disappointed that it includes neither Marc, who has made considerable progress, nor Evan, who now miraculously appears quite conversant in Arabic. Most of the less talented Brits are still there, toiling away at trying to master the basics of the language. Fortunately, both Marc and Evan again have Abu Walid as a teacher, and after a couple of days, he invites his favourite students to a dinner at his mother's home.

Evan nudges Marc when Hoda and Nadia enter the room with plates of tabbouleh, hummus, and kebab.

"Hoda's put on a little weight. And in the right places," Evan says.

Marc is deaf to the remark. His eyes fix on Hoda, and hers dart back and forth in a futile attempt to avoid returning his stare.

After Marc and Evan feast on the mountain of food, the conversation turns to politics over several glasses of Arak. Abu Walid is unsparing in his criticism of Kemal Jumblatt's decision to ally his Druze militia with the Sunni Muslims. Marc notices for the first time how attentive Evan is to the conversation. He has his suspicions about his friend's weekly meetings with the embassy. After all, they can't all be about imports of Australian wheat and lamb.

Hoda too joins the conversation to disagree with Abu Walid. She defends Jumblatt and castigates Arafat. Jumblatt has joined forces with the Sunni political parties only to counter the aggression of the Maronites. But the Palestinian leader has aligned himself with radical Muslim clerics, and now tolerates the PLO being referred to as the "Army of Allah." He is turning the conflict into a religious war.

"Hoda, I'm surprised to hear you say that," Abu Walid says. "You're a Muslim and a Palestinian."

"I may be born a Muslim, but in my heart all religions are equal. When they drive people to do good deeds, they're good; when they turn people to hatred and violence, they're bad. Political parties are the same. I'm against those who divide us along sectarian lines."

Marc looks intensely at the young woman. In the few letters that Marwan couriered back and forth for them over the past months, they had discussed many things—music, art, history, but not politics or religion. He's elated at how closely Hoda's beliefs reflect his own.

In his family, religion has always been a taboo, and for good reason. His mother was born into a Catholic family, full of priests and nuns, and his father's people were descended from the *conversos*—the converted Jews of Tarragona. Even after six centuries of Christian rule, some of his Spanish relatives maintain some distinctly Hebraic traditions and attend mass only at Christmas and Easter. When Marc's parents met in the anarchist circles in Barcelona, they both pledged to renounce religion and espouse the humanist creed. His father shortened his surname from the distinctively *converso* name of Lopez de Tarragona to simply Tarragon. A French official cavalierly decided to drop the second *r* when he registered Marc's birth.

Marc breaks himself away from his silent reminiscing to say: "*Tout à fait*—absolutely."

"Sorry, what did you say?" Hoda asks.

"I agree with you."

She smiles.

Abu Walid says: "Yes, it's good to be open to all religions, favouring none over the others. It is what Gandhi taught the world. But in Lebanon, that's not possible. Our people are brainwashed by their priests and imams. Every group believes heaven is reserved for them, and them alone. Even worse, they all believe martyrdom will guarantee them a place in their heaven." And then he adds the traditional Druze saying: "But let reason be above all."

"Religion is a waste of time," Evan says. "Marx was right. It is the opiate of the people."

For once, Evan has said something serious, Marc thinks.

A loud knock on the door interrupts the debate. Abu Walid rises to answer it. He comes back with the young son of the headmaster, who holds out a small slip of paper.

Marc takes it and reads it silently. "I'm sorry. I have to go."

"Is something wrong, Marc?" Hoda asks.

"It's from my mother. She wants me to call her. My father has had a stroke. The headmaster has offered me the use of his phone."

As he puts his jacket on, Marc can hear the soft incantations in Arabic from Abu Walid's mother and Nadia, asking for God's help for a speedy recovery for his father.

Evan starts to get up. Marc puts his hand on his friend's shoulder. "Stay, enjoy the evening."

When Marc turns to the door, Hoda is already there, her hijab wrapped around her head. "Marc, I'm coming with you." The determination in her voice is clear.

The night air and Hoda's company soothe Marc as they climb the steep street to the headmaster's house. Marc tells her of his parents' escape from Barcelona in 1939. They were part of twenty employees who ran the anarchist newspaper, *Iniciules*. When Franco's troops were on the brink of overwhelming the city's beleaguered defenders, the staff dismantled the printing press and put its key parts into flour sacks. Each of the twenty workers carried a sack over the mountains to France.

During the journey, several fell sick, exhausted and dehydrated. Marc's father and his companions took their comrades' burdens and continued on. They would have all perished if not for a group of French sympathizers who met the *refugiados* on the narrow mountain pass. In the small village of Rennes-les-Bains in the French Pyrenees, Marc's father supervised the setting up of the *Nuevas Inciales*. The paper continued to secretly publish spirited defences of the Republican cause and smuggle copies into Franco's Spain long after France fell to Germany and its allies in the Vichy Administration.

Hoda is drawn to every detail of Marc's story. She finds comfort that he's like her—a child of refugees. Marc's agreement with many of her political and personal beliefs increases her attraction to him. She is close to making her decision.

Marc is obliged to spend several more days in Shemlan. Air France flights from Beirut are becoming scarcer, but his friends at the French embassy intervene to finally get him a seat. He calls his mother to say that he is coming soon. His father is now in a coma, and the rest of the family are already in Rennes-Les-Bains.

To relieve the stress of waiting, Marc begins to walk daily the mountain paths near Shemlan. At times, his mind wanders back to the long hikes he would take with his father in the Pyrenees. There they would look into Catalonia, *la pàtria*. The day before his departure, he finds Hoda waiting for him around a bend on the path to the summit. She has packed a lunch of tabbouleh, hummus and flat bread. Together they begin the long ascent to the end of the trail near the summit. There is still snow on the ground. From the mountain, they can see the coast. The sea is free from the American and French warships that will later dominate the Lebanese coast. Small fishing boats from Sidon go about their business unimpeded. It's hard to imagine such a beautiful country at war.

"Do you like it here in Shemlan?" Hoda asks.

"Yes, I love being in the mountains."

"What do you like best about them?"

"I love the mountain flowers. They're so different. So fragile yet vibrant. And you?"

"I love them too. My favourite is the sawfar iris. Do you know it?"

"I've never heard of it. Are there any around here?"

Hoda stands up and scours the mountainside.

"Yes, there! Can you see those rocks up there. There is a sawfar iris growing between them."

Marc sees a glimpse of purple 20 metres up the rock face.

"You said it's your favourite flower, right?"

"Yes."

Marc begins to scramble up the steep rock face.

"No, Marc. Don't do that! It's too dangerous."

At first, Marc moves quickly. He has climbed many mountains in the Pyrenees. He jams, side-pulls and dynos his way up the first eighteen metres, but halts when the rock face becomes smoother and offers fewer footholds. He notices the clouds darken in the sky. Rain is coming and he should hurry. He hears Hoda's calls imploring him to come down. Then he sees it, a crimp just large enough for the tips of his fingers. He knows that the only way to get within reach of the iris is to mantle the smooth rock protrusion and scamper his feet to the ledge just below the flower. It is a dangerous manoeuvre, one he has never tried before. He presses his fingertips into the crimp and swings his leg over to the upper ledge. He makes it, but barely. Balancing on one foot, he stretches up to loosen the small rocks at the base of the flower. Then with a quick tug, he pulls the iris free. The sudden movement dislodges a sharp piece of slate, which falls, cutting his arm. It's not a deep cut, but it throws him off balance. He begins to bounce off the mountainside. Just before he hits the ground, he grabs a small shrub firmly rooted in the rock face. It's enough to break the fall, and with a large thump, he lands on his feet.

Hoda races to him.

"Marc, you could have killed yourself!"

"No, I'm fine."

"No, you're not. Your arm is bleeding."

Hoda quickly takes off her hijab and wraps it around his arm. Her long hair falls down to brush lightly against his skin, sending a sensation he has never experienced before. He moves his hand to her cheek. With the other, he offers her the iris. She looks into his eyes, then turns to kiss the palm of his hand. "Marc, you're completely crazy."

"Yes, crazy about you."

He leans in to kiss her, and she doesn't move back. It's the first time a man has ever kissed her. She feels his youthful energy. It excites her. She pulls herself against him and returns his kiss before pulling away. "We should go now. It's going to rain soon."

Marc nods, and watches her fold the picnic blanket. Adrenaline races through his body. He looks at the hijab wrapped around his arm. His blood seeps through the cotton. And he understands.

Hoda can't accompany Marc to the airport. The checkpoints are too dangerous, too unpredictable. Alliances are constantly shifting. And the Guardians of the Cedars have resumed executing every Muslim who crosses their path, provoking the Lebanese nationalists to retaliate—an eye for an eye.

Evan offers to drive Marc to the airport, taking the long route through the Druze-controlled Shouf down to the coastal highway. The trip is without incident. Marc's French passport ensures them safe passage through Damour, which is still under Phalangist control. He looks at the town's Christian inhabitants. The months of encirclement are taking their toll. Most residents are gaunt, with seemingly perpetual fear in their eyes. Marc touches the fabric of Hoda's hijab in his shoulder bag. He had forgotten to return it after washing out his blood. Now it gives him an odd sense of reassurance.

When they reach the suburbs near the airport, Hoda's cousin, Abdullah, meets them to give them a letter for the Palestinian and Druze checkpoints. The Lebanese army is still nominally in control of the airport, but it rarely checks the cars entering and leaving it. Marc thanks Evan for taking the risky journey with him. Evan shrugs it off. "Anything for a mate."

Part of the tarmac is pockmarked from the 1968 Israeli attack on the airport. There is no money to repair the potholes or clean up the debris of the sixteen destroyed airliners. Or perhaps, the Lebanese just relish the chance to tell the world that they, not the Israelis, are the victims of aggression. Despite the looming dangers of the civil war, the incoming Air France flight is full. Beirut is still the hub for business in the Middle East. Among the disembarking passengers, Marc recognizes the military attaché at the French embassy. Marc greets the colonel. His driver joins them.

Both have many questions for Marc. What did he see on the road through the Shouf and up the coast? Heavy arms? Mixed Palestinian-Shia checkpoints? Nervous Phalangist soldiers in Damour? Signs of evacuation?

Marc is candid about the seriousness of the situation but dodges explicit questions. He doesn't want the reputation of being a spy.

The colonel leans toward him.

"Marc, you should reconsider your plans to return. Our intelligence tells us that the country will soon be in all-out civil war.

"I appreciate the advice but I have other reasons for returning to Lebanon."

Chapter

13

Istanbul – February 2007

MARC HANGS UP THE PHONE. He's disturbed by what Marie has told him. Mossad agents here in Istanbul. How could they know she'd be here? Marc looks over at Bronstein who is checking the Israeli news on the internet.

"Jonathan, we have to change plans."

"Why?"

"The Mossad has tracked Marie Boivin here."

"I didn't know that she was part of this."

"Yes, she is here to do her second interview with me. I've asked her to pass a message to Abdullah."

"Why her?"

"I don't know. There's something about her that tells me I can trust her."

Bronstein looks at his friend. Taragon is not one who makes snap decisions based on emotions. Finally, he asks: "So what do we do now?"

"There is a place in Karpathos. I know half of the village, retirees from Canada. Greek Communists for the most part. I did a feature on them several years ago: "Little Montreal in the Aegean." I also know the local police chief, the son of one of the returnees. We get along very well, being both sons of political refugees."

"If they catch up with us there, it will take more than a small-town police chief to protect us."

"We'll have to take our chances. Nowhere else is safer."

"How do we get there? They may be watching the airport and ferry terminals in Athens."

"We can get to Karpathos by fishing boat from the Turkish mainland.

The Turkish and Greek fishermen have a friendly little smuggling operation going. For the right price, they'll take passengers."

"How are you going to get word to 'Akkawi?"

"Our Circassian friend will arrange it."

"When do we go?"

"Now. We'll take separate taxis to the coast. It'll be expensive, but it's
safer than by train. And travelling as a group is too dangerous."

Taragon walks down to the reception. He leans toward the young
man, who then calls up Café Esmir to order two coffees and baklava.
"Send Ahmet," the receptionist says. When the young boy turns up, the
receptionist whispers in his ear. Ten minutes later, 'Akkawi is handed a
new bill. On it the number of a taxi driver.

Although an experienced sailor, Bronstein has always dreaded the sea at
night. In the army, he was forced to conduct too many missions during
pitch-black nights, and those were before infrared goggles. But it wasn't really
the darkness that bothered him. Somehow water at night was stiller, more
menacing, more ready to swallow one up at the most unexpected moment.

Bronstein lays his head down near the bow. Sleep betrays him and
allows in dark dreams. The muffled breaking of the water as the paddles
slowly propel the dinghy forward. Beirut April 10, 1973—a moonless
night. Bronstein is the newcomer to the unit, recruited because of his
impeccable Arabic learned from childhood friends. It's ironic that he has
more Arab friends than Jewish ones, and yet his mission is to kill Arabs.

The dreams turn to the news brought by the police to a young boy—
both parents killed in a car crash in Haifa. Sent to live with his Aunt
Sadie in nearby Kiryat Tiv'on, he was at first incredibly alone. His aunt
ran a small hardware store on the outskirts of town. Many of her customers came from the new Bedouin township of Basmat Tab'un. The
government had cleared some land there for a rudimentary soccer field,
and the Bedouin customers, who took a shine to the young orphan,
convinced his aunt that he should join one of the town's soccer teams.
Bronstein became the first and only Jewish player in the village. How he
relished those days on the playing field, shouting "*Yallah*—Let's go," and
listening to his friends' mothers ululate whenever the team scored a goal.

The young boy was soon part of a world that few Israelis knew even
existed. From his friends' fathers, he learned to hunt with antique rifles
the red-breasted geese of the Alonim Hills. And after the hunt, the

women would feed them warm flatbread cooked on large upside-down cauldrons. After sunset, he would sit with the other boys listening to the old men speak of Bedouin honour, dignity, and hospitality. Then Abu Yassin, the local storyteller, would complete the evening with tales of Qahtan, the first of the Southern Arabs, and of Adnan, leader of the Northerners and grandson of the patriarch Abraham. And whenever he would mention Adnan, Abu Yassin would look at the young Bronstein and say: "You Jews, too, are of the family of Abraham. May God protect you!" Later he would serve with these same Bedouin youth in the Border Police.

Bronstein sees himself back on the beach outside Beirut, listening to Kasdan, the squad leader, give the order to hide the dinghies. Kasdan's squad was composed mostly of boys, fresh from their first year of intensive training in Israel's special forces. Bronstein himself was only nineteen, but he had already served in the Border Police long enough to demonstrate remarkable skill as a sharpshooter. At seventeen, he had killed his first *fedayee*. It had been a cold kill at a distance of five hundred metres. The Palestinian was barely visible in his scope. At first, he was unsure whether it was a man, woman or child, but when his sergeant, a Druze from Haifa, gave him the order, he pulled the trigger. The distant figure dropped, and the sergeant patted him on the shoulder and uttered laconically in Hebrew: "*Tov*—good."

Kasdan instinctively distrusted Bronstein who spoke Arabic flawlessly and was too at ease with the Druze and Bedouin army recruits. Kasdan didn't want someone so close to Arabs to be in on the actual assassinations. And he certainly didn't want an Arab lover witnessing whatever collateral damage they might have to inflict. He assigned Bronstein to guard the unit's escape route, and left with him another new recruit, Ari Epstein. The latter, a recent Moldovan immigrant, was a hopeless shot but was ruthless with a knife. Kasdan gave the two men their orders. If Palestinian or Lebanese fighters came by once the shooting started, Bronstein was to shout to them in his fluent Arabic that the Israelis had fled in the other direction. If he could, he was also to eliminate them when they turned their backs to him. Epstein was to clean up. Bronstein did his duty, and Epstein scoured the alleyway for those still alive, bending down twice to bloody his blade.

After Beirut, Bronstein returned to his studies. Kasdan went onto loftier things, and Epstein disappeared into the labyrinth of the Mossad, for a job suited for one without a heart. Bronstein never regretted the role he played, the lives he took. Perhaps, more lives than anyone he knew. His targets were enemies of Israel.

He parted ways with his former comrades in the special forces when Israel turned against its own non-Jewish population. The mayor of Kiryat Tiv'on, a right-wing fanatic from America, convinced the government to build a road directly to the Alonei Abba Moshav, bypassing Basmat Tab'un, but expropriating some of the village's best grazing land. Bronstein's young Bedouin friends were serving in the Border Police in Jerusalem, on the Golan and some on the border with Lebanon. They were too far away to challenge the expropriation order. In their stead, their fathers went to the authorities in Haifa, who turned them away. When the bulldozers arrived, twenty ageing men sat defiantly across the road. Young soldiers from Tel Aviv were called in. At first, the soldiers waited while a local interpreter tried to negotiate an end to the protest. But the old men were proud and would not budge.

The mayor arrived on the scene. Fat, sweaty, cursing in bad Hebrew, he bullied the soldiers to move forward and use their rifle butts on the old men. Bronstein was returning from the university in Tel Aviv when he heard the news. He immediately visited his friends' fathers in the hospital, and for the first time in his life, he felt shame.

Bronstein protested to the mayor, who only shrugged his shoulders, saying: "Why do you care? They're only Arabs. And we need the land for the new road." He held back from striking the man, from screaming obscenities, and instead, wrote a blistering letter of protest to the local newspaper. In it, he cited by name all the members of the tribe who were serving in the Border Police. To his surprise, the letter was published, and the prime minister himself ordered that the road be rerouted. The new minister of defence even sent a letter of apology to the injured protesters. Perhaps, that's why he chose journalism. It was an avenue to raise his voice over the clamour of blind nationalism.

A wave splashes over the bow awakening Bronstein. He looks up at the night sky, now bedecked with every constellation imaginable. He remembers their names in Arabic, but not in Hebrew. Taragon's presence at his side surprises him. Bronstein has been trained as a soldier to be always vigilant, alert to every sound and movement. How the Frenchman has passed unnoticed through his defences baffles him.

Silently they watch the lights of Karpathos flicker across the now placid sea. Only the soft rumble of the boat's diesel engine challenges the night's harmony. To their right, the small lights of a second boat appear, also heading for Karpathos. The Turkish captain of their vessel signals three times with his flashlight. Five short flashes come back from the other boat, now closing in on them.

As the second boat bumps up against their bow, a large figure rises from beneath a tarpaulin. Taragon stretches out his hand to the giant who quickly clambers aboard. Bronstein stares at the face that he hasn't seen for more than thirty years, a face so different from the one he remembers. A huge hand reaches out and grasps his. "*Salaam Aleykum*, my brothers."

14

Karpathos – March 2007

THE DISCUSSIONS HAVE GONE WELL in the small mountain village of Arkassa. Bronstein and ʿAkkawi now believe that a deal can be sold to the more reasonable in both their camps, and through their contacts in the media to the broader public. The hardliners in government will, of course, turn on them, and they'll need to take security measures. The Israeli settlers present an even greater danger—they'll stop at nothing to thwart a negotiated peace with the Palestinians. How Iran will act is difficult to predict. Its network of agents in the Middle East and Europe is extensive. Tehran is likely to see ʿAkkawi's involvement in the deal as treason. Its Quds Force is now 15,000 strong and operates clandestinely throughout the world. Its agents could well be ordered to assassinate ʿAkkawi. All the Israeli intelligence services also have a price on his head.

"Abdullah and Marc, there's a lot at play inside the Israeli intelligence services these past months," Bronstein says. "Rogue elements are operating within the Mossad, ones who no longer distinguish between Arab, Westerner, or Israeli when it comes to identifying enemies to eliminate."

"Many of our people have also been radicalized," ʿAkkawi says. "The influence of hard-liners in Tehran over much of Hamas and some of the Fatah movement is now stronger than ever. Many friends in Iran who are more pragmatic have been shoved to the sidelines."

Marc at first just nods his head. Then he leans back in his chair and says: "This is what we will do. You two will go into hiding until my journalist friends have a chance to make the story go viral. Abdullah, you'll go to Barcelona. My father's friends are in power there now. They're honourable men who won't bend to pressure from Spanish or foreign security services. Jonathan, you'll go to Montreal. I've a friend there. I trust her with my life. She'll keep you hidden until the news breaks."

"And you?" Bronstein asks.

"I'll go to France to speak to Kressmann. If he agrees to co-sponsor the plan, we can activate our newspaper and social media contacts to take it to the world. And Kressmann has the ear of the French Socialist Party."

The two other men sit silently. Both know Kressmann. The man is both saint and sinner. He worked as a doctor in the Shia slums of Beirut. His sympathies for the Palestinian refugees were well known back then. Admittedly, as a Jew, he has credibility with the powerful French Jewish community. But they also know Kressmann to be an unrepentant narcissist with unbridled political ambitions.

Taragon can see that his friends are uncomfortable about making Kressmann such a key player in promoting the peace plan. But there's no one else he could count on with the same level of political influence. The three men agree to call it a day. They'll meet again tomorrow. Taragon needs the time to make arrangements

The days pass quickly. Each brings new answers to the thornier of issues. Both 'Akkawi and Bronstein demonstrate such flexibility and empathy for each other's side that Taragon soon leaves the negotiations to them.

On the fourth day, 'Akkawi and Bronstein are grinning when Taragon approaches them in the village café.

"What are you smiling about?"

"We think that we've done it."

"A deal that will hold?"

"Yes!"

"Good. And just in time. We can't stay here undetected for much longer. I've got what we need next."

Taragon fishes out of his pocket two new passports. The forger in Athens had done a great job, and his Spanish contacts had come through.

"Thanks to a friend in Madrid, Abdullah you're now a resident of Spain. Your new Jordanian passport is complete with a five-year visa."

"Fantastic!"

"There's more," Taragon says. "A minister in the Catalan regional government will lend you an apartment in Barcelona."

"And me?" Bronstein asks.

"Here you go."

"What, a Russian passport? I thought I was going to Canada!"

"Don't worry. You are. Here are your Canadian papers. You're now a recent immigrant to Canada. You still speak Russian, don't you?"

"Barely, I haven't spoken the language since the death of my parents. And even when they were alive, we mostly spoke Hebrew."

"Don't worry. Just speak English to everyone and throw in the odd Russian word. And look tough. My friend in Montreal tells me that the Russians there have a reputation for being tough guys. Apparently, the Russian mafia is thriving in the city."

"And who is this friend?"

"Don't worry. You'll like her."

"We also have something for you, Marc."

Bronstein hands him an envelope.

Marc opens it. There's a printout of ten pages. The document, written in English, contains a few grammatical errors, but that doesn't matter. When he finishes reading, he looks up at his friends.

"This is amazing!"

"Glad you like it," Bronstein says. "Can you fix up the language so we can sign it today?"

"Of course, let me do that right away. Have you got it on a USB stick?"

"Here," 'Akkawi says.

Marc pulls out his laptop. He begins to re-read the text, tightening clauses, removing any potential ambiguity and restructuring the document so that its preamble captures the historical significance of the undertaking and spells out the basic principles underlying the agreement. Twenty minutes later, he passes his laptop over to 'Akkawi and Bronstein.

'Akkawi smiles as he reads the new text. "Marc, I once mocked you, saying that you thought your newspaper articles could end the killing in Lebanon. When I read this, I realize how wrong I was. My friend, you have the gift to move mountains with your words."

"Yes," Bronstein says. "Yours is truly the quill of the dove. May I read it aloud for all of us?"

"Yes!"

Bronstein adjusts his glasses and clears his throat, and then in his deep baritone voice, he reads:

The Pact of Arkassa

We choose humanity over hatred. Justice over greed. We recognize that peace never comes without compromise. The peoples of historical Palestine: Muslims, Christians, Druze and Jews have all suffered injustices. It is time to dam the river of enmity flowing from past wrongs and to embrace the future with the still water of peace.

We hereby agree:

Two states shall share the territory of our common historical homeland. We will build for present and future generations the State of Israel within its 1967 borders and the State of Palestine in the West Bank and Gaza.

The Basic Law of the State of Israel and the Constitution of the State of Palestine shall be amended to include a binding recognition of each state's right to exist and to forbid either country from entering into a military alliance against the other state.

Jerusalem shall be the spiritual capital of both States, but the political capital of neither.

The political capital of the State of Israel shall be Tel Aviv.

The political capital of the State of Palestine shall be Ramallah.

Jerusalem will be a demilitarized city. Its municipal police force will be composed equally of Jewish and Arab citizens, who will be unarmed and serve side by side. Any resident of Jerusalem who carries a weapon of any kind will be permanently expelled from the city.

A small armed emergency police force under the aegis of the United Nations shall be based in Jerusalem to protect the population from armed criminality and acts of terrorism.

Jerusalem within Israel's pre-1967 borders shall be governed by a municipal council elected by residents who are citizens of Israel.

Jerusalem outside of Israel's pre-1967 borders will be governed by a municipal council elected by residents who are citizens of Palestine.

All citizens of Israel and Palestine shall have the right to reside and own property anywhere in Jerusalem, provided they respect the law and keep the peace.

The two municipal administrations of the city shall appoint five members each to a Jerusalem Senate. The governments of the States of Israel and Palestine shall each appoint one member to this Senate, and the Secretary-General of the United Nations shall appoint a distinguished international person of neither Israeli or Palestinian nationality to chair the Jerusalem Senate.

The Jerusalem Senate shall be responsible for all matters related to the preservation of religious sites, the arbitration of disputes between the two municipal administrations of Jerusalem and shall appoint the Chief and Deputy Chief of the Jerusalem Police Force.

Non-Israeli and non-Palestinian citizens wishing to live in Jerusalem must obtain resident permits from the Jerusalem Senate.

Palestinian refugees living outside of Palestine shall have the options of returning to the Palestinian state; returning to Israel provided that they agree to accept Israeli citizenship; or accepting compensation for properties lost in the 1947 partition of Palestine.

Israeli citizens living in the Palestinian state at the time of the signature of this agreement will have the choice of remaining in this state provided that they agree to abide by Palestinian law and give up all arms that they possess. They will also have the right to obtain Palestinian citizenship if they renounce Israeli citizenship.

Still unsettled land in the State of Palestine expropriated by the State of Israel after 1967 shall be returned to the government of the State of Palestine.

The State of Israel shall compensate at fair-market value the Palestinian owners of land expropriated for Jewish settlements in the new State of Palestine. A UN commission will determine the value of the land.

The document continues with various dispute mechanism clauses and timetables. Bronstein, 'Akkawi and Taragon all realize how daunting the selling of this agreement will be. Still, they're confident that they can get their message to the people.

As they rise and shake hands, they fail to notice a young tourist with a backpack watching them from across the street. The woman suddenly walks into an alley and pulls out her cell phone. With a few quick keystrokes she sends a message to her boyfriend in the settlement of Ma'ale Adumim: *I just saw the journalist Jonathan Bronstein here in Karpathos. There was an Arab with him and that French journalist, the one who supports the Palestinians.*

Minutes later in Ramat HaSharon, Ari Epstein sees on his computer a new message: *Target found in Greece, beginning tracking.*

15

France – November 1975

THE BOEING 707 LANDS SMOOTHLY at Charles de Gaulle airport. Many of the Lebanese clap, much to the annoyance of the French passengers who disdain yet another Levantine extroversion. But Marc doesn't even notice—his mind is absorbed with thoughts of his father lying in a coma. Rennes is still a day's journey, and time is slipping by.

He recalls the last time he saw his father. It ended on bad terms. Diego Taragon, never an easy man, had become harder in his old age. His condemnation of everything right of the Socialist Party had escalated to the vitriolic, and compromise never natural to him was out of the question.

When Marc brought his Vietnamese girlfriend, Leyna, to Rennes, his father immediately queried her about her views on the South Vietnamese government. Leyna calmly explained that, although the government was far from perfect, the population was still firmly behind it as the only way to protect the country from falling to Communism. The older Taragon grumbled that the South Vietnamese president was an American stooge and all his supporters collaborators. This was too much for Leyna. Despite the profuse apologies of Marc's mother, Jacinta, and Marc's own entreaties for her to stay, Leyna took the first train back to Paris. Marc was furious with his father, but he spent two more days with his family at his mother's insistence. Each day, she tried to repair the damage, and convince her husband to write a letter of apology to Leyna. But Diego Taragon refused. When Jacinta pressed him harder, he said laconically: "Just remember My Lai."

Marc returned to Paris, angry that his father had made politics a wedge between him and his first love. He understood how American support for Franco in the fifties and sixties had outraged his father. So for Diego, the war in Vietnam was just another example of Washington propping up a dictatorship. Marc, himself, had demonstrated against the US atrocities in Vietnam. But Leyna was not part of any of that, and he continued to see her. The visit to Rennes had left its mark though, and a *froid* between them lingered on after he went to Lebanon. Still, they continued to write each other weekly. When North Vietnam launched their spring offensive against the South, Leyna became obsessed with getting her parents out of Saigon. In her letters, she voiced increasing bitterness that the French Left was undermining public support in Europe for the South Vietnamese government. He knew she expected him to write back agreeing with her, but he felt she was wrong and avoided the issue in his letters. By mid-April, her letters had stopped. By May, his letters were being returned by the post office.

When Marc clears customs, he's asked to accompany an immigration official to a small room. Inside a young man with dark glasses, who introduces himself only as Leblanc, sits beside a French border guard. The guard asks the questions while Leblanc jots down notes in a black book. *Has Marc met Palestinians in Lebanon? Has he been to any of the refugee camps?* Leblanc hands the border guard an envelope of photos, which the guard dutifully spreads across the table. Young men in keffiyahs, older men in ill-fitting business suits, and there in black and white is Hoda's cousin, Abdullah 'Akkawi. Marc has learnt from his father not to trust the French police. *They're all fascists* was his father's favourite mantra. Marc may have flinched when he saw 'Akkawi's photo, but he says nothing. Leblanc is silent too, but Marc can feel the man's eyes behind the dark glasses burn through him.

When the interrogation is finally over, Leblanc stands, utters a perfunctory *au revoir* and leaves. Marc rises, but the border guard motions him to sit. An official walks in with Marc's suitcase. It has obviously been opened, but Marc sees no point in protesting. He's happy to escape further questions and the relentless gaze of "Monsieur Leblanc." A few more banal questions, a warning about associating with terrorists and the interview is over.

As Marc makes his way to the bus stop outside the terminal, he ponders why he was singled out. Could the military attaché have tipped off

French intelligence? He remembers his father's advice when it came to politics —listen to everyone, say little and trust no one.

The last of the vineyards disappear into the rose-coloured roofs of the Toulouse suburbs. He's made this journey many times. In a few minutes, he'll arrive at the *Gare centrale* and transfer to the local train to Rennes. The hours on the train from Paris have given him the chance to reflect on what he really wants. He knows that he can't simply go back to Lebanon to be just a student. He needs to establish himself so he can earn a living, be with Hoda and then see where their paths will take them. Pondering over his future displaces worries about his father. Somehow, he's come to believe that his father will recover, and life will go on as if he never had a stroke. As the train pulls in, he's filled with hope for all those he loves.

16

Toulouse, France – November 1975

THE TRAIN TO RENNES-LES-BAINS is scheduled to leave in three hours. Marc decides to go into town for a quick supper. When he reaches the main entrance of the station, he sees his uncle Manuel coming toward him.

"*Hola,* Marc."

"Hello, Uncle Mani."

"I'm glad that I caught you. We need to get to Rennes tonight. There's no time for trains. My car is outside."

"How is he?"

"It's serious, very serious. Diego came out of his coma this morning, but he may not last long. He insisted on going home. The doctors agreed. They said that there's nothing more they can do for him. He's been asking for you."

Manuel steers his Citroën DS through the tree-lined boulevards of Toulouse. It is still light out, but soon night will fall and the winding mountain roads will be hazardous. They turn onto the Route d'Agde. Three hours to Rennes. Manuel isn't very talkative. Marc asks about his mother. Yes, she's holding up, his uncle assures him. The stroke came as a surprise. His father is known for his strength and endurance. No one had suspected that his heart was weak, but for the last few months, he hadn't been the same.

"It wasn't just his heart. Your father has also been depressed. He sees no change for Spain, even with Franco on his deathbed. He told me how the restoration of the monarchy under Juan Carlos would continue fascism for another generation. He also regretted how your last visit to Rennes ended."

"He spoke about that?"

"Yes, he acknowledged he had made a serious mistake in driving away your girlfriend Leyna. He wants to make amends. He wrote her a letter of apology, but I don't know if he's been able to send it."

Marc sits silently. Despite their frequent quarrels, he has always admired his father. Sure, he doesn't share his pessimism about Spain's future nor his absolute condemnation of France's centrist and right-wing parties. When Marc was sixteen, he crossed the border with a school friend. The Guardia Civil treated him courteously. The young people on the Spanish side of the border were really no different from him. A little more conservative, yes, but the tales of authoritarianism that his father would repeat incessantly seemed out of place. Spain was changing, and for the better. His father was furious with him. Marc challenged him with what he'd seen in Spain, even if it had only been for a day. Had his mother not intervened, he might well have been thrown out of the family home.

Marc is asleep when the Citroën pulls up in front of the small white cottage. Manuel reaches over to shake his shoulder. He immediately springs to life and jumps out of the car. He'd been dreaming of playing chess with his father, learning to fish in the mountain rivers and listening to him relate the history of Catalonia. He walks up to the door of his parents' house, but before he can knock, his mother opens it. She kisses him and holds him tight. Her tears and soft sobs seem endless. He wants to enter the house, but she prevents him. Manuel goes inside instead, returning a few minutes later.

"I'm so sorry, Marc. I should have driven faster. It's too late."

Marc takes his mother's arms from around his neck and pulls them down to her sides. He gently steps past her and heads to the bedroom. On the large bed in the centre of the room lies Diego, his face ash-grey, his hands folded on his chest. Marc bends over to kiss his father's forehead, and for the first time, he realizes his own mortality.

That night, Marc finds in his old bedroom a photo album left out by his mother. He leafs through the many old prints, but few include his father, always so busy at work. Marc stops at one where he is standing by his mother, with a cast on his arm. He had disobeyed his father and climbed the apricot tree in the neighbour's yard. Out of fear of punishment, he hid the fall from his parents for two days. Finally, his mother noticed that he could no longer tie his shoes, and marched him off to the town's doctor. It seemed that it was always that way: his fear of his father's wrath; his mother stepping in to save him.

When his mother touches his shoulder, he realizes he has fallen asleep over the photo album. She pulls back the cover of his bed and lays out some of his old pyjamas. Without saying a word, he kisses his mother good night and puts them on. Sleep comes quickly to him, and his dreams return, but this time, they are not of his father, his childhood and rebellious escapades, but of Lebanon.

Hoda notices the neighbour's son watch her. The young man has recently returned after working in Riyadh for three years. Her younger brother, Nabil, has warned Hoda that Saudi Arabia has changed him and he's no longer the polite boy they once knew. Akil is his name. It means intelligent, but Hoda has never found him to be very intelligent. He's nineteen, two years younger than Hoda, and has just opened a small olive oil shop on the main street. Since his father's death two months earlier, he's asserting himself as the head of the family. One of his first acts is to order his older sister, Sadira, to wear a niqab, the face veil so common in Saudi Arabia.

Hoda has known Sadira a long time. When the girl comes to her distraught, she knows she needs to intervene. At first, she thinks about going to Abdullah. Most of the young men in the camp either admire or fear her cousin. She holds off though. There's a rift building between leftists like Abdullah and more religious fighters. She doesn't see any point in aggravating it. Instead, she decides to talk to Akil's uncle who runs a small restaurant near the university where she studies. The uncle is sympathetic to his niece's dilemma and pulls aside her brother to scold him one day. From that point, Akil's watching changes. Resentment replaces desire.

The street is dark when Marwan drops her off. She thanks him for driving her back from Shemlan but asks him not to enter the main street. It's safer for him that way. The young men in the camp are increasingly wary of outsiders, especially at night. She begins walking the two hundred metres to her home. Almost all the shopkeepers have closed up and gone home for the Eid feast. She notices some young men still smoking in front of the Abu Sami's grocery shop, but can't make out their faces. She doesn't worry. Even in the middle of the civil war, Sabra is a safe place for young women. She pulls up her hijab and continues on her way.

In the days before the funeral, the skies over Rennes were grey and rainy as if the heavens also mourned Diego's passing. Today the sun has returned. Marc drinks his third coffee in the kitchen. The knock on the door doesn't surprise him. All morning, townspeople have dropped by to offer their condolences. He opens the door. Leyna stands there, her eyes red from the night's journey. Her hand clutches the letter of apology from his father.

"I thought that I should come. That you might need me."

Marc takes her in his arms. She holds him close and then pulls back to look up at him. She raises her hand to wipe away his tears. She seems ready for his kiss, but none comes. His mother joins them at the doorway, greeting Leyna and ushering her inside.

Marc stands there, gazing east over the grey shingled roofs of the neighbours' cottages. In the glare of the morning sun, he wonders what Hoda is doing. An elderly woman working in her garden waves at him. He waves back, and turns to enter his father's house.

The funeral has been delayed long enough for Diego's former comrades to fly in from as far afield as Mexico and Argentina. From Spain, many cross the border—Catalans, Basques, Spaniards. Old men with limps, young men with defiance in their eyes. Women once radiant in their youth, and still beautiful in the sorrow of the moment.

All gather in the open plaza before the *mairie* of Rennes-les-Bains. The mayor, himself a *refugiado*, officiates while the town's priest looks on from a safe distance. Diego's comrades come forward to deliver eulogies in Catalan, Spanish, and French. No word of God or the afterlife is uttered. To the end, the old men cling to their vision of a world free of divinities, one devoted to humanity.

After the ceremony, Leyna approaches Marc. His mother has explained to her that Marc has fallen in love in Lebanon. She's disappointed but not surprised. She realizes that she was at fault in having his letters returned to him. They sit together one last time before he must join the funeral convoy to Casteil. He asks her about her parents in Saigon. She hasn't heard from them in months and fears the worse. Marc offers to talk to some friends in the foreign ministry, although he knows that little can be done. She takes his hand in both of hers to thank him and ask if she can write him as a friend. Yes, he answers.

The hearse travels the winding road to Casteil where Marc joins Diego's old comrades to carry his father's coffin high into the mountains.

Along the winding path, under the tall firs, they struggle with the weight of the casket until they reach a glade bordered by a steep ridge.

"Our French comrades met us here in 1939," Manuel says. "We were exhausted and freezing. It was a miracle they found us in time."

"Your father was the strongest of us," the mayor of Rennes says. "He carried the sacks of others when they were too weak to continue."

The village gravedigger has carved a plot out of the rocky soil. It is sloped so that Diego can face the border he crossed thirty-six years before. Four strong boys hauled up a slab of *cenia azul*, a gift from comrades in Tarragona. On the blue limestone are engraved verses from *Bodas de Sangre* by Federico García Lorca.

Marc's mother passes her hand across the engraved letters.

"They're the words that your father whispered in my ear when he proposed to me, and the words he uttered with his last breath. Marc, will you read them to me?"

Marc leans down and brushes aside the dirt and leaves obscuring the words. He takes in a breath and recites in his best Spanish.

Vamos al rincón oscuro,
donde yo siempre te quiera,
que no me importe la gente,
ni el veneno que nos echa.

Let's go to the dark corner,
Where I will always love you,
I do not care for other people,
Nor for the venom that they cast on us.

To the end, Diego stayed true to the voice of the revolution, the affirmation of free will, the rejection of conformity, the sanctity of individualism.

Hoda walks toward her parents' house. The main street is now pitch-black. She sees a lighted cigarette several metres in front of her. A dark shape in a dishdasha is pulling down the metal door to a shop. It's the olive oil shop, Akil's shop. She moves to the other side of the street to avoid him. Too late. He calls out to her.

"Wait, I want to talk to you."

Hoda hesitates. Should she make a run for it?

"*Sharmouta*—whore, how dare you speak to my uncle!"

Hoda freezes. She doesn't know how to answer the angry young man.

He's now facing her, a padlock in his left hand. He grabs her arm.

"Come with me."

"Stop, Akil! You're hurting me!"

"I'll teach you a lesson."

Hoda swings hard at Akil. He blocks her blow. Intense pain shoots up her forearm. Then she feels the padlock in his fist strike the side of her face. When she comes to, he has dragged her back to his shop. She looks up. The place is crammed with bottles of olive oil and barrels of olives in brine. An old oil lamp on the counter offers a dim light. Beside it is the padlock. Akil paces in front of her. It is clear he doesn't know what to do next. He has struck a woman who defied him, but whose cousin is a Palestinian commander. Hoda feels for her hijab. It's gone. It must have fallen off in the street. Her hair tosses wildly on her shoulders. Her skirt is torn. Her legs are exposed. She desperately tries to cover herself.

"Akil, listen. I won't say anything. Just let me go."

"Quiet!"

The shop's door is still open. Hoda scrambles to her feet and begins running toward it. Akil grabs her shoulders and throws her back onto the floor.

"*Sharmouta*, you will pay for trying to dishonour my family."

He leans over her. His eyes burn with rage. She whispers, no, Akil, no. He pins her arms down. She screams. He clamps his right hand over her mouth. Her left arm reaches out searching for a weapon. Nothing. He yanks her over onto her stomach and presses one hand against the small of her back, pinning her to the ground and forcing the air from her lungs. She wants to scream again but she can't. She tries futilely to push away from the ground, but Akil's hand on her back forces her down. This time with such force, she hears one of her ribs crack. His other hand is fumbling to pull up her skirt. His knee pries her legs apart. Her mind races to find some means to defend herself as fear cuts through her like a razor. Her fingers reach the glass bottle.

Marc's father's last testament takes him by surprise. He had forgotten that Diego was the half-owner of *Le Matin de l'Occitan*, a small leftist

paper in Toulouse, and he certainly hadn't expected to be willed his
father's share. His father's partner, François Pelletier, makes Marc a fair
offer to buy the estate's share but on one condition. Marc must work for
one year as a journalist there. The paper is undergoing a transforma-
tion, and François needs a young man to get it on a solid footing. Marc
agrees and writes to Hoda that he'll have to stay in France a little longer.

Marc quickly excels as a journalist and helps François develop a
long-term plan to appeal to a much younger readership. But he can't
get Hoda out of his mind, and every night he writes to her. Her first
reply elates him. When a few days pass without receiving another letter,
he begins to fear that he's losing her like he had Leyna. When Hoda's
second letter finally arrives, he reads it eagerly. At first, her letters are
discreet, but in time they match the open passion that he puts in his
own. At night he looks at the photos she sends him, falling asleep to
dreams of what their life will be together.

After three months, Marc can take the separation no longer. He
walks into François' office to explain he needs to return to Lebanon,
and is ready to hand over his share in the paper. The violence there has
spiralled, and he must get Hoda out of the country. In the corner of
the office sits the foreign editor for *Le Nouvel Observateur,* Jean Simon.

"Excuse me for interrupting. François has told me a lot about you. If
he's comfortable with it, I would like to make you an offer."

"It's fine with me, Jean. Go ahead."

"Marc, would you like to be one of our stringers in Lebanon?"

"That would be fantastic."

"It wouldn't be full-time work, but you could also write for other
publications."

"What are you interested in?"

"The French people are conflicted. Naturally, many lean toward the
cause of the Christians in Lebanon. They speak our language and share
many of our values. But with our own history of colonial domination,
especially in Algeria, there's also a lot of sympathy for the Palestinians. Add to that, the considerable interest in French intellectual circles
about Israel. Many of our best people, including in my own magazine,
are Jewish. Can you give us the most objective reporting possible—articles that break down stereotypes and go to the core of the matter?"

"I can do my best."

Marc turns to François.

"So, Monsieur Pelletier, will you release me from my commitment? I can sign over my half in the paper today. I won't ask anything for it."

"Marc, it was your father's wish that you work with me for one reason. He wanted you to follow in his footsteps as a journalist. You've already learned everything I can teach, and now Jean can teach you much more. Taking Jean's offer is what your father would have wished."

Out of his cherrywood desk, François Pelletier pulls out a chequebook. He opens it to a cheque already made out.

"Here, this is for your share of the paper. I hope you'll find it fair."

Marc looks at the cheque. Two hundred thousand francs, much more than Pelletier had offered three months earlier.

"I don't know how to thank you!"

"You can thank me by making your father proud," François says. "He was my oldest friend. I'm happy that I could help his son. Now bring us the truth about Lebanon!"

Hoda tries to move out from under Akil's inert body. Shards of glass protrude from the back of his head. Her hand also bleeds from the bottle's broken glass. Olive oil now mingles with their blood. How many times she hit him with the bottle she doesn't know. She draws on all her strength to pull out from under him.

"Hoda?"

A thin dark figure holding her hijab stands at the door.

"Nabil?"

"Yes. What happened?"

"He, he … tried to rape me."

Nabil helps his sister to her feet. Slung over his shoulder is a wooden box of the paints and solvent he uses for his murals on the walls in the camp.

"I was just coming home when I saw your hijab on the street."

"What should we do, Nabil?"

"You should go home now. I need to see if he's still alive, and then I'll go to the police."

"No, don't! We can't trust the police. We should tell Abdullah instead. He'll know what to do."

"Okay, but go. Go now!"

Nabil watches his sister run down the street and turn the corner to their house. He walks to the counter, puts the padlock in his pocket and picks up the oil lamp. He kneels before Akil's body, and places the lamp close to his face. Akil's eyes show no sign of movement. He nudges the man's shoulder—no response. He places two fingers on the thumb side of his wrist. There is a pulse, faint at first and then a little stronger. Nabil looks for a telephone in the shop. It takes a minute to locate it amid the rubble of upset crates. He leans over and begins to dial Abdullah's number.

"You!" a voice behind him says. Nabil turns to see Akil on his feet, blood streaming onto his shoulders, his clenched fist ready to strike.

"Akil, wait!"

Nabil pulls back but too late to duck the blow. He crashes against the shelves of olive oil. He tries to get up but slips on the oil, smashing his knee against the broken glass. A hard kick to his stomach sends him flying onto his back.

Akil stands over him.

"Bastard, where's that whore, your sister?"

Nabil looks around and grabs the strap of his box of paints. With all his strength he swings it at Akil's legs, toppling him onto the oil lamp. The lamp's glass shatters and its flames set Akil's dishdasha on fire. Nabil limps out the door, ignoring the pain of the glass embedded deep in his knee. He glances back. Akil has torn off his burning clothes. Naked he looks like a rabid animal. The pool of spilt paint and solvent lies between them. Akil ignores the fire moving toward it and charges. Nabil pulls down the metal door just before an explosion engulfs Akil in flames. He tries to block out the man's pleading for his life on the other side of the door, but he can't. He begins to loosen his grip on the door handle. Then Akil chokes out the words. "I will kill all of you!"

Nabil takes the padlock out of his pocket.

Chapter

17

MARIE OPENS THE E-MAIL FROM TARAGON. Can she meet him in Paris for the next interview? He could put her up in his apartment if she wanted. Why not, she thinks. Her editor at Le Devoir loved her first piece on Taragon. And a new interview might be the fastest way to get to the truth. Besides, she loves Paris. But she certainly isn't going to stay at his apartment. She opens her laptop and books a room at the Hôtel Foch on Rue Malbeau. She quickly writes back that she'll see him on the seventeenth at Café Pergo, and politely declines his offer of accommodation.

Marie walks to the window of her Montreal apartment. The trip back from Istanbul had exhausted her. But that was two days ago, and she's starting to recover. She looks at her cell phone. There's a missed call from Minh Chau. Right, she remembers, her friend is coming down from Ottawa this weekend. She quickly calls her.

"Hello."

"Hi, Minh Chau. How are you?"

"Marie, I can't wait to see you. We had a blast in Istanbul, didn't we?"

"That we did, but seeing that Israeli again still gives me the chills. You really shouldn't have confronted him. You scared me to death!"

"Well, he's out of the picture now."

"I certainly hope so!"

"So *is* he?"

"What? Who?"

"The famous Mr. Taragon! Is he ... ?"

"I don't know yet, but I'm going to see him next week in Paris. I hope that I'll have the courage to ask him."

"I googled him."

"And?"

"He's incredibly attractive."

"I hadn't noticed."

"Really? I mean ... Of course, you didn't notice. You wouldn't, would you? Especially, since ..."

Marie feels a tinge of irritation, discomfort at the lie that she's just told her friend. Of course, she finds Taragon attractive. Who wouldn't? But it isn't something that she can share. She resolves to settle things as soon as possible.

"By the way, I can't make it until Sunday. Mathieu is arriving back from Vancouver on Saturday."

"How does he feel about becoming a father?"

"I haven't told him yet."

"What are you waiting for?"

"I'll tell him this weekend."

"Why don't you bring him down to Montreal?"

"Can I?"

"Of course, I'd love to meet him."

Marie hangs up, and pauses for a moment. She heads for the bookshelf with all of Taragon's books. His treatise on the Lebanese Civil War, his exposé on Israel's settlement policy in the West Bank, and his most recent book on the rise of Hamas. She opens the last to look again at the photo on the back flap. She searches for any resemblance to herself but finds none. She can see the Spanish in him—the thick wavy hair, the slightly hooked nose. He has the classic Mediterranean look that lets him fit into the crowds from Tangiers to Tel Aviv. Her own features are so different. Her eyes are dark, very dark, but her hair is blonde framing a china-white complexion. His lips are thin forming a sly smile. Hers are full and naturally red, always slightly parted to reveal immaculately white teeth.

She knows that she's beautiful—so many men have told her so as they awkwardly tried to win her heart. She knows that her summary rejection of suitors has earned her a harsh reputation and the occasional rumour of liking women more than men. Untrue. But there's so much lacking in the men she knows. Their fawning attempts to assert their political correctness, shallow proclamations of support for feminism. Their hypocrisy emasculates them. With Taragon, there is honesty, sincerity grounded in acts, not words.

Marie looks hard in the mirror and holds up the tattered photo that she always keeps with her. She searches in her own face that of the woman in the photo. It's there and then vanishes.

Marie remembers how simple her life was before her father gave her the photo. She understands that Jean Boivin was not her biological father, but he was the only father she had ever known. His absence still weighs her down. She decides to phone Carmen, Jean's wife. She no longer calls Carmen mother. A coolness plagues their relationship since Carmen moved back to Quebec City and began living with another man. Marie punches in the number, slowly, deliberately.

"*Allo?*"

"*Carmen, c'est moi.*"

"*Marie?*"

"*Oui.*"

"How are you? Where have you been? It's been a month."

"*Désolée.* I should have called earlier."

"It doesn't matter. You're all right though?"

"Yes, can I talk to you about Papa?"

"Is it the photo again?"

"Yes."

"Marie, I really don't know anything about it."

"But you knew that I wasn't your child, and you never told me."

"It was what your father wanted. He wanted to protect you. He wanted you to feel loved. We always loved you!"

"I know. I love you too." She wants to say *Maman*, but she hears movement in the background. "Is he there?"

"Yes, Philippe and I were just sitting down for breakfast."

Marie pauses. She doesn't want this intruder to overhear her conversation, but she's come too far. Time is pressing and answers are needed.

"Is the woman in the photo my biological mother?"

"I don't know. How could I? The first time I saw the photo was when you showed me it. Jean just told me that you were orphaned. That's all he ever said."

"Tell me again everything you know. It's important."

"All I know is that your father arranged the adoption from the Sisters of Charity when he served in Lebanon. I was surprised when he wrote me about the adoption. I said yes because your father couldn't have his own children, and in his letter, it was already apparent that he loved you. I knew that there was more to it, but I never asked. Sometimes, your father could be secretive, even with me. For a while, I wondered if somehow Jean had strayed, had an affair and you were born of it. I couldn't bring myself to ask him that. Before he left Canada, we'd had our problems. Every couple does. When he returned with you, life was perfect. Perfect until the end."

Her mother's sobs come through the line. Guilt overcomes Marie. Why is she putting her through this? Then she hears her say: "It's all right, Philippe." The intruder's presence angers her.

"Marie, are you still there?"

"Yes. I'm sorry, I didn't want to upset you."

"Will you come up to Quebec soon?"

"Of course, but I have another assignment first. In Paris, this time."

"Marie, *tu me manques.*"

"I miss you too … *Maman.*"

The pause, the silent reconciliation, lasts a short eternity, the blink of an immortal's eyelash, and then the line goes dead.

The room has grown larger as if to confuse Marie as where she should turn next. She feels her vitality escape from her languid limbs and slumps onto the sofa.

There on the coffee table is the photo album. A collection of what has been, false promises of what was to be forever. She flips through its pages. Tricycles to bikes to her first car. Bathing suits on sandy beaches to parkas in the snow. There he is, her father. He looks so handsome in his uniform. She turns to the end of the album. He's sitting up in his hospital smock, smiling through the pain. It was taken one day before he died from throat cancer. It's the keepsake of the last time she saw him, the day he gave her the photo. He could no longer speak. When she asked him what the photo was about, he summoned up the energy to write on a scrap of paper: *It was on you when I found you.* She wanted to ask him more about it, but when he closed his eyes and began to breathe calmly, she held back. She leaned over to kiss him on the forehead, then sat by his bed until he was fast asleep.

That night, Marie had her first dream of the boy at the wall. She had no idea where it came from or what it meant. She only knew it had something to do with the photo. When she returned to the hospital the next morning, Jean Boivin had passed from this world.

Taragon's taxi pulls to 10, rue de Solférino, the Paris headquarters of the French Socialist Party. Kressmann has agreed to meet him, but insists that a couple of colleagues also attend. He knows that these men will be sceptical, perhaps even cynical. They will have heard the entreaties of the Palestinians and the wild optimism of the Israeli Left before. Madrid in 1991 had infused everyone with excitement—an end to decades of bloodshed. Rabin's murder struck all peace supporters hard. The turbulent years of the Intifada, the rise of Hamas in Gaza, and the iron fist of successive right-wing governments have jaded most of them. And now he, a journalist, is going to present them with a blueprint for peace—another pipe dream? He readies himself for ridicule from these hard-nosed politicians.

He knows that Kressmann is putting his reputation on the line in meeting him, but Kressmann is indebted to Taragon in more ways than one. He also owes a debt to 'Akkawi for saving his life when the Phalangists surrounded his small clinic in Naba'a. To Bronstein, it is a *dette du sang*—two left-wing Jews who've both fought hard for their people to be part of, not apart from the world—to march on the righteous side of history and not sink into the role of oppressors.

Taragon will have to make a compelling case for Kressmann to bring his fellow Socialists onside. Then he can reel in the Spanish Left, and hopefully the Scandinavians. The junior senator from Illinois, Barack Obama, has also just announced his run for the presidency, and Taragon hopes to convince America's new voice of political moderation to endorse the initiative.

The questions that Kressmann may ask race through his mind. *How to convince Hamas and the Palestinian Authority? How to neutralize the settler movement? The Right of Return—what Israelis would ever agree to that?* He's been preparing his answers since leaving Greece.

"Twenty euros."

"Pardon?"

"The fare is twenty euros," the cab driver repeats.

"Yes, of course. Here you are."

Taragon's heart beats faster. He straightens his shoulders and brushes the hair from his forehead. He sees the shadows underneath his eyes in the reflection of the glass of the building.

f

18

Athens – April 2007

A GAINST TARAGON'S ADVICE, Abdullah 'Akkawi decides to
make a play to bring others into the initiative. So instead of
taking his new identity and heading to Spain as they agreed,
he island-hops the Aegean in a number of small fishing boats to the
southern coast of the Peloponnese. From there, he works his way up
to Athens, where his old friend Adil Nashashibi is vacationing. Dr. Nashashibi was the PLO's long-standing ambassador to Greece, and the
year before was elected Chair of the PLO's Political Committee. Since
Arafat's death, his influence has grown in the organization, and he's
one of the few Fatah leaders whom Hamas still holds in respect. He's
also one of the few accorded the privilege by the Greek government of
visiting Greece as often as he wants. He once succeeded in convincing
PLO dissidents to release a Greek passenger ship. Gratitude goes a long
way in the Greek memory. So does vengeance.

En route to Athens, Abdullah stops off in Tripolitza where, in 1821,
Greek nationalists massacred eight thousand Muslims and Jews. His
mother, Meryem, told him the story of how her grandmother escaped
to resettle in Algeria. But the rest of the Jews perished. It's a pilgrimage
he has wanted to make for a long time—a sober tribute to his mixed
heritage. Although it's been years since he abandoned his atheist youth
and submitted to Allah, Abdullah has also never denied his Jewish
blood. Why should he? It was Abraham who first submitted to the will
of Allah. He has merely followed in the Jewish patriarch's footsteps.
Truly, Allah does not distinguish between Jews and Muslims. Here in
Tripolitza, they were murdered as one.

Abdullah searches for some acknowledgement of the massacre—
some atonement of it, but there is none. Instead, statues of heroes of
the Greek War of Independence adorn the city. He cannot help but
think of Churchill's observation that "history is written by the victor."
He knows the success of the agreement negotiated in Arkassa is crucial
to the survival of the Palestinians, and now believes that it will be just
as important for his mother's people.

The train pulls out of Tripolitza's station. Soon, it is snaking its way
through the mountains and plains of the Peloponnese. A quiet land. A
land now at peace with itself, but it was not always so. In the low-lying
fog, he imagines Philip's Macedonian phalanxes spearing the Greek
citizen soldiers. From his train window, he can see the mountains of
Laconia, the frontier of the Macedonian advance. He hears again the
words of Father Jean, a French Jesuit, who visited his school in Beirut
to teach them the history of Greece and Rome: "Philip sent a message
to the Spartans saying: 'If I enter Laconia, I will raze Sparta.' They answered with a single word: αἴκα—if."

It was this example of ancient courage, Spartans' steadfastness that
pushed him to join the *fedayeen*. Forty-five years have now passed in
the struggle to regain his land. Against all odds, he is still alive. The
Arkassa Pact is now crucial to his goal—he must persevere. His eyes
grow heavy and he dreams of happier times, of holding Munir, Hedaya's
soft hands on his shoulder, and his cousin Hoda's graceful smile. The
train slows and then jerks as it changes tracks. And the Athenian suburbs in their concrete vacuity consume his dreams.

Bronstein curses Taragon as he walks up the snow-covered spiral staircase in Outremont. How did Taragon convince him into this frozen
exile? It's April. How can it still be so cold here in Montreal? At home,
the geese are plentiful in the Alonim Hills. The Bedouin of Basmat
Tab'un are cleaning their old rifles, ready for the spring hunt. He thinks
fondly of Abu Yassin, who taught him to hunt, to recite poetry and to
judge no man by his colour or religion. It's been a year since his mentor
passed away. Most importantly, he learned honour and respect from
the Bedouin leader. His teachings served Bronstein well when his world
shattered amidst the bickering of religious bigots and right-wing racists.

Bronstein shivers. His spring jacket offers little protection from the
bitter cold. He pushes the doorbell and waits. From the staircase, he

watches two Hassidic men walking with their sons. His entire life, he has never understood the *Haredim*. Like many secular Israelis, he resents how they exploit the state, avoiding military service and draining the government resources with their excessive demands for social services for their burgeoning families. Now Taragon has banished him halfway around the world to live among them. Suddenly, Bronstein feels ashamed. He's preaching reconciliation between Arabs and Jews, but is still plagued by his own bigotry.

"*Bonjour.*"

Bronstein turns to the face half-hidden in the partly opened door. The eyes are deep and alluring, despite the scars around them.

"*Puis-je vous aider?*"

"Marc has sent me."

"Oh. Please come in."

"Thank you."

The apartment is painted in the subtlest of pastels. There's an air of Provence. An elegance of Paris. And the scent—what is it? He watches his hostess walk to a small statue of a kneeling being. She puts out the burning incense in the clay saucer in front of it.

"Please forgive the smell. I was just completing an offering to the Buddha for my parents."

"It's a beautiful scent. What is it?"

"A blend of cinnamon, mango, and papaya."

"When did your parents pass away?"

"I don't know. I lost touch with them thirty-two years ago, so I pray for them on the day we lost our country."

Bronstein looks at a yellowed calendar on the wall above the shrine. In French and a language he assumes must be Vietnamese is the date April 30th. He struggles to understand its meaning. Then he remembers sitting with his young friends in the university's cafeteria when the radio announced the Fall of Saigon.

Leyna Nguyen looks up at her guest.

"Marc was vague about when you would arrive. Tonight, I've invited a couple of friends for dinner. I hope you don't mind."

"I can take a walk."

"In fifteen degrees below? I don't think so. You will join us."

"Is that a good idea?"

"Of course. I have it all up here. Your name's Anatoly Shostakovich.

You were born in Irkutsk and now live in Vancouver. We met on a vacation in B.C. last summer. We've a common interest in classical music."

"I didn't know that Marc had such a vivid imagination."

"Not Marc. He only said that I should call you Anatoly. The rest I made up. Does that work for you?"

"It's a great cover story."

"Good. It will be a little more convincing if you pay me a lot of attention during the dinner. They'll think that we're lovers and won't ask too many questions. I hope you don't mind."

"It'll be my pleasure," Bronstein says. There's something there, unexpected, a tiny spark between two exiles, the exchange of *chi* between them. Marc was right when he said: "You'll like her."

The doorbell rings, releasing them from the moment. Leyna quickly shows Bronstein to the guest room to put away his suitcase.

"Wait here. I'll come get you in two minutes."

Leyna rushes to the door and opens it to Marie Boivin, Minh Chau and a distinguished-looking man in his fifties who must be Mathieu Hibou, her new beau.

"*Bonsoir* Leyna. You know Marie, of course. And this is Mathieu."

Leyna steps forward to kiss Marie on the cheeks, hugs Minh Chau and stretches her hand to Mathieu. "*Enchantée.*"

She sees a serenity in Mathieu's demeanour. This pleases her. She's never seen Minh Chau so radiant. From the corner of her eye, Leyna notices the roundness of her midriff, a bump on her cousin's delicate frame. Is the life cycle beginning again? She looks into Minh Chau's eyes for the confirmation of her suspicion, and then leans in to whisper: "Congratulations!"

Leyna ushers everyone into the living room, then goes upstairs to knock on the guest room's door. Together they walk down to the living room, Leyna putting her hand around his muscular arm. Bald and missing a few teeth, Bronstein is not a handsome man, but there's a dignity in his movement that conveys strength and confidence. And he's someone Marc trusts so she'll trust him too.

"Everyone, I'd like to introduce Anatoly, a friend from Vancouver."

Bronstein freezes as Mathieu Hibou looks straight into his eyes.

From a café in the Plaka, Abdullah calls Adil Nashashibi. They agree to meet that afternoon in the Benaki Islamic Art Museum. There's hesitation in his friend's voice. It's been a full year since Hamas won the Palestinian legislative elections. In the last few weeks, while Abdullah negotiated the Arkassa Pact, tensions have been mounting between Hamas and Fatah. Adil is one of Palestinian President Mahmoud Abbas' earliest supporters. He explains on the phone that he'll listen to what Abdullah has to say, but the old man is furious with Hamas. An initiative from one of the movement's leaders will be a hard sell.

Abdullah listens calmly to his friend's caution, but inside he scoffs. Hamas gave Abbas every chance to rein in Fatah commanders in Gaza who filled their pockets with whatever they could skim off from the Gazan economy. When Gazans complained to Abbas, his only response was to reinforce his corrupt lieutenants. Now Gaza is on the brink of civil war.

Abdullah begins to weigh his options. Arkassa has the potential to change the landscape of the Middle East, but he doesn't share Marc's view that they should create momentum with the international community before seeking cooperation from the Palestinian leadership. The Palestinian factions must first form a united position. He needs the support of intellectuals like Adil to make this happen. Still, his absence from Gaza has left the field open to hotheads. Should he shelve the Arkassa initiative to return to Gaza to mediate an intra-Palestinian peace? No. Allah decided that he should join Marc and Bronstein on this journey. He will see it to its end.

Abdullah checks his wallet. He still has plenty of euros and his coded list of supporters in Europe. He'll wait to replenish his funds in Spain. It'll be safer there. Since the arrival of its Conservative government, decades of Greek support for the Palestinians have ended. It's now hard to believe that Greece once sent ships to evacuate the PLO from Beirut and gave Arafat a second lease on life. Slowly, the entire world is turning its back on the Palestinians.

Abdullah decides to walk to the rendezvous at the Benaki Museum. It's only twenty minutes away, and much of it is through the expansive National Gardens where pursuers will find it hard to hide from view. Abdullah touches the knife inside his jacket. How many has he killed with it? Ten, fifteen? Israelis, Lebanese, Palestinian informers. At first, he killed only in combat, battles of life-or-death. After Sabra, it was in anger as he hunted down his son's killers.

When the PLO left Beirut, he threw in his lot with the Shi'a fighters.

For years, he fought alongside the Hezbollah to drive out the Israelis from Lebanon and to track down the Guardians of the Cedars. He never learned which of them pulled the trigger to end his son's life and abducted his niece, but he interrogated enough of them to confirm their collective guilt—how his wife, his aunt, his cousin all fell under their knives. His anger consumed him and vengeance seemed the only reason to continue to live. Then one Friday in a remote village on the slopes of Mount Lebanon, an old man, perhaps the village *mukhtar*, came to him and said: "We will pray now." He turned to say no, that he never prayed, but he saw the man was blind. Out of respect, he rose to walk with the man toward the villagers gathered to pray outside their bombed-out mosque. The blind man placed his hand on Abdullah's shoulder and said: "Allah leaves no man behind. He sees you. He waits for you."

Perhaps, it was the simplicity of the mountain folk's faith, the unblemished act of submission to Allah's will in the cool spring air. No walls to stifle him. No rhetoric, Quranic verses or hadiths to confuse him. That day in the fellowship of the devout, his life changed.

The sculptured gardens and vaulted archways of the National Gardens guide Abdullah to his destination. He passes by the busts of the poets Dionysios Solomos, author of the Greek National Hymn, and Aristotelis Valaoritis, whose unfinished poem calling the Greeks to rise against Venetian rule graces the lips of every schoolchild. The glare of the noon-day sun is fractured by the hundred-year-old palms. There's a serenity here, no presence of danger, a sense of liberty. The gardens beckon Abdullah to stay, but Adil is waiting.

Abdullah quickens his pace for the last two hundred metres to the museum. Positioning himself just inside the park, he has a clear view of the building's entrance. He waits. Abdullah begins his three-hundred-sixty-degree surveillance of the meeting site. A taxi pulls up and parks one hundred metres from the museum, but the passenger doesn't get out. Down the other end of the street, a motorbike drives slowly up but stops a fair distance from the building. Abdullah doesn't like it at all. His cell phone begins to vibrate in his pocket. He looks at the incoming text message. *Stay away! They are here. Adil.*

Abdullah shoots one last look at the street. Another car is parked close to the taxi. He looks back to the centre of the park. Two men are walking quickly toward the museum, looking at a hand-held electronic device. They're headed straight toward him. A dog comes up, wagging its tail. Its owner is nowhere to be seen. Abdullah wipes his cell phone for fingerprints, tucks it in the dog's collar, and then throws a stick as far as he can. The animal dashes off to retrieve it. Abdullah watches the two men pivot. One is gesturing toward the tracking device. The other places a call. The cars and motorcyclist start moving to block the park entrance where the dog is now holding the stick in his mouth. Abdullah runs fast in the opposite direction, his hand firmly grasping the knife in his pocket.

Chapter

19

TARAGON LOOKS AROUND Kressmann's office in the Socialist Party's headquarters. Its high walls are adorned with fine pieces of post-modernist art. The French Socialists don't skimp on their luxuries. The magnificent mansion in the seventh arrondissement near the Musée d'Orsay seems so distant from Kressmann's decrepit clinic in Naba'a. Taragon wonders: Has his friend's altruism weathered his ascent to power or given way to political convenience?

Kressmann looks at Taragon. How they both have aged. What has it been thirty, no thirty one years since they first met? Then he'd thought that Taragon was going to die in the makeshift clinic in Naba'a. But his friend turned out to be much tougher than expected. And he's still the most tenacious person he knows. That tenacity has brought Taragon fame but has also alienated many people along the way. Now the man is sitting in his office trying to convince him to join a wild effort to bring about peace between Arabs and Jews. Maybe his old friend has gone too far this time.

Kressmann reads the document before passing photocopies of it to his two colleagues. He likes the agreement, although he knows they won't. It's so full of merit, so rational. For a moment his heart flutters. Could these pages change his life as much as Taragon's notebook had in Beirut? Five years ago, he'd have jumped at the opportunity to back such a plan, but there's now the call from the president's office. More is at stake, and he needs the support of the men beside him to realize his ambitions.

Taragon sits quietly, knowing that he can't rush the verdict of Kressmann and the others. These are sober men—men who take action only after much deliberation. He expected them to probe him, look for flaws in his strategy, provoke him with their scepticism and even ridicule the initiative to see how committed he is to seeing it through. But it's their silence that is now unnerving him.

Kressmann begins.

"Marc, is any of this real?"

Taragon's back stiffens. He's unsure whether Kressmann is playing the devil's advocate or expressing authentic scepticism. Perhaps, a clever opening move to navigate his friends into backing the plan?

Kressmann begins again.

"I mean, do you really expect us to believe that Abdullah 'Akkawi has signed on to a peace agreement with Jonathan Bronstein?"

Taragon looks Kressmann straight in the eye.

"Bernard, have you ever known me to lie?"

Kressmann retrieves the pages of the Arkassa Pact from his colleagues and hands them back to Taragon.

"So even if it's true, what do you want France to do?"

"You mean, what do I want Bernard Kressmann to do?"

"Now, that is one and the same."

"What do you mean?"

"I've been invited by Sarkozy to join his cabinet."

"Sarkozy? And you've accepted?"

"Yes, tomorrow the announcement will be made. Sarkozy has given me the Quai d'Orsay."

Taragon suddenly realizes where he has seen the other men before. They are not Socialists! Leblanc, now the head of the DGSE, France's CIA, is on Kressmann's left. And on his right is Carbone, Sarkozy's Corsican bagman.

"So you won't help?"

"Marc, I didn't say that. I asked you what you want us to do?"

"If you mean by us, the French Socialist Party, I want you to take this forward to all the Socialists in Europe,"

Kressmann pauses, then shakes his head.

"We can't blind-side Sarkozy on this. I'll speak to him tomorrow. If we do this, it will be on a non-partisan basis. But it won't be easy. Sarkozy isn't going to part ways with the Americans on this, or with the French Jewish community unless this is really going to fly."

"And the Socialist Party?"

"As of tomorrow, I won't be able to speak for the party, but if Sarkozy agrees, we will reach out to them."

Kressmann's sudden use of "we" and "them" unnerves Taragon. The man had always been on the Left, starting out as a convinced Marxist and moving to the Socialists when Mitterrand came to power. Now he was to be a minister in Sarkozy's government.

"Let me see what I can do, but 'Akkawi has to rein in Hamas," Kressmann says. "We can't sell your initiative if the suicide bombings start again."

"You know that Abdullah has nothing to do with the fanatics. Hamas is not monolithic."

"Maybe."

Kressmann approaches Taragon with his hand outstretched. A firm handshake, one that exudes confidence—and leaves you with an unsettled stomach like the kiss of Judas. Leblanc takes Taragon's hand too, clammy but not hostile. Carbone holds back. His eyes fixate on Taragon as if to read every movement he makes.

The secretary opens the door, and Taragon steps out into the world, alone with a dozen sheets of crumpled paper.

Chapter

20

H ODA WAITS NERVOUSLY with Evan's driver outside the terminal. She'd asked Marwan to drive her to the airport, but his uncle refused to lend him one of his taxis. Recently, the airport had become a dangerous place. So instead, Hoda asked Marc's friend, Evan, to drive her. He's now a third secretary at the Australian embassy and claims to have some influence with the airport authorities. Evan has been inside for over an hour, and Hoda begins to worry. The driver is also getting edgy. Hoda glares at him when he pulls out a package of cigarettes. He meekly puts them away.

"Where are you from?" he asks.

"Sabra."

"No, I mean in Palestine."

"My family is from Safad, but I was born here."

"My father lived in Safad as a boy."

"But you aren't Palestinian, are you?" she says.

"No, thank God! My father's family is from Kafr Bir'im, near Safad. We're Greek Catholics."

"Sorry, so then you are a Palestinian like me?"

"No, my mother is from Lebanon. I am Lebanese."

How silly it all is, Hoda thinks. Kfar Bir'im is only a few kilometres from Safad. Her grandfather, a country doctor, used to tell her of his trips there to visit patients. Yet this man sees himself as Lebanese. And he'll always see her as a foreigner, despite her having been born here. She hates this small-minded nationalism. She has also come to despise the pettiness of the Palestinian leadership. Arafat is revelling in his new status as the ruler of a mini-state. The leaders of the Palestinian Left are little better.

Most of all, Hoda hates and fears the fundamentalists who are growing in number. Their presence reminds her constantly of the assault by Akil. There were no witnesses to what had happened, and the camp came to believe that Akil had surprised criminals stealing from the shop, who had killed him. His friends elevated him to hero status.

Hoda now lives full-time in Shemlan, and keeps visits to Sabra to a minimum. She no longer trusts many of the young Palestinian men she's grown up with. She fears that one day someone will find out what happened on the evening of the Eid feast, and then Akil's friends will come for her and Nabil. On those rare occasions that she returns to Beirut, she visits first with Nabil who's now living with Marwan. It also gives her a chance to catch up with Marwan on what has been happening at the university. Hoda knows that her brother is safe with Marwan, and she also feels safe with him even when Nabil isn't there. The sudden opening of the car door interrupts her thoughts. She looks over to see Marc's smiling face.

Evan is at his most entertaining on the drive back into the city. Even the driver is laughing. Evan has learned by heart dozens of Juha jokes, the most beloved comic in Arab storytelling.

"When Juha was riding his donkey he passed some of the people. One said disdainfully: 'Oh Juha, I didn't recognize you, but then I saw your donkey.' Juha replies: 'Of course, that is normal because donkeys always recognize each other.'"

Marc listens in amazement. He can only catch about half of the jokes. How has Evan improved his Arabic so quickly?

When Evan starts into a joke about Juha, the Caliph Harun al-Rashid and his nubile new wife, Hoda bops him on the head with her purse before the joke gets too racy.

Marc sits back and thinks how wonderful his life will be in Lebanon. He's with a beautiful, intelligent woman. He has a great friend in Evan, who, despite all his flaws, is unshakably loyal. And now he has before him a promising career as a journalist. Beirut, despite the civil war, is still one of the great cities of the world. His exuberance puts an end to the months of grieving his father's passing.

They cross over into Fakhani, leaving behind the Palestinian and Shia checkpoints on the airport highway. Out of the blue, a truck pulls up beside them. The back is full of young fighters. Their leader sitting in the front seat waves for them to pull over. Evan mutters an obscenity in Arabic. The driver looks at Evan, who reluctantly nods to him to comply. They are in Fakhani, Arafat's stronghold. They should have nothing to fear here.

Evan is pumped, ready to bluster about diplomatic immunity when he recognizes the commander. *Fuck, it's that bastard Yassin Ayoub, the Mourabitoun leader who almost had them shot.* Ayoub trots over to the window. Something is different. He is no longer wearing the Mourabitoun insignia. Instead, he sports the red and white keffiyeh of the Popular Front. In one hand is an AK-47 and in the other a folded piece of paper. The driver is sweating. Marc straightens his back. Hoda pulls her hijab over her head.

"Marc Taragon?"

"Yes."

"This is from my commander."

Ayoub passes Marc a slip of paper, and nods respectfully to Hoda.

"What does it say?" asks Hoda.

"It's from your cousin."

"What?"

"Abdullah wants to see me right away. He says there's an important story unfolding."

"Don't go, Marc! You've just arrived. Let's go to Shemlan now. I'll explain it to Abdullah. Besides, how do we know that the note is really from him? Don't you recognize this man? This could be a trap!"

"It is indeed from Commander Abdullah," Ayoub says.

"You! You're Mourabitoun!"

"I was, but now I serve Commander Abdullah."

Hoda knows that what Ayoub is saying is likely true. Her cousin has risen in the ranks of the National Movement, and many non-Palestinian fighters are fighting for him. Still, she doesn't trust Ayoub.

"Hoda, I should see Abdullah," Marc says. "I'm a journalist now."

"Not without me!"

"Fine, come with me then."

"Thank you," Ayoub says. "Please follow us."

Hedaya tenderly treats her husband's wound, as she has done so many times before. This time the wound is deep. She's afraid of infection and pours more alcohol on it. Abdullah flinches but says nothing. He must show an example to his men. His young *fedayeen* stand guard all around the house and some have gone to the roof to take up positions as snipers. He curses himself for taking so many men away from the battle in Karantina. He will return that day despite his badly damaged shoulder. But first, he has to tell the young French journalist what's happening. He fears that only international media attention can prevent a wholesale slaughter of the Kurdish, Syrian, and Palestinian slum dwellers. The fanatical Maronite militia leader, Maroun El Khoury, from the neighbouring district of Dekwaneh, sees the Muslims of Karantina as an existential threat. He has vowed that no quarter will be given. And now El Khoury's followers are being reinforced by other Christian militias—Phalangists and Guardians of the Cedars. They're ready for the big push on Karantina, and then the nearby Shia community of Naba'a.

A hard knock on the door—Yassin Ayoub walks in.

"Sir, the Frenchman is here."

Hedaya puts her shoulder under her husband's arm to help him up and then stops when she sees Hoda precede Marc and Evan. Abdullah now standing on his feet, says: "Greetings, cousin." Hedaya moves forward, leaving Abdullah leaning against a table. Her round stomach proudly announces that soon she'll give her husband a child. She hugs Hoda, ignoring the men with her.

Yassin leads Marc to Abdullah.

"Do you remember me?"

"Of course, you're Abdullah 'Akkawi. You saved our lives."

When Abdullah sees Evan, peeking in at the doorway, he shouts: "You, *Jassus*, stop spying on us, come here." Evan steps forward, a little red in the face at being called a spy, and receives a friendly slap on the back from the gigantic fighter.

From the pocket of his blood-stained shirt, Abdullah takes out a dozen Polaroid photos of executed men, women and children. Scruffy-looking youths stand over the bodies. One is crouching holding a dead man by the hair as if he is a trophy. Marc and Evan look at the photos in horror. Is this Abdullah's work? Is he boasting of his gruesome conquests? They look more closely and notice the crosses around the young men's necks. The murderers are Christians.

"Who are the dead?" Marc asks.

"Syrian workers and their families who tried to leave Karantina."

"And the killers?"

"Maronite militiamen from the East Beirut neighbourhood of Dekwaneh. They're followers of the Maroun El Khoury Group."

Marc flinches. "The MKG?" He has heard the stories about them.

"Yes."

"How did you get the photos?"

"We took one of their fighters prisoner. We have him in the back. He can tell you what they did to these people. But that isn't the biggest problem. He also told us that the MKG wants to leave no one alive in Karantina, and its allies may send them enough men to do just that."

Marc pondered. So the Maronite factions are now working together. This is disturbing, especially the possible involvement of the Guardians of the Cedars. The followers of Étienne Saqr are by far the most ruthless fighters. More merciless than even the MKG. He knows that a large-scale massacre in Karantina will lead to reprisals elsewhere against Christians in Lebanon. He remembers the fearful faces of the people of Damour. Their town is now completely surrounded by Palestinian, Lebanese Muslim and Druze forces. Will the Christians of Damour pay with their lives for the impending massacre in Karantina?

"What do you want me to do?"

"Take the photos and tell the story to the world, and *inshallah* the Maronites might be intimidated from carrying out the attack. The Phalangists are particularly sensitive to stories in the French press. They're bigger than El Khoury's group and might just be able to pressure him to back off. We know that we can't defend Karantina for long, but a delay might give us enough time to evacuate the civilians."

"Okay, I'll do it, but first, let me talk to the prisoner."

"*Tayyib*. Ahmad and Hassan, stay with the foreigners. Yassin, we're returning to Karantina."

Hedaya protests, but Abdullah leans over and kisses his wife gently on the forehead. "*Kull shee, bitseer khayr*—everything will be fine," he says, reassuring her. But both know that the battle ahead will be deadly and that this could be the last time that they might see each other. Abdullah reaches down to touch his wife's belly and whispers: "Name him Munir."

Chapter

21

Beirut – January 1976

ARC IGNORES THE pleas of Hoda to return immediately to Shemlan. First, he must find out what's in store for the inhabitants of Karantina. He returns to the back room. The young Christian fighter slouches in a corner. He covers his bloodied face with his hands. Marc kneels in front of him.

"*Shoo smak?*—What is your name?"

The fighter looks up. His face is that of a boy—clean shaven for what little there is to shave.

"Are you a foreigner?" he asks in Arabic.

"Yes, I am French, a journalist."

The fighter shifts to French.

"*Je m'appelle Jean.*"

"Listen, Jean, you're in a bad situation here."

"I am innocent. I haven't even fired a gun!"

"Why were those photos on you?"

Jean pauses. His eyes shift to the left and the right before looking up.

"I swear I didn't participate in any of that! Commander El Khoury gave me the photos to take to the other militias. He wanted to show he was serious about wiping out the Muslims in Karantina."

Marc presses him.

"So you were going to join in on the killing in Karantina?"

"No, I had enough of that bullshit. I was deserting. I'm only half-Lebanese. My mother is Armenian. I was trying to reach the port to go to Cyprus and then to my uncle in Armenia."

"Can you prove that?"

The young man pulls out a wad of US dollars and a piece of paper with the name of a captain of a Greek vessel and another paper with a name and address in the Armenian capital, Yerevan.

"My mother gave me this. The Greek is a family friend. His ship's coming to Beirut tonight. Let me go. Take the money!"

Marc feels sorry for the young man. He said that he had no choice but to fight for the militia. All his school friends signed up after the first incursion by Muslim fighters. The Muslims had kidnapped a local businessman and left him mutilated in a rubbish heap by the port. The man lived long enough to tell his family that the kidnappers had come from Karantina. After that, refusing to sign on with the militia was considered an act of treason.

Marc tries to bargain for the young man's freedom with the Palestinian fighters whom Abdullah has left behind. But they have their orders to keep the prisoner until Abdullah's return. And then? The Armenian half-breed will pay for his crimes, declares a teen-aged fighter. Marc decides that he'll join Abdullah on the front to plead for the young man's life. And there he'll stay to witness for the world what will befall Karantina.

Evan reads his mind.

"Give me half of the photos. I'll make sure that Robinson gets them published in the Australian and international papers. Go!"

Hoda suddenly realizes what's happening.

"No! Marc, come with us!"

"I can't. I need to speak to Abdullah. I don't want this man's death on my conscience, and I need to see for myself what's happening in Karantina. If I don't go now, no other journalist will."

"You're so stubborn! This is not your fight."

"Hoda, innocent people have already died in Karantina. I need to get the story out so more won't."

"The photos are enough. This boy's testimony is enough. Write your story, but come with us now!"

"I can't."

Marc looks at Evan.

"Evan, keep her here!"

"No!" Hoda screams, struggling to free herself from Evan's grip.

"Take me to your commander!" Marc barks at a fighter, too young to challenge his authority. The other Palestinian fighters are unsure whether to stop Marc and free Hoda or join him on his trip to the front. Instead, they walk over to the young Christian captive who is now praying aloud in Armenian. They kick him until he stops.

Maroun El Khoury's cousin Samir surveils the street below. Maroun has taken most of his fighters with him to defend Dekwaneh against reprisals from the neighbouring Palestinian camp of Tel al-Zaatar. Two snipers and a mortar crew have been left under Samir's command. Their mission is to prevent the Muslims in Karantina from joining forces with fighters in West Beirut. Samir has sent his snipers to neighbouring buildings to triangulate their fire on the main road leading out of the slum. But the mortar is his real asset. That and the retired Lebanese artillery instructor who has joined them. As the morning wears on, the kills mount up. A dozen mortar strikes have stopped all the cars trying to run their gauntlet. His snipers have gunned down another dozen men and women trying to escape by foot.

Time is not on their side. Much of their munitions ran out during the initial incursion in Karantina. This has forced his cousin to postpone the next assault and to ask for reinforcements from rival militias. Maroun has sent out two couriers. One to Shaykh Pierre to implore the Phalangists to send their fighters. They're confident that the old man will hear their plea, even if the Phalangist areas are themselves thinly defended. Another courier, a half-Armenian, has gone to Étienne Saqr to seek the support of the Guardians of the Cedars. Saqr was well known for his disdain for half-hearted efforts so to win his support, Maroun executed a dozen prisoners and sent with the courier photos of the slaughter as proof that they're all in. Samir curses under his breath. His cousin has become reckless. Those executions will only stir up a hornet's nest, and Saqr can't be trusted.

"*Effendi*, look!" his adjutant says.

"Where?"

"There behind the cars."

A small figure in a dirty *jellabia* is crouching behind a burnt out taxi. Even from the distance, Samir can make out the boy's African features. Probably a Sudanese. There are many in the slum. He has no quarrel with the impoverished African workers, other than they're Muslims, and he knows that the Kurds and Palestinians will recruit them to fight against him. The boy is young, very young. Probably too young to be a fighter. But what is he doing there? Spying? Lost? No matter, they'll kill him when he tries to cross the road. They have no choice. The story of even one person escaping Karantina will encourage others to try the same. Samir's men don't have enough mortar shells and bullets to stem a large outflow. And he knows that once the slum dwellers escape, they'll begin plotting their revenge. All the men of Karantina must die.

Samir trains his guns on the road to the left of the burnt-out car. Come on, he says to himself, let's get this over with.

His young adjutant taps his shoulder and whispers: "Look, *Effendi*, the other side. We didn't get all of them after all."

The effort by Abdullah's men to relieve Karantina had gone wildly wrong. All of the Palestinian and Lebanese reinforcements were caught in a barrage of mortar fire when they reached the outskirts of the slum. Most of those who survived were decimated by the enemy snipers. The rest took shelter behind half-demolished walls, waiting to lull the Maronite snipers into believing that they had all been killed.

Abdullah focuses his binoculars on the one Maronite sniper position he has located. He sees the glint of the sun off metal as a gun is repositioned toward the direction of an arriving car. Abdullah signals his men to aim their guns at the sniper's position.

"Your friend, the *Franji*'s come," his adjutant Jamal says.

Abdullah turns to see Marc, walking quickly toward them, and waves his hand at him to keep low.

When Marc reaches Abdullah's side, he has a clear view of the street before them. Dozens of fighters lie dead across the pot-holed street. The rest, six at the most, have taken shelter in what was left of a corner store on the other side of the street.

Abdullah has positioned himself strategically behind a thick brick wall, the remains of what was once a police station. He can easily retreat without exposing himself to the snipers, but he won't leave his men. He can't leave them.

Marc presses his back against the solid wall, his Leica camera in hand. He senses Abdullah's displeasure that he has come, but the man says nothing. Instead, he shifts his huge frame to offer Marc some added protection from the snipers' bullets. Marc juggles the Leica into position. For a moment, the tobacco breath of the two young Palestinian fighters distracts him. They're now pressing their bodies against him, trying to

see what he's photographing. The smell of the sulphur of the recent shelling makes him gasp for a second. Then he sees Yassin Ayoub, two metres
from the store, his body cleaved in two by a mortar shell. Whatever
crimes he's committed, all is forgiven—he is now a *Shahid*.

The muscles in Abdullah's neck tighten. He wants to berate the
young Frenchman for coming. But he knows that any sound might
draw the fire of the Maronite militiamen. He's fairly certain that Marc's
imprudent arrival has probably alerted the snipers perched high in the
nearby buildings. Are there more hiding closer? And then he hears the
first click.

Marc has swung into action, rapidly snapping down the shutter-re-
lease of his Leica to record the sacrifices of the dead Palestinian fighters.
Before Abdullah can yank him back, Marc crawls to a mound of rubble
barely covering the bodies of civilians from the slum. He feels nauseous
but musters the courage to remove the rocks to document the killings.
A sniper's bullet whizzes by his ear. Abdullah pulls him back before a
second bullet can strike.

"You fool! They now know that some of us are still alive."

"Sorry."

"Forget it!"

"What can I do to help?"

"Just stay alive and get your photos into your newspaper."

Marc looks at Abdullah. The vein on the left side of his forehead
is bulging. He watches the Palestinian bite his lip before turning back
toward Marc.

"Listen, we may need to retreat," Abdullah says. "There's not much
we can do now, not without more men. But first, we need to find a way
for our comrades to cross this road. We need a diversion."

"And those still in Karantina?"

Abdullah looks Marc in the eyes. He has never run away from a
battle, but he isn't ready to lead his men to annihilation. The enemy's
ambush was well planned. He suspects that there aren't many of them
hidden in the buildings, but their aim is good and they have at least
one mortar.

He looks up the road. It is littered with his men's bodies and those
of the civilians who tried to flee. The Maronites will not give up their
strategic position without a real fight. Even trying to retrieve the bodies
of his fighters would be a death sentence. At least, he knows that the

enemy will not desecrate the bodies of those left behind—it's one line they won't cross. The war is still young, and both sides are respecting some time-honoured traditions.

"There, look!" Jamal says.

Crouching behind an old taxi across the road is a young boy. He wears a dirty grey *jellabia*. The boy looks five, no, maybe four and is clearly African.

Abdullah signals the boy to wait. A mortar explodes just in front of the taxi throwing up a massive cloud of dust. Abdullah lunges toward the boy, but Jamal pulls him back. A bullet hits the ground just where Abdullah was headed. The boy begins to race across the road. He freezes in his tracks when another sniper's bullet hits the ground in front of him. This time Marc sprints toward him, zigzagging to confuse the snipers. Two shots miss him. He grabs the child and turns. Both are thrown forward when a mortar shell strikes the abandoned taxi. Its fuel tank ignites. Marc shields the child, ignoring the searing pain as the flames reach him. The smoke of the burning diesel is blinding. The stench of his incinerated flesh makes him gag. For a second, he loses consciousness. Then the squirming of the boy under him wakes him. He hears the crackle of gunfire and pounding footsteps. Abdullah and Jamal have darted out, taking advantage of the billowing black smoke. They now have a clear view of the positions of the snipers, still firing wildly at Marc and the child.

Abdullah and Jamal pinpoint the first sniper and fire several rounds of tracer bullets at him. Abdullah's men from behind the corner store reposition themselves to several more secure positions. They watch the tracer bullets and then unleash their own volley of fire in the sniper's direction. He falls silent, but in the cacophony of the gunfire and the billowing smoke, the other two snipers don't notice and still focus their fire on Marc and the child. Abdullah identifies the position of the second shooter. More tracer bullets followed by concentrated fire from the dispersed Palestinian fighters take him out. The remaining enemy fighters launch one last mortar. It falls a hundred yards short of the Palestinians, hitting another vehicle and creating more smoke for cover. Abdullah's men advance, with guns blazing at their enemy's exposed position.

Samir El Khoury ducks the barrage. He turns to signal his men to gather up the mortar and retreat to Dekwaneh. Too late. Their bodies lie in a pool of blood around the mortar. He knows he can't abandon it. Aieee! A bullet grazes his forehead. He bends low and races across the floor, his arm scoops up the mortar, but another bullet pierces his arm, forcing him to drop it. He rolls on the floor in pain and then crawls his way toward the safety of the stairwell.

Abdullah now certain that the enemy is retreating, grabs Marc and the boy, and sprints to his fighters.

"Is the boy alive?"

"Yes."

"Merci, Abdullah," Marc says before falling into unconsciousness.

Dr. Kressmann looks at his new patient, one of many brought to his clinic in Naba'a from Karantina. The third-degree burns on the man's left arm and shoulder have sent him into septic shock. The nurse is already treating the burns with sucralfate cream and has prepared a tetanus shot. After giving the man a generous shot of morphine, Kressmann examines the burns. Through the man's delirium, Kressmann hears familiar words. He leans in to be sure—"*Hoda, attends. Je viens.*"

"Who is this patient?"

"A *Fransawi* like you, Dr. Bernard," the nurse says.

"Are these his things?"

"Yes."

Kressmann rifles through the leather bag. A Leica camera, some Polaroid pictures and a thick notebook. He flips through the notebook to the last entries. A confession by a Christian fighter of a massacre. He checks the man's passport—Marc Taragon, a journalist for *Le Nouvel Observateur*. Suddenly, Kressmann realizes the importance of the contents. He has warned the French embassy of the barbarity of the extremists. Now here's the proof. He nudges his new patient. No response. He knows that the man is slipping into unconsciousness and possibly a coma, but is unable to stop it. At that moment, he makes his decision.

"Nurse, take this film to Sarkossian and have him develop it right away. Ask him to duplicate these Polaroids and photocopy the notebook."

"Sarkossian doesn't have a photocopier. The Kanaan Pharmacy does though."

"Good! Take it there. I want two copies. Two copies of the photos as well. Wait!"

Kressmann quickly writes a note to his contacts at the embassy, stressing the need to prevent the impending slaughter. On another sheet, he writes to an Irish journalist, Martin Riley, asking him to get the notes and photos to *Le Nouvel Observateur,* and if he can't, then to publish them himself.

"When you have the photocopies and photos, take them to these two addresses."

"But doctor, we have so many patients here!"

"This is more important. Go!"

Chapter

22

Naba'a Clinic, Beirut – January 1976

H ODA LEANS OVER TO WIPE MARC'S BROW. The pain from the burns has been eased by generous doses of morphine. Marc floats in and out of consciousness. Hoda whispers to him that the international papers have used his notes and photos to run front page news for two full days. France is reportedly bringing pressure on the Phalangists to hold off from invading Karantina. "We'll be leaving Naba'a soon," she tells him. "Don't worry you'll be safe."

When the word on the street reaches the clinic that the East Beirut militias are hunting for Taragon, Kressmann doesn't hesitate. He insists that Abdullah 'Akkawi evacuate the heavily sedated Marc as soon as possible. He's not going to put his other patients in danger.

Sabra, far from the Maronite neighbourhoods, is the safest place to go, Hoda argues, and Abdullah agrees. When Hoda's parents learn of the plan to hide Marc in their home, they virulently object. How can they have a foreign man in the same house as their daughter? What will the neighbours say? Hoda shows them the newspaper clippings. Abdullah reassures them that Marc is a hero. He has given the Muslims of Karantina, many of them Palestinians, a reprieve from annihilation, and the young boy Marc had saved was not Sudanese after all, but the son of a *fedayee*, a respected martyr. Her brother Nabil argues with his parents in support of Hoda. They relent. But her father, who knows the recklessness of his daughter only too well, pulls her aside to say: "If you want to be with him, make sure he becomes a Muslim." Hoda suddenly feels an icy chasm between her and her parents. Their clinging to religion clashes with her own humanism, but out of respect, she remains silent and simply nods.

Marc's recovery is quicker than expected. Kressmann drops by on the third day to change the bandages and administer salves. He brings with him the tragic news that the Maronite militias have finally entered Karantina. The international community couldn't hold them back any longer. He has to get back to Naba'a. His clinic is already filling with wounded civilians. They're the lucky ones. The survivors are bringing tales of atrocities too horrible to describe.

Hoda never leaves Marc's side. She reads both the foreign and Lebanese papers aloud to him. Marc's Arabic is now reasonable, but when he looks puzzled, she reads more slowly and explains the more difficult words. She summarizes the Arabic radio broadcasts and shares the latest news from the front that Abdullah brings her. The Maronites are drenching Karantina in blood, but the war is going badly for them elsewhere. Lebanon's Muslims and Druze are rallying behind the PLO. All have had their fill of Maronite supremacy and are incensed over the slaughter of the innocent slum dwellers. Palestinians, Druze, and Muslims are closing in on the Maronite coastal town of Damour where three hundred Phalangist fighters are trying to defend the city. Another massacre is imminent.

On the fourth day, Marc overhears Abdullah tell Hoda's father that the order has been given for the assault on Damour. Abdullah will maintain discipline among his men, but he worries that the other Palestinian commanders will be blinded by vengeance, and Arafat won't restrain them. A slaughter would bring widespread reprisals. There are still many Palestinians in the Tel al-Zaatar refugee camp in East Beirut, and they'll be difficult to protect.

Marc is tormented by what he overhears. He knows Damour well. Whatever the Christian militias are doing in Karantina can't justify the slaughter of Damour's Christians. The next morning, Marc rises from the bed, as Hoda sleeps in the chair beside him. He dresses and checks his camera equipment. The pain from the burns still sears through him. He gives himself a shot of morphine and puts the rest of it in his bag. Damour is only an hour by car from Sabra. Even if he can't dissuade the Palestinians and their allies from attacking the town, he still has the duty to record the events there. The world needs to wake up and put an end to this mad escalation of violence.

It's five o'clock. He steps out into the morning's half-light. The devout meander toward the local mosque for dawn prayers. He recognizes

Hoda's father, leading some young men to prayer, and ducks into an alleyway to avoid discovery. Marc resurfaces to join a small column of stragglers, leaving them when they pass by a café. He reaches into his pocket to pay for the use of the café's phone. At first, the owner refuses. He too is late for prayers. Besides, what is this foreigner doing in Sabra? When he sees the fresh burns on Marc's neck and detects his French accent, he understands. News of Marc's heroism has spread quickly.

"Two minutes," he says.

The phone rings once, twice, three times before his friend's groggy voice answers.

"Evan, it's Marc."

"What the fuck, mate? It's five-fifteen in the morning!"

"I know. I need you to drive me to Damour."

"Are you out of your fucking mind! That place is crawling with Phalangists. And you're hardly in their good books."

"I need to report what is going to happen there."

"What is going to happen there is that those bastards are going to drag you into the street and shoot you like a dog."

"Evan, do this for me!"

"Fuck, mate. Okay, where are you?"

Marc looks up at the sign on the building. Café of the Return. He asks the owner for the cross streets and repeats them slowly over the phone.

"Got it! It's near Hoda's place, isn't it?"

"Yes!"

"I'll be there in forty minutes. Hold tight."

Marc looks around the deserted streets. The worshippers have all entered their tiny mosque. A stray dog stops to sniff some discarded vegetables and then wanders off. The streets have an eerie silence to them.

Evan's Peugeot pulls up to the café. Marc steps out. In the back seat of the car are two other men, cameras around their necks. Both look severely hung over. Marc hesitates.

"I didn't realize you were bringing others with you."

"Safety in numbers. Besides, you caught us in the middle of partying. It would've been impolite not to invite my guests to come along for the joy ride."

Marc looks at the three men in the car. They're unshaven, their clothes are rumpled and even from several feet away, he can smell the whiskey on them.

"Come on, get in!"

Marc walks to the passenger side, opens the door, sits and feels a hand on his shoulder. He cringes from the pain. The burns are still healing.

"Hi Marc, Remember me, Martin Riley, *Irish Post.*"

Of course, Riley, the Irishman with a big heart for the Palestinians and notorious for his drinking and philandering.

"And this is Owen Sharp. He's a stringer for the *Baltimore Sun.* Evan gave us a tip that you're onto something big."

Marc stares at the men, unsure how much he should disclose.

"They're good journalists," Evan says reassuringly.

"I know, but I wasn't expecting a posse."

"Riley was the one who got your photos to the *Nouvel Observateur*," Evan says. "You owe him."

"Correction," Riley says. "We owe you. Those photos woke up the world. Now everyone is clamouring for more news on Lebanon."

"What have you got?" Owen asks.

"I overheard something."

"And?"

"Today, Arafat and his allies are launching their big push on Damour. They plan to overrun the town by noon and avenge Karantina. No prisoners are to be taken."

"Even the civilian population?"

"No, the order is to spare them, but the fear is that the fighters won't hold back. Too much Muslim blood has been shed."

The silence is jarring. Both journalists had filed stories on the massacres in Karantina, but neither had been allowed to visit the slum. Their papers had re-run Marc's photos in the absence of fresh ones. Now, they could be in the front row of another atrocity. The world is watching Lebanon, and they know that if they break the story of a new bloodbath, it will again be front-page news. They also know the risks. Both have good ties to the PLO, but in the heat of battle, front-line fighters are unpredictable.

Evan says: "So folks, are you in?"

Murmurs greet him with a cautious affirmative.

Marc looks out the window. He can see Palestinian fighters climbing into trucks. Black-and-white keffiyehs for Fatah, red-and-white for the

Popular Front. Syrian-plated trucks with the Sa'iqa thunderbolt on the doors pull up beside the PLO fighters. It will be only minutes before they run into the first Phalangist checkpoint. Driver and passengers confer on whether to risk the checkpoint or hang back and follow the PLO fighters into the town. So far in the war, checkpoints on both sides have given journalists safe passage. Marc might be a liability though. His photos of the Dekwaneh killings have infuriated the Maronites. Riley asks him if he has a small photo of himself. Marc takes out his card for the French cultural centre and pulls off the photo in it. The Irishman fishes out a plastic badge from his bag and pries it open with a Swiss knife. He swaps the badge's photo for the one that Marc has just given him. Marc glances at it—"Richard Blacksmith, *Leeds Telegraph*."

"I always keep a backup press pass. The militias have a bad habit of confiscating them."

"Richard Blacksmith?"

"A friend in Leeds."

They're soon out of the city's southern slums. The mulberry bushes grace the mountainside. The car rides to the right to avoid oncoming trucks. It skirts the slope plunging down to the rocky shoreline. Damour comes into view against the aquamarine of the placid Mediterranean. The town's reputation as one of the prettiest on the coast is well earned. The steeple of Notre Dame de Damour and then of the five other Maronite churches bear witness to centuries of Christianity. The old palace looms over the town. There's a serene beauty, one that has long survived the guns of war.

The militiamen at the checkpoint barely look at the journalists' identity cards. Why should they? What danger could these foreigners be, with everything else happening? The defenders look haggard. Since the news of the Karantina massacre, they've been on full alert for reprisals. Now they seem resigned to their fate. Eyes hollowed out as if their souls have already departed. Honour-bound to make a last stand.

The journalists drive to Saint Elias Church. The priest is attempting to calm his parishioners. When they jump out the car, the women run up to them, crying: "*Sauvez-nous!*—Save us! *Ils vont nous tous tuer!*—They are going to kill all of us!" The priest introduces himself as Father Gabriel. He recognizes Marc from the photos in the newspaper and pulls him aside.

"You're Monsieur Taragon."

"Yes."

"You have connections to the Palestinians?"

"I know some."

"Will you take the women and children under your protection?"

Marc looks at the group. More are coming to the church. Soon there'll be over a hundred.

"I can try. What about you?"

"I'm going to take our young men's confessions."

The priest turns his back to his parishioners and marches up the highway, past where the older men of the town are erecting a new barricade. Some carry old hunting rifles. One or two have a new Kalashnikov. They're not prepared to let their sons die alone.

Evan pulls on Marc's sleeve. "This is suicide. Let's get out of here now!"

Riley is taking notes from the women and children. Their names. The names of their loved ones at the barricades. Owen is snapping photos like a madman. A sudden artillery barrage from the mountainside sends them scrambling for cover. The gunfire and then the approaching war cries unnerve them. They have a clear view of the road north of Damour. Scores of trucks are now barrelling toward the barricades. From the mountainside, sharpshooters are picking off the defenders like flies. Hundreds of Shia and Sunni militiamen are entering the town from the south. The Phalangists' defences are crumbling, but their men hold their positions until they're overwhelmed by superior fire-power. Some town people have gone to the beach in hopes of escaping the worst of the fighting. Marc watches in horror as the Palestinian fighters approach one group there and separate the men and older boys from the women and children. They push them into a circle a hundred metres from the women and force them to their knees. Each is asked a question. Some are then shot and others are spared. Later Marc learns that the Palestinians have killed only the Maronites, sparing the town's other Christians.

Father Gabriel comes into view again. An artillery shell hits a truck of Phalangist reinforcements sent to confront the Palestinians. He rushes up the hill to administer the last rites. The invading Palestinian fighters pay no notice to the priest as they drive by. But a pair of Japanese Red Army fighters in red-and-white keffiyehs jump out of a truck. They approach the priest. He looks up at them and crosses himself. They sling their Kalashnikovs over their shoulders and lift him up. They march the priest up the hill, stopping at each of the town's dying defenders long enough for him to administer the wounded fighters the sacraments. Then they finish them off.

Later, Marc learns from Abdullah that the Japanese are two brothers from Nagasaki. Raised as Christians, they had once contemplated joining the priesthood but became instead revolutionaries. In later battles, the brothers would repeat this ritual of finding a priest to drag along as they dispatch the mortally wounded. The Palestinians would name them the *Mala'ikat al-Maut*—the Angels of Death.

Evan's cajoling Riley, Owen, and Marc to head for the car when an artillery shell blasts a crater beside the Peugeot, sending it flying onto its side. Suddenly, it's clear that there's no escape from the advancing fighters. The local women gather around them, encouraging their children to cling to the journalists' legs. It's in this tangled mass of humanity that the Palestinian fighters find them. An officer walks up and asks one question.

"Are there men here?"

"No," Marc answers.

"*Yallah*," the officer says to his men, marching them off toward the town's centre.

Owen races after the officer and asks in broken Arabic for permission to accompany him, but the man raises his pistol and tells him to leave. He then shouts at Marc to take the women and children to the north edge of the town. And so begins a trek led by three foreign journalists and a diplomat of one hundred women and children. When the women walk past the slain Phalangist militiamen, many their sons and husbands, the wailing becomes unbearable. It draws the attention of some newly arrived Palestinian fighters. The women cower in fear as a gigantic man approaches them. Marc immediately recognizes Abdullah 'Akkawi.

"How did you get here?" Abdullah says. "We were looking all over for you! Never mind. You need to leave."

"Can you help us get these women and children to East Beirut?"

"Yes. Wait here. We can bring in buses. It will take some time."

"Fine. We'll wait with them."

"Walk first beyond that bend and stay out of sight. I'll leave some men with you. Be careful."

With that, Abdullah leads his men down the hill into the battle.

The winter sun offers little warmth to the huddled women and children. Then the rain starts. The curbside on the highway turns to mud.

Marc goes to each woman to ask her name and the names of her children. They also give him the names of their husbands and older sons, and beg him to find them. Marc promises to do so. He feels his heart wrench. These women, are they different from his mother, who escaped Franco's Spain, or from the refugee women in Sabra? He knows he'll find their husbands, but he doubts any will be alive.

Three hours pass. The women have no more tears to shed. They wander back to the crest of the hill where they can see their town. The guns go silent. Black smoke rises. Damour is burning. A woman becomes hysterical with grief. Others run up to drag her back. No one wants to attract the attention of the invaders.

Finally, the buses arrive. Red Crosses and Crescents are painted on their doors. Out of the first bus jumps Marwan Kanaan. Behind him, Hoda and her brother Nabil. A young girl follows them out of the bus. It's Marwan's cousin Selima, Marc later learns. Each wears a white armband. Marc embraces Hoda, who scolds him for disappearing that morning. Marwan tells Marc of the planned evacuation. The buses will be met at the entrance of Sabra by a truck of Social Nationalists and Palestinian fighters who will escort them to the Museum crossing. From there the women and children will walk to the Phalangist lines.

"I'll stay with the buses," Marc says, now holding Hoda's hand in his.

"Fine, Owen and I will head back to Damour to cover the rest of this disaster," Riley says. "Marwan, would you take this film to Sarkossian's to be developed? Marc, can you take our notes to our press office? Ask for Sarah. She'll transcribe them and get them off to our editors. There's still time to make the evening papers in Europe."

"Give them to me. It'll be faster," Evan says. "I'll use them to alert the embassies. Maybe the Americans can talk some sense into Arafat."

Hoda looks at the men, and then at the women and children climbing into the buses. She feels shame, a sense of guilt at what's happening in Damour. She knows that the journalists' reports will tarnish the image of the Palestinian cause, but she admires them for bringing the horrors of this war to the attention of the world. It is the right thing to do. She watches the men embrace and leave, and then slips her arm around Marc to pull him toward the buses.

23

Beirut – Winter 1976

THE KARANTINA BURNS have left horrendous scars. Kressmann tells Marc that he's done this to himself by returning to work too soon. There's nothing more Kressmann can do. Hoda doesn't mind. Her beloved's scars are badges of honour—proof to her parents that he's a hero, a man to be admired. When Marc also helps Nabil obtain a scholarship to study art in France, they consent to her seeing him. Secretly, they hope Marc will convert. They ask Nabil to speak to him of Islam. Nabil says he will but doesn't. After Akil's assault of his sister, he has quietly ceased to tolerate the moral hypocrisy of the believers.

Marc Taragon's standing with Hoda's parents is helped when his blow-by-blow telling of the Lebanese civil war rockets him to celebrity status in France. In Lebanon, his even-handedness in denouncing the excesses of both sides eventually earns him begrudging respect from most of the country's power-brokers. For the Palestinians, he becomes their conscience, the brake on their desire for revenge. For moderate Maronites, his articles bolster their calls for restraint.

Marc rents a room from Riley in the old Jewish quarter of Beirut. The synagogue is just down the street, open to the handful of Jews who venture to worship there under the protection of Fatah fighters. Arafat has sent out word that no Jew in Beirut is to be harmed. There Marc notices Abdullah 'Akkawi's frequent visits.

One Sunday afternoon, a quiet day, Marc turns the corner to see Abdullah enter the main gate of the synagogue. It's too late to greet his friend. Marc decides to wait outside for him to reappear. The guards know Marc well and appreciate his small gifts of cigarettes, but they will of course not let him into the compound when their commander is there. As Marc offers the guards a new pack of Marlboros, he overhears Abdullah speaking to the rabbi just inside the wall.

"Shalom, my son," the old rabbi says. "It has been too long."

"Rabbi, I was here just last week."

"Oh yes, I'm becoming forgetful. Forgive me."

"I'm worried. You're one of the last Jews to stay in Beirut. I can get you safe passage to leave if you want."

"No, there are others here who I must attend to."

"I haven't seen them for quite a while."

"Don't worry, they're still here. They're just reluctant to come to the synagogue with the guards outside, so I visit them in their homes."

"Do you have everything you need?"

"I could use news of those who have left."

"All I know is that the community in Montreal is opening a new synagogue soon. And those who have gone to Israel are allowing them-selves to be used for propaganda purposes."

"I'm sad to hear that. Lebanon is their home. When the war is over, I hope that they will all return."

"Rabbi, that may never happen. It's safe in Canada. You should go there."

"No, I must stay."

"As you wish, but please don't leave the synagogue again."

"My son, do you remember the Hebrew I taught you?"

"Yes, you taught me well."

"Wait a minute! I've something for you."

The rabbi returns with a piece of cloth.

"I hear you have a son. I'd like to give this to you for him."

Abdullah unravels the cloth. Embroidered in Hebrew are the words of Maimonides, one of the greatest thinkers in the Jewish and Islamic worlds:

Great indeed is peace, for as much as the purpose for which the whole of the Torah was given is to bring peace upon the world, as it is said: "Its ways are ways of pleasantness, and all its paths are peace."

Abdullah thinks about the words "all its paths are peace." He wishes that all who study the Torah would come to the same conclusion, but he knows that that will never be so. He'll give the cloth to his son, and teach him the goodness that still resides in the hearts of many of his grandmother's people. He turns to the rabbi.

"I need to join my men now but, next Shabbat, I'll return with my son for your blessing. After that, you should leave for your own safety."

"I will bless your son so that he may be like Menashe and Ephraim, two brothers who never competed with each other, who lived in harmony, just like we all should."

"And then you'll leave?"

The old rabbi looks to the soil in the garden. He stoops to pick up a handful and shows it to Abdullah.

"Leave? Can I leave this land, in which my family has lived for five hundred years? Their blood is in its soil, and so shall mine be when the time comes. Do not worry for me, my son. The Lord will protect me. *Shalom Aleichem.*"

24

Beirut – Winter 1976

M ARC WALKS BACK from the synagogue to his apartment. He feels unclean, ashamed that he eavesdropped on his friend. There's a bond between Abdullah and the rabbi that he doesn't fully understand.

Riley opens the door and looks down the street to see Abdullah leave the synagogue.

"Another visit? Doesn't Abdullah worry about how the other Palestinians see these visits?"

"I don't think so," Marc says. "I've asked around. Everyone knows his mother was Jewish, but it doesn't appear to be an issue with them."

"And with the Lebanese?"

"I'm not sure."

"Anyway, good for him. The Palestinian Left often pushes the idea of a bi-national state. At least, Abdullah is walking the talk, even if it is a load of rubbish."

Riley is a good flatmate and always ready to mentor Marc in the art of journalism and impart his political view of the world. He doesn't share Marc's pacifism though. Instead, he argues that the only way for Palestinians to achieve justice is to fight for it like the Irish did to end 700 years of British occupation. Despite his political views, Riley is a thorough and factual chronicler of the war. His articles spell-bind readers in Europe. But he doesn't have the sixth sense that Marc has when it comes to going to where things are about to happen, or the ability to connect the dots to predict what will happen next. The two flatmates are a formidable pair when they team up.

Riley offers Marc a Scotch.

"I heard that Hoda's found a teaching position at the university."

"Yes, but it's not permanent."

"So she won't be returning to Shemlan."

"No, and that's a good thing. The checkpoints are becoming too unpredictable."

"By the way, Marwan Kanaan and Nabil dropped by this morning."

"Really."

"Marwan's family has bought Sarkossian's photography studio, and he's looking to drum up business. A discount for photo developing at the studio if you do photocopying at his family's pharmacy."

"Good, he can have my business. He's a very reliable sort."

"And mine too."

"And Sarkossian?"

"The old man has gone to Canada."

"Pretty soon, half of the Armenians in Beirut will be there."

"It's a loss for Lebanon, but can you blame them?"

"Of course not. And Nabil?"

"Oh, he wanted to tell you that he's been accepted into the École des Beaux-Arts. He'll be leaving for Paris next week."

Marc leans back in his armchair, pleased with the news. He sips his Scotch. Good stuff, not as good as the Irish whiskey that Riley gets sent from Dublin, but still good enough for the daily fare.

Marwan passes over the list of clients to his uncle, Fouad Saadeh.

"So, have they all signed up?" his uncle asks.

"Almost all."

"It'll be important to get duplicates of their pictures."

"I know."

"We need proof of the militias' crimes, and where the forces are positioned. These journalists' photos are invaluable. Sarkossian wasn't willing to play ball with us. It left us blind—I'm glad that he decided to immigrate."

Marwan looks at his uncle. "Did you have something to do with his decision to leave?"

"No, of course not! He just read the writing on the wall. When this war is over, many will remember the Armenians for having raised the prices in their shops, and worse, some will blame them for selling to the militias the arms that sparked this bloodshed."

"That's not fair."

"Maybe not, but war doesn't encourage objective recollection of events or the actions of those involved in them."

"So how will the party use these photos?"

"First, we will analyze them for our own protection. If any of the other militias press us too hard, we can use the photos of their crimes to get them to back off. Second, we will send a set of them to Jumblatt once a week. His people in Mukhtara can use them in determining where to deploy his forces. It's always good to know where your enemies are and what arms they have with them."

Marwan nods.

"Have you spoken to the Palestinian girl?"

"Hoda?"

"Yes, that's the one."

"Yes, she's ready to work with us."

"And her brother, your room-mate?"

"His visa for France has come through. He's leaving next week. Anyway, he's not interested in politics."

"Never mind. It's the girl we want. We need her to take the photos to Deir Al Qamar to meet a contact there who'll take them to Jumblatt in Mukhtara. You can drive her, but she should keep the photos on her. The militiamen rarely check women at the checkpoints. Is that clear?"

"Yes, Uncle. I've to go now. I have a class at the university."

Fouad watches his nephew leave. He knows that he can trust him.

Chapter

25

Beirut – Winter 1976

HODA KEEPS HER RELATIONSHIP with Marc discreet. In Muslim Beirut, every neighbourhood has its moralists. Hoda and Marc begin to speak of marriage. She rejected his initial proposal, made the day of his return from France. No, she told him, let's wait—we need to be sure. Marc has offered to convert, at least on paper, but Hoda will have none of that. She's unsure of her own beliefs, and the more she frequents the Social Nationalists' meetings, the less Muslim she feels herself to be.

They steal moments away from their work for intimate dinners at Marc's place. Those evenings always end in long embraces and caresses, which stop just short of intercourse. One more year in Beirut, Marc says, and then he can ask for a re-assignment to Paris. In France, they'll marry, away from the madness of Lebanon. He has already chosen a spot for the wedding. It's high in the Pyrenees, a place of such splendour that every man, even he, would admit that God must exist.

Against the backdrop of their romance, the war continues. Lebanon begins to lose its soul, its humanity, and the international media can't get enough of it.

The Battle of the Hotels is the main story for much of 1976. Marc and Riley cover it by riding with the militias of the Lebanese National Movement. Owen moves to Ashrafiyeh to report from the Maronite side. Late every afternoon, the three confer by telephone on the day's events. It's a see-saw war between relatively small groups of armed men, but because it takes place largely from the rooftops of luxury hotels, the world stands up to watch.

Marc meets Hoda at their favourite café, just outside the university. The area is now secured by the Social Nationalist militia, which has grown in numbers as more Christians and Muslims join it to oppose the blind sectarianism of the other militias.

"My employers want me to get out of Lebanon for a couple of weeks to recharge my batteries," Marc says. "Have you been to Cyprus?"

Hoda smiles. "Have I been to Cyprus? I've never been anywhere."

"I've checked. There is no problem for Palestinians entering Cyprus. Come with me!"

"We would have to keep it secret."

"We can do that."

"I'll tell my parents that the university is sending me on a training course to Jordan. They don't know anyone there."

Hoda also needs a break from Beirut. The war's bred a lot of fanaticism on both sides, and loving someone outside one's community has become very dangerous. But she's not alone in loving a non-Muslim. Her brother Nabil now studying in France has confided how deeply in love he is with Selima, Marwan's cousin. They met first as Red Cross and Red Crescent volunteers, and then many times at Marwan's apartment when Nabil roomed there. Selima, well connected to Lebanese elite, helped Nabil set up several art exhibits before leaving for France. Now she too will be going to study in Paris.

Hoda likes the young Maronite girl. She'll be good for Nabil. He has never been physically strong, and the death of Akil has taken a toll on his mental health. She's told him again and again that he did what he had to do. And he did it for her and for the safety of their family. But since Akil's death, Nabil has estranged himself from the community. It has been harder on Nabil than her. Somehow, she has summoned the strength to black out the nightmares of the assault, at least most of the time. But when she visits her parents in Sabra and sees Akil's friends now all sporting long beards and skull caps, she cringes. She knows that she, like Nabil, can never live again in the camp.

Nabil sits on his bed in his tiny room in the Latin Quarter and re-reads the letter his sister has sent him. She tells him of the beauty of the divided city of Nicosia. She and Marc move constantly between the Greek and Turkish sectors. Hoda writes that leaving Cyprus to return to Lebanon won't be easy, but Marc's editors have heard that the Phalangists, who've lost the battle of the hotels, are now intent on launching their final offensive on the sprawling Palestinian refugee camp of Tel al-Zaatar. They've asked him to find out if the rumour is true.

Nabil puts the letter down. He limps to his easel. The injury to his knee is a constant reminder of the assault on his sister. On the easel is his present to Selima. He's counting the days to her arrival. He dips his brush in a rich red and dabbles it on the canvas. With a piece of cloth, he rubs in the red to fill in her lips. He stands back to admire the painting. He's worked hard to find the calming blue of her eyes, to sketch the perfect cherubim cheeks and capture her round chin. He's painted her from memory, but every detail is there, and then more.

Nabil rubs his knee. The room is cold. The pain in his other joints has also returned. He now worries about the rheumatic fever from his childhood coming back. He knows that he needs to take better care of himself. He counts the *francs* in his pocket and hesitates before putting another coin in the electric metre in the room. He has used up most of the money he earned from selling his paintings in Beirut, and Paris is much more expensive than he had expected. No matter, tomorrow he'll sell a painting at the flea market. Nabil leafs through several recently finished paintings against the wall. There's one he likes very much. A black figure of a young man climbing over a wall. In the teal background, the skyline of Beirut appears through a smoky nocturnal sky. He thinks of Sabra, of his parents still living there, of Akil's death. Is escape really possible? He puts the painting in his bag. Tomorrow, he'll barter his past for his future.

Chapter

——————

26

Tel al-Zaatar – August 1976

MARC'S STOMACH GRUMBLES as he marks off August 10 on his calendar. It's been two days since he has eaten anything but bread. He's been in Tel al-Zaatar for six long weeks. The camp's supplies are running dangerously low. Whatever provisions there still are go first to the children and pregnant women. The defenders eat what Marc eats, and that isn't much. It's clear that the camp won't be able to hold out much longer. The negotiations to evacuate the civilian population have faltered on one point. The Palestinians refuse to allow their women to be searched—a fatal mistake. The Syrians have now switched sides to help the Maronites and are blockading Muslim West Beirut. There'll be no relief for the camp.

Marc walks to the dispensary. He has lost a tooth during the night, and he's worried about infection. He can't remember the last time he saw a vegetable. If he can't find something to eat soon, he will at least ask the doctors to disinfect the hole left by the missing tooth. Gaunt boys stand guard with old rifles over the line-up of women and children waiting to see one of the camp's two remaining doctors. A month ago, the camp had six doctors. Two died when an artillery shell struck their clinic. Another died from an infection picked up on the makeshift operating table. And one, a Christian Palestinian, just vanished in the middle of the night. If the battle drags on much longer, the camp will face not just starvation, but widespread disease.

Two hours later, Dr. Ayad sees Marc. A quick rinse of homemade disinfectant and a shot of morphine for the pain. Opiates are in ample supply; antibiotics are not.

"Good news," Dr. Ayad says as he pulls out the syringe. "The evacuation is back on track. The Maronites have agreed to search only the women's bags but not their bodies."

"When will it start?"

"Tomorrow if all goes well."

"Thank you, doctor, I have a lot of work to do."

Marc leaves the clinic quickly and begins to interview everyone he sees. Their impressions on the eve of the evacuation need to be recorded. Some will be leaving homes that they've lived in since 1948. There are only a few who remain defiant. Most are ready to accept any conditions to avoid another day of hunger in the camp. Marc is down to his last roll of film. He chooses his subjects wisely: a grandmother cradling her daughter's newborn, a boy carrying an assault rifle in one hand and holding the hand of his little sister with the other. Marc's energy begins to ebb. The pains in his empty stomach grow stronger.

As the sun sets, he wraps up his last interview—a woman of seventy-three, who can still remember attending her Jewish neighbours' weddings in Safad. The old woman is overwhelmed that this starving journalist is risking his life to record her story. She offers him some dates she's been hoarding. He politely refuses. When he rises to leave, she calls her grandson to walk back with him. The young boy, who looks no more than twelve, brings a Kalashnikov and guides Marc back to the unfinished building that he has called home for the last six weeks. Along the way, Marc asks about the gun.

"It's my father's," says the boy.

"Where's your father?"

"He is a *Shahid*," chokes out the boy. "And I ... will be one, too."

Marc puts his arm around the boy's shoulders.

"What's your name?"

"Najib."

"Well, Najib, today you can't be a martyr because you're going to help me climb four flights of stairs. Is that okay?"

"Yes, Mr. Journalist. I'll help you. I'm very strong."

When they reach his building, Marc stumbles on the first stair. The boy catches him before he falls, and then slings the gun onto his shoulder to free his hands to hold Marc up. Together, they climb. When they reach the room, Marc collapses on a well-used mattress.

Najib stands guard over him as his grandmother has instructed him.

He moves to the window. The sun is setting. Slowly all of the camp turns pitch black, but the lights come on in Ashrafiyeh and in the villages of the Metn. They look magical.

Najib thinks of the stories that his grandmother has told him about Safad, about how the mountains are so beautiful. She always tells him that they are mountain people, born to breathe the pure air. He knows that he'll never see her mountains, never step foot in Safad. But he just wants once to go up into the Metn, and look down on Beirut from its heights.

Only twelve but here he is with a gun in hand—an orphan waiting to kill Maronite invaders before they end his life. He has never even met a Maronite. Why do they want to drive the Palestinians out of Tel al-Zaatar? He can't understand why the world is against his people, why his grandmother can't return to the city she was born in. He cries. He just wants to grow up to live his life like everyone else. The sound of the Frenchman turning and twisting in his sleep brings the boy back from his sorrows. He must be strong, like his father. His grandmother has given him the duty of protecting this man. He will make her proud.

The sun isn't yet up when Marc awakes to the artillery shells pounding the camp. He knows that this can mean only one thing. The plans for the evacuation have once again been dashed. From below he hears gunfire. He looks outside and begins to take notes. It's been two weeks since he was able to file his last story. His notebook is full of descriptions of life in the camp. He has interviewed hundreds of refugees, recording the stories of many who are living the last days of their existence. He's full of regret. His editors had only asked him to confirm a rumour, not to get himself killed. He'll never see Hoda again, and his stories will never be published. The tragedy of Tel al-Zaatar will be told by others.

From his balcony, Marc has a clear view of the eastern edge of the camp. He can see the massing of vehicles just beyond the camp's perimeter. The Phalangists have brought in reinforcements. Marc realizes that they're preparing for the last push. Some Palestinian defenders will fight street by street, but there's no way that they can hold out for long. He looks around him for Najib. The boy is nowhere in sight. Good, he must've returned home. It's better that he's there to protect his family when the enemy comes.

Elie Labaki brushes the dust off his uniform. The thread of the Phalangist patch on his shoulder is beginning to fray. He thinks of his mother who had reluctantly sewed it on. He checks his gun again. Oiled and ready for action. He throws a rock in the air and blasts it with a single shot. For weeks, he's been preparing for the assault. He sleeps little these days. The nightmares are too many. To stay alert, he takes amphetamines shipped in from Haifa, courtesy of their Israeli advisers. Elie doesn't care for the Israelis, even if they are now providing a lifeline to his people. He doesn't even care about Lebanese politics. He fights now only to avenge his fiancée's murder in Damour.

Elie looks over the young recruits he's been assigned. They're just boys from the mountains, lost in the city. Abu Antoine, the group's commander, passes by. He whispers to the men that the order has come from the top—no boys over the age of twelve are to be spared. For the young, unmarried women, three short words are given—"Make them brides." Elie shakes his head. He pulls together his squad.

"Listen. You will forget that order. If one of you touches a woman, I will put a bullet in your head!"

"And the men?"

"Did they spare our men in Damour?"

"No."

"Do what is in your hearts, but leave the young ones unless they are carrying weapons."

Another officer walks up to Elie's men. Over his shoulder is a duffel bag of ski masks.

"Abu Antoine says everyone is to wear them. The assault will begin at dawn. Tell your men to get some sleep."

As Abu Antoine's man leaves, Elie kicks the masks aside and spits on the ground. He has no intention to lead faceless killers into the coming battle.

"Please, Abdullah, get Marc out of there," Hoda pleads.

"It's impossible. He'll have to take his chances with the other evacuees."

"No, when they find out who he is, they will kill him."

Hoda turns to Marwan. "Can you do something?"

He looks back at her. It will be risky, but there is a chance. It's hard to say no to Hoda. Since Marc has been stuck in Tel al-Zaatar, she has confided more and more in him. He'd like that to continue. He suddenly feels ashamed of his feelings for Hoda—a man's life is at stake.

"I know a priest," Marwan says.

"You know a what?"

"A priest, a Maronite priest. He can travel anywhere in East Beirut.

And the Phalangists and other Maronite militias show restraint whenever he's present."

"Because he is a priest?"

"Yes, but also because he's related to Shaykh Pierre and enjoys his personal protection."

"Why would this priest help us?"

"He is Selima's cousin on her mother's side."

"He'll do it if Selima asks him to."

"And will she ask him?"

"If you ask her, she will. She adores you."

"What exactly do you want this priest to do?"

"To accompany me into Tel al-Zaatar so I can find Marc before Maroun El Khoury's men and their allies overrun the camp. As long as the priest is with me, I won't have anything to worry about and neither will Marc when we find him."

Suddenly, it all makes sense. Even Abdullah agrees that it's worth a shot. He'll radio a message to the camp defenders asking them not to fire on the priest.

Elie leads his men out from the crumbling building. They have *cleaned* it. The sight of the priest accompanied by a civilian surprises them. The priest walks toward him. Father Tobias from Bikfaya. He must distract the priest from entering the building and witnessing what they've just done. He whispers to two of his men: "Hide the bodies." Then he walks out to meet this man of God.

"Father, you shouldn't be here. It's not safe."

"I came to supervise the evacuation of the children."

"There'll be no evacuation. We've been ordered to take the camp."

Father Tobias pauses. He knows only too well what this will mean for the children. He braces himself. He knows that as long as he's with the militiamen, they won't kill the innocent. He regroups and says: "I am also looking for a French journalist. Have you seen him?"

"No. You should leave!"

"No. And I insist that you hand over any children you capture to me. Do you understand?"

Elie is frustrated. What is he to do with this stubborn priest? He shrugs his shoulders. Priest or no priest, there is more cleaning to do. They'll take their chances with the children, and pray that those they spare will not shoot them in the back. For the adult civilians, none will be overlooked. Let the priest complain to Shaykh Pierre if he wants. The old man knows exactly what's going on today.

"Then follow us, but stay close to the walls. Watch out for the snipers. And don't interfere with our work!"

"The children?"

"Yes, yes. You can have any who are not carrying guns."

"The journalist?"

"If we stumble across him, you can have him too, but I'm not putting my men's lives at risk to search for him. Is that clear?"

Father Tobias realizes that this is the best he can get from the tough young fighter. He turns to Marwan.

"Stay by my side. They don't know you."

The young fighters bow their heads as they pass in front of the priest. Two even kiss his ring. Father Tobias, in turn, blesses them with the sign of the cross. He knows that he'll prevent their excesses today, and prays that God too will forgive them for those they've already committed.

Marwan watches the priest fall in line with the fighters. As they move forward, he can see inside some homes with bodies of men, women and children strewn across the floor. He wonders what other depravities he might witness this day.

Marc has a clear view of the assault. Waves of leather-jacketed gunmen dart in and out of the warren of concrete homes inside the camp. The Palestinian defences are crumbling under the sheer weight of the invaders. He can see handfuls of defenders, many young teens, even children, huddling behind the broken concrete of bombed buildings. The clinic he visited yesterday is now debris. A woman's hand pokes out from the rubble. A militiaman walks over and tries to pull off the wedding ring. It is stuck. His commander tells him to hurry up. He pulls out a knife and slices the finger off.

Marc can see a group of eight men approach his building. They have to be Maronites. But something is odd. It can't be. A priest? He curses Gemayel. Is the old man now sending in priests to bless the massacres he condones from the safety of his mansion in Bikfaya? Close behind the priest is a man without a gun. A civilian? Marc puts the telephoto lens on his camera to get a better view of the approaching group. He focuses in on the man in the rear. Marwan Kanaan! What the hell is going on?!

The group occasionally takes cover to return fire at the remaining camp defenders. It doesn't last long. The defenders quickly run out of ammunition and retreat under the barrage of superior gunfire. Marc refocuses the camera's lens on the group's leader. A face he knows, but from where? He needs to decide. He could surrender to this group. Would they dare to kill him in front of a priest? Or he could attempt to join the remaining defenders and die with them. He could hide and hope for the best. That wouldn't work. He knows that the militiamen will search every building in the camp and dynamite most of them.

Marc starts down the stairs. He's still frail and nauseated from slow starvation. He stumbles down the last flight, falling flat on his face. Lifting himself up from the dusty floor, he staggers along the corridor toward the entrance. And then he sees it. A small body lying face down just inside the front door, clutching a Kalashnikov. Najib had stayed after all to protect him. He stoops down to check the boy's pulse. Not a beat. He turns him over. A large hole in his chest reveals a bloody pulp of flesh, lungs, and fragments of a mortar shell. Marc looks around for a cloth to cover the body. Nothing. He takes off his shirt and places it on the boy's face. Marc pries the gun from the boy's fingers and stands it in a corner. He summons all his strength to pull Najib inside a first-floor apartment and put him down on a mattress that had once served as a family sofa and bed. He searches the boy's clothes for something to take back to his grandmother. All the boy has on him is an UNRWA ration card: *Najib Safdawi. Born 1963, Beirut, Lebanon. Status: Refugee.*

The hot muzzle of a recently fired gun pushes against the back of Marc's skull. One shot will scatter his brains across the room. It's a quick way to die. Resigned, he closes his eyes and thinks of Hoda. The softness of her body pressed against him.

Feet begin to shuffle behind him. The gun is pulled back from his head. The footsteps of a second man. Marc keeps looking down at the floor. Two well-polished boots appear.

"*Marc Taragon, le journaliste?*"

He nods his head, still waiting for the bullet.

"We found him!" The shout goes out.

Marc feels four hands pull him up. Blood rushes to his head. A familiar voice. Jumbled words. Marwan's smile. He leans back. Father Tobias steps in just in time to catch him from crashing to the ground.

Chapter

27

Beirut – September 1976

H ODA TYPES UP MARC'S NOTES and sends them with his photos to Le Nouvel Observateur. Marwan translates the notes into English for Riley, who files a separate story for the Irish Post, adding Marc's name to his on the byline. The story is syndicated throughout the English-speaking world. Offers of employment flood in, but both stay true to their publishers. Over the next year, the two journalists become inseparable and travel across Lebanon in search of the latest escalation in the conflict.

The Syrian Army is entrenched in West Beirut, but it has left all of South Lebanon to the PLO. Israel is also building a buffer state with the Maronites in the villages just inside the Lebanese side of the border. With Israel's encouragement, a Christian officer, Major Saad Haddad, deserts the army to set up a new paramilitary force dubbed the Free Lebanon Army. Israel quickly begins to provide arms and cash to enable Haddad's forces to stop *fedayeen* attacks on northern Israel. But the Palestinians soon find ways to bypass Haddad's men, and their cross-border attacks grow bolder.

The Syrians take their share of Lebanon. By 1977, they've increased their troop presence in Lebanon to forty thousand. Damascus has two goals. It wants to prevent the rise in Lebanon of a Sunni state, which could give refuge to opponents of its Alawite-dominated regime. For this, it needs Lebanon's Christians to be a counterweight to growing Sunni power. Under the guise of restoring peace, President Assad deploys his soldiers to form a protective ring around the Maronite mini-state in East Beirut and the Metn.

Damascus's second objective is to prevent the Israelis from flanking the Syrian defences in the Golan Heights and making a direct run on Syria through the Beka'a Valley. Syria's control of Lebanon becomes an obsession for President Assad. The Druze leader of the Lebanese National Movement, Kemal Jumblatt, allies himself with the PLO to resist Syrian domination. The Syrian Socialist National Party splits between a pro-Damascus wing, allied to local Baathists, and a pro-Jumblatt wing. Hoda and Marwan Kanaan put their faith in the Druze leader.

Marwan and Hoda alternate in travelling to the Shouf to provide Jumblatt with the intelligence he needs to counter Syrian moves against him. They don't see Jumblatt himself. This would compromise them and him. Instead, they meet in Deir al-Qamar with Professor Abu Walid and occasionally with Nadia. The Shouf is still a patchwork of control by different factions, but Deir al-Qamar stands out as a relative haven for all and is only a half-hour drive from Mukhtara.

They meet their Druze friends in the inner courtyard of the long disused synagogue in Deir al-Qamar. On Saturdays, Hoda hands over copies of the international press photos developed by Marwan in his studio. On Wednesdays, it's Marwan's turn. Occasionally, they bribe local employees in the press offices to photocopy for them some of the correspondents' notes before the stories are written. Increasingly, the photos that interest Jumblatt the most are of Syrian army positions. Marc, a prolific photographer, has taken many of them.

Abu Walid asks Hoda to convince Marc to take even more photos of the Syrian presence in the city and along the highway near Aley where their troops are in close proximity to the Druze militia.

"No, I won't do it!"

"Why?"

"It'd put Marc at risk."

"How?"

"Local Baathists have been visiting Marwan's studio. They may be putting two and two together, although even that much math is a challenge for Assad's friends."

"Move the developing of the special photos to another location."

"We could, but there's more. The Syrians are detaining me longer at checkpoints. More than once they've asked if they've seen me before. This morning one guard wrote down my name and ID number."

"And?"

"If they find a few photos from various journalists on me, they'll assume that I have stolen them to sell to local papers. They might detain me for a while to get a bribe and then let me continue on my way. But if they find dozens of photos with the same markings, they'll want to know who the photographer is."

"I see. Well, things are getting complicated on the ground, and we need to know where Assad's troops are. Jumblatt has only five thousand men, and he needs to concentrate them where they'll provide the most protection for his people."

"This is what I can do. I'm working on a map with all the locations of the checkpoints. I can share that with you if Fouad Saadeh agrees."

"Good, but how are you getting the information?"

"Fouad's drivers are logging where the flying checkpoints are and the main routes taken by Syrian convoys. They do it to avoid getting stuck in the traffic. I also talk to the drivers of journalists who are Marc's friends. We're getting a much better understanding of Damascus's deployments inside the city and the routes used to move the troops around."

"Excellent! Well, when will the map be ready?"

"In about two weeks."

New banners with the face of the Lebanese Shia cleric Musa al-Sadr hang off the balconies of the modest apartment buildings as Evan turns onto Army Street and then into the Jewish quarter of Wadi Abu Jamil. There aren't many Jews left. Most have moved to Jounieh or emigrated to Canada. Shia refugees from the South have begun to move into the empty buildings.

Taragon still rents a room in Riley's apartment in one of the more prestigious buildings in the Wadi. The rent is low, and the apartment is vast by Beirut standards. The landlord has left behind some priceless pieces of Levantine art and some beautiful mother-of-pearl furniture. Having international journalists living in his home is the best insurance against looting.

Evan climbs the twisted metal staircase to the second storey. He didn't phone ahead. Riley comes to the door in a bathrobe.

"Hey, Evan. Nice to see you. A little early, isn't it?"

Evan looks inside. The table is full of half-empty whiskey glasses. A woman's scarf is draped over one of the chairs.

"Is Marc in?"

"He left this morning to see a Shia leader in Sidon. Come in and have a drink!"

Evan walks into the flat. To the landlord's elegant furniture, Riley has added memorabilia from throughout the Middle East. Jambiah daggers from Yemen, Bedouin carpets from Jordan, and an extensive collection of Palestinian embroidery. He's been almost ten years in the region, starting with coverage of the '67 war. He's a sought-after journalist, but he has burnt his bridges with a couple of major papers because of his strong views on Palestinian rights. He now plans for a long stay in Beirut as the *Irish Post* correspondent, provided he can convince his young Swedish wife to join him. But his philandering isn't helping his case. Gossip is reaching her, even in Stockholm.

"What's your poison?"

"Have you got any single malt scotch?"

"Only the finest. I'll fetch some clean glasses."

"It looks like you had quite the party last night."

"Just entertaining some of our Italian colleagues."

Evan smiles as he inspects the silk scarf with the letters *S.G.* embroidered in the corner. Sabrina Giametti, *La Stampa's* Beirut correspondent. Half the city's press corps has been chasing after her. Evan himself has on more than one occasion tried to talk her up. How this cantankerous Irishman has bedded her is beyond him.

"Mate, you have a great flat here."

"Thanks, Evan. It's not quite the luxury lodgings the embassies provide you folks, but it will do."

"The Americans and French yes, but Canberra is not quite that generous with us. So, are you working on any big stories?"

"We're keeping our eyes on the Israelis. We're not sure how much longer they'll put up with the cross-border raids."

"Yes, I hear that the Israelis are losing patience, but they should think twice about getting bogged down in Lebanon. Ever been to Mukhtara?"

"No."

"You should go. It's quite beautiful."

"I'm not sure many taxi drivers are going through the Shouf these days. Tensions are high between the Druze and Maronites there."

"I'm driving up later today if you're interested."

"Are you going to see Jumblatt?"

"No, but I will be seeing one of his advisers, Abu Walid. He was my Arabic teacher up to a few months ago."

"Really? Let me give it some thought."

Riley pulls out some notes that he was working on for a story on Jumblatt's criticism of Damascus. There it is. *Jamal Seifeddine, known as Abu Walid, new Jumblatt adviser, ties to the Syrian Social Nationalist Party. Sister Nadia, American citizen, vice-chairperson of the Progressive Women's Union.*

"Have you ever met Jumblatt, Riley?"

"Yes, on several occasions."

"What's he like?"

"An oddball. Far more of a Buddhist than a Druze. At times, he seems completely un-Lebanese, just a philosopher uninterested in local politics. But when things get tough, he changes and starts to micro-manage every political move and counter-move on the local scene. A lot of Western journalists underestimate him, writing him off as a local warlord."

"So what is he then?"

"Well, first he's highly intelligent. There's no doubt about that. If anything, he's driven by a deep passion for bringing Lebanon out of its petty sectarianism so it can find its place in the world."

"Sounds lofty, but the fellow is truly pissing off Damascus. Canberra asked me to get a word through to him."

"Really. Aren't you a little junior to be talking to Jumblatt?"

"That's precisely why they're sending me. Anyone more senior might seem like we're giving him a direct order. My visit will only be to warn him and then not even directly. I'm hoping Abu Walid will pass on the message."

"Warn him of what?"

"That Damascus has lost patience, and he should watch his back."

Riley looks over at Evan. He has never known him to be so candid.

"So why do you want me to tag along?"

"I could use a witness to the fact that I actually went to Mukhtara. My boss-man, Robinson, is a hard case, always accusing me of dodging difficult jobs. Meanwhile, he sits on his butt, slugging down Cuban rum at the marina."

"Sounds like a prick."

"You've got that right, mate."

"If I go with you, will you introduce me to Abu Walid?"

"Sure. He loves the Irish. A big Joyce fan. He's been translating *Ulysses* into Arabic for the last ten years."

"Wonderful, a man of letters in the turmoil of a crumbling country. All right, I'm in."

Hoda re-reads the letter from her brother Nabil. He tells her of how wonderful Paris has become since Selima's arrival. She delights at her brother's happiness. She looks forward to the day that she too will live in France. But for now, there's important work to do.

She waits outside Marwan's photo studio. She pulls out her hijab. Downtown Beirut is more conservative now that the Sunni militiamen are fired up with the idea that they're the vanguard of Islam. The studio was once surrounded by many Armenian shops. Some opted to emigrate to Canada. Others moved to Ashrafiyeh. Sunni merchants have moved in, often investing money that they or their relatives earned in Saudi Arabia. West Beirut is losing its cosmopolitan caché. Sleeveless tops and mini-skirts have been replaced by kaftans and hijabs, but Prada knock-offs are still in vogue. For a moment, she thinks she sees Sadira, Akil's sister, but she's mistaken. Akil, will she ever forget what he tried to do? She pulls her hijab off and puts it back in her pocket.

Marwan's white Mercedes pulls up beside her.

"Hoda, I'm sorry I'm late."

"That's fine. We still have time. Do you have the photos?"

"Yes, but today I can drive you myself. It'll be safer that way."

"Are you sure? There might still be some flying checkpoints."

"We'll be fine."

Hoda jumps into the back seat of the taxi. Marwan passes her the photos, which she slides inside her blouse. He watches her through the rearview mirror. Her hair is flowing free today. It has been a while since he has seen her that way. He takes a deep breath, starts up the Mercedes and heads toward Aley and then Mukhtara.

Chapter

28

Beirut – December 1976

THE MOUNTAIN ROAD FROM MUKHTARA twists and turns as they head back to Beirut. Normally, Evan would be enjoying the drive, but the trip to Mukhtara was a bust.

"You look upset," Riley says.

"It didn't go well."

"What happened?"

"Abu Walid blew me off. Instead, he sent his sister Nadia to meet me. She told me point blank that nothing would change Jumblatt's position on Syria's presence in Lebanon."

Riley shifts in his seat. Evan is pushing the car pretty hard, barely clinging to the road on each new turn.

"Take it easy, man. Get us to Beirut in one piece, for Criss' sake!"

"All right. Keep your panties on!"

Fecking bastard, Riley thinks, *I can't wait until ...* A blast hits them before he can complete his thought.

The Peugeot rolls off the road, doing three-sixties until it hits an enormous cedar. Masked men scramble down the slope. They pull open the driver's door. Evan, dazed, can barely make out their words.

"*Mish huwi*—it's not him," the first masked man to reach them says, cursing. The second aims his gun.

"*Khalee-hun li halhun*—leave them be."

"Why?"

"Killing foreigners is not what we're being paid to do."

Evan hears the boots jamming into the mountainside as the men scramble back up to the road. He waits until the tires screech away before he finally exhales. Riley's bloodied face is now staring at him.

"Sweet mother of Jesus! Who the fuck were those guys?"

"Palestinians and Syrians. Probably Sa'iqa."

"How do you know?"

Evan holds back. He isn't ready to reveal how well or why he can distinguish local accents.

"I don't know. Just a guess."

"Let's get the hell out of here!"

Riley tries to move his hand to open the door, but an excruciating pain shoots up his arm. "Feck, I think my arm's broken."

"Hang in there, mate."

Evan eases the driver's door open, noticing in the side mirror that his forehead too is covered with blood. He climbs out of the car. The grass is wet. He starts to slip down the slope but grabs a low-hanging branch of the giant cedar. He looks around. The tree has blocked the car just two metres from the edge of the ravine, an easy two hundred metres deep. He notices the gasoline leaking from the fuel tank.

"I'll be there in a sec, Riley," he says as he hoists himself onto the tree trunk to get to the passenger side of the Peugeot.

A small rock bounces off Evan's shoulder. He looks up the mountain. Nothing and then faint voices. Riley hears them too.

"Jesus," Riley says, groaning. "Are they coming back to finish us off?"

The phone is ringing when Marc enters the apartment. He rushes to pick it up.

"Yes … Okay, I'll be there shortly."

It's been an exhausting day of work in Sidon. He has spent hours with fishermen protesting against the Israeli seizure of their boats. Things aren't going well in the South. With the PLO's support, the Mourabitoun have moved into Sidon and Tyre to set up checkpoints and collect local taxes. In the towns and villages closer to the border, Saad Haddad is forcing Shia villagers to enlist in his Free Lebanon Army. Those who refuse are quickly expelled from his mini-state.

Marc's dispatches on South Lebanon can wait. He changes shirts, gives his face a good scrub, and rushes into the street to hail a taxi.

"Where to, *Effendi*?"

"Berbir Hospital."

The entrance of the hospital is full of patients. A harried nurse points Marc to the emergency ward. The hospital's corridors are spotlessly clean, but a few cracks are showing on the walls. As he turns the corner, he sees Hoda, Marwan, and Evan waiting outside a room marked "minor trauma." Hoda walks to Marc.

"Don't worry, Riley's going to be okay."

"What happened?"

Evan steps forward.

"Some fucking Syrians and their Palestinian lackeys blew us right off the road!"

Hoda glares at him.

"They weren't our people," she says.

"Probably Sa'iqa and Syrian intelligence," Marwan says. "Do you have any idea why they attacked you?"

"They probably thought we were somebody else. I heard them say it's not him, and they just took off."

"You were lucky."

"No kidding, and then the cavalry arrived." Evan looks to Hoda and Marwan.

Marc studies their faces. They twitch a little and avoid his glance.

Marwan explains how they were returning from Mukhtara. An errand his uncle had asked him to run. Marc looks to Hoda.

"I asked to go along. It's been a long time since I've been to the Shouf," she says. There's an unevenness in her words. A tightness around her mouth. Her eyes dart up to the left. Evan knows that she's lying. He's been trained in these things.

Marc doesn't press her.

Riley limps out of the trauma room, assisted by a nurse. His arm is in a cast, but he's smiling.

"Don't worry, folks. I'm not dying, at least not yet. Just *banjaxed* my arm."

"Let's get to the office," Marc says. "We need to file a story on this."

"Can you leave our names out of it?" Marwan asks.

"Sure."

"Marc, I need to get back home now," Hoda says. "I want to make sure that my parents are okay. I'll see you later."

"I'll drive you," Marwan says.

She leans up and kisses Marc. Marwan shuffles his feet. Marc feels something forced in her kiss. He watches Hoda and Marwan leave.

The nurse insists on pushing Riley in a wheelchair to the exit while Marc trails behind. Riley scribbles his phone number on a piece of paper for her.

Evan sidles up beside Marc. "Don't worry about Hoda and Marwan, it's not what you think."

"I'm not thinking anything."

"Those two weren't sightseeing in the Shouf, but they're not fooling around either. It's something political, I bet. I can find out for you exactly what they're up to if you want."

"No, Evan. If there's something I need to know, she'll tell me." Marc walks quickly ahead of him. His friend's presence suddenly irritates him. His words were too close to how Marc really feels. He knows that Marwan took great risk in getting him out of Tel al-Zaatar, but it grates on him that his wife-to-be spends so much time with the man. He takes in a deep breath. He will talk to Hoda *one day*.

Months fly by, and Marc and Hoda are as busy as ever. She has graduated and is now teaching at the university. Riley recovers and pulls Marc along on every lead he has. Evan frequently goes to Damascus. The embassy there needs a helping hand. He's met a nice local girl. Cheaper booze in the duty-free zone. Too many pretexts to ring true. Marc doesn't care. Whatever Evan is up to, he trusts his friend. Marwan isn't much in sight. Perhaps, Hoda has finally felt Marc's discomfort about him.

Hoda's cousin, Abdullah 'Akkawi has taken over responsibility for Mieh Mieh, a camp of five thousand in the hills overlooking Sidon. The camp has become a listening post for everything happening in the South, and journalists from everywhere stop there when they can. But rarely does Abdullah agree to see them. There are just too many covert agents posing as journalists. Marc and Riley are the ones he truly trusts. He welcomes them in his modest quarters, and often sends back with them boxes of oranges from the local orchards for his wife Hedaya to sell in the market in Sabra. During the lulls in the fighting, life seems close to normal, or for what passes for normal in Lebanon.

Dawn is breaking when Riley walks into Marc's room.

"They fecking did it!"

"Did what?"

"Those bastard Syrians just killed Jumblatt."

Marc scrambles out of his bed.

"Who did you hear this from?"

"Marwan just called me. He told me to stay out of the Shouf today. The Druze are mobilizing."

Silence fills the room as the two journalists begin to realize just how serious the situation is. Jumblatt was no local warlord. He had thousands of armed militiamen, who were ruthless when it came to reprisals. And no act of retaliation would be greater than avenging the murder of their leader. The Syrians are out of reach, hunkered down behind fortified lines, but the Christian population of the Shouf is easy prey. Their isolated villages are only defended by local youths, reinforced by a few hotheads sent up from East Beirut.

"We can't just stand by. There's a story out there that the world needs to hear," Riley says as he paces around the room.

"Can Marwan get us there?"

"No, all of Fouad Saadeh's drivers are now suspect. The rumour is that Damascus used the pro-Syrian branch of the Social Nationalists to carry out the attack. Fouad's guys are party members, although none of them side with the Syrians."

Marc and Riley ponder the situation.

"Let's call Abu Walid. He can at least give us the Druze version of what's happening."

Riley nods his head in agreement and walks to the phone.

Marwan pours the tea and puts out the pita bread and hummus. But neither of them has much appetite.

"Hoda, the situation is bad, really bad."

She nods.

"The Druze will drive all the Christians out of the Shouf, and the Phalangists will retaliate against West Beirut."

"And they'll attack the Palestinians first," she says. "Massacre us again like in Tel al-Zaatar."

"Uncle Fouad is trying to work something out. He's asked me to go to Mukhtara to talk to Abu Walid."

"He should go himself."

"He can't. He's on the Syrian hit list now. Besides, he needs to organize the party's militia. We could be heading for an all-out war."

Hoda rises up. "I need to go. I want to make sure that Marc doesn't do anything foolish."

Marwan watches her as she walks to the door. She has begun wearing traditional Palestinian dresses, which flow to the floor but accentuate her curves. His body begins to ache. How long has he known her? Five years. He remembers when he saw her on her first day of university. She was wearing tight-fitting jeans and a loose summer blouse. Her hair tumbled to her shoulders, and her eyes lit up the room. He wasn't the only boy whose head she turned. He had thought many times of asking her out. She was a Muslim though, and he a Maronite. Others had bridged that divide, but Marwan had been more cautious, always waiting for the right moment. Then Marc came into the picture. She's still here in his life, but not as he wishes. He knows one day soon, she'll leave for France with Marc, and perhaps never return. His chest constricts at the thought.

Elie Labaki and his men arrive too late. They took the long way around to avoid the Lebanese army checkpoints and drove the muddy back roads for the last ten kilometres into the village. The disorganized Lebanese army has been trying to create a buffer between the belligerents. The army's efforts keep the Phalangists and other Christian militias from reinforcing their positions in the Shouf, but the better-armed Druze militiamen just drive around the army checkpoints. When Elie and his men arrive in Maaser, the Druze fighters are already gone, leaving behind them a devastating scene of destruction, and evacuating the handful of Druze families still living in the village.

Twenty-one bodies lie face down along the wall of St. George's Church. The village women come out of hiding when they see Elie's men. They rush to the wall, seeking signs of life from their loved ones. There are none. The wailing begins. The male survivors, very old men, load cars and tractors with whatever can be carried. Some of the men try to add the bodies of the dead children, but their mothers resist, holding them tight against their breasts. No, the women will carry the children with them in the cars. Elie tells the villagers to hurry. The Druze could return at any time.

Compared to the bloodshed in Tel al-Zaatar, Maaser is a minor massacre, but unlike Tel al-Zaatar, no one among the victims carried a gun. It was a mindless killing to quench the Druze's thirst to avenge the death of their leader. They came in by foot from Mukhtara, walking in the middle of the night through the dense cedar forests to surprise the villagers at dawn, and retreated the same way. Elie looks at the trail and considers pursuing the killers, but it's too treacherous. Instead, he sends his sappers to mine the trail to delay the henchmen's return. Most of the villagers clamour to leave for Beirut, but a few want to stay and insist that Elie and his men remain to protect them. Elie explains they're too few to defend the village.

An old woman walks up to him. She's toothless and hard to understand. She waves her cane at him.

"It's your fault! We lived in peace with the Druze. You have ruined everything. And for what! So you can sunbathe on the beaches of Jounieh with your women undressed for all the world to see. Go away! Return to your whores! Leave us in peace!"

Spitting at the ground, she heads for the church. There she'll pray for the husband she's lost, for her murdered sons and grandson, for the end of life as she has known it. Elie watches her. Is her anger any different from his? He too has cursed the politicians who've led them into this war. He calls on the old woman to return to the cars. But she continues walking, her back to those who are deserting their village. Then she falls. The other villagers run toward her. A young woman, her granddaughter, Elie later learns, puts her ear to the old woman's chest. Nothing. More women gather round, and the ululations begin. The old men glare at Elie, who turns away from them.

"*Yallah, Shabaub.* There's nothing more we can do here," Elie shouts to his men. He takes one last look around. He thinks, here are the best cedars, the oldest and tallest in the Shouf. Like the Christians of this village, they've been here for centuries. But how long will they last in the fires of war? How long will any of them last?

Chapter

29

Paris – March 1978

NABIL COUGHS AS HE READS THE NEWSPAPER. The news from the Middle East isn't good. A group of Palestinians have attacked Israel again. This time they're led by a young woman from Sabra. He remembers Dalal Mughrabi well. She's only a year younger than him. Now she and her comrades are all dead and more than thirty Israeli civilians, including thirteen children, have perished in the failed mission.

He looks over at Selima quietly sleeping in his bed, her perfect body curving under the sheets. They've found peace in Paris, but those they left behind are still caught in the cycle of violence. He worries for his sister Hoda and for Marwan. It's clear from her letters that they're now deeply involved in the Syrian Social Nationalist party. She writes of joining him in France when she marries Marc. But she also speaks often of Marwan and the importance of the work that they're doing. When he lived with Marwan in Beirut, he saw how Marwan would look at his sister, how he would speak of her. And at times, she would also look back at him. He wonders if Hoda really knows what she wants.

Images of Dalal Mughrabi and her comrades are already painted on the walls of Sabra when Marc and Riley arrive to interview her family. At first, the family refuses to speak to them. But as Dalal's mother is closing the door on Marc and Riley, Hoda appears. She asks Dalal's mother to tell them why her daughter left her nursing studies to become a fighter. Right or wrong, the world should understand why young Palestinians are taking up arms.

The mother's story differs little from that of hundreds of thousands of refugees driven from their homes by the violence of the 1948 war.

The Mughrabi family had intended to return when the fighting was over, but Israel's victory prevented that. In vain, they waited for the international community to force Israel to recognize their right to return. But supported by the West, it flouted UN resolutions and humiliated the Arab states in three wars. The build-up of the PLO in Lebanon gave young Palestinians like Dalal the hope that they could do what the rest of the Arab world couldn't.

The Mughrabi family claims no knowledge of the planning of the attack and is horrified that their daughter was involved in the death of the Israeli children. But they know that they'll never be able to express their views publicly. The PLO has already elevated their daughter to martyr status, and her actions are beyond criticism.

Later, Riley will learn from senior PLO sources that the goal was to disrupt Egyptian President Anwar Sadat's peace talks with Israeli Prime Minister Menachem Begin. The target wasn't civilians but the Israeli Ministry of Defence in Tel Aviv. The plan went awry when bad weather forced the zodiacs carrying Dalal and her comrades to make an emergency landing forty miles north of the city. Determined to continue the mission, Dalal's group hijacked a civilian bus. In the ensuing confrontation with the Israeli Army, most of the fighters and dozens of civilians were killed.

Riley turns to Marc as they leave the cinder-box structure, which has been the Mughrabis' home for almost thirty years.

"The PLO is out of control. That girl was only nineteen and they made her into a killer. These suicide missions will turn the world against the Palestinians."

"You're right, and the Israelis will now use the massacre as the pretext to invade Lebanon."

As they wait for Hoda, a group of Popular Front fighters led by Abdullah 'Akkawi approach them.

Marc embraces Abdullah, as they always do, while Riley looks on. Hoda comes out of the Mughrabi house.

"What is it?" asks Hoda.

Abdullah pulls the three of them out of earshot of his men.

"I'm recruiting as many men as I can for Mieh Mieh. We'll be ready when the Israelis come."

"You're insane. The Israelis will overrun Mieh Mieh," Riley says.

"No, we don't think so. The camp is of no strategic importance.

Normally, it has only a small group of local men defending it. The Israelis won't count on a significant force being in the camp and will likely just pass by it as they push north. Then we can launch our attacks from behind their new lines."

"That's a huge gamble," Riley says. "Are you ready to take it?"

"Yes."

"So why are you telling us this?" Marc asks.

"It is possible that I may be fighting for weeks behind Israeli lines, and Riley's right, I might not make it out alive. If I die, I want you and Hoda to look after Hedaya and Munir and take them to France."

Hoda looks at her cousin, realizing the gravity of what he's saying. Abdullah has already escaped death a dozen times, but fighting the well-trained Israeli army from behind its lines is virtual suicide. She also realizes that for the first time her cousin accepts her eventual marriage to Marc. She feels warm inside for his understanding and honoured by his entrusting his small family to them. She looks at Marc, who nods his head in agreement, and then turns to Abdullah.

"We'll do it."

Abdullah asks to borrow Riley's Polaroid camera to take a picture of Marc and Hoda. As he focusses the lens, he's struck by the beauty of the young couple. Hoda's silky black hair graces her shoulders. Her skin, tanned like that of the women in the fields, is splendid in the lavender dress she bought in Cyprus. Marc's Spanish features stand out, projecting strength, only to be softened by his green-blue eyes. Their children will be beautiful. He hopes to live long enough to see them born and then watch his son Munir play with his cousins. Abdullah has taken up the gun to defend his people, but today he abhors war. Perhaps, it's the senselessness of the coastal road attack—the death of the Israeli children. If there were only another way.

The telex machine in Riley's office is hammering away non-stop. As everyone expected, the Israelis have made their move. Operation Litani, they declare, will rid South Lebanon of the PLO. The pundits are already predicting a total Israeli victory in forty-eight hours. After all, how can the Palestinians succeed where all the Arab armies have failed? But Riley isn't so sure the Israelis will have an easy time of it. After all, Arafat and the other Palestinian leaders have been expecting the invasion for a long time and are prepared to hold their ground. And most of their men have cut their teeth battling the Christian militias, and have usually won.

A knock on the door causes Riley to turn. Marc stands there loaded with cameras and a pack-sack of provisions.

"Are you coming?"

"Give me five minutes. Who's our driver?"

"A Shiite fellow from a village near Marjayoun. Evan found him for us. He knows the South like the back of his hand."

"And if we encounter Haddad's forces?"

"Half of this fellow's family have been conscripted by Haddad, and he's on good terms with the local Christians in Marjayoun. He can negotiate for us."

"And the Israelis?"

"We'll take our chances with them. They may not like everything we write, but so far they haven't harmed any foreign journalists. Let's hope it stays that way."

"Have you let Abdullah know we're coming?"

"Yes. We shouldn't have any difficulties getting through the Palestinian checkpoints. The Israelis haven't reached Mieh Mieh yet, and if they do what they're announcing on the radio, they'll stop at the Litani."

"Good, we can use Mieh Mieh as our forward base then."

Riley fetches his pre-packed bag from the back of the office and picks up an unsigned letter that he wrote the night before. It's a plea to his third wife, living in Stockholm, not to proceed with their divorce. In it, he tells her that he still loves her, and will see her as soon as he can. He signs it and hands it to his assistant.

"Please mail this today."

Riley walks to the door to join Marc. He senses that there will be difficult times ahead for both of them.

Hoda touches herself as she lies in bed, looking at the ornate ceiling in Marc's room in Wadi Abu Jamil. She can still smell his semen oozing from inside her—the scent of apples. It was the first time that they completed the act of love, and it felt wonderful. His commitment to taking care of Hedaya and Munir convinced her that his promise to marry her is real, that she can trust him completely. They've agreed to spend six months more in Lebanon before leaving for France. It'll be difficult to leave her parents, but she loves Marc too much to live without him. She knows though that marrying and living with a non-Muslim husband in Lebanon is almost impossible. But in France, they can live free.

The BBC announced the news of the invasion in the early morning. Marc's bag was already packed. For days, she's known of his plan to cover the invasion from Mieh Mieh. He's promised to return to Beirut if the Israelis advance beyond the Litani. Still, she worries.

She showers, dresses and leaves a short note for Marc. In front of the neighbourhood grocery store, she hails a taxi to take her to Fouad Saadeh's office. She will rendezvous there with Marwan to receive their new orders.

Chapter

30

MARIE OPENS THE WINDOW to let in some fresh air. It's cold but soothing. She looks out at the last snow of a long winter coating Clark Park. Soon it'll be spring. From the guest room come the soft murmurs of Minh Chau and Mathieu making love. It's five in the morning, and they probably think that she's still sleeping. But she can't. Bronstein told them why he was in Canada after Mathieu discovered him at Leyna's. He decided to trust in their discretion. As Bronstein explained the Arkassa Initiative, Marie began to see Taragon in a new light. She knew that he was altruistic and a maverick, but she never imagined that he would be the driving force behind a plan that could change the Middle East forever.

She walks to the kitchen and turns on the kettle. A strong coffee will do her good. As she waits for the water to boil, she bathes in the light penetrating the frosted window pane. Slowly, thoughts of Taragon give her a tingling feeling. Intellectually, she wants to ascribe this to a sense of pride nested in the possibility that he might just be her father and is taking great risks in the name of peace. But there is more. A sensation that she can't accept—one she has known too infrequently in her life or perhaps never really. She must see Leyna and Bronstein again. They could have the answers she is seeking.

She hears the shower. Muted laughs betray her guests' intimacy. She smiles. They'll soon join her in the kitchen. She wants to talk to them about Taragon, but it's too soon.

Taragon's new instructions from Paris are clear. 'Akkawi is to wait for them in Spain. With Kressmann out of the game, they'll announce the Arkassa Initiative to the world from the relative safety of Barcelona. Taragon will bring his contacts in the Catalan government up to speed.

'Akkawi is worried. He's received news that several of his closest supporters have disappeared. He doubts that it's the work of the Israelis. He knows their tactics too well—don't waste time on subordinates, strike at the leaders quickly and unexpectedly. How many Palestinian leaders had met their deaths from those targeted assassinations? Thirty, forty, perhaps fifty. No, the deaths of his people aren't the work of the Israelis, at least not this time. He's been away too long, and his opponents in Hamas are taking advantage of it. He's always been a thorn in their side—never a true Islamist. But he still commands the loyalty of many in the movement.

He can also count on the support of the leftists in Gaza. Co-existence still has currency with them—the dream of a secular bi-national state. The Arkassa Pact provides at least an opening for that. No doubt others will try to play spoilers. Corrupt Fatah officials will feel threatened by an agreement not of their own making, and one that will undermine their ability to milk the system for personal benefit. Few of the Islamic Jihad militants will ever come on board. Most of them are already in the pockets of Iranian hard-liners. 'Akkawi knows he could still walk away from Arkassa, retire in Gaza, maybe take a new wife and be honoured by his countrymen for what he'd done in Lebanon. No, that would be a life for another man.

Perhaps, he has already seen the shadow of his own death, flanked by the fleeting ghosts of his fallen comrades. And just maybe, the Arkassa Pact is the only gift to his people that he has left to give.

Leyna shifts to her side. How it happened so quickly is still a mystery to her. Yes, she was attracted to Bronstein as soon as she saw him. Perhaps, Marc's description of him, of what he'd done in his life, had impressed her. After the first evening, they spent several more exchanging views, not just on politics but also culture and art. He had time to talk. He was waiting for news from Taragon—what they would do next. Besides that, his only role was to lie low.

When did it happen? She isn't sure. During those long conversations, time stood still. In that mist of words, ideas and beliefs, there had been the first touch—his—and then her hesitation. Had she been flirting with him? Was her need so apparent, and he just reacting to it?

She wants to sleep, but the morning light won't let her, and for some inexplicable reason, she doesn't want to shut the blinds. It's as if the daylight is determined to bring her back from the darkness, the loneliness that she has felt for so long.

Last night was the first time she'd made love since the brutal beating by a Chinese thug had left her scarred twenty years ago. At first, she turned off all the lights hoping that Bronstein would imagine her as she was in her youth—immaculate skin, not these hideous scars. But he turned the lights back on. He brought her to the bed. In the brightness of the room, she found reassurance in his gaze and succumbed to his kisses. When they had finished making love, she opened up to him about the scars, how she'd been beaten into betraying to the Triad killer the location of a friend. Her friend survived, but it did little to alleviate her guilt. It was the first time that she'd told anyone outside her family about it. He listened. He understood.

Leyna looks over to her lover. He's not there. She sits up and scans the room. He's nowhere. Then from the kitchen, she hears his voice on the telephone. She throws a robe around her shoulders and quietly walks down the stairs.

Bronstein is pacing the kitchen floor, his cell phone pressed to his ear.

"I understand. I'll come as soon as I can," he says and hangs up.

Leyna feels her heart drop. Is he leaving her already? Are her scars too ugly to bear? Doubt drowns the joy that she experienced this night. She yearns to be in his arms again, to feel his desire for her, to restore her belief in herself.

Bronstein sees her. He walks over and kisses her softly on the lips.

"How are you, my love?"

She looks up at him.

"Are you really leaving?"

"Marc just called. Things are not going well. Kressmann won't sponsor the initiative. We have to go ahead with Plan B."

"Which is?"

He hesitates. Again he kisses her, and whispers in her ear: "I can't tell you. It would put you at risk."

Leyna pulls back.

"I would never tell anyone anything!"

"Still, it's too dangerous."

"When do you leave?"

"Tonight."

She hesitates and looks down. The question within her can't be asked, but he senses it. He takes her shoulders and turns her so that she's looking straight into his eyes.

"I'll come back. I love you."

A joyful sigh escapes her, and she looks at him as a bride to her betrothed.

"I'll help you pack."

"Not now. We still have time. Come."

Bronstein's face beams as he guides Leyna back to the bedroom. The radiance in Leyna's eyes tells him that she too has found something that both had thought long lost—the whisper of belonging to someone else.

Chapter

31

MARC LOOKS AT HIS CELL PHONE. There's a new text message. He opens it. Marie. He doesn't need a distraction now. How did she get the number? Bronstein, of course. He reads Marie's message carefully. It is cryptic. Marie understands the need to maintain secrecy through ambiguity.

Cher M, I think I can help the AI. Will be in P tomorrow. Can we meet at the tourist trap at the same time as in N.?

He remembers in their conversation in Nicosia, she asked him if he had ever been to Harry's Bar in Paris. He had. She said that it was number twenty-five on her bucket list of places to visit in the world. Her editor had told her that every journalist should make a pilgrimage to the birthplace of the Bloody Mary. He had smiled and said that it was a tourist trap, but he would buy her a drink there if ever they were in Paris at the same time.

He had planned to tell Marie about Arkassa on the seventeenth, the day he had hoped Kressmann would stand by his side to inform the entire world. No matter, tomorrow will do instead. Maybe she can help.

He taps into the phone *oui*.

He sips his coffee and tightens his fist. Three days have passed since their meeting, and not a word. The announcement of Kressmann as Sarkozy's foreign minister is front-page news across Europe. He has already announced his priority: peace in the Balkans. Not a word about the Middle East. It's clear that Kressmann won't be able to bring Sarkozy around, even if he wanted to. Taragon has asked Bronstein and 'Akkawi to meet him in Barcelona in two days. He now has to ensure he can leave Paris undetected. He worries about Leblanc. Why did Kressmann include him? Then he recalls Kressmann once told him how Leblanc had helped get the word out about Karantina. Taragon has no doubt there are many layers to the man, some good and undoubtedly some evil. As for Carbone, he shrugs off the thought that the Corsican bagman can do him much harm.

Ari Epstein hangs up the secure phone. It has been a very good day. Bronstein has been spotted in Montreal, and they have a full report of Taragon's meeting with Kressmann in Paris. Ari calls up the cyber unit. He gives them the coordinates of Taragon's new cell phone. The Corsican had obtained them from a French service provider, which has the roaming contract and depends heavily on French government largesse. Tomorrow he'll send the agreed amount to Carbone's Swiss bank account. He's amazed how much easier it'll be to track Taragon from this point onward. As for Bronstein, they've dispatched agents to watch the airport. When he leaves, they will have him. Only 'Akkawi has been too clever for them. He escaped them in Athens, but it won't be long before the trap closes in on him too.

Ari calls in David. It's time to put him to work.

32

Paris – April 2007

H ARRY'S NEW YORK Bar is filled to the brink with tourists, wowing at its inlaid ceiling and in awe of the beautiful workmanship of the thirty-foot counter. Taragon isn't there for the aesthetics or the cheap thrills. He anxiously glances at his newly acquired Blackberry. He's about to ditch his cell phone. He no longer trusts it after using it to contact Kressmann. Leblanc's presence at the meeting alerted him to take more precautions. Kressmann is ambitious, and Taragon is no longer sure what games his old friend might decide to play, especially now that he's currying Sarkozy's favour.

Ten past noon. Marie's late. He considers leaving, but then she appears in a stunning red dress. She stands by the entrance and scans the bar. Customers, men and women, turn their heads to get a better look at her. Taragon realizes for the first time how beautiful she is. In Nicosia, he only noticed her eyes. There was something familiar about them— something he couldn't place. Perhaps, he suppressed any other feelings he might have had. He's been with many women but has only loved one. In any case, it isn't the time to indulge in that sort of thing. He has more pressing matters to attend to.

He waves his hand toward Marie. She sees him.

"Marc!"

She saunters over to him. There's a lightness to her walk, exuding an unmistakable happiness.

She kisses him on both cheeks and sits close beside him. He feels the warmth come off her body.

"Is it safe for us to talk here?"

"It's fine."

"Jonathan told us about what you're doing."

"He shouldn't have."

"Don't worry, we're all one hundred percent behind you. Minh Chau, Mathieu, and Leyna."

"Mathieu?"

"Mathieu Hibou. He says that he knows you from Gaza."

Amazing, the world is a small place. Of course, he knew Hibou.

She's speaking to him again. Her words pull him back to the present.

"I can help you. When are you going to announce the initiative? I'm sure that I can get the Montreal media to run the story right away."

"Marie, *du calme*. I don't think that you understand the dangers."

"I'm sorry if I'm getting carried away. It's fantastic what you're doing!"

"Look, I'll let you know, as soon as I can, when we'll make the announcement. It won't be long, but we have a problem. We need at least one major international figure to immediately endorse it. We tried Kressmann, but he won't do it."

Marie sits back in her chair. No one comes to mind.

"Do you know someone who can get to Senator Obama?"

Again Marie thinks hard. She has few American contacts. Only journalists, and none whom she can trust in any case. When it comes to Israel, US journalists are reluctant to take chances. But there is one exception.

"I know one who might."

"Who's that?"

"A journalist called Owen Sharp. He's a bit of a radical."

The name is familiar. Taragon searches his memory. Sharp, of course! Riley's old sidekick in Beirut. The one who had gone with them to Damour. Taragon pulls from his bag some stapled sheets of paper. He pens a quick note on a blank sheet and attaches it to the others.

"Take this. Send it to Sharp tomorrow."

Marie reads the note.

"Is this really it? I mean, is it the Arkassa Initiative?"

"Yes."

Marie holds the paper in her hand for what seems to be an eternity and then puts it in her bag.

For a moment, both sit in silence. The crowd in the bar is growing. The chances of getting served anytime soon are slim. The noise level also rises, as tourists and French locals become animated in their discussions. Taragon speaks up

"Would you like to go someplace else?"

"We can go to my hotel. There's a quiet bistro there."

"Can we walk?"

"Yes."

"Marie, will you excuse me? I'll be back in a minute."

Taragon leaves a few euros on the table. He walks to the washroom. It's empty. He looks around and sees a heating vent. He pries apart the metal with a pocket knife and pushes his cell phone through it. A bounce off the metal, once, twice and then nothing. He bends the vent back into shape. The phone was clean of contact information. He was careful about that. If the call to Kressmann had compromised him, the trail would end here.

When he returns to the table, Marie's standing with their coats in her arms. In her heels, she's almost as tall as him. Their eyes meet, but she looks away.

Marie involuntarily feels the same tingling as when she thought of him in Montreal. She shudders. What is she thinking? It's getting harder to close down these thoughts. He can't be—he really can't be. If he were, she would immediately know it, wouldn't she? She needs to get this uncertainty out of the way.

Chapter

33

Paris – May 2007

DAVID LEANS OVER THE FRENCH TECHNICIAN. Taragon's cell phone's location flashes on the computer screen. They've succeeded in remotely downloading state-of-the-art tracking software. The technician hands David a new cell phone. The same map appears on its screen.

"Done! You can track him from anywhere now."

David hands him a thick envelope, generously filled with euros.

The technician raises his hand in protest.

"I'm not doing this for money."

"Take it."

Bronstein kisses Leyna one last time before going through airport security. He has decided to fly from Montreal to Cuba and then from Cuba to Spain. It's a good plan. He knows that the Mossad's ability to operate in Cuba is quite limited. He glances back. Leyna is still watching him, smiling. He didn't expect to find someone like her. They share instant trust—something that he'd never felt before.

Bronstein sits back in the airport bar and watches the TV screens as he waits for the boarding call. CNN is flashing pictures of more killing in Afghanistan. The Taliban are far from being beaten there. NATO is increasing its troop levels to prop up the Karzai government and, in doing so, is inflaming tensions throughout the Muslim world. The images change. More bombings in Baghdad—two hundred dead. Bronstein begins to wonder if it's not already too late to reverse the violence overwhelming the Middle East.

The loudspeaker announces his flight and invites passenger to begin boarding. Bronstein finishes his drink, stands up and squeezes by the luggage of a young girl in ripped jeans immersed in reading a text on her cell phone.

When Bronstein exits the bar, the girl taps into the phone: *gate forty-three, Havana*. Ramat HaSharon won't be happy that Bronstein's heading to the one place barred to them.

'Akkawi checks out the municipal hall, as Taragon has asked him to. He doesn't like what he sees. There's no real security there, just a few old guards. He trusts Taragon for a lot of things, but not for this. Taragon has never been a soldier. 'Akkawi has already activated his network in Spain and planned his escape route if things go wrong. Three men will come in from Zaragoza, two from Madrid, and one from Valencia. Half the group will be at the press conference. The others will wait outside in the cars that'll ensure an escape if one is needed. A Basque comrade will bring in the guns from Pamplona. If the opposition tries something, blood will be spilled.

34

Beirut – March 1978

THE WHITE MERCEDES PULLS UP just as Hoda reaches the entrance to Fouad Saadeh's office. The car's front wheel scrapes the curb. Marwan sits in the driver seat; small beads of sweat appear on his forehead.

"Come, Hoda, we don't have much time."

"Marwan, what's the matter?"

"We have a new assignment."

"Where?"

"Damascus. I'll explain on the way."

"Wait, shouldn't we first see Fouad?"

"No, he's not there."

"Where is he?"

"He's meeting with Kemal Jumblatt's son, Walid. The killing of Kemal has thrown everything into disarray."

As soon as Hoda sits in the car, Marwan pulls out into the traffic and pushes hard on the accelerator. Erratically, he navigates the narrow streets, dodging the poorly parked cars and odd donkey cart until he reaches the Corniche.

"What's the matter, Marwan?"

"It's our orders."

"What about them?"

"Sending us to Damascus doesn't make any sense!"

Hoda realizes the danger for any Lebanese Social Nationalist to travel to Damascus. Assad is furious most members of the party in Lebanon had sided with Jumblatt and continue to support his son Walid.

"We are to deliver this letter to the party's leadership in Syria. Fouad wants them to mediate with Assad to end this feud with the Jumblatts. He says that the Israelis are trampling on our sovereignty with impunity and murdering our people with their bombs from the sky, so now is not the time for disunity."

"And you think that Fouad is wrong?"

"The Syrians killed Kemal. How can we trust them?"

"Not all Syrians are the same."

Marwan looks straight ahead. Hoda waits for a response, but none comes. She also doesn't trust Syrians, but she can see Fouad's point. The Social Nationalists, although banned in Syria, still have a large following there and maintain a dialogue with the regime. As for danger, the shifting of political alliances makes all of Lebanon an unsafe place for the courier work that she and Marwan do for the party. Is Damascus really more dangerous?

The Mercedes climbs the steep hill toward Aley. They'll soon pass Baabda, where Lebanon's president, Elias Sarkis, sits powerless in his palace. After Baabda will be the first Syrian checkpoint.

The lead Israeli tank comes into view, then another and many more. From their hilltop position outside of Deir Qanoun, Abdullah, Marc, and Riley have a clear view of the armoured column. It's now three kilometres to the west. Its destination is clearly the Leontes Bridge, which connects the South to the rest of the country.

Marc and Riley had caught up with Abdullah in Mieh Mieh just as he was heading with his fighters to the South. He has a sizeable force under his command—two hundred seasoned fighters, well-armed and with an excellent knowledge of the terrain. If the Israelis' announced intention of stopping at the Litani is true, the group will serve no purpose staying in Mieh Mieh, 40 kilometres to the north.

Abdullah briefs Marc and Riley on the way to Deir Qanoun.

"Syrians are not going to move out of their positions in the Northern Beka'a valley. Any troops moving through the valley to the South would be easy prey for the Israeli jets. Besides, Assad might want to teach Arafat a lesson after last week."

"What do you mean?" Riley asks.

"Assad is fed up with Arafat, and letting him get bloodied by the Israelis might teach him a lesson. Arafat's approval of last week's attack was sheer madness, another in a long list of bungled operations. I knew that girl Dalal. She was green and never should have been put in charge of the mission. There is no way that it wasn't going to end in a blood-bath involving civilians."

"And now the world's supporting the Israeli invasion," Marc says.

"What is your strategy?" Riley asks. From his US intelligence con-tacts, he already knows how bleak the situation is for the Palestinians. Once the Israelis take the bridges on the Litani, they'll be able to box in the three thousand PLO fighters south of the river.

"We have an ace up our sleeves," Abdullah says. He walks over to a few antiquated pieces of artillery, salvaged from an abandoned Leba-nese Army warehouse.

"The Israelis won't be expecting these guns. From this hill, we can pro-vide at least some cover for our men when they try to cross the Litani."

"And how are they going to cross the river?"

"Look!" Abdullah points to a dozen of his men who are descending the narrow dirt track to the river. Over their shoulders, they have rope and in their hands axes. "We're going to cut down some of those pines by the river to make rafts."

Within minutes, Abdullah's men have thrown together the first raft and are testing it on the water. One man swims across the river and attaches a rope around the branch of a large fir and then swims back with the rest of the rope. A rudimentary pulley system is now in place. On the hilltop, the four old Howitzers are pulled into position.

"Over there!" one of Abdullah's men shouts.

Below, they can see a man making his way through the orange groves toward the river. He's naked to the waist. It is difficult to tell whether he's an Arab or Israeli. His frantic darting about suggests that he's a fugitive. One of the Palestinian fighters looks through the binoculars.

"I know that man. He's a Fatah fighter from Sidon."

"Look," Marc says.

"Where?" Abdullah asks.

"There!"

An Israeli jeep with four men comes into view. It is slowly moving through the orange groves toward the river. The jeep stops and three men fan out into the trees. They're obviously tracking the fugitive.

Abdullah picks up the radio receiver.

"Cross over and bring back the man running toward the river!"

"*Na'am*—yes," the fighter leading the raft-making crew replies.

Marc and Riley watch four of the men below pulley their way across the river. The fugitive sees them and begins swimming toward the raft.

Abdullah picks up the radio again.

"Send a second group to head off an Israeli jeep about one kilometre inland on the dirt road leading to the river. Be careful! There are four men. Do you see the road? It is fifty metres downstream."

"Yes, should we kill them?"

"No, take them prisoner. They might have valuable intelligence."

The first group meets up with the fugitive and takes him to the other side of the river while six other fighters pole a second raft across it.

The Israeli jeep stops. The passengers fan out on either side of the vehicle, and the driver advances slowly. This gives the Palestinians time to position themselves in the orange groves where the dirt road meets the river. The Israelis are heading straight into their trap.

Abdullah jumps into a jeep, signalling Marc and Riley to wait. Four husky fighters squeeze into the vehicle, and the group moves down the narrow road to the raft-making camp.

Marc and Riley watch the unfolding of the operation, scribbling furiously and snapping photos with their telephoto lenses. Abdullah's men crouch in wait for the Israelis. As soon as the enemy passes, the Palestinians hurl their grenades, killing three of the Israelis instantly. The driver guns it, but slides off the road to crash into an orange tree. When he groggily looks up, blood flowing down his forehead, the Palestinians are already on him. They pull his arms behind him and bind them with rope. Downstream, Israeli tank crews have heard the gunshots, and Marc and Riley can see two tanks leave the armoured column to head toward the site of the ambush. The Palestinians also hear the distant rumbling of the tanks. They drag their prisoner to the raft and push off, poling furiously to reach the other side.

The Israeli tanks bulldoze their way through the orchards to the river bank and turn south. The lead tank's commander spots the raft when it reaches the halfway point in the river. The tank turret swivels and fires a 105-millimetre shell. It just misses the raft and hits a boulder in the water. Rock fragments fly everywhere, knocking one of the fighters into the water. The other Palestinians rescue their comrade and resume poling with all their force.

The fugitive is waiting for them on the opposite shore. He grabs a large knife from one of his rescuers and begins wading through the water toward the raft. Like a mad man, he tries to climb onto it to reach the Israeli prisoner, but the other Palestinians push him back. Abdullah's car pulls up to the river bank.

"Put down the knife."

"No, they tortured me. I'm going to kill the bastard!"

"Put down the knife, or I will have you shot now," Abdullah says.

The man looks baffled, but when all of Abdullah's men point their guns at him, he throws the knife into the water. Another Israeli tank shell comes whistling toward them, again missing the men, but destroying a half-finished raft. Abdullah rushes into the water, pushes the fugitive aside and pulls the prisoner to shore. Marc and Riley can hear him shout to his radioman with the artillery crew: "Shell those tanks!"

The old guns still pack quite a punch. The first shell hits the lead tank, setting it on fire. The other tank pulls away from the river, and the second and third artillery rounds miss it entirely.

On the hilltop, the Palestinians go into action, picking up and repositioning the old artillery pieces. The next salvo results in a direct hit on the retreating tank. The success is ephemeral. Two Israeli warplanes appear out of the clouds. Their bombs destroy all four guns—their crews escaping seconds before the bombs hit.

With the raft-making operation disrupted and their artillery destroyed, the Palestinians aren't going to wait for the Israeli jets to return. Abdullah orders fifty of his men to go east to set up new crossings to rescue the remaining PLO forces fleeing from the south. A smaller group of ten is told to take the Israeli prisoner to Mieh Mieh for interrogation. The remaining 140 men join Abdullah in what will be an ill-fated attempt to retake the Leontes Bridge from the Israelis. The Israeli prisoner is bundled into Riley's car, and guarded by a young fighter from Sabra. Riley and Marc protest that as journalists, they cannot be implicated in the taking of a POW, but Abdullah replies: "We need your car."

The prisoner is still groggy and bleeding from the forehead. Marc takes out a bandanna to wipe the blood away while Riley fishes out a first aid kit from his bag. They stem the bleeding and give the Israeli some water. He still looks stunned when he asks: "Who are you?"

"Riley, *Irish Post*, and this is Marc Taragon from *Le Nouvel Observateur*. Who are you?"

"Bronstein, Lieutenant Jonathan Bronstein."

"What are you, an infantry officer?" Riley asks.

Bronstein narrows his eyes and stares at the two journalists.

"Sorry, I didn't mean to interrogate you," Riley says. "But if you give us some information, we can put it in our reporting. It might just help you."

Bronstein knows that revealing that he's an intelligence officer could be a death sentence—one from torture. So he reverts to his well-practised cover story.

"I'm a reservist. I'm on assignment for Israeli Army Radio."

Riley looks at him sceptically. "Where's your sound equipment?"

"Back in the jeep."

"Wait. You're not the Jonathan Bronstein who writes for *Haaretz*?" Marc asks.

Bronstein feels a sense of hope—perhaps, these journalists could be useful after all. "I'm surprised that you know that."

"A couple of your pieces on Palestinians in the Galilee have been carried by my magazine."

"Are you also prisoners?"

"No, we're just covering the story. We're based in Beirut."

Bronstein studies the two western journalists. Is the PLO now so savvy as to convince Western Journalists to accompany it on dangerous frontline missions or are these just two hard-core Palestinian supporters?

"One of them nearly killed me by the river. The commander stepped in to stop him," Bronstein says.

"Yes, Abdullah."

"Why did he do that?"

"Killing prisoners is not his thing."

"Count yourself lucky, Bronstein. Not many Palestinian officers would have saved you."

Bronstein sits back and tries to adjust himself to compensate for his bound arms. He can feel the young guard trembling beside him, jittery from so much foreign conversation. Marc decides to put the guard at ease by speaking to him in Arabic.

"*Huwi Suhufi*—He's a journalist."

"*Suhufi, wallahi?*—A journalist, really? *Bas huwi Isra'ili*—but he's an Israeli?"

"That's right, he's a war correspondent."

Bronstein joins in Arabic. *"Minayn inta, ya shaab*—where are you from, young man?"

The eyes of the guard widen. Not just one Franji speaking good Arabic, but two, and the second is an Israeli with a heavy Bedouin accent.

The Syrians have tripled the checkpoints along the Beirut-Damascus highway. Marwan's and Hoda's cover story is pretty tight though. They are a newly-wedded couple on their way to visit relatives in Bab Al Sharqi, one of the Christian quarters in Old Damascus. The Syrian soldiers at the checkpoints don't pay too much attention, gratefully accepting the cartons of Marlboros that Marwan offers them. It's at the border that they'll face the greatest scrutiny.

"Do you know our contacts in Damascus?" Hoda asks.

"No, I only have their names and addresses."

"Can we trust them?"

"Uncle Fouad does."

Hoda has an uneasy feeling in her stomach. She's risked being captured by Maronites, Mourabitoun and numerous other groups in Lebanon, but Syrian intelligence is something else. Assad has agents everywhere in Syria. It's hard to imagine that she and Marwan can simply drive into Damascus and meet up with Assad's political opponents without being detected.

At the Lebanese border crossing at Masnaa, the line-up is longer than usual. They notice a lot of license plates from Sidon and Tyre. The inflow of people fleeing the Israeli advance has already begun. The Lebanese gendarmerie checks their papers. All is in order. Lebanese can still enter Syria without passports, so it's fairly routine. Down the road at the Syrian border post in Jdaidet Yabous, things will be different.

Abdullah spares Bronstein the physical abuse that goes along with the usual interrogation. Capturing an Israeli officer is an achievement in itself, and Bronstein will be an important bargaining chip in the prisoner exchange that'll inevitably follow the ceasefire. In any case, it's unlikely that Bronstein knows anything of value. The Israelis are already at the Litani River, the objective of their current operation, or so they've proclaimed to the world. The Palestinians have now seen their enemy's order of battle, and they're employing the guerrilla tactics that they've learned from earlier skirmishes along the border. Palestinian and Lebanese spies throughout South Lebanon are watching every move made by the Israelis and their allies in the South Lebanon Army. Each day that the Israeli forces stay between the Litani and Israel's border with Lebanon is a day well spent by the Palestinians studying their enemy's vulnerabilities.

Bronstein is confused about the privileged treatment he's being accorded. He had expected at the least to be beaten by his interrogators. Instead, they just sit there asking the same questions over and over again. The interrogation lasts four hours before he's sent back to a makeshift cell, where Riley visits him a few hours later.

"Was it rough?"

"No."

"What did you tell them?"

"Nothing."

"What would you like to tell the people in Israel?"

"Tell them that I'm safe."

"Okay, we'll put that in. Anything else?"

"No, that's it. Thanks."

Riley offers him a cigarette, which Bronstein refuses. "Not good for the health."

"I thought soldiering was not good for the health."

"We serve our country," Bronstein says.

"You know, he's half-Jewish."

"Who?"

"Your captor—Abdullah 'Akkawi."

"How is that?"

"His mother was a Jew from Algeria. Married a Muslim in Haifa. That's where Abdullah was born."

Bronstein starts going through in his head the dozens of intelligence files that he's read on Palestinian fighters. 'Akkawi. Yes, a Popular Front fighter in close contact with the rabbi in Beirut. An atheist. But he hadn't read anything about him being part Jewish. It would explain a lot of things. So both he and 'Akkawi are from Haifa and share Jewish blood. Neither believes in God. And yet both are fighting on different sides of a conflict fuelled by religion. Bronstein grins at the irony.

Marc visits Bronstein on the fourth day. He hands Bronstein a copy of the *Irish Post*. A four-paragraph article by Riley has made the front page.

"Riley did you a huge favour. I heard *Haaretz* has run a translation of the article. There's already talk of a prisoner exchange."

A knock on the door interrupts them. Abdullah enters.

"You leave tomorrow."

"To where?" Bronstein asks.

"To the airport. Your government has agreed to our conditions."

Chapter

35

Barcelona – May 2007

TARAGON TRAVELS LIGHT. He doesn't want to be caught waiting for luggage. He goes straight to the taxi stand and asks to be taken to the Plaça de Catalunya. There he can mingle with the crowd and lose anyone following him. During the ride into the city, he sends a text message to Aleix Mas, the head of media relations in the Catalan government, to give him the green light to release the media advisory. The press conference will start in an hour. Mas will officiate. He hopes that Bronstein and 'Akkawi will be there on time, but not a moment sooner. He's counting on the presence of the journalists to protect them. It's a huge risk for everyone.

The plan is straightforward. Aleix Mas will introduce them. Taragon will present the Arkassa Initiative to the journalists, and Bronstein and 'Akkawi will field the questions. During the question period, the Secretary General of the Spanish Socialist Party, Pablo Suárez, will announce his support for the initiative. Simple. Certainly not the elaborate launch Taragon had planned for Kressmann. When he sees Marie, he'll ask her if she's heard from Sharp. He knows that it's a long shot, but if he can get the young American senator onside, things could move very fast.

"Are you new to Barcelona?" the taxi driver asks.

Taragon stiffens.

"Yes, I'm here for a few days on business."

The driver switches to Catalan.

"But you are from here, correct?"

Taragon hesitates.

"Not really," he replies in Spanish.

The driver nods.

"I've seen you before. On television. You're that French journalist, the one always reporting on the Middle East, aren't you?"

Taragon's immediate reflex is to ask the driver to pull over.

The driver protests. He didn't mean to cause offence.

"Now!" Taragon insists. He hands over a twenty-euro bill and jumps out of the cab to disappear into a *callecita*. He runs for twenty minutes, ducking in and out of the narrow side streets before he disappears into a tapas bar.

He takes a seat by the window and watches the street. Perhaps he's too cautious, even paranoid. The driver's recognition of him was normal. He's often appeared on Barcelona TV to talk about the Middle East. And he's the only international journalist who speaks good Catalan. He curses himself. His reaction may have attracted unneeded attention. He looks at his watch. Twenty minutes to the launch. He checks the GPS on his Blackberry. He can make it by foot, but just. He looks up and down the street. Nothing suspicious stands out, but for good measure, he heads out the back of the bar.

Suárez begins to worry. The room is full of journalists. Taragon is a known figure in Spain. Several of his books have been translated into Spanish. Taragon has even written a book in Catalan, a short biography of his father. Could he have been spotted? Could they be tracking him now? Suárez had offered him a bodyguard, but his old friend was too stubborn. Neither of the other two guests has turned up. The old Socialist curses. It took a lot to bring on board the party's executive. It has been fifteen years since the Madrid Conference. Peace is more distant today than ever. Why should the Socialists take another gamble, especially for an initiative to which they haven't even been given the full text? Suárez called in many markers to swing the vote to endorse the Arkassa Initiative, and even then he was short of a majority on the first vote. It was the old warhorse Gonzalez, a veteran of the resistance to Franco, who swung over the others. "I knew the father," he said. "A good man. We should trust the son."

Suárez sees a giant of a man approach. Matias, his personal security, steps out to intercept him. Suárez signals Matias to stop.

"*Señor 'Akkawi?*"

"Yes."

"*Mucho gusto.*"

"Thank you."

'Akkawi looks beyond Suárez. Bronstein is coming down the corridor from the other entrance. Seeing the hulking figure of 'Akkawi, hovering over the diminutive Suárez, Bronstein stops and waves.

'Akkawi steps forward to clasp Bronstein's forearm. Several photographers begin to take pictures of Palestinian and Israeli joining forces for peace. They'll make brilliant headlines in the morning papers. Suárez looks at his watch. Where the hell is Taragon?

David adjusts his glasses. He doubts that Taragon will recognize him in the crowded room. If Taragon even saw him in Nicosia, it could have only been for a second, and now he's sporting a full beard. Taragon had given him the slip in Paris. He'd searched Harry's Bar inch by inch before he saw the damaged vent. He was about to fly back to Israel when Ari called him. Mossad's research team had dug up Taragon's Catalan ties, and based on their psychological profile of him suggested that Barcelona would be his most likely destination. When a sympathetic journalist tipped them off about the press conference, David was already on the ground.

David's orders are clear. Stand by the entrance for a quick exit. Disrupt the press conference as soon as it starts. He has placed an incendiary device near the fire alarm. A small hand-held detonator will set it off, making a loud explosion, triggering the alarm and creating havoc. But he has one other order—more difficult to execute.

David bends his elbow to take the detonator out of the pocket of his jacket, only to be jostled by someone rushing into the room. The device flies from his hand.

"*Excusez-moi.*" The man apologizes in French. David checks his gun. The man is now moving quickly toward the front of the room. Shit, it's Taragon!

From behind the curtains walks out 'Akkawi, followed by the traitor Bronstein. They join Taragon at the podium. It's time. David looks for the detonator. Taragon begins to speak in Spanish.

"*Estimados colegas de la prensa.* I would like to present to you today a plan to change the path of history in the Middle East."

A young woman begins to distribute photocopies. Her curvaceous figure distracts David for a second. Where is the damned detonator?

Finally, he spots it on the floor just in front of a heavy-set journalist. Should he risk calling attention to himself by going after it?

The journalists are listening attentively to Taragon. Two cameramen have started recording the event. One is filming the audience. David raises his arm to conceal his face. It's too late to disrupt the press conference. The photocopy girl is looking straight at him. It's the Canadian! She turns toward Bronstein and points at David. No time left. He must execute Plan B. 'Akkawi must not leave alive.

Bronstein is talking to Suárez. The tall man is slightly in front of them. Damn it! He won't have a clear shot. David notices the bulge in the tall man's jacket. A bodyguard! Then he sees the others in the corners. Men who aren't onlookers. Men with an intensity in their eyes. He watches them scan the room. Are they looking for him? He turns to walk away. No point in getting killed here. There are few places for the Palestinian to hide in Barcelona. He'll track down 'Akkawi later. He hopes that Epstein will order him to kill all three.

The big journalist shuffles in his chair kicking the detonator forward. The woman in front of him turns to glare and in doing so, steps on the remote. The loud explosion and alarm send the journalists running for cover. When David recovers from his shock, he looks for his target. Gone!

'Akkawi has been watching the young, bearded man since Taragon bumped into him. The man's reflex to check his pocket is the first clue; his nervous look at the floor the second. When Marie points at him and quickly rushes away, it confirms his suspicion.

'Akkawi was ready then and there to gather his men and leave the press conference, but he'd noticed how intently the journalists listened to Taragon. There must be a way to neutralize the Israeli to allow the press conference to continue. His men stationed in the corners haven't noticed the Israeli yet. The explosion allows 'Akkawi to make his move. Bending low, he races quickly but quietly down the left side of the room.

David has now recovered fully from the explosion. His eyes dart around the room, but only at the last second does he see 'Akkawi in his peripheral vision. The giant is moving quickly toward him from the left. He gets off a single shot before 'Akkawi slams into him. The bullet hits a bystander in the shoulder. As he falls under 'Akkawi's two hundred and fifty pounds, he aims inward to stop the giant. A second shot. David hits the floor hard. His skull cracks.

'Akkawi's men help him to his feet. He stands straight up but then falters. Blood gushes from his neck. The second shot has severed an artery. He hears the shouts around him and collapses. A strong hand turns his shoulder to lay him on his back. He can barely make out Taragon's blurred face above him. Beside him is another familiar face. It's the first time that he's seen them together. The perfect image from the photo he took thirty years ago. He gasps: "Hoda. Marc. *Allah Karim*— God is merciful." The bright light forces him to close his eyes. His throat constricts as he whispers the *Shahada*.

There is no god but God. Muhammad is the messenger of God.

Marie's warm hand presses hard on 'Akkawi's neck to stem the bleeding. His voice is gone, but his lips move to say in silence: "Hedaya, Munir, Hoda, I failed you. Please forgive me."

36

Barcelona – May 2007

THE MEDICS IN THE AMBULANCE do what they can for Abdullah, but he's lost too much blood. For a second or two, he comes back to consciousness. Hoda, he whispers. Taragon pales when he hears the name. The medics begin to close the back doors. Taragon attempts to climb in. No! No one can ride in the ambulance. One medic turns to Aleix Mas and whispers in Catalan: "Tell them that it is too late for his friend." 'Akkawi's men overhear this and vanish into the crowd.

The journalists crowd around Taragon and Marie. They unleash a flurry of questions. Who was the bearded man? Is Abdullah 'Akkawi dead? Will you continue with your peace initiative?

Marie holds Taragon's arm, pushing her left hand out to fend off the reporters. Suárez and Bronstein join them, and the security guards from the convention centre provide a protective circle around them. A SWAT squad enters the room. The TV cameras roll. Tonight the world will learn of the Arkassa Initiative, launched amid the deaths of two men. 'Akkawi's men in Barcelona will report back to Gaza that a hero of Palestine has fallen, and the calls for vengeance will begin.

Ari looks in disgust at the television. Fragmented reports of Arkassa are all over the news. Images of the assailant flash across the screen. CNN speculates that the man must have been an Iranian agent, citing his beard as proof of membership in the Iranian Revolutionary Guards. Absurd, yet already the Mossad is supporting the story. They'll discreetly recover David's body, and give him a proper funeral in Israel. But for now, it's better to pin all of this on Tehran.

"Meir wants to see you."

Ari's shoulders droop. He knows his time has come. One too many screw-ups. The director of the Mossad is a hard man. Ari curses Taragon and Bronstein. They will walk away as heroes. And he, who gave everything to Israel, will be pensioned off. At least, that *Shmendrik* David took 'Akkawi with him. Ari vows to take care of the other two.

Leyna Nguyen sits motionlessly in the immaculate office of her downtown medical centre. Since hearing of the attack in Barcelona, she has cancelled her morning appointments to wait for the call. The gentle vibration of the cell phone in her pocket puts an end to her anguish.

"It's me, Jonathan."

"Oh my God! I saw it on television. Are you all right?"

"I'm fine."

"And Marc and Marie?"

"They're fine too. Our friend Abdullah 'Akkawi gave his life to save us. But it's over. Arkassa is finished. Gaza is exploding over Abdullah's death. His supporters are marching to celebrate his martyrdom and calling for vengeance against Israel. The Israelis are spinning his death as an Iranian assassination attempt. No one's listening to what Arkassa is really about. Even the Spanish Socialists have pulled back their support. Things have become too hot for them."

"What will you do?"

"I want to come back. Will you have me?"

"Yes! And then?"

"I don't know. I'm talking to Marc. It's hard to see how we can salvage anything from this situation. Maybe it's time I face up to reality."

"Come back, Jonathan. You know I love you, but I don't want you to give up! I know what Arkassa means to you."

Bronstein feels her words—a salve for the all-encompassing fear of yet another failure. How long has he waited to find someone like her? Someone who already knows him, even if they have only been a few days together. He'll tell Taragon of his decision. He won't abandon the cause, but for now, he needs to return to Leyna.

Marie stands close to Taragon as Bronstein's flight to Montreal takes off. She slips her hand under his arm. The three have spent the night sending out press releases about Arkassa, but none have been picked up by the media. Hezbollah has shelled northern Israel to commemorate the martyrdom of Abdullah 'Akkawi. An Israeli child has been injured. Those are today's headlines. Arkassa is already just a footnote in a long history of failed peace initiatives.

Their Circassian friend has intervened with Erdogan to allow a Turkish freighter to take Abdullah's body from Spain to Northern Cyprus and from there by speedboat to Beirut. His old comrades are preparing his grave site in Sabra, next to his wife and son. Marc and Marie accompany Abdullah on the sea journey.

On the freighter, Taragon tells Marie about Abdullah. His heroism during the siege of Beirut. His resistance to the Israeli occupation of South Lebanon. Finally, Marie asks: "Who is Hoda?"

Taragon hesitates. She can see him twitch.

"Abdullah's cousin."

"Why did he say her name when he looked at us?"

Taragon looks at her, brushes a hair from her forehead.

"Well, there's a resemblance. She was like you. Beautiful. Perhaps, Abdullah just wished to die remembering someone he loved."

Marie freezes. Hoda, someone Abdullah, not Marc, loved? Hoda, perhaps just a cousin of a friend? She takes in a deep breath as she ponders the possibility that she may have been on the wrong track all this time. Then something else Marc has just said begins to fill her with a warm sensation—*She was like you. Beautiful.*

Chapter

37

S EA SPRAY WAKES MARIE. The harbour comes into view. She leans against the metal casket containing Abdullah 'Akkawi's body. Her hand stills when she touches the steel. She ponders his last words Hoda. Allah Karim. The cutting of the waves breaks the silence. The twilight reveals the contours of the town's minaret. Soon the muezzin will call the faithful to prayer, but for now, Kyrenia sleeps. Marc sits at the bow with his back to her. His black figure merges with the night sky. She tries to imagine his face, but for the first time, she can't.

The launch will dock at the Chimera taverna, where Taragon and Bronstein began their quest. The speedboat from Beirut won't be long in joining them. The freighter from Barcelona has taken a full three days. Enough time for Marie and Marc to get to know each other. It's rich background material for her next article on him, this time against the backdrop of an important peace initiative. But Marie still hasn't asked about the photo. True, both have been too caught up in the moment, debating how they can put Arkassa back on track. Or is it that she just doesn't want to know?

She watches Marc approach her, swaying from side to side as the waves rock the launch.

"Marie, I spoke to my editor. If you want to work with us, you can. It'll pay you a lot more than *Le Devoir*."

"Do you mean as a team?" There a flutter in her heart, the thrill of the unexpected offer and …

"Yes, at least for the short term. You'll want to branch out on your own after a while, I imagine."

"Can I think about it?"

"*Bien sûr.*"

She leans back in the launch. Working with Taragon would be a fantastic opportunity, but that is not why she sought him out. Maybe she's already learned enough. Taragon was 'Akkawi's friend, wasn't he? And it was 'Akkawi who loved Hoda. Isn't that what Taragon said— *Loved*? But how far did that love go? She looks at the metal container. What if the man inside is the one she's been looking for?

Marie feels Taragon's presence beside her. He sits and passes his hand across the casket, a caress, a gentle caress. Involuntarily, Marie does the same. Their hands come near, and Marie feels an urge to touch his. She turns to see if he feels it too, but Taragon doesn't look up. Instead, he stares at the black metal as if he can see right through it. Thirty years of friendship now extinguished by an assassin's bullet. Were it not for Arkassa, 'Akkawi would still be alive. Time can't be turned back, and even if Taragon could wish it so, 'Akkawi wouldn't want it. His friend believed in the predestination of all human existence. And he had died a true *Shahid*. Taragon leans forward to touch his forehead against the cold metal.

Marie watches him. She can't hear his words but feels his tensed body relax. She knows that he's making peace with 'Akkawi, with himself. She wants that peace too—all of it. And she wants more …

The launch slides up along the quay. Taragon helps the crew lift 'Akkawi's casket onto it.

"Marie, let me help you," a familiar voice says in French. She turns. Ibrahim. His face is beaming and his teeth shine in their immaculate whiteness. She grasps his outstretched hand and pulls herself onto the quay. An older black man walks over to join them. Taragon embraces him.

"Come here, Marie," Taragon says. "I want to introduce you to my friend, Khalid Murat, Ibrahim's uncle."

"My pleasure," the older man says. "What a relief to see both of you safe. I feared for the worse when I heard about Barcelona."

"Khalid, Abdullah's assassin was one of the two Israelis you detained," Taragon says.

"*Bok*! I knew I should have disobeyed my orders and kept them longer in Cyprus."

"It's not your fault. Their influence is everywhere."

"Look, I'm sending Ibrahim with you to Beirut. You can use the protection. But you must leave soon for your own safety. The boat to Beirut will arrive shortly."

Taragon walks off to confer with Khalid in private while Ibrahim brings up a folding chair and a blanket for Marie.

"You must be very tired, Marie."

"Yes, I haven't slept much."

"Marie, it's good seeing you again."

Ibrahim kneels beside her and smiles. He's a beautiful man, but the attraction she had for him in Nicosia is no longer there. She turns to the water and watches the lights of an approaching speedboat come into view. The last leg of the journey will soon begin.

Chapter 38

Sabra Refugee Camp, Lebanon – June 2007

MARIE LOOKS AROUND HER. The concrete walls of the camp dwellings are barren, except for two posters announcing 'Akkawi's martyrdom. One is from Hamas, the other from the Popular Front. The funeral procession will start soon. The camp women separate her from Marc and take her to a large room. It's covered with carpets and cushions and now crowded with many women. Some come to speak to her in Arabic. She tries to explain that she can't speak their language. And they look puzzled. An old woman stands in front of her and stares. Only seconds pass, but Marie feels the weight of the old woman's presence. The woman looks bewildered and yet vaguely familiar. She points at Marie and says: "Zayy Hoda." A fashionably dressed woman escorts the old woman back to her seat.

The elegant woman returns to sit beside Marie. She says in good French: "Um Amin says that you look like her niece."

"Do you mean Hoda?"

Marie's blunt question unnerves the woman. She takes a moment before answering.

"Yes."

"Tell me about her."

The woman looks out a glassless window as if to find something in the blue sky beyond. She turns back to Marie.

"*Nous croyons qu'elle est morte*—we believe she's dead."

"When? How?"

"When they all died."

"In the war?"

"Yes, after Arafat abandoned them."

"The Sabra and Shatila massacre?"

The woman becomes agitated.

"*Je ne veux pas*—I don't want to talk about it. It was a long time ago, and nothing is certain."

Marie suppresses her next question, not wishing to upset the woman. She looks around the room and wonders how many loved ones these women of Sabra lost in the massacre.

A knock on the door. The women rush to put on their hijabs.

"*Tfaddelu*—come in!"

A young man in a red and white keffiyeh pokes in his head, and says in English: "Marie Boivin?"

"Yes."

"It's time to go. The procession will start in five minutes. Mr. Taragon is asking for you."

Marie tenses her muscles. Leave? Should she? There could be others among these women who knew Hoda. Maybe the answer isn't with Taragon, but with them. She asks the elegant woman for her phone number.

The woman looks at her obliquely and then writes her name and number on a sheet of lined paper.

Selima 'Akkawi 710697 Bikfaya.

The back of the Armenian's shop is dark, barely enough light to see the glass of mint tea in front of him. Ari picks it up and sips slowly. He doesn't like the taste of mint. It reminds him of the antiseptic scent of the morgue—a place he's visited too often to identify foe and friend. He drinks the tea nonetheless. It's the Mossad's tradition to drink tea with their Arab hirelings.

The Director has given Ari Epstein a reprieve—one last assignment to make good his blunders. He looks at the morning's Arabic paper, *Al-Quds*. On the front page is a photo of Taragon marching in the funeral procession in Beirut. He's flanked by bearded men wearing Muslim skullcaps and others sporting red and white keffiyehs. Many carry Kalashnikovs; others signs denouncing Israel. The killing of 'Akkawi has united the fundamentalists and the leftists. Further down the page is news of rockets launched from Gaza into Israel, a kidnapping of American tourists hiking near the Green Line, and the closure of the Al-Aksa mosque for two days. A new *intifada* is beginning.

A young boy brings him a copy of *Le Monde*. He gives the boy a ten-shekel note. Unlike his Arabic, Ari's French is rusty. He learned it long ago, but it's still good enough to make out most of the lead article. Kressmann is trying to calm the Muslims in France. One hundred cars have already been set aflame in the suburbs where many French Muslims live. 'Akkawi has become larger in death than in life. Kressmann tells the protesters that he knew 'Akkawi well and recently learned of his involvement in a new peace initiative called Arkassa. Kressmann says that, although this initiative has some fundamental flaws, peace advocates on both sides should launch new ideas like it. Ari despises Kressmann—a Jew who would sell out his own people for a few headlines in the newspaper is not a *Mensch*.

It was hard convincing the Director to give him another chance. The old man imposed on him two conditions. First, to spirit David's body out of Spain. This was easily done—Israel has friends everywhere, even in Catalonia. The second will be the real challenge. He must negotiate with Muhammad Shehadi to silence Taragon.

The Fatah commander arrives.

"What do you want?"

Ari hates the insolence in Shehadi's voice. Haven't they paid him well enough over the years? Besides what is he now? Just a failure chased out of Gaza by Hamas.

"Sit down. We have something for you to do."

"I don't work for you anymore."

"Calm down, my friend. This is also in your interest, and you want us to help you take back Gaza, don't you?"

"Gaza! You should've given me the weapons I asked for when we still controlled it."

"We gave you enough. Your men were incompetent."

Shehadi gives Ari an ice-cold stare. He feels like ripping out the old man's throat. Instead, he leans back and sneers. "If they're so incompetent, why are you here now?"

"Good. Listen."

Bronstein strokes Leyna's back as he tunes into the BBC World Service. 'Akkawi's funeral in Beirut has brought out a hundred thousand mourners. Many more are marching in solidarity in Gaza. The whole of the Middle East is watching, but is the rest of the world? And the power brokers in Washington, London, Paris and Moscow—do they care?

Leyna props herself up on a pillow and pulls the sheet to cover her exquisite half-moon breasts.

"What will you do now, Jonathan?" she murmurs.

Bronstein leans in to kiss her shoulder and replies: "I have talked to my editors. They've agreed to make me the paper's North American correspondent."

"Is that what you want?"

"I want to be with you."

"And Arkassa?"

"We'll see if Marc can generate some support for it in Europe. If he can, I can try to promote it here. If not, it's time to make a new start. I can no longer imagine returning to the madness back home. I want to stay here."

Leyna likes his answer, the reassurance that he'll be with her.

"Did you know 'Akkawi well?"

"I met him in Lebanon. He spared my life when I was captured."

"Captured?"

"I was with Israeli military intelligence when we invaded. 'Akkawi's men ambushed our car when we were chasing an escaped PLO fighter. Everyone else was killed, and I was taken prisoner."

She wonders if she should ask more.

"Leyna, those were hard times. Both sides used gruesome interrogation techniques. The escaped prisoner was tortured. When he saw me, he tried to kill me. But 'Akkawi stopped him."

"Wait, you tortured someone?"

"No, not me, but he wanted to take his revenge on any Israeli."

"Why did Abdullah save you?"

"I don't know, but he kept me safe until a prisoner swap was arranged."

"And Marc?"

"He was travelling with 'Akkawi when I was taken prisoner. He interviewed me, and that interview was instrumental in convincing my government to do the prisoner exchange. At first, I didn't trust him. He was close to the Palestinians, but his reports were always fair. When he became the Jerusalem correspondent for *Le Monde* and I went into politics, we became friends."

Leyna watches him as he moves closer to her.

"But enough with politics. Come here."

Leyna feels Bronstein's strong arms embrace her. She opens up to him, pulling his hips toward her. She feels him enter her, slowly at first and then rapid deep thrusts. Her heart beats faster as the adrenaline fills her body. She moves in perfect unison with him, like she never has with a man before. As she is about to climax, he brushes her lips with his and whispers her name.

Chapter

39

Cairo, Egypt – July 2007

NEWSPAPERS AND MAGAZINES throughout the world republish the photo essay by Taragon and Marie of 'Akkawi's funeral in Sabra. The images go viral on the internet. The royalties pile up, and *Le Monde's* editors couldn't be happier. Bronstein has done his part in interviewing Lebanese and Palestinian Montrealers who knew 'Akkawi in Beirut. His reporting is a direct challenge to the dead terrorist narrative of the mainstream Israeli press, and the Israeli right demands Bronstein's head. But die-hard peace activists defend him. Some even call on him to return to take over the leadership of the faltering Meretz party.

The Mossad's attempt to deflect blame onto Iran has faltered. Not only does Tehran deny that it had anything to do with 'Akkawi's death, but a Russian hacker releases intercepted e-mails between Ramat HaSharon and an intern at the Hospital del Mar in Barcelona, attesting to the conspiracy to "disappear" David's body. Then David's aunt goes public demanding that he be given a hero's funeral. Only the most right-wing Israeli papers continue to print the concocted story of Iranian involvement. Meretz MPs call for an inquiry into the young man's death but stop short of accusing the government of ordering 'Akkawi's assassination.

Arkassa is dying a lingering death. No rational observer will deny the value of the initiative, but the killing in Barcelona has changed everything. European politicians are simply not prepared to back it without a prominent new Palestinian interlocutor.

Taragon looks around La Recyclerie bar for his editor, Pierre Chevrier. The bistro is a popular attraction for left-wing journalists. He says hello to a few as he moves toward the table in the back that Chevrier normally takes. There he is, sitting with his back to the wall, positioned to see all who come into the café. Taragon appreciates his editor's precautions. Both of them have more than a few enemies.

"*Bonjour,* Pierre. Sorry to keep you waiting."

"No problem. Please sit. The duck is very good here."

"Before we order, can I tell you what I want to do with Arkassa?"

"If you must. It's lunchtime though, and I've barely had anything to eat today."

"Thanks."

"Well?"

"We're going to Gaza."

"To Gaza? The Israelis will never let you through."

"I don't plan to go through Israel."

"Then how?"

"Egypt and then the tunnels."

"How do you plan to get Egyptian approval for illegally crossing an international border?"

"Don't worry. I have contacts there. It's only a matter of money. All Egyptian officials can be bribed."

"Okay, so you get to Gaza, then what?"

"Akkawi's closest supporters are there. They'll listen out of respect for him. And there are other voices of reason in Gaza, others who see hope in compromise and oppose the religious hard-liners."

"Marc, it's too great a risk. The Israelis have denied foreign journalists entry to Gaza since Hamas drove out Shehadi's men. It's convenient for them. This way, no Western journalist can confirm the civilian deaths in the drone attacks on Hamas leaders."

"All the more reason to send me there."

Chevrier pauses. Taragon is tenacious. He will argue his point all afternoon if needed. And Chevrier is starving. What does he have to lose by allowing Taragon to pursue his crazy plan?

"Fine. Do it! Now let's order."

"There's one other thing. I want Marie Boivin to come with me."

Chevrier looks Taragon straight in the eye. Why does he need the girl? Then it strikes him. What a man will do for a woman!

On the ride in from Cairo airport, Taragon carries on the usual banter in Arabic with the taxi driver. Marie watches him closely. She wished she knew the language. Oddly, some of the words sound familiar. She feels honoured that Taragon has asked her to come with him, and is determined to do her best to support selling Arkassa to the Palestinians. For the first time in her life, she feels truly alive. She senses that they're about to accomplish something historic.

Taragon and Marie take adjacent rooms at the Hotel Longchamps in the central Cairo neighbourhood of Zamalek. From Cairo, they'll travel to El Arish and then through the tunnels to Rafah in the southern end of the Gaza Strip. The plan is to surface in Canada Camp in Rafah, named after a contingent of Canadian peacekeepers who once had their barracks there. Taragon knows the place well. He recalls walking with Mathieu Hibou and Bronstein around a sewage-infested pond in the camp. Hibou was explaining how, with volunteer community labour and building material from his NGO, they'd soon drain the pond and turn it into a soccer field for the local kids. Taragon pointed to the Israeli sniper positions on the roofs of an unfinished building at the north end of the pond. "What about them?" he asked. "Oh them," Mathieu said. "They'll get free admission to the games." Bronstein quoted Mathieu in his *Haaretz* article on Canada Camp. The snipers were recalled before the story was picked up by the international press.

On the first night at the Longchamps, just knowing that Taragon is sleeping a few feet away disturbs Marie. She feels his presence, and despite her best efforts, he enters her dreams. In them, he stands on a balcony overlooking the ruins of Beirut. Smoke and fire are everywhere. She sees herself approaching him from the bedroom. He turns to her, his face is that of the boy, Munir. The fires in the background are quickly extinguished by a flash storm. Taragon's face returns to the figure on the balcony. He steps towards her. She falls to the ground. A grey mist sweeps over her. The coolness calms her. The sun over the Nile ends her fantasy. She hears Taragon already hard at work in the adjacent room.

Shehadi's man waits in the lobby. He was starving for work—no, he was literally starving when the call came through. Like all of Shehadi's men, he was forced to flee Gaza after Hamas put down the attempted coup. His funds have run out, and he's ready to do anything to get something to eat. He studies the photos. Taragon, he already knows. The woman looks like the fair-skinned girls in Beach Camp, whose families fled Jaffa in 1948. The daughters of Crusaders, they used to call them. He is to guide them through the tunnels to Canada Camp. He knows the tunnels better than anyone in Gaza. He and his relatives helped dig them so that Shehadi could smuggle thousands of weapons, and other things—alcohol, drugs, fancy lingerie for Shehadi's favourite women. He hates the man, but he belongs to him—he is owned by him—and will do what he's told.

The lobby is free of the usual presence of the Egyptian *Mukhabarat*, Mubarak's secret police. Shehadi has dished out enough money to bribe them to take the day off. They'll be back tomorrow though, looking to line their pockets again, but by then Taragon, the girl and he will be gone.

Selima 'Akkawi pauses before looking again at the photo album. She was disturbed when she saw the Canadian girl. The resemblance to her sister-in-law is remarkable. She doesn't understand why Taragon doesn't see it too. She tried to talk to him at the funeral, but they were constantly interrupted by men and women offering condolences. It's not that every feature of the Canadian's face is the same as Hoda's nor is their complexion at all similar—still her sister-in-law's remarkable beauty is there.

It's a quiet morning in Bikfaya—a good day to visit Nabil's grave and talk to him. If there's a connection between the Canadian and his sister, Nabil will give her a sign. She longs for signs from him, some sense that beyond this world he still exists and waits for her.

Selima walks down the stone steps to the street. She hears a voice.

"*Bonjour Madame Selima.*"

"*Ah, bonjour Monsieur Labaki.*"

"It's beautiful out, isn't it?"

Selima lets her neighbour walk beside her for a few blocks to the stand to catch a taxi for the cemetery.

"Your husband was a great artist. His death was a loss for all of us."

Selima finds it hard to believe the man. She knows his past. How he led the Maronite fighters against the Palestinians—how ruthless he was. It is true that later, as a minister in the government, he achieved many good things. More recently, he's been pivotal in the reconciliation process. But can a past like his ever be forgiven? He lives beside her now, as she wiles away the days in her dead father's house, and he seeks out her company at every opportunity. She tries always to be polite to him—she can't afford to do otherwise. Many in the town still reject her for having married a Palestinian, and worse a Muslim. But Elie isn't one of them. She doesn't know why, nor does she understand the sadness of this man who was once a monster. True the sense of loss he projects dilutes his sins, but she isn't ready to forgive him. Still, he could be useful to her.

When she reaches the taxi stand, she turns to him.

"Monsieur Labaki, there's someone I lost track of during the war."

"Who was it?"

"Nabil's sister, Hoda. I need to find out what happened to her."

"When did you last hear of her?"

"In 1982. We heard that she had returned to Sabra."

Elie Labaki frowns. Is this a trap, a veiled accusation?

Selima sees the sudden change in his demeanour.

"I only want to find out what happened to her. Nothing more. I understand that many bad things took place during the war, and that is behind us, all of us."

Selima's words reassure him. If Hoda 'Akkawi was in Sabra during the "cleansing," then her identification papers might be still in the movement's archives. They had catalogued many of these documents, along with field reports of that dreadful day, in the event that they would ever have to defend themselves in an international court.

"Madame 'Akkawi, can you get me a photo of your sister-in-law?"

"Wait, I have one here."

Selima brings out of her purse an old black-and-white photo of herself, Hoda, and Nabil. How young they were!

Elie looks at the photo. He instantly recognizes Hoda, but from where? He then compares the young Selima in the photo to the woman standing beside him. The years have not worn away her beauty. If anything, she's more beautiful now.

"I'll see what I can do and let you know in a week."

"Thank you."

Selima looks at Elie. There's a determination in his face, but also a softness. That he was brutal during the war, there's no doubt, but now in the tranquillity of Bikfaya, she sees a fleeting dignity about him—a sense of pained honour.

The taxi arrives. It's crowded but there is one place left. The passengers in the car stare disapprovingly at Selima. They know who she is, who her husband was. A woman passenger edges her large frame over into the free seat. The driver politely asks her to move back to make room for

Selima. She shakes her head and says she'll pay for both seats. Two of
the other passengers nod in approval. The driver looks at Elie and raises
his hands. Elie leans into the window and whispers something to the
men in the car. They know who he is. The large woman stills refuses to
budge, but the men move closer to free up just enough space for Selima.
The woman utters something unintelligible. The men's faces redden. Elie
holds the door open. Selima takes her place beside them. The car pulls
away. She glances back. He's still standing there … watching.

What his contact in Israeli military intelligence has just told him worries Bronstein. Can it really be that the Mossad has hired Shehadi to
eliminate Taragon? Have they gone mad? Bronstein must warn his
friend, but where is he?

He stares out the window. It's summer and children play in T-shirts
and shorts. Large oak trees shade the streets of Outremont. Sparrows
chirp their happiness and discontent. The harmony of it all calms him.
For a moment, his mind drifts away to the hills of Alonim where the
red-breasted geese of his childhood fill the sky in perfect V-formations.
A scent of lavender wakes him.

"*Ça va, mon amour?*"

"Yes," he answers.

Leyna places her hands on Bronstein's shoulders and squeezes them
ever so gently.

"You looked peaceful just now."

"I was, but I now have to find Marc."

"Is he in danger?"

"Yes."

"He's with Marie Boivin."

"Leyna, how do you know that?"

"She told Minh Chau."

"Where are they?"

"Somewhere in the Middle East on a special assignment. She was
very secretive. She just wanted Minh Chau not to worry."

Bronstein thinks hard. Who might know where they are? Of course,
Pierre Chevrier, Taragon's editor. He could warn Taragon through him.
That's if Chevrier has the means to get a message through.

"Look I might need you to translate for me. I need to talk to Marc's
editor in Paris."

Chapter

40

Gaza – July 2007

S HEHADI'S MAN KNOCKS on the bottom of the hatch. It has taken
them an hour to crawl through the tunnel from Egypt. Their
clothes are full of dust. The oxygen in the tunnel is thinning out.
Cold perspiration covers their foreheads. All this is a small price to pay
to enter Gaza safely.

"Don't worry. I can hear them coming," Shehadi's man says to
Taragon and Marie.

The hatch opens slowly. Two faces peer down.

"*Marhabba. Ya Shabaab!*" Shehadi's man says.

The men above pull him up and reach down to offer their hands to
Taragon and Marie.

Shehadi's man soon realizes that his cousins are not alone. Three
armed bearded men stand by the unlit doorway to the rest of the house.
He turns to his cousins. "What's going on?"

"Sorry, we didn't have a choice."

One of the bearded men steps out of the shadows, toting an AK-47.
The muscles in his face are tense.

"Mohammad Zarzawi, you're under arrest."

"For what?"

"For conspiracy to murder these two foreigners."

For a moment, Shehadi's man looks down at the hole.

"Don't do it, cousin. They'll catch you and kill you."

The other two men by the doorway move into action, grabbing
Zarzawi's arms.

The third man extends his hand to Taragon.

"I'm Adnan Barghouti. Abdullah 'Akkawi was my friend."

"He was also ours."

"There was a plot to have you murdered. Your editor in Paris tipped us off."

"Thank you."

"How did he know?"

"He just said that Jonathan had heard about it from his sources."

Taragon makes a mental note to call Bronstein as soon as he can safely do so. His friend must be mobilizing his support network in Israel. He knows that Bronstein's connections inside the labyrinth of Israeli intelligence services are extensive, but will any of them actually support the initiative? Would any of them dare to stand up to the Mossad, which must have been behind the assassination of 'Akkawi in Spain?

"Do you know why we're here?"

"Yes. Arkassa."

"How do you feel about that?"

"Like I said, Abdullah was my friend. I'll listen to you, but I don't know if anyone else in Gaza will."

Marie shakes off the dust on her clothes and moves beside Taragon.

"Adnan, this is Marie Boivin."

"Yes, we've been expecting her. Salwa, come!"

A young woman in Islamic clothing steps into the room.

"Salwa, you're to accompany this woman everywhere."

"Yes, brother."

"Let's go."

Leyna brushes her hair. Long strokes to straighten it. She looks at the wisps of grey. She's now fifty-two. So much time has passed, and, until recently, each day has gone by faster than the last. But since he entered her life, time seems suspended. She touches the scars on her face. They seem less visible now. Is it her imagination? She looks over her shoulder toward the bedroom. She hears him move in the bed. She smiles, puts away her brush and removes the towel from around her. Naked she tiptoes to the bedroom and turns the doorknob. Bronstein is spread out on the sheets. She covers his body with hers, and he awakes to take her in his arms.

The love-making lasts for an hour before both are satiated. Bronstein gives her a last, long kiss before rising up. She joins him in the shower, and again they make love. Neither can remember such pleasure, such closeness.

Like teenagers, they walk down to the kitchen hugging each other and kissing. Bronstein tries to hike up her dress. She puts her finger to his lips. "Later! We have the whole day in front of us." Bronstein puts on a sad face. She kisses him and whispers: "Please! I won't disappoint you."

Leyna puts on the kettle, as Bronstein checks his cell phone for messages. A missed text message from Taragon—*Call me when you can.* Bronstein shows the message to Leyna. She nods. He goes to the living room and dials Taragon's number.

"Yes?"

"It's me. Is it safe to talk?"

"Yes, but let's keep it short."

"You asked me to call."

"Listen, first, thanks for getting the word to Abdullah's followers. Do you know who was behind the plot to kill us?"

"The Mossad. They paid Shehadi to arrange it."

"Are you certain? I can't believe that the Mossad would make a deal with a butcher like Shehadi."

"Don't fool yourself. They've been supporting him for years. And now they're in a panic. No one ever thought that a Hamas leader would make such far-reaching concessions. Arkassa risks undermining all the Mossad's work in convincing the West that the Palestinians will never agree to a lasting peace."

"Unfortunately, Abdullah's followers don't appear to share the same willingness to compromise as he did. It's going to be tough."

"How are they treating you?"

"With a great deal of respect. It's clear that they idolize Abdullah, even in death, and he'd told them of our friendship."

"What do we have to do to convince them?"

"I'm not sure. Unlike Abdullah, few of the new generation here lived through the civil war in Lebanon. Some still believe that other Arabs will rally behind them to force a better deal with the Israelis. They're also less concerned about Jerusalem than Abdullah was. Most are refugees from Ashkelon just across the border. Others are from Jaffa. They still dream of a full return to the 1948 borders."

"Well, that's a non-starter."

"I know, but that's what they want."

Bronstein looks down. Is this how it was going to end—a peace initiative that no one wants—then the hounding by his enemies in Israel until they can find a way to discredit him or eliminate Marc and him like they had Abdullah?

"Jonathan, I need to get into Israel."

"Why?"

"I need to convince Abdullah's supporters that there are Israelis ready to come on board. All the Gazans have seen is Israel's iron fist and the fanaticism of settlers. When I spoke about you and what you, an Israeli, are doing to make Arkassa work, they didn't believe me. They want reassurances that there are Israelis who are ready to come on board. Then, maybe they'll compromise."

"Let me get back before you attempt to cross into Israel. I can try to mobilize people. We need to work together. Remember, Arkassa is as much mine as it is yours."

"Can you get me into Israel?"

"Yes."

"How?"

"The Palestinians aren't the only ones getting people in and out of Gaza. Let me talk to a couple of people in Tel Aviv. In the meantime, keep your head down."

Marie moves beside Taragon.

"Ask him if Leyna is there."

"Did you hear that, Jonathan?"

"Yes. I'll put her on."

Marie takes the cell phone from Taragon.

"May I have a moment, Marc?"

"Certainly, I need to speak to Adnan anyway."

Marie waits until Taragon leaves the room before returning to the call.

"Leyna, are you alone?"

"Yes."

"Can you get a message to Minh Chau?"

"Of course."

"She's supposed to go to Beirut in a couple of days. I want her to meet a woman there called Selima 'Akkawi. Her number is 710697 in Bikfaya. It's about an hour north of Beirut."

"And what is she to do when she meets this woman?"

"Ask Minh Chau to show the woman the copy of the photo I gave her. Maybe this woman has the answer I've been looking for."

"Don't worry. I'll get the message to her today."

"What photo is that?" asks Marc asks, having suddenly reappeared behind her.

Before she can respond, Adnan interrupts them.

"It's time to go. You've been too long on the phone. The Israelis monitor these calls. Then the drones attack."

Adnan leads them through an underground passage to the basement of a neighbouring building. Like most of the neighbourhood, it's covered with debris from recent aerial strikes. They wait. No drones attack this time.

Minh Chau looks through the window as the Airbus makes its descent to Beirut. From the sky, the city is as beautiful as ever. The cars race down the Corniche, as if to escape from the nightmares of the past war and make the most of the present. There's a sense of eternal youth in the city. She's looking forward to the weekend in Beirut before her conference starts on Monday. Soon she'll not be able to fly. A small bulge is already noticeable, and she's been questioned by the airlines about how far along she's in her pregnancy.

Minh Chau reflects on the last message that Leyna sent her from Marie. She looks at the old photo. She, too, sees the resemblance between the young man and Taragon, and also one between the young woman in the picture and Marie. Minh Chau won't fail her friend. She'll find Selima and obtain the answers that Marie is so desperately seeking.

Elie has selected the small café in Jounieh to be away from the prying eyes in Bikfaya. But even here, people recognize him and come over to shake his hand. No matter. When she arrives, he'll suggest that they walk down to the marina. It's quiet there at this time of the year. He'll share what he's discovered, but not all of it.

Elie takes out of the envelope reports in Arabic, French and Hebrew. The conclusion is irrefutable. Hoda 'Akkawi, Selima's sister-in-law, was a courier between the Social Nationalist leadership and the Druze leader Kemal Jumblatt. In 1979, she disappeared. There was one sighting after that—in Bsarma in northern Lebanon in the company of Marwan Kanaan, a fellow Social Nationalist. The Bsarma report contains a blurred photo, in which Hoda 'Akkawi holds the hand of a very young child. It isn't clear if it is a boy or girl. In 2005, a civil rights association obtained the right to dig for mass graves in the refugee camps. More than thirty bodies were found. There the searchers found a copy of Hoda 'Akkawi's UN *laissez-passer* on the decomposed body of a young woman.

"Hello, Monsieur Elie."

He looks up. *Wallahi* (by God), she is beautiful.

"Madame 'Akkawi, you are radiant today."

"*Merci*. You're too kind."

"Would you like to take a walk to the marina in Keslik? I know a spot there where we can talk freely."

Selima watches Elie put the papers and photographs on the table back into the manila envelope. She manages to get a glimpse of one of the photos—a young woman with a child. Could that be Hoda?

The streets of Jounieh are quiet. The party-goers from the night before are still sleeping, and the tourist buses from Beirut haven't yet arrived. As they descend the steep street, the Casino du Liban across the bay comes into view. It's a massive structure, a monument of defiance to all the bloodshed that has plagued Lebanon. Selima looks at Elie, who stares ahead. Today, there's a serenity to the man. The haunted, hollow look is no longer there. It's as if he's come to grips with his demons.

When they turn on to the seaside road, Elie says: "It's not far."

They walk along the seawall to a small blue boat. On it, an old man is unknotting a net. Elie nods to the man, who jumps ashore, shakes Elie's hand, bows to Selima and walks to a café across the road.

"We can talk on the boat," Elie says as he steps aboard.

She hesitates, looks around. There are a few older men taking their morning stroll along the seaside. Some fishermen are repairing their nets on nearby boats. She steps on board.

"It's my cousin's boat. He's in Canada now. I pay that man to take it out occasionally so we can keep it registered as a working boat."

"We're not going out to sea, are we?" Selima asks.

"No, we can discuss everything here."

Elie spreads the documents on a small table in the galley.

"Do you want to read them first, or should I summarize them?"

"I'd like to read them myself."

"Go ahead, please."

"Can I keep these copies?"

"No, I have to return them. They can't fall into the wrong hands."

"Thank you, Monsieur Elie, for helping me."

"It's nothing, only my duty."

Selima looks again at this man, who's detested by much of the Lebanese population, but considered a hero by others. Has she misjudged him? Who is she to judge others for what they did during the war? She and Nabil had the good fortune to escape to France. There Nabil's art earned him international acclaim. In a small town outside of Paris, they discreetly married in a civil ceremony, one never recognized in Lebanon. Some fanatics decried her marriage to a Palestinian Muslim as an act of treason against the Christian cause, but Monsieur Elie wasn't one of them. She remembers an article that he wrote in a Lebanese newspaper praising Nabil's work as a fine example of Middle Eastern impressionism. It was only after her husband's death that she was able to return to Lebanon and live under the protection of her relatives in Bikfaya. Many of them had stood by Monsieur Elie when the Maronite leadership passed him over for the sons of the old oligarchs. She doesn't share his politics, but he's more honest than the others who emerged from the war rich and arrogant.

She works her way through the documents as Elie prepares them coffee. A tale of espionage and intrigue emerges. She never realized how deeply involved Hoda and her cousin Marwan were with the Social Nationalists. The reference to Hoda being in Bsarma perplexes her. What was she doing there with Marwan? And who was this child?

Elie places a small cup of coffee in front of her.

"Have you found what you wanted?"

"Some of it, yes. Do you know who Ari E. is?"

"Who?"

"The man who filed one of the reports in Hebrew."

Elie hesitates. He hadn't anticipated she might be able to read the Hebrew documents. And there are many secrets that he isn't prepared to share with Selima.

"How well can you read Hebrew?"

"Some, but it's rusty. I studied linguistics at university. So do you know who Ari. E. is?"

"Does it matter if I do?"

"Yes."

"Why?"

"He might know more of what became of Hoda."

Elie realizes that Selima hasn't grasped the meaning of all the evidence. Perhaps, she overlooked the report from the NGO? He hesitates before saying: "Your sister-in-law died in Sabra. Many others died there, including children. It was a bad time."

Tears begin to well up in Selima's eyes. His confirmation of Hoda's death is the deepest of cuts. Then *une petite espérance* comes to her.

"I think that I may have found the child."

"Pardon?"

"The child from Bsarma."

"I see."

"There's a young Canadian woman who bears a resemblance to Hoda."

"A Canadian?"

"Yes. Monsieur Elie, what happened to the orphans from Sabra?"

Elie drew a breath. Did he really want to relive it all?

"I mean, could some of the children have escaped?" she asks.

"Of course, not all the children were killed. I know that some of the orphanages took in young children after what happened. During the war, families from abroad would adopt orphans from here."

"So it's possible that this young woman could be Hoda's daughter?"

"Anything is possible."

"Will you help me find the records from the orphanages?"

"I can help with those in East Beirut. I'd not be welcome at the others."

"Can we start tomorrow?"

Before he could answer, Selima's cell phone rings.

"Hello. Yes, this is Selima 'Akkawi. I see … Are you in Beirut? Of course, I can meet you. Tomorrow at 3 p.m. at the St. George Hotel."

Elie looks at her.

"That was a friend of the Canadian girl. She's something to show me."

"I'd like to meet her too."

"Monsieur Elie, I think I should meet her alone. Believe me though that your help is important to me."

The words warm his heart. He's done so many cruel things in his life. So much blood in the name of protecting his community and the avenging of his fiancée. Perhaps, he could atone for some of it now.

Chapter

41

THE FIRST TRIP TO DAMASCUS GOES WELL. The local representatives of the Social Nationalists agree to intercede with Assad. The old man has shown more willingness to compromise since Operation Litani. The ease with which Israel was able to flex its muscle and flaunt international opinion disturbs him.

Hoda and Marwan soon find their courier services in high demand. A relatively small group, the Social Nationalists rely heavily on diplomacy to achieve their objectives. Fouad Saadeh has managed to maintain good relations with the PLO and most of the dissident Palestinian groups. Damascus is now happy to provide the *laissez-passers* for Hoda and Marwan to move freely through any checkpoint of the Syrian Army and its surrogates. While both have qualms about how quickly their party has forgotten Jumblatt's assassination, the first trip to Damascus convinces them that Fouad knows what he's doing.

For Marc and Riley, who together have developed an impressive network of contacts among most of the warring factions, Lebanon has become a journalistic Eldorado. Both have received substantial raises from their employers, who are syndicating their stories to a world enthralled with what will happen next in the Middle East. Marc and Hoda decide to put off their plans to move to France. Instead, they decide to take another vacation in Cyprus to escape the stress of Beirut.

During the holiday, the house of cards collapses.

The party's leadership in Damascus invites Marwan to speak to Aleppo's Maronites. The community there is divided between joining the ranks of the Syrian Social Nationalists, like many of Syria's

Christians are doing, or sending aid to their co-religionists in East Beirut. As a Maronite Social Nationalist, Marwan is seen as the ideal candidate for making the case for the party. Marwan arrives in Aleppo on June 16, the day that the Muslim Brotherhood orchestrates the massacre of thirty-two Alawite army cadets. Assad's security forces go on a rampage. When they stumble across Marwan walking in the Salaheddine quarter, where Muslim Brotherhood support is strongest, they immediately take him into custody. Marwan hides his real reason for being in Syria and disappears into the notorious Syrian prison system.

Hoda smiles as she reads the latest letter from Nabil while Mark showers. Her brother has just had a fantastically successful exhibition at one of Paris' best art galleries. His paintings have sold for fifty thousand francs. He'll send half of the money to their parents in Sabra. The rest he'll keep to rent a larger apartment for Selima and him. They've decided on a date for their wedding but don't know how to tell their parents. Hoda jots a quick note to tell them to keep the marriage secret for the time being. There'll be time enough to make it public when the fighting in Lebanon subsides.

Hoda hears a knock on the door. She opens it to the grandson of the owner of the pension.

"Madam, there's a call for you downstairs. Can you come now?"

Hoda follows the boy down the narrow staircase. She hands him the letter to Nabil with money for an envelope and stamps.

"Mail it today please."

At the base of the stairs, the septuagenarian owner of the pension stands by a small table with a telephone. He hands Hoda the receiver.

"Hoda?"

"Yes?"

"It's Fouad."

"What's the matter?"

"Marwan has disappeared."

"Where? How?"

"It's my fault. I sent him to Aleppo to help out our Syrian friends. Have you heard the news about what's going on there?"

"Yes, it's horrible."

"Marwan got caught in the middle of it."

"Who has him?"

"We think that he's held by Syrian military intelligence."

"I can help. Send me to Syria. I have a lot of contacts there."

"It's too dangerous. Our comrades in Damascus are feeling the pressure since the killings in Aleppo. Assad's brother Rifaat is going after all non-Baathists. His paramilitary forces are ruthlessly eliminating anyone suspected of supporting the insurgency, and Rifaat still sees us as a threat."

"I want to go. I've relatives there who can help. Trust me."

"I'll think about it, but you should come back to Beirut first."

Hoda puts down the receiver. The names of dozens of party contacts in Damascus race through her mind. Many of them will help if they can. And then there's her cousin, Mustapha, a Sa'iqa commander. She met Mustapha several times as a child. She remembers him as being a gentle man. That was before his parents died in an Israeli air raid. Abdullah also knows Mustapha as well as many Popular Front sympathizers in the Yarmouk refugee camp. With their help, she might find a way to free Marwan. She feels a hand on her arm. She turns to Marc, his hair still wet from the shower—a quizzical look on his face.

"That was Fouad Saadeh. Marwan has disappeared in Syria. I need to find him. I need to go to Damascus."

"Did Fouad ask you to?"

"No."

She looks at him, her eyes imploring him to understand.

He brushes the hair on her brow behind her ear, looks into her eyes, and says: "Then I'll go with you."

The director of the foreign prisoners wing, Abu George, puts his notebook aside. The Maronite had refused to cooperate so they intensified the interrogation, moving it from constant beating of his feet to cramming his body into a tire. It's a technique that usually breaks a man in minutes. The Maronite still maintains his cover story. Abu George scratches his day-old beard. Could it be the man is just who he says he is—a tourist, taking a break from the stress in Lebanon? Abu George shakes his head. The man's story doesn't jive. Syria is the last place that Maronites would holiday in.

His subordinates are asking permission to move to the next step—the metal chair and electrical cables. Abu George abhors this method.

The smell of burning human flesh nauseates him, and the permanent damage to the prisoner's genitals repulses him. But he has his orders, and he can't trust his guards not to go over his head.

Since coming to Sednaya Prison, he's been able to end the practice of rape here. The first time a prison guard suggested it, he shoved his pistol against the guard's genitals. Still, Abu George is careful. Although a Baathist, he's a Christian. It's one thing to stand up to a Sunni prison guard, but another to defy the Alawite intelligence officers, who demand quick results. And since the massacre of the cadets in Aleppo, they're more demanding than ever. His thoughts are interrupted by the appearance of his adjutant.

"The Maronite is ready."

Ready, yes ready for another round of interrogation, one that would lead to nothing. Abu George has had enough.

"Bring him here."

"Here?"

The adjutant looks at the director's pristine office, with its beautiful Persian carpets.

"Should we clean him up first?"

"No, just bring him now."

Abu George has decided that he'll give the Maronite one last chance to confess or find someone who can raise the twenty thousand Syrian pounds he can hand over to his superiors to secure the prisoner's freedom. The alternative to these two options is bleak. Without making a confession or paying the money, the prisoner will be crippled by the beatings and then disappear into the notorious network of prisons. And few come out of it alive. Abu George is not ready to let this happen to a fellow Christian, even a Maronite.

The adjutant returns with the prisoner, whose clothes are caked with blood.

"Sit here," Abu George orders.

He scans Marwan's face for some recognition that he knows what his fate will be if he continues to resist.

"Listen to me. I'm a Christian like you. I know that you can't be supporting those Muslim fanatics. But you're also not a tourist. Why don't you just tell me why you were in Aleppo. Are you a smuggler? A thief? A spy? Who were you going to see in Aleppo?"

Marwan looks at his interrogator. He doesn't sense in Abu George the sadism that the guards have shown him, but he can't trust the man. The Syrians will pick up any persons he names and subject them to the same torture he's just gone through.

Abu George shuffles the papers on his desk.

"Look, if you don't want to talk, then you can pay for your freedom, but it'll be costly."

Marwan perks up.

"How much?"

"Twenty thousand pounds."

Marwan knows that Fouad will pay that amount and even more, but how can he get a message to him without compromising their network in Syria? The Syrian jailer still doesn't know who he is and who his contacts are. He looks at the man's face for a sign of honesty.

"You say you're a Christian. Is that true?"

"Why would I lie to you? I'm a Christian and a Baathist."

"Then bring me a priest from your church, and I'll tell him who to contact for the money."

"Why do you make it so hard on yourself? You know that I can't do that. I'll give you one last chance. Tell me who you are and what you were doing or tell me who to contact for the money."

"I can't."

"Guard! Take the prisoner back. And bring out the chair"

Evan O'Shea reads the telex from Nicosia again. Marc and Hoda are coming to Syria and need his help. He's been at the Australian embassy in Damascus for only three months and hasn't consolidated his network yet. He's unsure about how much he can help. He still needs to secure his cover as the agricultural attaché before he can start nosing around and asking Syrian officials for favours. Besides, his Ambassador is a moron and doesn't have a clue what Evan's real responsibilities are. Robinson in Beirut is still his control officer, and he's ordered Evan to lie low for the first six months, enough time to lull everyone into having confidence in him. Well, Robinson is a prick, and Marc is his friend, so Evan feels no compunction in disobeying his superior.

Evan makes up his mind. He'll find out what hell-hole they have Marwan in. After that, it'll be up to Marc and Hoda to secure his release. Money will do the trick.

Marc's decision to involve Evan is a dilemma for Hoda. She wished that he'd consulted with her about it, but she wouldn't have been able to explain her objection anyway. Even with Marc, there are some things that she has kept secret. Through her work for the Social Nationalists, she'd found out exactly who Evan is, but has never told Marc. Yes, perhaps Evan could help, but the less Marc knows about her role in the party, the better.

Marc pulls out his maps of the Middle East. He's always so organized.

"We'll take the ferry from Limassol to Tartus. It'll only take a day to travel from Tartus to Damascus."

"Are you sure? That will take us through the Sunni heartland. Some of the cities are already rebelling against Assad."

"It's still our best bet. There will be less surveillance at the port in Tartus, and fewer checkpoints from Tartus to Damascus. Besides, I know an Armenian merchant in Limassol. He can facilitate the trip for us."

Hoda pauses. It doesn't surprise her about the Armenian. Marc has connections everywhere. Besides, he's right about Tartus.

"Yes. Let's go to Tartus."

Rough weather delays the ferry's arrival. As they pass the island of Arwad, the last Crusader stronghold in the Middle East, Marc slips his hand behind Hoda's back, but she pushes it away.

"Not here."

"Why not?"

"Don't worry, we'll have time for that later. The people in this area are extremely conservative. We need to be careful."

Marc smiles. He looks forward to when they'll walk down the Champs d'Elysées, and stop and kiss for the whole world to see. He loves the Middle East, but the loss of personal freedom chafes him. Hoda takes out a white hijab, and buttons up her blouse. Soon they'll be travelling through areas loyal to the Ikhwan, where men and women are rigidly segregated. And these fanatics are becoming stronger and more daring in their efforts to impose their will on the population. He'll restrain himself, at least until they reach Damascus. Assad has many failings, but his Baathist regime guarantees that men and women can freely express their emotions at least in the Syrian capital.

The bump of the ferry against the dock shakes Marc. Within seconds, a tall immigration officer boards. The captain points the officer in the direction of Marc and Hoda. There's nothing friendly in the way he walks toward them. Sweat forms on Marc's brow and he feels Hoda tremble beside him.

"Documents please."

They hand the man their passports.

He whips out the immigration seal and stamps them before they can say another word. The man's face softens as he says: "Welcome to Tartus, and give my thanks to our Armenian friend."

Chapter

42

Mieh Mieh – July 1979

ABDULLAH WATCHES HIS MEN TRAIN. They've learned much from fighting the Israelis during Operation Litani. He feels confident leading them into battle again.

He picks up the letter from Cyprus. Hoda has decided to disobey Fouad Saadeh and go to Syria. She wants to contact Popular Front members there who still have influence with the Assad government. She and Marc must obtain Marwan's release, but first, they have to locate him. The Syrian prison system is a bewildering maze of institutions run by different groups within the government and military. Abdullah is unsure how to reply. His Popular Front movement is no longer in good standing with Assad. Any day now, the Syrian president might decide to throw all their leaders in Damascus into prison. There's no point in Hoda contacting them.

Hoda also suggests in the letter that their cousin, Mustapha, the Sa'iqa commander in the Yarmouk refugee camp, might be in a position to help. It's a long shot, but better than trying to enlist the beleaguered Popular Front leaders in Damascus. Abdullah has not seen Mustapha since they were boys, and more than once the Popular Front and Sa'iqa have found themselves on different sides of the barricades. Still, blood among Palestinians often runs stronger than any political ideology.

Abdullah calls in his second-in-command.

"Do we have any men from Yarmouk?"

"Yes. Why?"

"I want to send a message to my cousin, Mustapha."

"The Sa'iqa commander?"

"Yes."

"Why Sa'iqa? Remember what they did in Tel al-Zaatar."

"Trust me on this."

"Well, Ghassan Ajluni is from Yarmouk."

"Yes, Ghassan. He fought well against the Israelis. Bring him."

Abdullah folds Hoda's letter. He takes a pen and paper and begins to write a letter to Mustapha and another to her. He's careful to write in a cryptic style that won't reveal too much if intercepted. He feels a hard knot in his stomach. From Mieh Mieh, there's little he can do to protect his cousin. He hopes that Marc will keep her impulsive nature in check.

Hoda takes the key from the shopkeeper in Bab Sharqi. The room's perfect for them. It is hidden inside the courtyard of a magnificent Ottoman house. Marc carries their bags in from the taxi. Renting rooms to tourists is common in Bab Sharqi. And they're able to pass as young French honeymooners, raising no suspicions.

When Marc brings the bags into the room, he's taken back by just how beautiful it is. The armoires and chairs are in-laid with mother of pearl in the most exquisite patterns. The poplar panels of the ceiling are carved with Arabic calligraphy—a Kufic script that he has trouble deciphering. Later Hoda will explain that it is poetry, and she'll read it to him in the evenings ahead of them. The room's broad beams are at least a foot thick. *They must be centuries-old*, he thinks. Marc lies back on the bed. He knows that the coming days will mark his life. Damascus is an enchanting city. Despite the risks they're running, their time here will be magical.

"Hoda, let's go to the Umayyad Mosque this morning. I've never been there. It's only fifteen minutes away."

"We have more important things than tourism to do."

Marc is surprised by the curtness of her tone and feels a little chastised. Lately, Hoda's moods have been unpredictable.

"When will you see Evan?" she asks in a calmer voice.

"This afternoon. We'll meet at the Beit Jabri Restaurant in Qaymariya. Do you know where that is?"

"Yes, it's not far. About a twenty-minute walk. I hope that Evan has some answers when we meet him?"

"*We* don't meet him—I do. He asked me to come alone."

"Why?"

"He doesn't know if Marwan has told them anything yet, but he's afraid that they might already know about you."

Hoda stares at Marc. She knows what Evan has told him makes sense, but it still irritates her that she's being left out. Her desire to find out what Evan has learned about Marwan is burning inside her. Besides, Evan is a spy and she doesn't trust spies of any kind.

"Look, I'll come right back after seeing Evan. If he's learned anything, we can begin right away with speaking to our friends here."

Hoda nods her head, resigned that she'll have to wait a little longer. Slowly she unpacks their clothes, meticulously putting them away.

Marc takes out a map of the old city. He glances over at Hoda. Her figure has become more shapely, her breasts fuller. They haven't been intimate since learning of Marwan's disappearance.

"Come, *mon amour.* Show me on the map where the restaurant is."

Hoda slips beside him. He circles her waist with his arm and strokes her belly as she points to the location of the restaurant and indicates other major landmarks in the city. Suddenly, he pushes away the map and kisses her. She pulls back for a second to gaze into his eyes, then presses her body against his. She quivers as he lifts her onto the bed. The worries of the past days vanish.

Evan drums his fingers on the table. Marc is uncharacteristically late. He begins to worry that everything is unravelling and his friend, and perhaps soon he too will be in real danger. The Syrians are no fools. He's been careful to play perfectly his own role of the junior commercial attaché, pretending to be more interested in meeting Syrian importers of wheat and beef than politics. Hoda's presence in Damascus threatens to upset that. She's now a top operative for the Social Nationalists. His contact inside the party has told him as much and more. Evan realizes that he probably knows many things about Hoda that Marc does not, and it worries him.

The swaying of a waitress carrying a tray of appetizers distracts Evan for a moment. God, the women in this country are beautiful. His eyes begin to track her movements from table to table as he sips his third glass of Arak. His girlfriend, Raja, is refusing to visit him in Damascus, and his loins yearn for something new.

A hand lands on his shoulder. "You should stop staring!"

Evan whips his head around.

"You bastard! You scared me."

"Did you think that I was the morality police?"

"Not quite. Around here, the Muslim Brotherhood does that job instead, and right under Assad's nose."

Marc sits as Evan pours him a glass of Arak.

"No thanks."

"Drink, my fine French friend. You'll need it when I tell you what I've learned."

Marwan leans against the wall of his narrow cell. Only six by three feet, it is a coffin. Still, it's large enough to house a family of rats, which scurry up and down the walls. He can't see them, but he hears them all the time. He pulls his knees to his chin to avoid contact. Two of them are mating at the far end of the cell. He's grown accustomed to their routine. For a moment, he ponders disturbing their love-making, but no longer has the strength to do so. Besides as long as they leave him alone, why should he? He searches for a ray of light through the metal grate that serves as a ceiling. It's his only connection to the rest of the world.

He hasn't slept for days. He doesn't know how much more he can take. That morning, he overheard the guards talking about electrical cables. He's seen how these cables have reduced once proud men to quivering figures hiding in the shadows. Through the walls, he hears their moans, silent entreaties to their divinity to save them.

Marwan no longer knows night from day. It's always cold in the coffin. Occasionally, he hears the voice of another prisoner trying to speak to him through the wall, but he never replies. The Syrians are crude, but they're also cunning. To protect everyone he cares for, he knows that he must say nothing, even in his sleep. To still the pain from the beatings, he thinks of Hoda. He thinks of her all the time. She has become the only reason to stay alive. He regrets never telling her how he feels. But he knows he's deluding himself. There's no doubt that she deeply loves Marc, but if only … Sleep silences his regrets, the what-ifs that will never be. And time is running out.

Abdullah's instructions are clear. Ghassan is to find Mustapha 'Akkawi, the Sa'iqa commander. It's been nine years since Ghassan left his home in Yarmouk to join the Popular Front in Beirut, but the streets of the sprawling refugee camp are still familiar to him. He has to be careful to avoid meeting his relatives before delivering his commander's message to Mustapha. The Syrian intelligence services have turned many of Yarmouk's residents into informers, and he's sure that some of his family are among those reporting regularly to the Syrians.

Ghassan glances at the sketch map. He'll take a taxi to Al Kadam Railway Station, an old stop on the Damascus-Medina railway. From there, he can approach Yarmouk across the farmers' fields. From Salahaddin Ayoubi Street, the main thoroughfare on the west side of the camp, it's only a five-minute walk to Mustapha 'Akkawi's neighbourhood. Ghassan realizes that the commander's house will be surrounded by bodyguards, but as least, they will all be Palestinian. There he can identify himself as a messenger from the commander's cousin.

Ghassan feels a presence beside him. He realizes that he's been careless, looking too long at the map. Two heavily armed Sa'iqa fighters have boxed him in.

"Can we help you, brother?"

"Yes."

"And?"

Ghassan sees no point in obfuscating.

"I have been sent to see Mustapha 'Akkawi."

"Sent by whom?"

"His cousin in Beirut."

"Which cousin?"

"Abdullah."

The two fighters look at each other. Abdullah 'Akkawi's reputation as a courageous leader with little love for the Syrian regime is well known.

"Will you take me to Commander Mustapha?"

The young fighters shrug their shoulders. "Come. He'll be angry if you're not telling the truth though."

Abu George is a pragmatic man. His threat to use the iron chair is a bluff. When they strap Marwan to it and test the electrical cables, sparks fly into the air. Abu George studies the face of the Maronite. It betrays no sense of fear. He doesn't flinch, even when one of the guards bends down to push the cable under the open seat of the chair. Abu George wonders where such courage comes from, and calls off his overzealous guard.

"Fine, we'll get you the priest, but the price's now forty thousand."

It only takes one day for the priest to get the message to Fouad

Saadeh. The Orthodox Church's network in the Middle East is better than any postal system. Fouad doesn't hesitate to arrange the ransom. Getting it to Abu George will be another matter. Syrian banks never accept such large personal transfers. And the money changers in Beirut and Damascus are all under Syrian control. Nevertheless, he sends a message that the money will arrive within a week.

Fouad needs to contact Hoda. He knows that she's already in Damascus. He'll use a Canadian supporter to have his cousin make the money available from a supermarket in Chtaura, but he will still need someone to take it into Syria. There's one person in Damascus who would certainly know where Marc and Hoda are, and maybe he's also the one person who can bring money unchecked through the border. He calls in his son.

"Do you remember the Australian who was always with Marc Taragon?"

"Yes, the one who loves to ogle the girls, and speaks Arabic like a Syrian."

"Do you know where he is?"

"He's now at the Australian embassy in Damascus."

"That's what I thought. His name was Evan, wasn't it?"

"Yes, Evan O'Shea."

"Do you know how we can contact him discreetly?"

"We can ask his girlfriend in Shemlan. She's a party member and keeps tabs on him for us."

Fouad smiles at the irony of how easy it is to spy on spies.

Chapter

43

Beirut – July 2007

IF MINH CHAU WAS WORRIED about Marie in Gaza, she's determined not to show it. She looks around the bar in the Saint George Hotel. She craves a drink, but she's sworn off alcohol during her pregnancy. She looks down at the photos. There's in the woman in the photo a striking resemblance to Marie, but nothing of the man in her. She turns to the book flap with Taragon's photo. Again she sees not the slightest resemblance. She wonders if Marie is on a wild goose chase. Will the meeting with Selima 'Akkawi clear things up? She hopes so. She's sensed Marie's fighting an attraction to Taragon. Would she act on it if Taragon had nothing to do with the woman in the photo?

Minh Chau is far too lost in her speculation to notice Selima hurrying down the hall toward her.

"Ms. Nguyen? I'm sorry I'm late."

"*Bonjour* Madame 'Akkawi. I was just enjoying the atmosphere. It's a beautiful hotel. Please sit. Can I order you something?"

"No. Thank you. I'm fine."

"You said that you had something important to share with me."

"I do."

"And I have something to show you."

"Please."

Minh Chau puts the faded photo on the table. The gasp from Selima is audible. She gingerly picks up the photo. There's no doubt—it's the one Abdullah took thirty years ago. Carefully, she lifts it closer to examine the fine lines of her sister-in-law's face.

"Please. Please tell me. Where did you get this?"

"It's from Marie."

"From Marie? How?"

"Yes, this photo was with her when she was adopted."

"Where?"

"Beirut."

Selima feels her heart contract. There's no need to visit orphanages to rummage through dusty files. The proof is here. She catches her breath, straightens her shoulders and looks across the table at Minh Chau.

"The woman's name is Hoda 'Akkawi. She was my sister-in-law."

"Could she be Marie's mother?"

"Yes, but when Hoda disappeared, she didn't have a child. How old is Marie?"

"Twenty-seven."

Selima does the math in her head. Something is wrong.

"When was she found in Beirut?"

"September 19, 1982."

The date jolts Selima. The day after the massacre. It's the bitter confirmation that she had sought, but no less painful to hear.

"How did Hoda die?" Minh Chau asks.

Suddenly, Selima feels paralyzed. She wants to answer Minh Chau's question, but no words come out. Tears gather in her eyes. Her chest again feels like it's collapsing. Minh Chau reaches quickly over to catch her before she slips out of the chair.

Selima wakes to the cool napkin on her forehead. Soothing words. A gentle pat on her cheeks. A waiter helps her into a chair. A small crowd has gathered around them, but Minh Chau asks them to leave.

It's the first time that Selima has fully accepted that Hoda is gone. For thirty years, she's harboured the hope that one day Hoda would walk back into her life. Elie has shown her evidence suggesting Hoda's death, but somehow it's too clinical, too unreal to be true. She thinks of Marie—her fresh, beautiful face so much like Hoda's. Through the narrow channel of her grief, Selima sees a ray of hope emerge. Hoda has left in this world something of herself.

"Here. Drink some water," Minh Chau says.

Selima sips from the glass. The water is cool and laced with mint. The vaulted arches of the hotel come back into focus. The spotless marble floor. The cherrywood furniture. The touches of elegance soothe her.

"I'm sorry," Selima says.

"Relax. Take your time. Drink some more water."

Selima swallows the cool liquid and then places on the table the blurry picture of Hoda and the infant in Bsarma, the one that Elie said one of his own men had taken while spying on the village.

"This is the last picture of Hoda we have. I only saw it myself for the first time this morning. I don't know for sure who the child is, but I now believe that it's probably your friend."

"And the man in Marie's photo?"

"That's Marc Taragon?"

"He must be the father then?"

"I don't know. They were together only until 1979. And there was talk that Hoda left him for another man."

"Another man?"

"Hoda vanished in Damascus. It was rumoured that she left Marc for a man, who'd been her friend for many years."

"And the man was?"

"My cousin, Marwan."

"I don't understand. Are you saying that Marc Taragon and Marie's mother were together, but he isn't her father?"

"I can't say for sure. Maybe the rumours were false. Maybe Marie is simply older than she thinks she is. I was living in France when Hoda disappeared. It was such a long time ago."

"Please tell me what else you know."

"I will. Please, may I have a moment?"

Chapter

44

Kibbutz Zikim – August 2007

TARAGON LOOKS AROUND the spartan room. He finds it hard to believe how easily he's been smuggled into Israel from Gaza. The rendezvous point was only two kilometres from the kibbutz, just south of the Shikma reservoir. Taragon had emerged from the tunnel in the middle of the night and crawled his way through the sand dunes to the edge of the dirt road. There he waited.

It wasn't an operation without risk. The Israelis had lined much of the border with landmines, but the human smugglers in Ash-Shiafa had worked as agricultural labourers in Kibbutz Zikim before the border was closed. The Kibbutzniks had shown them the mined areas to avoid. At six o'clock sharp, an old woman drove a small tractor along the road. As planned, Marc darted out of the dunes and jumped into the trailer behind it.

Before leaving Ash-Shiafa, one of the Gazans had pressed a ripe mango into Taragon's hand. "Give this to Aunt Sadie," he had said.

Taragon reaches out for the mango now sitting on the table. A knock on the door. The old woman enters. He offers the fruit to her.

"Jamil asked me to give this to you."

"Thank you. I miss him. He was a good worker. A good person."

"Thank you for bringing me here. You took a big risk."

"Not really. The border guards are mostly Bedouin. I've known them for a long time."

Taragon looks into the woman's face. He sees the resemblance to his friend. "You're Jonathan's aunt from Kiryat Tiv'on."

"Yes."

The old woman steps forward and offers her hand.

"Sadie Kalman."

The hand is fragile, somewhat cold. There's a slight tremble. He notices a large lump on her neck. He remembers what Bronstein had said. Stage four. Incurable. He wonders how much longer she has.

"Why are you helping us? Is it just for Jonathan?"

"I want peace. Too much blood has been shed. And for what? So that the hard-liners can make us complicit in oppressing the Palestinians!"

The old woman begins to pace the room. His question has clearly upset her. She turns around and looks straight into him.

"You asked me if I'm doing this for Jonathan. Yes, in part I am, but I'm also doing this for Israel. I came to this country as a young girl with my older sister, Jonathan's mother. My parents were sent to the camps. My sister had to sleep with a Hungarian officer to get us on the train out of Budapest. She sacrificed herself to save me. Family was everything to her. Jonathan is now my only family and Israel is my only country. I will help Jonathan and you because I believe what you're doing could save this country from self-destruction."

"Do you understand the risks in what we're doing?"

"Of course, I do. Do you think that I'm a senile old woman? Do you think I'm afraid? I believe in Israel as a place for the Jews, but I believe that the Palestinians should have equal rights in this country, and those in Gaza and the West Bank should have their own state."

Taragon feels the old woman's passion. She must now be in her eighties but is still driven by the strength of her beliefs in equality and fairness. Could there be enough like her in Israel to give real momentum to Arkassa? He remembers the news footage of the demonstration in Tel Aviv after Sabra and Shatila. Four hundred thousand Israelis demonstrated against the massacre and called the Israeli government to account. Could Arkassa bring along these people? He turns again to her.

"When is Jonathan coming?"

"In two or three days. First, he has a meeting in Jerusalem, and he has to be sure he isn't being followed. It's best that you stay here until he arrives. Others are coming from *Yesh Gvul* and Peace Now. The chairwoman of our kibbutz's council is on board, but there are others here who don't share our beliefs. Just be patient. Don't go outside. I don't want to explain why you're here to anyone."

Chapter

45

Damascus – July 1979

A T FIRST, THE FIVE ONLY share pleasantries and watch the other café patrons. When nothing appears amiss, they begin. They share what they know. Marwan is in the political prisoner section of Sednaya, and a senior prison official is willing to release him for twice the standard bribe. The official will expect the money to be delivered by a priest from Sednaya. Evan offers to bring the money in from Lebanon in a diplomatic pouch. Hoda and Ghassan can then take the money to the priest and accompany him to the prison. Mustapha 'Akkawi is leading a convoy of fresh Sa'iqa troops into Lebanon that evening and can hide Marwan among them. The border is still a risk. Syria is awash with competing intelligence services, all of whom have agents there. Mustapha will try to co-opt Syrian General Intelligence and Marc will speak to his contacts at the foreign ministry to reduce the risk at the border.

"So, that's it. We all know what we have to do," Marc says.

"Right," Evan says. "I should be off now if I'm to bring in the money from Lebanon later this afternoon."

"We're leaving too," Mustapha says, taking Ghassan in tow. "We're meeting with our contacts in Syrian General Intelligence in less than an hour."

"Are you sure they won't sell us out?" Hoda asks.

"Don't worry. They owe us too many favours and will still need us for a very long time."

Hoda briefly speculates about the types of favours that Mustapha and his men have done for the Syrian intelligence services, but says nothing.

As the others leave, Marc looks across the table at her. Neither speaks for a long time. Finally, he says: "I don't like the idea of you returning to Lebanon without me. We don't know if Marwan talked. You could be compromised."

"Marc, I'll be fine. It's more important that you ensure that the Syrian foreign ministry is onside in case we have problems at the border."

"I don't know. Maybe I should stay with you?"

"Don't worry. I'll see you in Beirut in just a few days."

The words give him little comfort. Hoda hasn't been the same for the last few days, often waking up in the night to vomit. He asked her about it, but she was evasive. Finally, he asked their landlord if he could arrange a doctor's appointment for her. He did so with his personal doctor, a man known for his discretion, especially if you paid him in hard currency.

"Aren't you getting back the results of your medical tests today?"

"Yes."

"Let me know if there is anything. I can arrange for the French embassy's doctor to see you in Beirut once we are back."

"Marc, you worry too much. Let's stay focussed on Marwan."

Hoda sips her coffee. The nausea is coming back. She's fairly certain that the tests will confirm what she already suspects, and then it'll be time to tell him. A sense of joy overcomes her. She leans over and kisses him on the cheek and says: "It's time for you to go. Your meeting at the foreign ministry is in twenty minutes."

Marc rises from the table, uncertain whether he should leave Hoda alone. But she's right that getting the Syrian foreign ministry to cooperate is important. He looks back at her toying with a piece of pita bread. He thinks of the incredible nights that they've spent in Damascus. Their frenzied love-making has reached a crescendo that surpassed his imagination and brought him to the point of physical exhaustion. Waiting for their plan to free Marwan to come together, they've spent their days wandering in the Al-Hamadiyeh Souk. Five hundred metres from east to west, the bazaar's arched ceiling of iron beams and corrugated metal covers hundreds of shops filled with embroidered cloth, spices, sweets, carved rosewood chessboards and in-laid mosaic boxes. Their favourite place is the Bakdash ice cream shop. They visit it every day to taste *booza*, the exquisite Syrian ice cream served with crushed pistachios, and covered with honey for those with the sweetest of teeth. Ironically, here in this city so tightly under the grip of Hafez Assad, they've felt freer than ever before.

"Marc, you should really go."

"Ah yes."

He looks at her, sitting at the table and leans down to kiss her again. She pats his cheek. "Go."

Hoda watches her love disappear in the crowded winding street and takes a small box of jewellery out her handbag. Inside the box is her wedding gift to Selima, an Ottoman necklace adorned with red carnelian beads. She writes a note to Selima to wish her all the happiness in the world and to tell her that she'll soon share happy news of her own.

The priest didn't expect that the bribe would be delivered by a woman. This unnerves him. Men know the ways of the world, and even a priest has to play that game, but women are a gentler lot. He takes the time to show her his modest church in Sednaya and explains that he's only transferring the money as a favour to a parishioner.

Hoda lets him play his game a little before telling him that a car is waiting outside to take them to the prison, seven kilometres away. At first, the priest is reluctant to be driven to the prison by a stranger. He wants to take his own car and meet her there. She insists that they go together. It's safer that way. Ten thousand dollars is a lot of money. Reluctantly, he walks with her to the car. Her things are in the trunk, ready for the onward trip to Beirut. Ghassan is sitting beside the Damascene taxi driver whom Mustapha recruited.

Ghassan jumps out to open the doors. Hoda scans the street. No sign of surveillance. But then, why should there be? The Christians in Sednaya are strong supporters of the regime, seeing it as a bulwark against Muslim fanatics. There's little need for Assad's men to watch the goings-on in their neighbourhoods.

The taxi descends the steep winding side streets, joining the town's thoroughfare near the main square. From there they can see the Cherubim Monastery perched high above the city. As they leave the town, Damascus's fertile plains open up before them. Beyond are Lebanon's mountains and freedom. When the road bends a few kilometres later, the sinister concrete monster that is Sednaya Prison looms.

"Don't worry about the men at the checkpoints," the priest says. "They're local boys. Most are Christians, and I'm sure that I've baptized quite a few of them."

The priest is right. At the first checkpoint, the soldiers simply wave the car through. At the next two checkpoints, the soldiers politely ask them about their business. When the priest mentions Abu George's name, they nod and wave the car through. At the prison's gate, the guards are more cautious. These men carry no crosses around their necks. "Alawites," the priest whispers. The guards train their guns on the driver and ask the priest and Hoda to step out.

"We're here to see Abu George," the priest says.

"Who's the woman?" the guard asks.

"She's here to accompany one of the prisoners back to Lebanon."

Five large army trucks with the Sa'iqa insignia pull up. Mustapha steps down from the cab.

"Is everything in order?" Mustapha asks Hoda.

"Yes, the good Father was just explaining why we're here."

Mustapha looks at the priest with disdain.

He turns to the guard. "Do you know who I am?"

"Yes, *Effendi.*"

"Good. Take us to Abu George."

The guard returns to his hut and picks up the phone. It's clear that he's soon on the receiving end of an animated conversation. Several nods of the head later, he returns.

"The priest goes in alone."

Abu George glares out the window at the entrance of the prison. His ears are still burning from the news that the dreaded Sa'iqa commander, Mustapha 'Akkawi, is here for his prisoner. Who the fuck is this man? He clenches his fist and curses again. Perhaps, he had asked too little for his release. Perhaps, he shouldn't be releasing him at all. He watches the priest walk across the prison courtyard. He hears a knock on the door.

"Yes."

The prison warden walks in.

"Abu George, why are there Sa'iqa fighters outside the prison?"

Fuck, he thinks. How is he going to explain this away?

"Is it the Lebanese prisoner?"

Abu George hesitates. He looks the warden in the eye.

"Yes, it's the Lebanese."

"You told me that he was a nobody. A catch-and-release case."

"That's what I thought."

"Get rid of him and the Palestinians. And make it quick!"

The priest appears at the door.

"Father, it is good to see you," the warden says.

"Yes, it's good to see you too. Am I disturbing you?"

"No, I was just leaving."

The warden glares back at Abu George before closing the door.

The priest takes a chair and hands Abu George a thick envelope. Ten thousand dollars—twice what he had asked! This Lebanese must mean a lot to someone. He'll find out who later. Now, he just wants to be rid of him. He hands two thousand dollars back to the priest. "This should cover the re-tiling of the church's roof."

"Thank you, my son. You're most generous."

Abu George calls in his secretary. "Please bring me the prisoner."

"He's in the interrogation room. They're not finished with him yet."

"What?! I told them to leave him alone."

"Yes, Director, but the warden ordered another interrogation."

That distrustful bastard, thinks Abu George. He couldn't leave well enough alone.

"Bring the prisoner now. I don't care if they're finished or not. Tell them that the warden has personally ordered the man's release."

Five minutes later, a bloody heap of a man is frog-marched into the office. Abu George can hardly recognize him. His eyes are just thin slits in swollen balls covered in blood. His right leg is twisted horribly out of shape. His left hand has only two fingernails left on it.

"Tell me what you told them," Abu George says.

At first, he can't understand the prisoner's response. Just a gargle of strange noises. Finally, he hears it. "*Wala shee*—nothing." Abu George looks at his adjutant, who nods.

Abu George notices the unease of the priest still in his office. "I'm sorry, Father. I had nothing to do with this."

Abu George rises and goes to the window again. Mustapha 'Akkawi, now with dozens of his men around him, is pacing outside. Enough! He'll escort the man out himself and speak to 'Akkawi.

"Bring the prisoner water. And tea. And towels and bandages," he orders his adjutant. The priest is already wiping much of the blood off Marwan's face and uttering a prayer for his recovery.

Mustapha 'Akkawi can barely hold back his anger when he sees the bloodied figure of Marwan being held up by the priest and Abu George.

Behind the three are several armed guards. Mustapha knows that if he gives the order, his men will be more than a match for them, but what would that serve? No matter, he'll soon have Marwan and Hoda safely back in Lebanon.

Before the three reach Mustapha, Hoda darts out and grabs Marwan, dragging him into the protective circle of Mustapha's men. The priest approaches Mustapha and whispers.

"This is not Abu George's doing! The warden ordered it."

Mustapha marches forward to Abu George, towering over him.

"Is that true?"

"Yes."

"Fine. Tell your warden that we will meet one day."

The threat is clear. Abu George shudders at the anger in the Palestinian commander's voice. He doesn't need this. "No, wait!" He walks to Mustapha and gives him the envelope of cash. "Take it! I don't want it." The priest also steps forward, "Yes, this too."

Mustapha takes the two envelopes and gives them to Hoda.

He turns to Abu George, and says: "Promise that we'll have no trouble between here and the border, or I'll return to Sednaya with all my men."

"Promised."

Mustapha turns. Hoda is easing Marwan into the back of the taxi.

"No, put him in the truck with the other men. It's safer that way. Cousin Hoda, you and Ghassan will follow in the car. *Yallah*—let's go!"

Chapter

46

Road to Damascus – July 1979

MAHMOUD HOMSI'S MEN are still bleary-eyed from the overnight journey from Idlib. They met with their local contact only three hours earlier. The contact, a young boy, gave them the instructions from the leadership in Aleppo to kidnap Christians on the road from Sednaya to Damascus. The boy is only thirteen and is full of rage. That very morning, he learned that the police had returned his father's corpse from Sednaya Prison. The boy insisted on going with them. Mahmoud reluctantly agreed—he needed someone who knew the terrain. Now he worries about the boy's anger. When the boy asks for a gun, he pulls his cousin, Muawiya, aside and whispers: "Give him the old hunting rifle, but no bullets, and keep a close eye on him!"

Mahmoud regrets having joined the Ikhwan, the armed wing of Syria's Muslim Brotherhood. He isn't a religious man, but his whole village had turned to the Brotherhood for support when their crops failed. For all the socialism that the Baathists preached, their government did nothing to help the impoverished villagers. Instead, the Alawite officers continued to conscript the young men into the army to serve in Lebanon, leaving their families to scavenge for food. Mahmoud had been one of those conscripts.

Without the Brotherhood's generosity, many villagers would have starved. When Mahmoud returned to the village to ask for his cousin's hand in marriage, her father refused, saying: "You're unworthy. You've served in the Alawite Army. Prove yourself first that you're a true Muslim." So Mahmoud formed a small band of other former conscripts, all being similarly blackmailed by the village elders and reported to the

Ikhwan commander in Aleppo. Mahmoud had hoped his group would be assigned light duties, perhaps some simple surveillance of Syrian army movements. Instead, the commander dispatched the new recruits to the regime's heartland in the South.

The local boy waves his hand. Something is coming down the road. The plan is simple. They will stop the car. If there are Christians inside, they'll take the richest one hostage. His ransom will finance their next operations and provide funds for the men's weddings. If the passengers are Alawites, they'll kill them. Mahmoud doesn't like the thought of killing anyone, but he has his orders.

Mahmoud gives the order to move forward. The local boy is already on the road with his old rifle pointed at the bend where the vehicles will first come into view.

It's a military truck, the Sa'iqa thunderbolt painted on its hood. Shit, thinks Mahmoud. He tries to wave his men back, but it's too late—the boy is frantically clicking the trigger of his empty gun, and is about to be hit by the truck. Muawiya steps forward to push the boy to safety, turns and fires a round into the cab of the truck. The windshield shatters, and the driver slumps forward as the truck swerves off the road. All of Mahmoud's men start firing their weapons. Two Palestinians stagger out of the back, only to be cut down by the barrage of bullets. Suddenly, a taxi appears around the bend in the road. Mahmoud can see three men and a woman in it. Civilians, he thinks. The car distracts his men long enough for two more Palestinians to scramble out of the truck, their guns blazing. The local boy is the first to be hit. Then Muawiya takes a bullet to the shoulder. Palestinians stream out of the truck firing away in all directions. Most are cut down by the guns of the Idlib fighters. Shots come from the direction of the taxi. A lone gunman has taken position behind the passenger door. He has a clear view of all of Mahmoud's men. One after another, he guns them down.

Soon other trucks of Palestinian fighters pull up. Mahmoud curses. All his men are now dead or wounded, and he hasn't fired a single shot. At least, none of the Palestinians have noticed him, hidden in the rocks halfway up the hill. He knows that he doesn't have much time to make his escape. As the Palestinians finish off the wounded attackers, Mahmoud vanishes into a thick stand of mountain pines. His men will have their reward in heaven, and he will spin a fine tale of his own heroism to his uncle and the village elders. He'll praise the courage of their dead sons and have his bride.

Perhaps, the guilt of his cowardice forces him to take one last look back at the carnage before he reaches the top. The woman from the car is tending to the wounded. A man with a bandaged face squats beside her and does what he can to help. Even in that horrendous scene of death, he can see that the woman is graceful, elegant, more beautiful than his cousin. He lingers for a moment, then scrambles to the top to speed away on his motorbike. Allah is merciful. This war is now over for him.

Chapter

47

TARAGON'S MEETING with the chairwoman of the kibbutz goes well. He feels that he has her trust. Sadie walks beside him back to the house, passing the avocado and mango trees at the edge of the fields. The combined fragrance of musk and tanginess fills the night air. He wonders what life is like here. Separated from the world. Hard work for little reward. The putting of the community before oneself.

Sadie picks a few ripe mangoes from the trees. There's a nobility in the way she moves—a serenity in her demeanour that calms him.

"The fruit looks delicious," Marc says.

"Delicious, yes, but they don't have the special taste of those in Ash-Shiafa. We tried to grow the Gazan mangoes here, but without any success. It's only four kilometres away, but the soil is different there. I'd like to go there one day to test it, to learn what makes their mangoes so special."

"I didn't realize that there was a difference."

"We'll share Jamil's mango when we get home. You'll see what I mean. It's ironic. No matter, how much we try to reach out to each other, we're different—the Palestinians and us—just like our mangoes. Can Arkassa change that?"

"Would you like that? I mean, breaking down the barriers between Israelis and Arabs."

"Of course. I have always liked Arabs. At my hardware store in Kiryat Tiv'on, they'd make my day when they came in. And they were wonderful to Jonathan when he was a boy. They helped make him the man he is today."

"He speaks fondly of you, you know."

Sadie smiles. She likes her nephew's friend.

"So, tell me about your colleague, Marie."

He's surprised by the question. Obviously, Bronstein has shared something with his aunt. Perhaps, a suspicion of feelings that are growing stronger inside him.

"Actually, I don't know too much about her. She normally works for a major Montreal newspaper, but she's now on a leave of absence to work with me."

"Is she pretty?"

Taragon looks at Sadie. She has a mischievous smile.

"She's a beautiful young woman."

"*Tov.*"

Sadie's white adobe house comes into view, illuminated by the security lights on the kibbutz's watchtowers. They enter the dwelling, Sadie bids Taragon good night and goes into her room. He decides to sit on the porch for a while. Sadie's house is at the edge of the kibbutz. The sand dunes, which stretch to the Mediterranean, are only a stone's throw away. His mind drifts to Marie. On the boat to Cyprus and the few days in Gaza, he felt something. He shakes his head. What foolishness. Marie is very young, and she's his colleague. He leans over and picks up a stone to toss into the dunes. It disappears in the sand as the smell of freshly cut mango caresses his nostrils. He looks up at Sadie's outstretched hand. She sits at his side, and they bite into the sweetness of the Ash-Shiafa fruit, and dream of what could be.

Minh Chau fiddles with her cell phone as she waits for her flight to Paris. She doesn't know what she'll say to Marie. What she learned from Selima won't bring closure. Marie deserves certainty about who her father is. Is it Marc Taragon? Marwan Kanaan? At least the evidence seems to point conclusively toward Hoda being Marie's mother. She looks at her watch. Marie's flight will have already arrived in Amman. But is the telephone really the way to give Marie the news? Minh Chau texts Marie instead: *Hi Marie, spoke to Selima. Still unclear. Coming to Amman. Luv MC.*

Bronstein looks at the empty meeting room in Jerusalem. He's twenty minutes early. The secretary was kind enough to open the door for him. He looks at his notes again. He knows most of the players who'll be there. All Mapai old-timers—the deans of the left-wing elite. Some had cut their teeth under Ben Gurion's leadership. Most lost a lot of influence though when the Labour Party drifted to the right. One, now ninety-five, had even negotiated the inclusion of Arabs in Israel's first government. These old men are the true Zionists, so unlike the self-serving demagogues now running the country.

Doubt battles hope in his mind. Can he really pull this off? Can he re-kindle the dream of Jews and Arabs living side by side in peace? He knows that the leaders of the Israeli Left need a sign from the Palestinians, especially from Hamas and Popular Front supporters. They need to hear directly from the Palestinians that they're ready to put Arkassa on the negotiating table. He hopes that Taragon can deliver this before the settlers, the psychopaths and rogues in the intelligence community join forces to bury Arkassa once and for all.

Chapter

48

Tiberias – September 2007

TARAGON LOOKS ACROSS the Sea of Galilee. There's an absolute calm to it as if to invite the sceptics to walk upon its waters. The trip from Kibbutz Zikim was uneventful. Inside Israel, no one questions him. Why would they? He glances in the mirror. He looks as Israeli as any of them, and through years of personal study, he's learned enough Hebrew to pass as a new immigrant.

Bronstein and the old Mapai leaders had agreed in Jerusalem on Tiberias for its proximity to progressive Arab villages and kibbutzim in the eastern Galilee. Far from Tel Aviv and Jerusalem, the people of the Galilee have minds of their own when it comes to the issue of co-existence.

He watches the delegates arrive at the Scots Hotel. What better place to promote the Arkassa initiative. Built originally as a hospital by missionaries to serve equally patients of all religions, the building was converted by the Church of Scotland into a luxury hotel in an effort to maintain the church's foothold in the Galilee. The church's Middle East Secretary, a strong defender of Palestinian rights, insisted that the first Arkassa support conference be held at the hotel.

"Mr. Taragon, your friends would like you to join them," the young Glaswegian receptionist says.

"Yes, I will be there shortly."

Taragon looks around. No sign of surveillance. How is that possible? In Barcelona, the opponents of the initiative committed murder to sabotage Arkassa, and now not a sign of them? From the corner of his eye, he sees Bronstein walking toward him. He has a cell phone in his hand.

"Marc, someone wants to talk to you."

He hands him the phone.

"Marc, it's Selima."

"Selima, how are you?"

"I'm fine."

"How did you get this number?"

"From Leyna."

"What is it, Selima?"

"We found out what happened."

"What happened?"

"What happened to her."

"Selima, you're speaking in riddles. What happened to whom?"

The line goes silent for a moment. Then a hushed name, too faint to be understood. A sob, and another. It's the language of absolute grief that finally makes him understand.

"Selima, what did you learn about Hoda?"

"It's what we always expected. She returned to Sabra."

"Did she die there?"

"Her papers were found in a mass grave."

"*Merci*, Selima. We'll talk again. I have to go."

He hears her say something as he hands the phone back to Bronstein, but doesn't catch it.

"I need a few minutes, Jonathan."

"Of course. Come when you are ready."

Taragon wanders into the hotel's garden. His chest tightens. He leans against a stone pillar. It has been many years since he last punished himself with nightmares about Hoda's fate. For months, he searched for her. He never believed the rumour that she'd abandoned him for Marwan. He never stopped loving her, but time stills the mind—no question is eternal. A sawfar iris stands out in the hotel's garden. He picks the mountain flower and puts it into his pocket.

Ari Epstein goes through the reports. Taragon again. His fucking peace proposal is gaining momentum, and now even inside Israel. He could have had the bastard arrested for illegally entering the country, but his superiors ordered him not to. And that traitor Bronstein, he deserves a bullet in the head. Ari is tempted to reach out to his settler contacts in Ma'ale Adumim. They would do the job, but they're reckless, convinced that no Israeli court would ever convict them of any crime. And maybe they're right, but he couldn't risk being implicated because of their arrogance. His bosses are no fools. Ever since the David fiasco in Barcelona, they're watching his every step.

Ari still can't believe that Shehadi screwed it up in Gaza. There's no point getting in touch with him again. Mossad's top brass would never tolerate a hit by Palestinian underlings inside Israel. And besides, Shehadi is getting greedier.

Ari decides to play his last card. He dials the one individual he can trust, the one man with no ties to Israelis or Palestinians. No sum of money can buy this man, but Ari has something more valuable to the man—something that he's kept secret for twenty-five years.

If Marie is jet-lagged from her flight yesterday from Montreal to Amman, she isn't showing it. Nor is the now rotund Minh Chau who's exiting the baggage room. The two women rush to embrace in the middle of the concourse.

"So tell me everything!" Marie says.

"The woman in the photo is Hoda 'Akkawi, Abdullah's cousin."

"And the man?"

"It's definitely Marc Taragon, and Selima even remembers when the photo was taken and who took it."

Minh Chau pauses before continuing.

"Hoda and Marc were together for several years."

Marie hunches her shoulders and looks away.

"So he's my father then?"

"Not necessarily."

"What?"

"Hoda disappeared during the civil war and was said to have left Marc for another man. And that seems to have taken place before you could've been conceived."

"What happened to her?"

"There's a rumour that she returned to Beirut several years after disappearing in Syria, and died shortly after."

Minh Chau avoids mentioning the massacre in Sabra. She doesn't want her friend to relive in her mind how gruesome a death her mother may have suffered. That can be dealt with later.

"What else did you learn?"

"There's a photo of Hoda with a very young child. It's unclear whether it's a boy or a girl. It was taken in a Christian village in northern Lebanon. What she was doing there is a mystery."

"Could it have been me in the photo?"

"Maybe. Selima has begun visiting the orphanages in Beirut to look for documentation that could clear up things. In any case, she sees Hoda in you. She's adamant that you must be Hoda's daughter."

"And my father? Who does she think is my father?"

Minh pauses again. This time, it grates on Marie's nerves.

"Well?"

"The man who Hoda is rumoured to have left with. His name was Marwan Kanaan."

"Was?"

"He disappeared with Hoda during the war and was never heard of again. Selima believes that both died about the same time."

"Who was he?"

"Selima's cousin."

"Is that it?"

"Yes, for now."

What Minh Chau has shared throws Marie for a loop. The woman in the photo now has a name, a history, and is almost certainly her mother. Moreover, she and Taragon were once a couple. But that's where the path ends. The math doesn't add up. Hoda's separation from Taragon seems too soon for him to be her father. But that's only if she isn't older than she thinks. And now, there's another man, Marwan Kanaan, who could be her real father, a man she knows almost nothing about.

Minh Chau looks at her friend. She places her hand on Marie's shoulder and says firmly: "You know you could resolve this once and for all by asking for a DNA test."

"I can't do that. I haven't even shown Marc the photo."

"Show it to him then! You've had lots of opportunities to do so. Show it to him tonight and get it over with!"

Marie resents Minh Chau's directness. It isn't her friend's life that'll change once the truth is out. No, she won't be rushed. She needs time to think out how she'll approach Taragon. There is just too much and yet too little information now. She needs to get her mind around all of this.

Their driver walks up and takes their bags.

"Ladies, it's time to leave for the Allenby Bridge if you want to get to

Tiberias today."

"Will we make it in time for the conference?" Minh Chau asks.

"Yes, my cousin will take you from the other side of the border to Tiberius. You'll arrive just before the conference starts."

Marie knows that, by the time they arrive, many of the delegates will have made up their minds for or against Arkassa. There's nothing she can do about that, but what she can and will do is broadcast the message to the world that Arkassa isn't dead, that there are Arabs and Israelis determined to give it a chance. Her editors are pressing her to get the story before the other media outlets, and she's also determined to give the conference as much exposure as humanly possible. And then, she'll ask Marc about the photo, about her mother, and everything will be solved. Just a few more hours.

Chapter

49

Bsarma, Northern Lebanon – October 1979

H ODA LOOKS AROUND at the stone walls of the old house. She's still stunned how badly things went wrong three months earlier.

As soon as Marwan's wounds had healed, the local Maronite militia, the Marada, pressed him into service. At least, the militia pay is keeping them from starving. The local fighters are loyal to former Lebanese president Suleiman Franjieh, now embroiled in a full-scale war with the Phalangists. The year before, a Phalangist force attacked the Franjieh stronghold in nearby Ehden. They brutally murdered the president's son and his family. It's now Maronite against Maronite in a struggle that cuts off Bsarma and many of the neighbouring villages from all contact with Beirut and most of the outside world.

Nowhere's safe—certainly not the nearby city of Tripoli now under the control of Sunni militias opposed to any Christian faction, and at war with the Syrians. Still, Hoda finds it hard to believe Marc hasn't found them. She'd left a letter with Ghassan to tell Marc that, after the attack on the road and Mustapha 'Akkawi's death, they had to change plans and decided to cross the border at Arida on the road from Tartus to Tripoli. Their new rendez-vous would be in the Koura not in Chtaura. She also wrote of her condition.

Isolated in Bsarma, she and Marwan agree to resume the charade of man and wife until Marc can reach them and take Hoda out of Lebanon. Marwan knows only a few people in the village, but some, like their neighbour Um Amin, fondly remember Marwan as the young boy who would visit his grandfather on school vacations. The villagers take their "marriage" at face value. Soon they're also congratulating Hoda on her obvious pregnancy. None asks why she and Marwan never attend Sunday mass. After all, the couple are "city folk."

"Things are getting worse," Marwan says as he shakes the rain off his khaki jacket and puts his rifle against the inside of the door. "These Marada fighters are just gangsters. They won't last long."

"Is there any way to get out of here?"

"Only through the Syrian-controlled Alawite parts of Tripoli."

"No, we can't trust the Alawites. Is there at least a way to get word to Beirut, to Marc?"

"The Phalangists have cut all the telephone lines in the valley. They're preparing for a major push."

"What about the Palestinians in Nahr al-Kalb? They could help us."

"No, the camp has fallen under the firm control of Muslim extremists. They would kill both of us. Me for being a Maronite and you for carrying a foreigner's child. For them, we are the worst kind of *kuffar*."

"*Kuffar*—infidels," Hoda mutters the word under her breath. Is that how she'll be seen?—a woman who has abandoned Islam and is now carrying the child of her non-Muslim lover.

Hoda feels her belly. She's six months pregnant. She wants desperately to escape this place. Damn Marc, why hasn't he found them yet? He has connections everywhere. He could certainly have found a way across the lines. Perhaps, he doesn't want to. They never talked about having a family. Would he betray her when she needs him most?

Marwan sits beside her.

"Don't worry. Maybe, I exaggerated. We'll stay here. Bsarma is just a small village. Perhaps, we will be left in peace."

Hoda begins to cry on his shoulder.

"Marwan, I'm so afraid for the baby."

"Don't! I'm here with you."

Travel within Lebanon has become almost impossible. In the north, the Phalangists are pressing the Marada militia hard for control of more territory. In Beirut and its southern suburbs, the Shiite Amal Movement have come to blows with the Syrian Army. Elsewhere the usual sectarian violence and petty gangsterism are running rampant. The respect for journalists at the beginning of the war has long since faded, and Marc's name tops the kidnapping lists of several militias he has lambasted in his articles.

The quiet refugee camp of Mieh Mieh comes into view. There Abdullah 'Akkawi will be able to help him find Hoda.

Fighters from the checkpoint outside the camp jump into the taxi for the last stretch to Abdullah's house. Although two of them know Marc, no one approaches their commander's house unaccompanied.

The gigantic fighter appears at the door to his quarters. Marc jumps out of the taxi and marches up to him.

"Do you know where Hoda is?"

"Come inside. I've prepared tea."

Marc follows the tall man's orders. Abdullah eases himself to the cushions on the floor, the wounds from last year's invasion are still not completely healed. Marc sits beside his friend.

"What do you know, Abdullah?"

"About Hoda?"

"Yes."

"Things went awry after Mustapha was killed outside of Sednaya. Hoda, Marwan and my man Ghassan survived the attack, but Mustapha's men refused to take them to the border. They blamed their commander's death on them."

"And?"

"They took their chances with the Damascene taxi driver. He took them to Aridha where crossing the border is much easier."

"And you learned this from Ghassan?"

"No, Ghassan didn't make it back to Mieh Mieh. His mutilated body was found on the road from Ba'albek to Chtaura, not far from the Christian town of Zahlé. The local villagers buried him and gave his identity papers to the Lebanese police. We found out about Aridha from the driver in Damascus."

"So where's Hoda now? When can I see her?"

"We lost track of them after Aridha. They didn't want to tell the driver where they were going next."

Marc waited.

"Don't look at me that way! Don't you think that I wouldn't leave any stone unturned until I found her? We'll find Hoda, but we must wait. There are too many things happening, and the Israelis could return at any time."

It's not what Marc had hoped to hear, but he understands that Abdullah is stuck in Mieh Mieh, coordinating the preparation of the next Israeli invasion. Abdullah is his last lead. He has already tried Fouad

Saadeh, who knows nothing more, even after putting out the word to every Social Nationalist in Lebanon and Syria. He thinks about Aridha. Why that border crossing? Safer yes, but could there be another reason? He recalls that Marwan had once spoken about spending much of his childhood with his grandparents in the Koura Valley. What was the name of that village again?

"Abdullah, can you get me to the north?"

"Where?"

"The Koura Valley."

"The Koura is inaccessible. The area is defended by Suleiman Franjiyeh's forces, and he's clearly in the pockets of the Syrians. Your problems with Damascus aren't going away anytime soon. Besides everything between Beirut and the Koura is in the hands of the Phalangists, and they're pressing hard to expand their territory north and northeast to box Franjiyeh in."

Marc knows what Abdullah is saying is true. The Phalangists have succeeded in bringing other Christian fighters under the umbrella of the newly formed Lebanese Forces. Only Suleiman Franjiyeh and his Marada militia are holding out. The fighting in the North is bound to get a lot worse and very soon. He'll need to wait out the worst of it before trying to reach the Koura.

Chapter

50

I
T HAPPENS SO SUDDENLY. A whizzing through the air. Hoda
doesn't even have time to look up. The mortar shell smashes into
the wall of the old house, knocking her down. She instantly feels
the wrenching in her abdomen. She clutches herself and sees the blood
on the floor. Hands are lifting her toward the bed. She looks up to see the
faces of her neighbour Um Amin and her daughters, Amal and Najwa.
She can hear their soft reassurances. Don't worry. Everything is fine.

When the child comes, it is already dead. The impact was too great.
When Hoda comes back to consciousness, Um Amin tells her that a
priest sprinkled holy water on her child.

"Don't worry, my little one. We even gave him a name."

Hoda's eyes turn up to the old woman.

"Yes, a beautiful name. Rami. It was Marwan's grandfather's name."

Um Amin's youngest daughter, Amal, blurts out: "And you'll see him
in heaven. God is merciful to the innocent!"

Marwan, who'd left the fighting as soon as he heard what had happened, now sits holding Hoda's hand. He sees her lips move, but without sound. He leans down to hear better.

"Rami," she whispers as she slips into unconsciousness.

The days pass. The first snow blankets the mountains above the
Koura. The Phalangists return to their warm homes in the Metn. The
Marada militiamen also return to their loved ones, but many fewer
men than the summer before. Marwan now is always by Hoda's side.
In her semi-lucid moments, she confesses to him her fear that Marc

has abandoned her. She wants to return to her parents' home in Sabra. Winter comes and goes, and the melting of the snow on the mountain passes promises another season of blood-letting. The militiamen pay their respects to Hoda but insist that Marwan must return to the front. Marwan has become a good fighter, and they need everyone to repel the Phalangists' spring offensive.

Under the warm Koura sun, Hoda's injuries heal. The Phalangists retreat, and Marwan returns home. Hoda decides to stay in Bsarma. It isn't that it's too dangerous to return to Beirut. The roads have re-opened during a ceasefire. It's that she no longer wants to see Marc. In her mind, the loss of the child, their child, ends everything between them. She can't believe that he couldn't find them. The directions to Bsarma were clear in the letter she gave to Ghassan, and she trusted Ghassan. The young man had stood by her on the road from Sednaya and risked his life to bring them to Aridha. He wouldn't betray her. He would certainly have found a way to deliver the letter. Yes, it's Marc who's failed her, turning his back on his unborn child. Had she really ever known him?

In the recent months, Marwan has become every day more caring, more tender in his language and attentive to her needs. They no longer speak just of politics and the good times in Beirut, but instead, in-creasingly of the everyday goings-on of the village. Despite the war, the hearts of the villagers have not hardened. Many come to visit Um Rami, as they now call her. Their warmth and simple manners win her over. Even in war, these villagers never hesitate to reach out and share their love of life. And for a while, she thinks that she can live with them for-ever. When she is strong enough to walk, Um Amin and her daughters take her to the cemetery. As they stand there by the tiny plot with a carved wooden cross, Hoda panics—she has nothing to put on her son's grave. Um Amin speaks quickly to her daughters. Najwa and Amal run into the nearby forest. Within a few minutes, they return with wildflow-ers. There are so many to choose from, but Hoda takes a single sawfar iris and lays it on the rough stones covering the son she's never seen.

Um Amin and her daughters begin to recite prayers in the Syriac language that the priest has taught them, but Hoda puts her finger to her lips, takes their hands in hers, and recites to her son the words of Gibran Khalil Gibran, Lebanon's greatest poet.

You would know the secret of death.

But how shall you find it unless you seek it in the heart of life?

The owl whose night-bound eyes are blind unto the day cannot unveil the mystery of light.

If you would indeed behold the spirit of death, open your heart wide unto the body of life.

For life and death are one, even as the river and the sea are one.

Chapter

51

Bsarma, Northern Lebanon – December 1979

IT HAPPENS MUCH QUICKER than they expected. Maybe it was inevitable—as Abdullah would say "Maktoub." Hoda thinks back when she first saw Marwan. He was a handsome young man with a brilliant mind. That he was a Maronite had dissuaded her from any other thoughts. Marrying a foreigner who could take her away from Lebanon was one thing, but falling in love with a Christian Lebanese is another. Now in the eyes of all the villagers, they're a happily married couple. When they look at each other, they begin to feel the same.

Marwan is still a traditionalist underneath his revolutionary idealism.

"I will find a way," he proclaims.

"A way for what?"

"For us to marry."

"You know that's not possible. There's no civil marriage in Lebanon."

"I know, and the local clergy will ask to see our identity cards. Mine as a Christian and yours as a Muslim. But I will find a way. I could ..."

"Stop! Don't even think about converting!"

"It would only be on paper. We could go to Tripoli and ..."

"No, I said no! I'm not asking you to risk losing your community over something that I don't even believe in."

"Okay, but I will still find a way."

Hoda begins to invite Marwan to her bed, but he refuses. At night, she hears him pace the floor in the next room, trying to find a solution to their dilemma.

After a week, Marwan surprises Hoda in the kitchen as she chops parsley for tabbouleh.

"I found it."

"Go on."

"I met an American missionary in Zghorta. He can do it."

"What church does he belong to?"

"He's a Quaker."

Tom was the young Quaker's name. And he wasn't quite a missionary. He had worked in Ramallah at the Friends School and had come up to Lebanon to volunteer in an orphanage in Zghorta. Marwan had asked him how Quakers married. Tom explained that Quakers had no clergy to officiate a wedding, but instead, other Quakers simply witnessed the marriage. Marwan asked how many witnesses were needed, and Tom answered: "Just one."

So it's decided. Marwan will ask Tom to come to Bsarma to witness their marriage. Hoda is delighted. She knows that the ceremony isn't necessary. In her heart, she's already married to Marwan. But she loves the effort that he's gone to make things right.

"Marwan, you know that I love you. If you want to bring Tom here, that's fine, but come with me now."

Hoda pulls on his army jacket to take him to the bedroom. She takes off her clothes and lays them on the commode. She lets his eyes wash over her. Her excitement grows. It's clear that his desire for her is strong, very strong. But he backs away.

"Wait, Hoda, I'll get Tom now. We'll be together tonight."

Before Hoda can pull him back into the bedroom, he's gone.

Four hours later, the young blond American follows Marwan into the house. The ceremony lasts ten minutes—just brief declarations of love and fidelity, a sheet of foolscap inked with the date of the marriage and the signatures of Hoda, Marwan and Tom.

"Are we really married?" Hoda asks.

"God joins man and woman together. All I've done is witnessed this so that you'll be married in the eyes of the Society of Friends."

"Tom, I don't know how to thank you," Marwan says.

"It's nothing. Look, I haven't seen Bsarma before. I'll be back in a couple of hours," Tom says with a shy grin.

Hoda walks up to Tom and kisses him on the cheek. "Thank you."

With Tom's departure, Hoda takes her husband by the hand to the bedroom. With the tenderest of care, she undresses him. He wants to turn off the light, but she refuses. When she removes his shirt, she sees the deep scars from the interrogation in Sednaya. He tries to pull it back on to hide them. No, she whispers that his scars witness his loyalty to her—the refusal to speak even under torture. He shivers when she touches them. She realizes that this is the first time that her *traditionalist* has ever been with a woman, and it excites her. She places his rough hands on her shoulders and pulls them down to her breasts. She meets his lips with hers and then guides his hand beneath her skirt. He pulls her closer, lifting her skirt high. She unbuckles his belt and slips her hand inside his pants. Her fingertips stroke his penis. It is hard and beautiful. She pulls him onto the bed. And lost in the moment of ecstasy, she drinks every gasp from his lips.

Chapter 52

Allenby Bridge Border Crossing – September 2007

MARIE AND MINH CHAU step down from the bus at the border. The driver unlocks the luggage compartment and pulls out the bags one at a time, under the watchful eye of two Israeli soldiers. Arab porters take the luggage of the Palestinian passengers off to an outdoor conveyor belt where teenage soldiers rifle through them. It's nearly forty degrees Celsius, and the soldiers are irritable. Each time they come across unlabelled liquids and electronic gadgets they shout at the owner to step forward. If the answers don't please them, they toss the objects into large storage bins. The bags of Marie and Minh Chau and the five other foreigners are taken to counters inside the building. As they wait for their turn, Marie again quizzes Minh Chau about what Selima told her in Beirut.

"So Selima really doesn't think that Marc can be my father?"

"That's right."

"But she did say that Hoda 'Akkawi and Marc were a couple?"

"She said that they were together. I assume she meant as a couple."

Marie looks at the floor.

Minh Chau gives her friend a minute before asking: "Does it bother you they were a couple even if he's not your father?"

Marie doesn't answer.

"Oh my God! Marie, you have feelings for Taragon. I knew it!"

Marie stiffens. She's unsure how to respond. Minh Chau is now crossing the line. She resents her friend's uncanny ability to read her and worse maybe even decipher what she herself can't come to grips with.

"Next," the Israeli immigration official shouts.

Marie steps up and Minh Chau is called over by another official.

The grilling goes on for forty minutes and each is given a thorough body search. A lone taxi is left in the parking lot, and its licence plate doesn't match the one they've been given for their new driver. An Anglican priest who was on the bus steps up beside them.

"Don't worry. I thought that this would happen when I overheard you say you were in Lebanon. I asked my driver to wait."

"Thank you. That was very kind of you," Marie says.

"Are you just headed for Jerusalem?"

"No, we need to get to Tiberias today."

The priest converses quickly in Arabic with the driver.

"Ahmed can take you there after he drops me off. The fare is one hundred shekels to Tiberias. Is that all right?"

"Absolutely!"

The priest shares with them the latest news about the faltering peace negotiations. There's talk of the Americans getting more involved in the mediation efforts and even hosting a new peace conference at a place called Annapolis. No one holds out much hope for a breakthrough. But there's a rumour of a much more ambitious private peace initiative called Arkassa.

Marie sits quietly. She's no longer thinking about the news from Beirut. Instead, she's unsure just how much she can trust this priest. It seems unusual that he has already heard of Arkassa. Maybe everyone now knows what Taragon is trying to do in Tiberias? She shudders at what this could mean. The Mossad had killed 'Akkawi in Barcelona and tried to kill Taragon in Gaza. Would they just stand aside while he and Bronstein mobilized support inside Israel itself?

"It's done. Now do your job! I don't care how, but just get it done quickly," Ari Epstein says on the phone.

"Are they all dead?" Hussein Harb asks.

"Yes."

"How?"

"It doesn't matter. They're dead."

"I want to know if they died slowly like my son."

"I don't know. All I know is that they were taken care of."

"How long have you known who they were and where they were?"

"You ask too many questions. We kept our end of the deal. Now keep yours."

"Don't worry. I'm ready for it."

"And destroy the burner phone I gave you. I don't want this coming back at me."

"I will. Thank you."

"For what? They were just scum and deserved to die. Goodbye."

Hussein hears the click of Ari hanging up. He walks to the kitchen pantry and takes out a meat cleaver and a cutting board. He lifts the cleaver high and smashes the phone, once, twice, many times. He'll scatter the pieces from his car when he drives to Tiberias.

He walks to his bedroom and kisses his son's photo on the dresser. From under the bed, he pulls out a metal box. The lock is old and rusty, and it takes a lot of effort to open it. He takes out the contents—khaki, coils and *plastique* crudely put together. He remembers the body of the Hezbollah attacker, shot in the head before he could detonate the vest. At first, he had hoped to sell it as a souvenir to his Israeli overseers. No one wanted it. Now, he would use it for his last act. He looks at the other package, which arrived this morning. He knows what it contains. No traces will be left of what they have planned.

53

Tiberias – September 2007

MARIE AND MINH CHAU get out of the taxi and stand before the hotel. It's an impressive structure for a small place like Tiberias. A dozen ancient palm trees guard the facade of the century-old brick building. The terrace with its exquisite vaulted pillars is already full of Jewish and Arab delegates sharing glasses of tea. Both women feel a dynamism to the place, a sense that something important is going to happen.

Although Marie has maintained a certain coolness toward Minh Chau since her friend's comments at the border, she's still happy that her friend is with her in Tiberias. She'll need all of her support after she speaks to Taragon. She must choose the right moment. Taragon is in the midst of negotiating an agreement that might bring into play at least a chance for peace. She's come too far to put Arkassa at risk, and yet she can't leave Tiberias without answers. She'll wait until the end of the day's deliberations before doing anything.

"Marie, I'm going to call Selima," Minh Chau says. "Perhaps she's learned something new."

"Yes, go ahead. Give me your passport, I'll check us in."

Minh Chau walks down the hallway, eases into an over-stuffed chair covered in Palestinian embroidery and pulls out her cell phone.

Marie waits for her turn at the hotel reception. Suddenly, she feels a familiar presence. She turns to see Bronstein's crooked smile.

"Jonathan!" she exclaims, planting a warm kiss on his cheek.

"Marie, it's wonderful you're here. Things are going better than expected. Marc made a compelling presentation of the initiative to some of the early arrivals this morning. There are fewer sceptics than we thought there'd be."

"And no interference from the government?"

"No, that's the surprising thing. At any moment, I thought that the police would barge in and arrest Marc for being illegally in Israel. But no, nothing of the sort."

"They must be afraid of making him a hero."

"Yes, that's what I think. But we'll use it to our advantage."

"Where is he?"

"He's mediating between the Meretz representative and delegates from the Arab Democratic Party. Do you want to see him now?"

"No, I can wait."

Marie wonders about Selima. She's close to Marc. Could she have already spoken to him? She probes Bronstein.

"Has Marc said anything recently about me?"

"What do you mean?"

"I mean anything new that he's learned about me?"

"Well, he called you his right hand, and said that you did remarkable work in Beirut and Gaza."

"Hmm."

Minh Chau joins them, giving Bronstein a huge hug.

"*Mazel tov*, Minh Chau. Leyna told me that you're expecting the baby very soon."

"Thank you, Jonathan." She adds with a wink: "I hear that you and my cousin are now a thing."

With his crooked teeth, he betrays the smile of a man in love.

As the two women leave, Bronstein wonders whether he should've said more, but it wasn't his place to betray his friend's confidences.

Chapter

54

Tiberias – September 2007

MARIE AND MINH Chau decide to take separate rooms. Marie will need her privacy if she's to reveal what she knows to Taragon. Minh Chau has just spoken to Selima and learned that she has indeed spoken to Taragon about Hoda's death, but nothing more. Marie appears even more nervous when Minh Chau tells her this. She hasn't seen Taragon yet, and probably won't until the start of the late afternoon session. Bronstein has warned that this session will be the toughest. The organizers decided that there should be a challenge function—a final chance to ask the hardest questions in a group setting. A video link has been set up with Gaza where a Hamas representative will join the discussion for the first time. A lot is riding on Taragon's ability to convince the delegates that Arkassa is a viable solution.

Marie looks out the window at the road leading to the hotel. A Citroën with a French flag arrives. Two minutes later, a Mercedes with a Spanish flag. Word has reached the diplomatic community that history is being made in Tiberias. How can this all be happening right under the nose of the Israeli government? Someone must have intervened at a very high level to keep the local police at bay. Finally, she sees it and understands. A small convoy of three armoured vehicles, with the American flag on the hood of the middle one, pulls up before the hotel. A tall black man steps out. Sharp succeeded! Marie's heart soars. It all seemed so hopeless four months ago when they buried Abdullah 'Akkawi in Beirut. Now things are moving much faster and better than anyone expected. She calls Bronstein's cell phone.

"Jonathan, I want to participate in the proceedings."

"Of course. You can pick up your press pass at the reception."

"No, I mean I want to be a delegate. I want to express my personal support for Arkassa."

"But you are neither an Israeli nor a Palestinian."

"No, you're wrong about that."

"Pardon."

"I'll explain later. I want to sit with the Palestinian delegation."

"If you wish, that shouldn't be a problem. Meet me at the reception and we'll have a pass made up for you. We have to hurry though. Marc is about to speak to the plenary session."

Marie slips into a pair of black linen pants and a violet-blue blouse. Looking into the mirror, she brushes her hair and applies red lipstick. There's a glow to her cheeks and her eyes are bright with life. She takes a white scarf out of her suitcase and wraps it around her neck.

Marie has made her decision. She will stand with the Palestinian delegation and declare she's the daughter of Hoda 'Akkawi, killed in Sabra, and the second cousin of Abdullah 'Akkawi, martyred in Spain. She'll speak in favour of Arkassa and her pride in her Palestinian heritage. She'll urge the delegates to not let the sacrifices of her mother and Abdullah be in vain. Then she'll see what Taragon has to say.

Marie herself is surprised at her determination to reveal what she's only learned a few hours ago. She glances at the mirror in the hallway as she walks to the elevator, there it is—the face of Hoda in her reflection. When she presses the button to call the elevator, she glances sideways. An older dark-haired man, more likely an Arab than an Israeli, stands beside her. There is a musty smell about him. He wears a trench-coat over his bulky figure. She looks down at his scuffed shoes covered with a thin layer of dust. When the elevator is slow in coming, the man heads toward the stairs.

Bronstein already has her pass in hand when she arrives at the reception. He escorts her quickly to the entrance of the conference room where the hotel security guards check her credentials. There's been no time or money to set up scanners at the door, and the hotel personnel don't want to offend the guests with body searches.

The room is filled with more than fifty delegates. The technicians are doing the final sound checks and the image of the Hamas delegate from Gaza appears on the large screen at the front of the room. Marie smiles—it's Adnan Barghouti, the man who saved them in Gaza. She remembers his parting words: "Bring us proof that there are Israelis ready to listen to Arkassa." She studies the room. Israelis make up at least two-thirds of the delegates. Some wear yarmulkes, two are Hassidim. Taragon walks up to the podium. He taps on the microphone and begins. His eyes lock on Marie as she sits among the Palestinian delegates. A slight shake of his head, and then the faintest of smiles. He straightens up and scans the room. He is ready. Today, it's all or nothing.

"My dear friends, what you decide today can shape the future of the Middle East for your children, for your grandchildren, and the generations who will follow us, all of us. If you are here, you're here because you realize that violence is not the solution. Compromise is. Earnestness is. Sincerity and commitment will give the people of the Middle East what they all deserve—peace. We've called this session a challenge session, a chance for any and all of you to ask the tough questions about the Arkassa Initiative, but the hardest question is the one we must all first ask ourselves. What happens if we fail today? Do we return to our decades of hatred, of killing?"

A thin man stands up and speaks in Hebrew: "You speak wisely, Mr. Taragon, but I ask my colleagues here another question. Are you ready to sacrifice your prejudices and pre-conceptions to accept peace?"

A woman in a hijab beside Marie rises and says: "I am ready for peace. I am ready today." She returns to her seat, and Marie clasps her hand.

The audience begins to murmur louder and louder. In Hebrew and Arabic, the refrain "I am ready" reverberates. The words in Arabic flow to Marie's lips, at first slowly then with more fluency as if freed from decades of being buried in her subconscious. On the screen, she sees that even Adnan Barghouthi is repeating the words.

A man moves slowly forward. She recognizes him from the elevator. Perhaps in his sixties, the man looks haggard. At first, his steps are short, hesitant, almost lethargic. Then his pace picks up. He is clearly heading for the podium. He too is uttering alternatively in Arabic and Hebrew: "I am ready." She's unsure of the man's intentions. Is he just caught up in the moment, eager to express his desire for peace or ...? He stops a dozen feet from Taragon and opens his coat to reveal a vest of wires and explosives. The man looks at Taragon and says: "Miracle-maker, can you give me back my son?"

Marie begins to move toward Marc, ready to throw herself at the man, but Bronstein pulls her aside. He holds her firmly and allows dozens of panicking men and women to push them both toward the exit. Unable to free herself from Bronstein's grip and the weight of the crowd, she looks over her shoulder to Taragon. He's standing perfectly still, alone with his assailant. He raises his hand in a gesture of calm. There's no fear in his face or in the bomber's. Both are the same height and build, the same dark features and aquiline noses. As the man draws within a few feet of Taragon, their profiles look like the mirrored image of the same being. Taragon still makes no effort to flee. Instead, he steps slowly forward, his hand reaching out as if to touch the assassin's shoulder.

Chapter

55

T HAT SUMMER, Hoda gives birth to a girl. They name her Meryem after Hoda's aunt. Marwan reluctantly continues to serve in the Marada militia while Hoda devotes herself to her daughter. The girl grows quickly, bringing joy to the young couple and to the villagers around them. But the situation near Bsarma deteriorates. The front is getting closer. They begin to speak of going to France after the war. Nabil and Selima are still there. They've heard that Nabil is doing very well. Perhaps, he could help them. They consider trying to smuggle out a letter to him, but all the mail is being regularly read by the militia.

The fall of Aaba eighteen months later shocks the village. Aaba is less than four kilometres away. Its capture will now allow the Phalangists control over much of the road from Tripoli to Kfar Hazzir. More threatening, there's a rarely used dirt track off that road, which leads straight into Bsarma. The militiamen on leave are quickly mobilized to defend it. Marwan, now the most experienced among them, is chosen to lead the defence.

Hoda packs Marwan's knapsack while he cleans his gun.

"I've put food for three days," she says, turning away to hide her tears.

"Hoda, don't cry. I'll come back, but I have to join the men now. The Phalangists may have already discovered the back road."

"Wait, let me get Meryem."

Several men are gathered outside the front door. Some are seasoned fighters working for hire. Others are local boys, still in their teens.

Hoda brings their daughter in her arms and closes the door on the waiting fighters.

Marwan lifts up his daughter.

She says: "Papa, papa, you go?"

"On a little trip, my darling."

"No, Papa. Stay! Play!"

Hoda takes Meryem.

"Your father will play with you when he returns. Now, back to bed."

Three hard knocks on the door. The militiamen are impatient.

Elie looks at the debris blocking a passageway up the hill. There's no doubt that there's a road, one not used for a long time. He sends one of his men up it. Two minutes later, the man returns.

"It keeps on going up the hill, Commander."

"To the east."

"Yes."

Elie ponders the situation. His orders are to advance on Bterram, a village just a kilometre away, but Bterram is of no strategic importance. Its young people are making their fortunes in Beirut, Australia and Canada. There are no trained fighters to put up resistance. Most of the village's inhabitants are Greek Orthodox, trying to avoid being dragged into the intra-Maronite struggle. He respects the people of Bterram who've provided many of Lebanon's intellectuals. He looks at his motley group of fighters, mostly mountain peasants. They're still fired up from their victory in Aaba. Twice he had to step in to prevent them from killing civilians in Aaba. He would like to spare the cultured people of Bterram a visit from these brutes. Bsarma is different. For years, the Marada fighters based there have been a thorn in the Phalangists' side. He pulls out the radio to speak to Beirut.

The scout returns to their position at the crest of the hill. Marwan pulls him aside.

"Did you see them?"

"Yes."

"Where?

"At the base of the hill. They found the entrance to the road and are removing the rocks that we put to block it last winter. "

"Dammit! How many are there?"

"Only ten."

Marwan calculates. He has six men with him. He'll need to send one back to warn the village. Still, they have the high ground and could hold off the invaders until reinforcements arrive.

"Marwan, there's something else," the nervous militiaman says.

"What is it?"

"They have a radio. I saw them use it."

The odds could soon change against Marwan's small group. He has no time to lose.

"Go to the village. Tell everyone to climb the eastern escarpment. They'll be safe there. Get a message to the commander in Ehden to send us reinforcements. Do you understand?"

"Yes."

The Marada commander in Ehden peruses the press card before him. Richard Blacksmith, *Leeds Telegraph*. The face in the photo is vaguely familiar, but the name means nothing. What on earth is this journalist doing in the Koura? He picks up the phone to see what his headquarters know about this man who's mysteriously popped up in the town, asking all sorts of questions. The line is dead, *again*. He doesn't have much time to spend on this matter. There are reports that the Phalangists are on the move again.

"Bring him in!" he barks at the young militiaman waiting at the door.

As soon as the journalist enters his office, the commander recognizes him. Marc Taragon, the French journalist.

"Monsieur Taragon. What are you doing here under a false identity?"

Taragon comes clean.

"I'm sorry. I didn't have a choice. I needed to get through the Syrian checkpoints."

"Just tell me what you're doing here!"

"I'm looking for someone."

"Who?"

"Her name is Hoda 'Akkawi."

Marwan adjusts his binoculars. Three trucks are coming up the road from the south. They bear the cedar in a red circle insignia of the Lebanese Forces, the new identity that the Phalangists work under. He realizes that his small group could soon be outnumbered ten to one. He prays that the trucks will continue past the men now clearing the entrance to the back road. The trees hide those men from his sight, but he can hear the trucks come to a grinding halt. Then comes the distant muffled sound of boots hitting the ground.

"Let's go back to Bsarma," a seasoned Marada fighter says. "We won't be able to hold them off here."

"Go if you want, but I'm staying here," Marwan says.

The fighter confers with the rest. Two young fighters opt to stay with Marwan. The other four decide to return to the village and try to get word to Ehden to send reinforcements.

Marwan turns to the two remaining fighters. They're brothers still in their teens. One has been courting Najwa, Um Amin's daughter.

"Why have you decided to stay?"

"It is better that we die here if it delays the Phalangists," the younger brother says. "It'll give time for our friends to evacuate our families." The other brother nods in agreement.

Marwan pats them on the shoulders. His decision is no different. He knows that falling back on Bsarma now would only allow the enemy below a free run on the village. He thinks of Hoda and Meryem. Will they leave with the other villagers? He should've given the departing fighters a special message for them. Too late. Perhaps, they can still hold off the Phalangists. After all, the enemy doesn't know how many men he has with him.

There's a lull as the forces below cautiously probe their way up the dirt track. Marwan keeps his eyes fixed on the invaders. But for a moment, his attention lapses. He thinks of the time he lost, standing on the sidelines while Hoda was with Marc. If he'd only been courageous enough to ask her out when they first met at the university. Two years together are not enough. And now there's Meryem in their lives.

After they married, Marwan wondered whether he was only Hoda's second choice and if Marc turned up one day, she would fall in love with him again. It bothers him that the priest had named the dead child Rami after his grandfather, and now all the villagers greet him as Abu Rami. The child was Marc's son, not his. Each greeting is a constant reminder that he isn't the first in Hoda's life. He knows that it's petty to resent the dead child for having to live this lie in his grandfather's village. It's a lie to protect Hoda, and he would live a thousand more lies for her. One day when she returned from her weekly visit to Rami's grave, he confessed his doubts. She reassured him that her love was unconditional and that she'd never felt with Marc what she now feels with him. But his doubts continued to resurface, and lately, he's felt Marc's presence. He knows that this is irrational, but somehow it's as if his rival is closing in on him. He banishes these fears and delusions from his mind. He must defend Bsarma with action, not thoughts or words. His family is there.

The Marada commander is growing impatient with this famous journalist.

"I told you. I don't know any Hoda 'Akkawi. Besides, you say she's a Palestinian. The Palestinians know we don't want them any more than the Phalangists do. Why would she come here?"

"Let me stay in Ehden for a while," Marc says. "I'm sure that she's somewhere in the Koura."

"Look, I can't have you running around here. If you're caught by the Phalangists, they'll force you to tell them what you have seen of our defences. You must go now!"

A young fighter bursts into the commander's office.

"Pardon me, Sir. The Phalangists have taken Aaba and now control the main road to Kfar Hazzir. They've also discovered a backroad into Bsarma. Our men there are urgently asking for reinforcements."

"Are they defending the village?"

"Yes, they have a few men in the hills who are trying to delay the Phalangists' advance along the back road."

The commander turns to Marc. "You heard him. We have an attack to deal with. You must go now!"

Marc grabs the man by the shoulder. "No, it's taken me two years to get here. I can't leave now!" The commander lashes back, smashing Marc's face with his fist. Several of his men grab Marc's arms. *No one touches me*, the commander thinks. He turns to his men.

"Teach this *Fransawi* a lesson and then put him in a taxi out of here. Make it quick! We're going to Bsarma."

Hoda watches the villagers pack provisions for their trip to the escarpment to the east of the village. Even if the Phalangists take Bsarma, they won't risk following the villagers up the escarpment. This has been the village's escape route for hundreds of years, and everyone knows what to do. Hoda has made her decision to wait for Marwan. Several other villagers, including Um Amin and her daughters, have decided to stay as well.

Hoda looks at a photo of young Marwan on the wall. It was taken by his grandfather. She now realizes how deeply she loves him. How foolish it was to waste the years with Marc when she could've been with Marwan. In her mind, there's no doubt that Marc has abandoned her. If not, he would have found her by now. She knows that her husband would never abandon her. The fighters returning from the hills have told her that he's there right now defending Bsarma, defending her and her daughter. She feels a tug on her leg. Meryem is looking up, her eyes drowsy and her hair tousled. How she resembles her father!

Elie's men are only fifty metres up the back road when they come under fire. This confirms what he suspected. The road must lead right into Bsarma. It's his lucky day. If his men can take two villages from the Marada in a single day, Beirut will take notice. Since Tel al-Zaatar, he's risen through the ranks to company commander. Now he has greater ambitions.

Marwan has the Phalangists' lead man in his gunsights. He hesitates. It is never easy to take a man's life. But he thinks of Hoda and Meryem and squeezes the trigger. Pats on his back from the young fighters.

"You got him, Marwan!" they shout. Their joy is brief. A hail of bullets strikes down both of them. Marwan is now alone. He returns fire. His aim is deadly. One, two, three Phalangists fall under it. Then a bullet rips through his left shoulder. He breathes hard and continues firing.

Elie pulls his wounded men to cover. Four boys, all from his home town of Bikfaya. Losing more men to this ambush isn't worth it. Today, they'll liberate Bterram instead.

The reinforcements from Ehden emerge from the trees, firing in the air to proclaim their victory. Hoda picks up Meryem and rushes to them. On stretchers are the two brothers, one of them Najwa's fiancée. The young girl weeps hysterically by his side. Her mother desperately tries to console her. Then the hand of Amal, Um Amin's youngest daughter, pulls Hoda's arm.

"This way. Marwan is over there!"

They scramble past the militiamen to a stretcher laid on the soft green grass. The doctor beside it looks up at Hoda.

"Your husband is still alive, but not for long. I can do nothing more for him."

Hoda kneels to the ground with Meryem still in her arms. She mouths the words, I love you. Meryem crawls out of her mother's arms. Marwan motions to Hoda to bring Meryem closer. To his loved ones, he whispers the simple poetry of Nizar Qabbani.

Before you came
The world was prose
Now poetry is born

Chapter

56

Bsarma – Spring 1982

THE VILLAGERS BURY MARWAN next to his grandfather and
Rami. Hoda carries Meryem in her arms during the funeral
procession. People swarm around her to offer their condolences. The commander from Ehden speaks to her of Marwan's courage.
He asks her where she's from. Beirut. Beirut is big. Where in Beirut?
Hoda turns away from him. She notices several Marada fighters watch
her as if to say they know who she is, have always known. One walks up
to the commander and whispers in his ear. He then steps forward toward her. But Um Amin stands in his way and tells him to let Hoda be.

Tom joins Hoda in the funeral procession. She takes his arm and
walks with him. He tells her that he is leaving Lebanon. The road to
Beirut via the Beka'a Valley has just re-opened, and he wants to get out
before it closes again.

Hoda knows she can no longer stay in Bsarma. Nothing will happen
to her today or tomorrow or perhaps for weeks. But she knows that
suspicions will grow, and they may come for her when the allure of
being the wife of a hero wears thin. She says softly to Tom: "Take me
with you!"

Tom looks at her uncertain what to say.

"Take me to Beirut," she says. "My parents are there."

"Okay, I can do that, but are you sure? Do you really want to travel
with an American? There are still a lot of checkpoints."

"Yes."

"I leave tonight."

"We'll be ready."

The trip takes longer than expected. Tom is right about raising suspicions. Most of the militiamen think that he's CIA, but no one wants trouble from the Americans. After some lengthy questioning, Christian, Muslim and Druze militiamen let the couple through.

Tom insists on driving Hoda all the way to her parents' house in Sabra. Even the *Death to America* banners with gigantic photos of Khomeini in the poor Shia neighbourhoods don't deter him.

They pull away from the checkpoint at the entrance to the camp and drive toward Bir Hassan Street. As they pass Akil's old olive oil shop, she shudders. Is she doing the right thing?

They miss the turn-off at Café al-Awdah.

"Stop!" Hoda says. "Can you back up to the corner?"

Tom shifts into reverse.

"Thanks, turn left here," she says.

They pass some young men returning from the mosque. She recognizes a few. Akil's friends. But they no longer wear the skullcaps and dishdashas. Instead, all are in the army fatigues and keffiyehs.

Tom is speaking but not to her.

"How are you doing there, Meryem?"

Her daughter looks up at the big American and claps her hands.

"Hoda, are you nervous about seeing your parents again?"

"Yes."

"Do they know about Meryem?"

"No, they don't even know that I'm alive. I couldn't take the risk of contacting them when we were in Bsarma. Besides, explaining that I married a Christian isn't an easy thing."

"Do you intend to tell them now?"

"Yes, I'll have no choice when they see Meryem. Turn here. It's the third house on the right."

"Should I stay with you?"

"No, let's say our goodbyes here."

As Tom pulls in behind an old blue Peugeot, he can see the curtains of the neighbours' windows open. He walks to the trunk and opens it to take out Hoda's old canvas suitcase, a gift from Um Amin. Hoda is now at his side. Her hair is covered with a white scarf. It's the first time that he's seen her in a hijab. She steps forward and presses the silver crucifix into his hand. "Take it, Tom. I won't need it now."

He feels a tug on his pants. A tiny voice speaks. "Tom come?"

"No, my love. Tom must leave," Hoda says.

Meryem wraps her arms around Tom's leg. "No, Tom come!"

He bends down and lifts the young girl high in his arms. He whirls her around. She spreads her arms, and screams in delight: "Airplane! *Ana Tayara*—me airplane."

"Hoda?"

Hoda turns to see her mother walking slowly toward her.

"Mama!"

That night in Sabra, Hoda writes the first of many letters to Um Amin. She tells her that reuniting with her parents has proven much easier than she had thought. Their love for Meryem is immediate and unconditional. At first, they assume that Tom is Meryem's father, but Hoda quickly clears that up. And Tom is free to be on his way but not before, at her mother's insistence, he shares a modest meal with them.

In the morning, Abdullah's wife, Hedaya, comes over with her son, Munir. When she sees Hoda, she runs over to embrace her, and Munir walks cautiously up to Meryem. The two children look curiously at each other. Hoda places her hand on Munir's shoulder and says: "Munir, this is your cousin. Meryem, say hello to Munir."

Meryem holds out her tiny hand, but when Munir reaches out to shake it, Meryem pulls it away. She raises her arms and cries out: "*Ana Tayara! Ana Tayara!* Lift, lift!" Munir looks at his mother who nods her head, and dutifully he lifts his young cousin high into the air.

Hoda and Meryem spend every day with Hedaya and Munir. The young boy proudly assumes the role of his cousin's protector, especially after they tell him that Meryem is named after his grandmother. In the morning, they go to the market to take new orders from the vendors for the oranges that Abdullah sends them from Mieh Mieh. Supplying citrus to the Sabra merchants has become an important source of income for the whole family. Even Munir has set up a small stand in front of their house where he sits like a pasha counting out coins.

When Abdullah finally makes it back to Beirut, he immediately embraces Meryem. With one hand, he lifts her high into the sky, and she responds by flying like an airplane. Hoda walks up to Abdullah. He throws his free arm around her shoulders and pulls her tight.

"I'm so honoured that you named her after my mother."

"Abdullah, your mother taught me so much. Now I will teach my daughter to be like her, strong, wise and open to the world."

She can see the tears in his eyes.

"Hoda, we all thought you died, like Ghassan."

"Ghassan is dead?"

"Yes, murdered on the road from Baalbek. There was nothing on him, but a Shiite fighter recognized him, and informed us a week later."

"Nothing was found on him? Not even a letter?"

"A letter? No, there was no letter."

"And Marc?"

"It took him several weeks to find a way to return to the Middle East after Syria expelled him. He came to see me right away."

"It hurt me that he didn't look for me," Hoda murmurs.

"Oh, he looked for you. In fact, just a couple of months ago, he was looking for you in the Koura in the midst of the fighting between Gemayel's men and Franjiyeh's people. Marada fighters caught him asking questions in Ehden and nearly beat him to death."

Hoda pauses to take in all the information. It's overwhelming. To think that Marc had come within a few kilometres of Bsarma.

"I can contact Marc for you," Abdullah says. "Right now, he's in Afghanistan covering the Mujahideen's Jihad against the Russian occupation. We have friends who can get a message to him."

"No! Listen, Marc is the past. Marwan was the real love of my life. He's the father of my child. I don't want to confuse things now. Swear to me, Abdullah, that you will never tell Marc where I am."

"Excuse me, Hoda. I must speak to Abdullah," Hedaya says, interrupting.

"Yes, *Ruhi*, what is it?"

Hedaya hands her husband a small note. He glances at it and then looks over to the doorway where one of his men is waiting for him.

"What is it, Abdullah?" Hoda asks.

"I have to return to Mieh Mieh. The Israelis have crossed the border."

"An incursion?"

"No, this time, they've crossed in full force."

Hoda embraces Abdullah. "Be safe!"

As Abdullah's car starts on the long trip to Mieh Mieh, Hoda's father brings out an old transistor radio. He dials it to the Israel Broadcasting Corporation's English service.

"Can you tell us what they're saying, Hoda?"

She turns up the volume.

A man with a South African accent says: "The Israeli Defence Forces have crossed into Lebanon to stop the shelling of our northern settlements. Operation Peace for the Galilee has begun."

By mid-June, the Israelis reach the outskirts of West Beirut, and the inhabitants prepare for a long siege. Hoda writes to Um Amin about the many hardships that the city endures. The citrus shipments from the south stop immediately. Other food grows scarcer. The constant artillery shelling shatters any sense of normalcy. Both Lebanese and Palestinians feel abandoned by the world.

That is until Marc returns to cover the story. In the evenings, Hoda listens to his voice on the radio, recounting the latest violations of the ceasefire and the fear and deprivation felt by the civilian population. But he also doesn't hesitate to report on how Palestinian fighters are positioning their own artillery in densely populated areas, endangering tens of thousands of civilians. Of all the journalists, he takes the most risks to get both sides of the story. Despite what she told Abdullah, Hoda is tempted to see Marc again, if for nothing else to explain what had happened and to thank him for speaking up for the people of Beirut.

Two months into the siege, the unspeakable happens. Arafat capitulates and agrees to the evacuation of the PLO forces.

When the departure date arrives, the ululations from mothers, wives and sisters fill the streets of Sabra as the men climb aboard the trucks that will take them to the port.

Hoda brings her parents their morning tea, unsure of what to tell them, afraid to alarm them.

"What is all the noise outside?" her mother asks.

"It's nothing, Mama."

"Can you bring the doctor? Your father's not well today."

"Yes, Mama. I will get him, but later. He's still at the hospital."

It's a lie. She knows that their only doctor, a prominent member of the Popular Front, is also leaving. Were he to stay, he would certainly be imprisoned when the Israelis move into the city. She's heard though that Abdullah has refused to leave and is now hiding among the Druze in the Shouf, looking for a way to return to Sabra. When he does, perhaps he can find a new doctor for them.

Hoda thinks about trying to contact Marc for help, but the multinational forces brought in to secure the evacuation of the fighters won't let ordinary refugees from the camp enter the city.

She walks over to her suitcase and looks for the photo, the one that Selima took of them. She considers attaching a note to the photo for Marc and entrusting it to one of the departing fighters. She could ask him to give it to the French legionnaires who are escorting Arafat's troops to the port.

"Hoda, please come."

She turns to see Hedaya standing at the door to the bedroom.

"Your father is asking for you. He doesn't sound well at all."

Hoda pockets the photo and goes to the bedroom.

Chapter

57

Tiberias – September 2007

THE BLAST COMES just as Bronstein helps the last person out of the room. He hears his ribs crack as it throws him against the doorway. He pulls himself up. The chairs and tables in the room are piled up, obscuring the view of the podium. Bronstein pushes several aside. He sees Taragon's bloody form propped up against the far wall. The bomber's body parts are strewn over a radius of ten feet. Bronstein knows the chances of another bomb are high, one timed to explode just as the first responders turn up. He is about to leave when he hears the moan. It can't be. He turns, and for a moment thinks he sees Taragon's shoulder move.

Bronstein staggers forward. The distance to Taragon seems like an infinity. Through the constant ringing in his ears, he strains to listen for another sign of life. Maybe he has imagined it? How could Taragon have survived the blast? He's about to collapse when he finally reaches his friend's body. The bomb has inflicted a massive chest wound. The left side of Taragon's face is a tangle of veins, flesh and torn skin. Bronstein kneels down and presses his index finger on the artery of his friend's neck. Nothing. He tries to administer CPR, but when he places his hands on Taragon's chest, the bones shatter. His hands sink deep into the cavity and press against the heart. He cups the heart for a moment in a desperate hope to feel a sign of life. Again nothing. He angrily looks at the remains of Taragon's murderer. Who was he? Bronstein knows that he won't rest until he discovers the assailant's identity and who ordered the assassination. He knows what he must do, and reaches over to pick up the severed digit.

The SWAT squad rushes into the room to whisk Bronstein away before the second bomb hidden in the ceiling turns the room into flames, charring the remains of Taragon and his assailant.

58

France – October 2007

T HE SUN RISES as the train passes Limoges. Still four hours before they reach Toulouse. Leyna's head is resting against Marie's
shoulder. As the train changes tracks, Leyna wakes and looks
into the young woman's eyes. "Are we there?"

"No, go back to sleep," Marie says.

"Are you all right?"

"No."

Leyna sits up and takes Marie's hand.

"It hurts me too, but there's nothing to do except bring him home."

"Have you ever been there?" Marie asks.

"Where?"

"Rennes."

"Yes, twice when I was very young."

"You loved him, didn't you?"

"Then, I thought I did. I mean of course I loved him, but then I
thought we would be always together."

"What happened?"

"He fell in love with someone else. It was a long time ago."

"Did Minh Chau tell you?"

"That you thought that Marc could have been your father?"

"Yes."

"Do you still think that?"

"No, I don't, but after we bury Marc, I'm going to Lebanon to be sure.
Someone there is going to help me find the truth."

"Selima?"

"Yes, you know?"

"Minh Chau told me. She told me everything."

"So you must know that my mother was Hoda 'Akkawi. Was she the woman who took Marc from you?"

"Yes. It was a long time ago, Marie. I learned to love Marc another way after that. He was my friend, my best friend. He was always there for me. Always so easy to love."

Leyna wipes her tears and turns to Marie. The young woman's face is ashen, her eyes hollow, so empty. Leyna squeezes Marie's hand and melds her grief into her own.

Marie and Leyna descend from the train and walk to the baggage car. The porters are already unloading the casket. Marie freezes when she sees it. It is still so hard to believe that he's gone. She feels Leyna squeeze her arm, then a slight tug to turn her around. A small woman, perhaps in her eighties, leads a group of men toward them. At her side is a tall, thin man. Marie recognizes him immediately—Kressmann.

Leyna walks ahead to bring the old woman forward.

"Marie, this is Madame Taragon. Jacinta, this is Marie Boivin."

"I know. She's exactly like Marc described her."

The old woman walks purposefully forward, places her hands on Marie's face and pulls her down to kiss her cheeks. Marie feels the tears well up in her eyes, *in their eyes.*

"Little one, let's not cry. We must be strong."

Marie cannot hold back any longer. In the arms of the diminutive Jacinta Suárez de Tarragona, she collapses.

Chapter

59

I T'S JUST A FEW MORE KILOMETRES until they reach Bsarma. Selima looks at the young woman in the driver's seat. It isn't just Hoda that she sees in her. She sees Nabil as well. She wishes he'd lived long enough to be with them now. But the bouts of rheumatic fever during his childhood finally took their toll on his fragile heart. Selima had visited Nabil's grave before picking Marie up in Beirut. He spoke to her. He asked that something of his be given to the young woman, the last of their bloodline. Selima went back to her house on the hill to go through his paintings. She knew right away which one she'd choose as Nabil's gift. It sits beside her now, wrapped in plain brown paper.

Marie fidgets. She feels strange to be beside this woman who claims to be her aunt, this woman who has assured her that she'll find in Bsarma what she's looking for. Marie had pressed her in Beirut for details, but Selima insisted that she should hear it first-hand from people who knew Hoda during her years in the village.

The road flattens out as they pass by Amioun with its centuries-old hand-carved monk caves. The beauty of the valley quiets Marie's nerves. It's a place in touch with nature and the past.

"They call the Koura, the holy valley. The Christians here are very devout. They're mostly Greek Orthodox and Maronites."

"Maronites? Were they Phalangists?"

"No, the Maronite population here fought hard against Gemayel's forces. But they weren't saints either."

"You're a Maronite, aren't you, Selima?"

"Yes."

"You said Hoda was your sister-in-law. She was a Muslim, wasn't she?"

"That's right. I married her brother Nabil. And yes, he was a Muslim. Neither of us cared about religion. We escaped together the madness of the civil war here, and lived many wonderful years in France."

"Is your husband still alive."

"He died two years ago from heart complications."

"I'm sorry."

Selima gazes at Marie and takes her hand in hers.

"You would have loved your Uncle Nabil."

Uncle. The word sounds so strange to Marie.

"Look, that is Bsarma," Selima says.

Marie slows her rental car. The road now has many people walking along it, but few young ones. Most have immigrated.

"Our hosts were very excited when I told them you were Canadian. Almost everyone here has family in Montreal."

Marie says nothing. It's still hard for her to believe that it was only three days ago they buried Taragon. At his mother's insistence, they marched high into the Pyrenees to lay him beside his father. Kressmann walked beside her the whole way, denouncing the bombing in Tiberias. But he told Marie to forget Arkassa. The focus was now on American efforts in Annapolis. The right of return for the refugees and separate status for Jerusalem would never be accepted by the majority of Israelis. With American support at Annapolis, the Palestinians still had a real chance for a state of their own.

Marie was disappointed with Kressmann's dismissal of Taragon's initiative. She can't understand his faith in the Americans. Perhaps, he's just naïve. Perhaps just another tired politician too cynical to stand up for what is right. She's looking forward to seeing Bronstein again. She knows that he won't give up on Arkassa. Leyna is already on her way to Tel Aviv to help him convalesce. She'll join them soon and together they'll plan the next steps.

Selima tells Marie to stop the car in front of a stone house covered with climbing vines. An old woman emerges from it, propped up by a girl in her late teens. Selima is out of the car and walking up to the woman. Marie follows slowly.

The old woman squints her eyes and leans toward Marie.

"*Mashallah*—What God has willed." She reaches out to take Marie's hands and stands there with her mouth open for a moment.

"Come, grandma," the girl says, leading the old woman back to the house. Then she says to Marie and Selima: "Please come. We have tea and sweets inside."

They walk into the modest house. The girl brings a teapot and a plate of baklava.

"Marie, this is Um Amin and her granddaughter Nadine," Selima says. "Um Amin speaks very little French, but Nadine can translate."

Marie pulls out the photo that she had wanted to show Taragon.

Um Amin falls into her chair and pats her chest.

When the old woman recovers. She looks intensely at Marie.

"I see Marwan in you, and Hoda too."

"Marwan?" Marie says.

"Your father."

Marie looks at Selima who raises her hand to wait.

Um Amin slowly tells Marie what she has wanted to know for so long. A mother of exquisite beauty who'd loved her. A father who died heroically defending the village. But also a brother who died at birth. The old woman tells Marie the name her mother gave her—Meryem. Marie repeats the two simple syllables of the origin of her being, and looks into the faded grey eyes of the old woman.

"And the man in the photo?"

"*Ma b'arifu*—I don't know him."

Marie quietly explains that he's a French journalist called Marc Taragon.

No, the old woman explains, Hoda had never mentioned a Frenchman. She was Marwan's wife and the mother of his children. That's how she knew her. That's how everyone in Bsarma knew her. She was a good woman, a good mother.

Marie politely asks the old woman for more details. She asks her what happened to Hoda when she left Bsarma. Wait, she answers and whispers to Nadine. Two minutes later, the girl returns with a stack of letters. One after another Selima translates them for Marie. They speak of Hoda's happiness at being reunited with her parents. How handsome and big her nephew Munir had become. *Munir*—the boy's name triggers her memory. The last kiss from her mother before being sent off with her cousin. Hoda's face is as vivid as if she were standing there before her now. Dark hair, olive skin, coal-black eyes as piercing as they were beautiful.

"Wait, Meryem!" Um Amin says. She walks over to a cedar chest. She opens it and brings back a photo.

"*Votre père*," she says.

Marie freezes. Selima takes her hand.

"He was so handsome, your father."

Marie stares at the young Marwan Kanaan. He is perhaps fourteen. His curly dark blond hair flows over his ears. His high cheekbones give him nobility. His eyes betray the curiosity of youth.

"Do … do you have other photos?"

The old woman shakes her head, but Selima opens her purse.

"Meryem, this is your father at university." Selima too has begun to address Marie by her birth name, and when she says it, it sounds so real.

Marie takes the photo in her hand. It seems unbelievable to her.

"Would you like to visit him?" Nadine asks.

Marie looks confused.

"I mean his grave," Nadine says.

"He's buried here?"

"Yes, come."

Marie processes the new information as she walks with the women toward the church. The small cemetery gate is in a bad state of repair. It takes a jolt to open it. They walk up to a small engraved stone bearing her father's name. Beside it is the name Rami Kanaan.

"Is this my brother?"

"Yes."

Marie searches her memory for a prayer to recite. It's been years since she was inside a church. Her mind draws a blank.

Selima senses her frustration.

"What is it, Meryem?"

"I can't remember any prayers. I should say something, shouldn't I?"

"Your father wasn't a religious man, but he loved poetry. Do you know Gibran Khalil Gibran?"

"Yes."

"Then say this with me. It was your father's favourite poem. I remember him reciting it once at a poetry reading at the university. He had such a beautiful voice."

Marie listens to Selima begin, and then repeats her words.

Where are you, my beautiful star?
The obscurity of life has cast me upon its bosom.
Sorrow has conquered me.
Sail your smile into the air; it will reach and enliven me!
Breathe your fragrance into the air; it will sustain me!
Where are you, my beloved?
Oh, how great is Love!
And how little am I!

Chapter

60

Bsarma – October 2007

THE WORDS OF GIBRAN'S POETRY give Marie a sense of completeness. She smiles at the women, and silently thanks them for their kindness.

"Can we go back?" she asks.

"Yes, you will want to visit your house first," Nadine says.

"My house?"

"Yes, your great-grandfather's house now belongs to you. You can stay there tonight. We've cleaned it for you."

The women return to the small house next to Um Amin's. Outside it is a tall olive tree.

"Your father planted this tree when he was a young boy," Um Amin says. "It's now strong and bears a lot of fruit. It will live a long time, like you. I'm old, and God willing, I'll soon see your father and mother in the other world. I'll tell them how beautiful their daughter has become. They'll be very happy."

The old woman opens the door and then presses the rusty key into Marie's hand. "Meryem, it's your home now. You should come often. You're a daughter of Bsarma."

"Thank you."

Selima and Marie decide to stay the night. It's far too late to return to Bikfaya, and the mountain roads can be treacherous.

As she lies on the bed, Marie feels like she's always lived here. There's a knock on the door. She opens it to see Selima holding the thin rectangular package she had in the car.

"Marie, I have something for you. Something … from your … uncle," she struggles to say.

Marie takes the package. It feels light, delicate. She gingerly takes off the tape, careful not to tear the paper. Inside is a small painting, exquisite in its simplicity. Just the black outline of a man climbing over a wall to a city somewhat obscured by smoke.

"It was one of the first impressionist pieces your uncle sold. I came across it last year at an auction and bought it back."

"It's beautiful. Does it have a name?"

"Yes, turn it over."

On the back of the canvas, in pencil is written: *Évasion de Sabra, Nabil 'Akkawi, Paris 1976.*

Selima leaves Marie. She knows that there's much that the young woman has to think about. It is better she's alone. Selima opens the door to the courtyard and goes to the olive tree. There she feels the urge to see Nabil's face. She looks into her handbag and finds the photo of Nabil and her by the Eiffel Tower. It was taken just after they left the *Mairie* with the piece of paper signed by the magistrate to bear witness to their love. She knew that she loved him the first moment she saw him. A thin boy, his fingernails covered with paint. He never had his sister's beauty, but his pale lips, narrow eyes, the rising of his eyebrows when she approached enchanted her. Her family disowned her after her marriage to Nabil, but her cousin Tobias, a Maronite priest, intervened to reconcile them to her choice. The years passed and their love grew stronger, even when he entered his dark period after the news of his parents' death in Sabra. She nursed him back to life and he returned to paint with more passion than ever. When his heart started to falter, she was always by his side. When the end came, she refused to let him go. He's still with her. His voice answers her over the snow in the mountains, through branches of the cedars and against the stone walls of the villages. She will never let him go.

Marie watches Selima stand in the courtyard. She hears her speaking, but can't make out the words. She momentarily wonders who's with Selima, but her interest wanes as fatigue overcomes her. She falls back on the bed and looks around the room. Moonlight casts shadows of the tall olive tree on the walls surrounding her. The wind picks up and the shadows move like Javanese puppets. She imagines in them her father and mother playing with her in the courtyard. Um Amin's girls join them. Sleep brings colour to their smiling faces.

The happy images fade into a different dream. She's back at the wall, but Munir isn't with her this time. Her hand is bleeding. She hears gunfire all around her. The flares illuminate the night sky. She looks in every direction but is afraid to cross the street into the city.

From the shadows, a dark shape emerges. Then another and a third. She looks at their faces. Young faces. Abdullah, Bronstein, Taragon. She wants to go to them, but her legs won't move. A boy's voice whispers from the darkness behind her: "Go, Meryem." She gathers her strength and walks slowly toward them, and they turn into alabaster statues. She touches Abdullah. He disintegrates into white sand. Then Bronstein, again her touch reduces him.

She reaches out to the immobile Taragon. His face is so beautiful, like a Greek god. She pulls back from fear of destroying this ivory vestige of what he had been. Starlight replaces the rivulets of red that grace her palm. She presses her hand against his cheek and breathes into him her fragrance of olive trees and cedars. For a droplet in time, Taragon comes to life. The light fades. Sand fills her open wound.

Chapter

61

Beirut – 1982

RILEY LOOKS AT FOUAD SAADEH sitting in his living room. He's never seen the old leftist leader look so desperate.

"We can't let this happen," Fouad says. "We have to stop the election of Bashir Gemayel. He'll destroy Lebanon."

"I don't think that you have any options left. Arafat and the Syrians are gone. The multinational forces have already left. The nationalist members of parliament have been cowered into submission. They'll vote for Gemayel as ordered."

"It can't happen, it can't happen," Fouad mutters.

Riley hands him a Scotch. "Drink. It'll make you feel better."

"No." Fouad rises up. "I tell you that we won't let this happen. I have things to do." He picks up his coat and embraces Riley before leaving. Riley wonders if he will see his friend again.

He thinks about contacting Marc, but forgets which hotel in Tunis he's at. Like much of the international press, Marc is covering Arafat's move to the Tunisian capital. Riley decided to stay behind in Beirut, waiting to see what the Phalangists and Israelis will do next.

The knock at the door is soft, so soft that first Riley doesn't hear it. Then it comes again. Riley picks himself up from the sofa. He pulls a revolver out of the side drawer. These days, he can never take enough precautions. Since the departure of the PLO, looters have become bolder.

He looks through the peep-hole. *It can't be.* There in Israeli fatigues is Jonathan Bronstein.

"Jonathan, is that really you?"

"Yes, open up. I came for that scotch you promised me."

Riley opens the door. The two men grab each other by the forearms and embrace. Down on the street, an Israeli army jeep with a driver and two heavily armed soldiers stand guard. At either end of the street, Lebanese Forces militiamen are setting up barricades.

"What are you doing here?"

"I came to see if you were okay. Wadi al-Yahoud is being secured by our allies. Some of them don't like your reporting, neither does General Sharon. I suggest that you relocate to the King George Hotel. We can escort you through the Lebanese Forces' lines."

Jesus, thinks Riley. He certainly doesn't want to be there when Bashir Gemayel's thugs come knocking.

"Okay. Give me ten minutes."

"Take your time. As long as we're here, you've nothing to worry about."

Munir bounces Meryem on his knee. He loves his young cousin. Hedaya and Hoda listen to their children laughing. It alleviates the daily stress of scavenging for food and medicine and caring for her bedridden parents.

The music on the radio is interrupted by the announcement that the parliament has just elected Bashir Gemayel as President of Lebanon.

"It won't be long before the Phalangists enter West Beirut," Hedaya says. "I need to check on my parents. Can you take care of Munir?"

"*Tayyib,* but return before dark. The old men and boys out there can't protect the camp. There have been reports of more looting."

"Don't worry. I'll be careful."

Abdullah waits for Fouad Saadeh. Things are going too fast. Bashir Gemayel is under pressure to sign a peace deal with Israel. Although the new Lebanese president resisted in the meeting with Begin in Nahariya, it's clear that he's going to cave in to Israeli demands. In exchange, the Lebanese Forces will be given free rein to quash the Muslims while Syria watches helplessly from the sidelines.

Fouad's car pulls up. The Druze militiamen recognize him and wave him through to the empty store where Abdullah has set up camp. Abdullah hears the car, looks through the curtain and walks to the door to unlatch it.

"May God preserve you, Fouad."

"And you."

"Why are you here?"

"I need to warn the people in the camps."

"About what?"

"We've decided to stop Bashir. You need to rearm the camps. After we strike, the Phalangists will take revenge on all of us. We can defend ourselves, but they'll also come after your people."

"When?"

"Tomorrow."

"Can you give us men?"

"No, we need all of them to defend our areas against the Phalangist backlash, but I have a trunk full of arms. How many men do you have?"

"None. I'm alone."

"What about the reports of hundreds of fighters infiltrating back?"

"Israeli propaganda."

Fouad looks at his friend, realizing what'll happen, but it's too late to call off the operation.

"Take the guns anyway, and get your family out of Sabra."

"I'm trying to."

"Go in peace, my friend."

"Thank you."

Chapter

62

Beirut – September 1982

HODA AND HEDAYA sit in shock around the radio. Lebanon's new president, Bashir Gemayel, and twenty of his top commanders have been assassinated.

"Hedaya, go bring your parents here. They shouldn't be alone."

Munir starts to follow his mother, but Hoda holds him back.

"*Habibi,* your mother will be back soon. Stay with Meryem, please. I need to check on my parents."

"Yes, Auntie. Will mommy be long?"

"Not long. I promise."

Hoda enters the bedroom. Her mother is awake, but her father sleeps soundly.

"Hello, Mama."

"Hoda, come here. Sit with me."

Hoda takes her mother by her hands, and looks into her eyes.

"Mama, I have some bad news."

Hoda's mother pats her hand and nods her head.

"They killed Shaykh Pierre's son."

Her mother looks over to her sleeping husband. She understands immediately the hopelessness of the situation.

"Hoda, you must leave Sabra. Take Hedaya and the children, and find Abdullah. He'll protect you."

"Mama, I can't leave you."

"You must. We'll be fine."

"No. Now go to sleep, and don't worry. I'm not going anywhere."

Hoda leans over, kisses her mother on the forehead and lets her sink listlessly back onto the mattress.

From the far end of the street, Abdullah watches the Merkava tank lead the convoy of trucks into the Fakhrani district. Gemayel's assassination is proving the perfect pretext for the Israelis to break the agreement to stay out of West Beirut. Abdullah ducks behind the wall as the trucks drive by. He weighs his options. Should he head for Sabra now or wait until dark? Fouad has given him a lot of guns. If he could get them into Sabra, perhaps then even the old men there could stave off an attack long enough for the women and children to get away. But how? The old street vendor comes into view, slowly pushing his cart along as if invisible to the Israelis passing by. Abdullah thanks God for his luck.

For the last hour, Bronstein has gone over the preliminary intelligence reports with his adjutant Aaron Rabin. There's no doubt that the bomber is the Social Nationalist Habib Shartouni. Israeli troops accompanied by Phalangist militiamen are now combing the downtown area to find him.

A young corporal comes up with a piece of paper. Bronstein reads it.

"What the fuck!" he blurts out. "What shit is this?"

A cocky lieutenant walks in. "Those are your orders, Captain. We're going to secure the perimeter of the southern camps."

Epstein, that bloodsucker. What's he doing here?

Bronstein crumples the paper and walks to the window. The trucks are already lining up in the street below.

Bronstein looks dismissively at Epstein and then waves to Aaron to follow him down the stairs. Most of the trucks are empty.

"Where are my men?"

"I've already sent them on their way. These trucks are for our allies," Epstein says. "They're going into the camps for us."

Bronstein glares at the man, barely holding back from smashing his face. He knows precisely who's left in the camps. He's written the reports to the General Staff himself, confirming that there isn't a single *fedayee* still there—just women and children and a few old men and young boys with rusty guns. The Phalangists will slaughter everyone if they're let into the camps. He has to reach the General in charge of this insane operation. He jumps into the first truck and sets off with Aaron toward Sabra. The engine's roar drowns out Epstein's protests that the truck must go first to Ashrafiyeh.

The General quickly shuts down Bronstein. He doesn't care for this Arab-loving intelligence officer. All this protest about not trusting the Phalangists and how there are no fighters left in the camps. What does he care? He's Sharon's man, and he has his orders. Epstein has now joined them on the rooftop. He's accompanied by three of Gemayel's men. They greet the General. Bronstein stands to the side. He doesn't want any part of this. Below, a street vendor pushes his cart. He studies the man. There's something familiar about his large frame. He decides to investigate. It's probably nothing, but he needs to buy some cigarettes anyway.

Abdullah watches the Israeli officer walk toward him. It's unbelievable—the same man he freed four years earlier. Bronstein. Jonathan Bronstein. Will the Israeli recognize him? It's too late to run. The trucks are arriving with reinforcements. Dozens of Phalangists, Guardians of the Cedars and even SLA militiamen jump out and march right by him. He can smell the alcohol on their breath and see the wide amphetamine-induced look in their eyes. Bronstein is now only two metres from him.

"Cigarettes? Do you have some cigarettes to sell me?" Bronstein asks in perfect Arabic.

Abdullah tries to look away, but it's too late. Bronstein immediately recognizes him. Unsure what to do, Brownstein reaches for his gun. Abdullah's right hand also disappears into the back of the cart. Just then Aaron catches up with them.

"They're insisting that you come back. The General is muttering something about a court-martial."

Bronstein stares at Abdullah. If he arrests him, the General will just hand him over to the Phalangists. He knows what will lie in store for the Palestinian fighter. After all, Abdullah has killed dozens of their men, and he was at Damour. Worse, Epstein is here, and will certainly volunteer to help with the interrogation. Knives are his speciality. The man is a psychopath, but he has a reputation for getting results so the General will let him join the Phalangist interrogators. He can't let this happen. If it wasn't for Abdullah, he wouldn't be alive today. He decides that it's time to repay his debt. A life for a life. Besides, Abdullah is only one man. There are no other Palestinian fighters left in the city. Israel has already won this war. He pulls himself together and plays the charade.

"Give me one pack and then leave immediately. This is a military zone. Aaron, please accompany this man out of the area."

Bronstein watches Abdullah wheel the cart down the street, Aaron dutifully walking behind him, gun in hand. He knows that Abdullah will find a way to return, but hopes that they won't meet again. He heads back to the command post. If he can't stop this madness, at least he will bear witness to testify later on what is about to occur.

Chapter

63

Beirut – September 1982

THE NIGHT'S LONG, but there's no sleep for any of them. The General has ordered all his officers to wait up with him, watching with binoculars the militiamen do their work. The Lebanese Forces commanders stand on the roof in a corner, sharing cigarettes and bottles of Arak. They're drunk on alcohol, power and vengeance. Epstein curses them—Arabs. He hates them, both foes and allies. But at least these animals will do the dirty work that has to be done, the work that his countrymen won't do themselves.

"Epstein, Bronstein, come here!"

The General has had enough watching the two pace like tigers eyeing each other in the night.

"Ari, I want you to take these friends with you into the camp, and find out what is happening."

Epstein looks at the new arrivals, South Lebanon Army fighters flown up from Marjayoun. One stretches out his hand and says in broken Hebrew: "I am Hussein." Epstein ignores the man's hand. "*Tov*, now let's go."

Bronstein is about to follow them.

"Wait! I've another job for you. Take your man and check the perimeter. Bring back anyone who tries to get out of the camp."

A Guardians of the Cedars officer overhears them.

"That's not necessary, General. I've sent my men to watch the wall. No one will escape."

"Fine! Just bring me any prisoners."

The militiaman looks at the General with disbelief. Prisoners? Can the Israeli be so naïve? He then curls his mouth into a disparaging smile, and says: "*Tayyib, Effendi.*"

Bronstein understands immediately what that means.

"I'll go," he says and sets off down the stairs before the General can change his mind.

Hoda looks in horror at Munir and Meryem. Hedaya hasn't returned. She fears the worst. Since the PLO left, marauders have been abducting women from the camp. She tells Munir not to worry but knows better. Whining sounds followed by small explosions. Through the windows, she watches the night sky light up. At first, she doesn't understand, and then she hears the crackling of rifle shots.

Hoda lifts Meryem in her arms. She kisses her several times, and her daughter laughs. She puts her down and gives Munir a hug, whispering in his ear: "You must take your cousin away from here. Run along the wall until you find an opening. Hide in the city until morning. When you see men from our side, ask for your father."

"Are you coming with us?" Munir asks.

Hoda looks toward her parents' bedroom.

"No, I can't. But you're a man now. Be brave. Take care of Meryem! Here, take these photos with you."

Munir looks up at Hoda.

"Auntie, I'll be brave. I'll make you proud of me. And Papa too."

She kisses the boy one last time. She lifts her daughter and places her in Munir's arms. Meryem waves at her mother as they leave quickly through the back door. A dagger strikes deep into Hoda's heart. What has she done? Sending the children into the darkness! Perhaps straight into the hands of Bashir's men. In her mind, a thousand scenarios race by. Even if the children reach safety, will they find Abdullah? Alone how can she protect her parents from what's coming? She remembers the pistol Abdullah left with his wife. She rifles through Hedaya's possessions until she finds it. She closes the bedroom door behind her, sits down beside her parents and waits.

Epstein and Hussein cross into Sabra. Three militiamen follow them. They inspect the first houses. Nothing is moving inside. Epstein smiles. The Phalangists are doing a good job. Then a moan. In a corner, a small shape begins to stir. Epstein approaches it. A bloodied head with a jawbone blown off turns toward him. He signals to Hussein to step forward. A single shot puts the child out of her misery.

Epstein and Hussein continue "mopping up." They pass some Phalangist militiamen resting from hours of "cleansing." They're now deep inside the camp. The houses are deserted. No matter, the fleeing inhabitants will run into the militiamen coming in from the opposite entrances. No one's going to escape. From a distance, they watch a boy run from a house, with a small girl in his arms. Epstein holds Hussein back. "It could be a trap." They proceed to the door of the house and break it down. Hussein orders the three other militiamen inside. No one's in the main room. There's another room. Its door is locked. They aim their guns and listen.

Hoda sits in the darkness. She hears them whispering. The horrors of Tel al-Zaatar pass in front of her. Then Akil's face, his heavy body on top of her. She will not submit to these animals. She looks at the pistol and then at her parents. She bites her lip and takes aim.

Bronstein and Aaron proceed cautiously down the street. Every two hundred metres, a Guardian of the Cedars emerges from the shadows to begrudgingly greet the Israelis. It's clear that the militiamen don't appreciate being checked up on by their "overlords."

After half an hour, Bronstein decides he's seen enough. He takes a look at the camp's wall as Aaron shares a cigarette with a young Guardian. A head bobs up over the wall. Instinctively, Bronstein reaches for his pistol. Another head appears and then a body. A young girl is being lifted onto the wall. An older boy pulls himself behind her. Bronstein turns away. He has no intention of bringing children back to the command post.

"Aaron, let's go."

The two Israelis turn to head back when they hear a thud. The boy has jumped and is now raising his arms to catch the girl. A shot rings out. The Guardian lowers his gun and walks to the wall. The boy lies on the ground, clearly dead. The girl is still in his arms. The militiaman continues toward her, knife in hand. Bronstein calls on him to stop, but he keeps moving forward. Bronstein raises his pistol and squeezes the trigger just before the killer reaches the child. The dead man lurches forward, his knife frozen in his grip. He falls on the young girl who helplessly raises her hands to ward off the blade.

Aaron races forward to pick her up. Other Guardians menacingly approach the Israelis. Bronstein screams at them to back off. Aaron is now at his side, cradling the girl in one arm. Blood flows from the cut across her palm.

One of the militiamen kneels over the dead man at the wall.

"*Sharmout!* You've killed Fadi."

There are more than a dozen armed men now on the scene. The situation is turning ugly. Three shots in succession ring out from just inside the camp. Bronstein and Aaron seize the distraction to move behind a parked car and fire into the air. The militiamen duck for safety. As they begin to race toward the command post, a bloodied photo falls from the girl's tiny hand. Aaron grabs it in mid-air while Bronstein takes out the lead pursuer with a clean shot to the head.

Chapter

64

Tel Aviv – October 2007

AARON RABIN SITS PATIENTLY in the hospital chair. His old friend will soon awake. He has time. Better to let him sleep a little longer. His injuries are extensive. He's found what Bronstein had asked for. A name, a motive, irrefutable proof of a conspiracy. The fingerprint and DNA had pointed them in the right direction.

The nurse enters to change the bag of IV fluid and morphine.

"Your friend is still not out of danger. His heart was badly bruised. His ribs are healing slower than they should. He told us he wanted a discharge. You should convince him that it's too soon."

Aaron nods politely as the nurse leaves, but he knows that Bronstein wouldn't listen to him anyway.

"She's a pretty one," Bronstein says, his voice gravelly.

Aaron looks at the hospital bed. Bronstein is smiling through his pain and trying to pull himself up. The morphine is working its magic.

"Good to see that you noticed," Aaron says. "But take it easy. Lie back. I have what you want."

"Show me!"

"It's all up here," Aaron says, pointing to his head.

"Fine, tell me then."

Aaron walks Bronstein through Hussein Harb's file. The bomber was a poor farmer coerced into serving in Haddad's South Lebanon Army. He was given refuge in Israel when the Hezbollah and Lebanese army regained control of the South. Palestinian gunmen returned to his village and took their retribution out on his seventeen-year-old son. After that, Harb was never the same. In Israel, he eked out a pauper's existence by occasionally working as an informant for the Mossad.

"So why would he kill himself to attack us? What was Arkassa to him?" Bronstein asks.

"It wasn't Arkassa at all. It was vengeance. I mean, it was Harb's payment for the vengeance that he couldn't exact himself."

"I don't understand."

"The day before the bombing, three Palestinians were assassinated in Sidon. They were the men who had murdered the son."

"Who killed them?"

"Our people."

"What? On whose orders?"

"I think you know who. There's only one person in the Mossad so insane to make a deal like that."

Bronstein rolls his eyes to the ceiling. *That Moldovan psychopath!*

"Look. I need you to get me something."

"Do you mean this?" Aaron pulls a rectangular case out of a small gym bag. He stands up and opens it.

"What's its range?"

"Two kilometres. It's the best that we have, and it's completely polymer. You can take it even through a metal detector."

Bronstein puts his hand on his friend's forearm, and whispers: "Thank you. Now tell that pretty nurse to get me out of here."

Chapter

65

EVERYTHING'S THERE. AARON is a real professional. The building's roof offers a direct line of sight to the parking lot. Bronstein takes out Epstein's current photo and his daily schedule. On it is written the type and plate of his car. He adjusts the scope on the gun. Within seconds, he locates the vehicle. It's twenty metres from the entrance. Twenty metres for Epstein to walk. He checks the schedule again—5 pm. It should be all over in a few minutes if Epstein keeps to his routine, and the Moldovan is a creature of routine.

Bronstein bolts shut the roof's door and sets up the gun mount. The building is a full kilometre away, but it'll be child's play for him. His skills have not waned over the years. Not these skills at least. The pain shoots through his chest, distracting him for a moment. He hasn't taken his morphine today. He needs all his focus. Then he feels it. A small tremor like a hand squeezing his heart. He stumbles forward for a moment, but it passes.

Epstein packs up his things. The inquiries by Military Intelligence have reached his bosses. They don't have any proof of his involvement. They don't need it. They've had enough of Epstein, and jump on the chance to kick him to the curb. Even his friends in the cabinet can't save him this time. It doesn't matter. Why should it? He's achieved everything he set out to do. Arkassa is dead. Taragon and 'Akkawi are dead, and when he has the chance, he'll put a bullet in that traitor Bronstein. He doesn't need his employers for that. He knows the seaside apartment building where Bronstein lives, the cafés he frequents, his news-stand by the beach. One day, he'll take a morning stroll and cross paths with the traitor.

Epstein wipes the corner of his mouth. It bothers him that he has recently started to drool. He reminds himself to see a doctor. He looks back at his desk. It's clean. He's always valued cleanliness—purity. He walks to the elevator and says goodbye to the two young agents still in the office. They don't acknowledge him. He curses them. How easily they dismiss him. Don't they know what he's done for Israel, now and thirty years ago. He holds his head high.

Bronstein's hand shakes a little when he adjusts the scope. It has never shaken before. Is it the impatience—the waiting? The target has stayed much longer in the office than expected, and the parking lot is almost empty. All the better. He'll have a clean shot. The sun beats down on his uncovered head. Sweat rolls down his brow, and the back of his head begins to throb. The pain from his chest and ribs has returned, this time in full force. He feels the pressure around his heart, like a hand pulling to jiggle it free. Impatiently, he shifts positions.

Epstein looks out the door. The sky is bluer than he's ever seen it before. For a brief moment, he feels good, free to do whatever he wants. No one will be able to hold him back now, to tell him what to do and to scorn his advice. He's the master of who lives and who dies, just like so many years ago in Lebanon.

His elation passes. The finality of his last step out of the building pulls him down. He wipes the drool from the corner of his mouth. There's not much left for him. Years of bitterness have driven off all his friends, at least those who hadn't died as warriors. Good deaths. He would've preferred to die like them, still serving his country. Instead, he'll probably rot away senile in a filthy apartment.

Bronstein watches the man stand at the entrance, still three-quarters inside the doorway. What is he waiting for? He puts a bullet in the chamber, 43 grams of copper-clad lead that leave no chance for survival. Just one step forward, come on you bastard, take that step!

Epstein isn't a remorseful man, but suddenly a scene from years ago disturbs him—a woman covering with her dead body the corpses of her two elderly parents. He remembers ordering Hussein to turn the woman over. He wanted to see the face of a woman who would defy them even in death. He recognized her immediately from the many photos he'd studied. He recalled she had a young daughter, but no child was with her then. Now that child has ruined his career. He curses the woman. He curses Nicosia … and steps forward.

The dove swoops down as if it has been waiting for him. He pulls back to avoid the bird, just as the bullet whizzes by.

Bronstein swears and puts another bullet in the chamber. Too late. His target has ducked inside the building. Bronstein's anger flares. He's never missed before. His chest tightens. He rolls on his back and struggles to breathe. He sees the bird fly high into the sky as the iron grip twists his heart. The blood flow to his brain slows. He closes his eyes and allows the sun to pull him up. He is flying, flying with the dove. Cities appear beneath them—Tel Aviv, Haifa, Beirut. The roads between them fill with throngs of people, human chains making the land one. No boundaries. No walls. Anger leaves him. The flesh abandons. And high above the hills of Alonim, he is free.

ACKNOWLEDGEMENTS

Novels are rarely written in isolation. In my case, I was lucky to have benefited from the comments of more than 25 fellow writers who volunteered their time to read wholly or partially one or more of the novel's three drafts. I hope that I have done justice to the suggestions and insights that they generously shared with me. I am especially grateful to the early readers from the Deux Voiliers Publishing writers' collective, the Ottawa Independent Writers and the Quebec Writers Federation, all of whom are part of my literary family and companions on my writer's journey. In bringing *Quill of the Dove* to fruition, I had the privilege of benefiting from the editorial direction of Michael Mirolla of Guernica Editions. I hope that the novel has lived up to his expectations and Guernica Editions' quest for publishing literature with no borders, no limits.

I am thankful to the many good people I met during my travel, studies and work in the Middle East. They are the inspiration for this novel. One of them was a young Israeli girl living near the border with Gaza in 1994. I was returning to Gaza from Jerusalem and pulled into a roadside nursery to buy some plants for my garden. The young girl helped bring the purchases to my car. When she saw the Gaza licence plates on the car, she asked me what I was doing there. I told her that I ran a development program for Palestinians. She returned to the nursery and came back with a gift of six more plants. I asked her why. She said, "Your work is important. It will help improve the conditions for the people there who will be our neighbours. We want to live in peace with them." When I told my Palestinian staff of this encounter, each and every one of them echoed the Israeli girl's sentiment. It rooted my belief that the starting point for peace is empathy and the common people when given the chance can rise above the petty narcissism of their political leaders and reach out to their neighbours. I hope that in some small way *Quill of the Dove* will encourage just that.

Printed in October 2018
by Gauvin Press,
Gatineau, Québec